I think about telling her I love the warm air blowing through the windows when we drive together, and the smells of things alive and scary and waiting for me out there. I think about telling her I love the Chevy's red upholstery, and the scratchy, far away music coming from the radio, and the shiny chrome on the front of the radio, and the way her black hair whips around her face in the wind. I think about asking her a lot of questions. Why does Grandma Hollister have headaches, and when is Grandpa Hollister going to smile, and will he ever let me shoot his gun, and what does he do when he goes to work, and are we going to talk about last night? I just say, "I like it here. It's exciting."

My Aunt Delia laughs, and her laugh sounds like I know the water will sound running over those flat stones I saw from the bridge. She says, "You're sweet, Travis. It's sweet of you to say that."

sweet dream baby

a novel

STERLING WATSON

SOURCEBOOKS LANDMARK™
AN IMPRINT OF SOURCEBOOKS, INC.®
NAPERVILLE, ILLINOIS

Music copyright notification at back

Published by Sourcebooks, Inc.
P.O. Box 4410, Naperville, Illinois 60567-4410
(630) 961-3900
FAX: (630) 961-2168
www.sourcebooks.com

Watson, Sterling.
     Sweet dream baby / by Sterling Watson.
          p. cm.
     ISBN 1-40220-017-X (Hardcover)
     1. Grandparent and child—Fiction. 2. Southern States—Fiction. 3. Teenage
girls—Fiction. 4. Aunts—Fiction. 5. Boys—Fiction. I. Title.
     PS3573.A858 S94 2002
     813'.54—dc21

                                                              2002003852

                Printed and bound in the United States of America
                     MV 10   9   8   7   6   5   4   3   2   1

For Kath, again

Acknowledgments

My thanks to Jamie W. Gill, Melisandre Hilliker, and David Henderson for patient and resourceful help with research; Dr. Karl Sohlberg, M.D., for advice about pathology; Suzan Harrison, Bill Miles, and Dennis Lehane for insightful and generous criticism; and editor Jennifer Fusco for her intelligent, sensitive, and artful alchemy in transmuting a manuscript into a book. It is almost certainly true that this book would never have seen the light of day had it not been for the energy, insight, and belief given it by Ann Rittenberg, a literary agent of unparalleled gifts who loves stories, knows business, and is good to writers. This book and its author owe her a debt that can never be fully repaid.

Dream lover, where are you,
With a love oh so true,
And a hand that I can hold,
Through the years as I grow old.

I want a girl to call my own,
I want a dream lover,
So I don't have to dream alone.

Some day, I don't know how,
I hope she'll hear my plea.
Some way, I don't know how,
She'll bring her love to me.

Dream lover, until then,
I'll go to sleep and dream again,
That's the only thing to do,
'Til all my lover's dreams come true.

DREAM LOVER

—Music and Lyrics by Bobby Darin
—Recorded by Bobby Darin

JUNE

I love you darling, baby you know I do,
But I've got to read this book of love,
To find out why it's true.

Chapter one says you love her,
You love her with all your heart,

Chapter two you tell her, you're never,
Never, never, never ever gonna part,

Chapter three remember,
The meaning of romance,

Chapter four you break up,
But you give her just one more chance.

I wonder, wonder, um-be-do-oo-who,
Who wrote the book of love.

BOOK OF LOVE
—Music and Lyrics by Charles Patrick, Warren Davis, and George Malone
—Recorded by The Monotones

one

I look out through the back door screen to see if the Pultneys are there. One of them is, Jimmy. I'm scared of the Pultneys, but I don't say so. Dad says never say you're scared and you won't be. Jimmy Pultney has a chicken in one hand and a hatchet in the other. He holds the chicken by the neck, and the neck stretches long. The chicken doesn't try to get away. It hangs quiet, knowing it can't. The chopping block is an old hickory stump. My dad says the Pultneys probably dragged it with them from some holler in the Ozarks. He calls them Okie trash.

I can hear him in the bathroom getting ready. He's humming, and that means he's shaving. I like to watch him shave, but not this morning. I like the scratchy sound and the blue color of his jaw coming out of the white soap. I like the smell of Barbasol. I'm watching Jimmy Pultney, and I'm scared, and I wish I had a way to kill him.

Yesterday, Jimmy tried to kill me. He had the bow and arrow he got for Christmas. It's a nice one with real feathers and steel-tipped arrows. I went over to the fence and said, "Hey, Jimmy, let me see that bow you got."

He was standing over by the back porch. He had an arrow across the string. He turned and said, "See it?" He shot the arrow at my head. I don't think he can shoot a bow. I think he was just lucky. I could see the steel tip coming at my face and the feathers turning slowly, getting larger. The voice in my head said, "Down."

The steel tip went through my hair. It left a hot scratch across the top of my head. Dad won't see it because it's under the thick black hair, and I won't tell him. When I reached up and touched, there was blood and a piece of feather in my hair. I wasn't scared until the arrow was behind me, sticking in the ground. I went to get it, and my knees started to sink. I had to make my feet push them back up. I pulled the arrow out and turned to tell Jimmy I was going to break it.

He was standing at the fence. "Kid, you better gimme that arrow back."

I said, "No, I'm keeping it." I raised it up to break it over my knee. Jimmy's eyes got that way they get. The way all of the Pultneys' eyes can get. Small and cold and don't care. I held the arrow over my knee.

Jimmy said, "Kid, don't make me climb over this fence."

There's a fence between our yards to keep out the Pultneys and their animals. My dad hired a man to build it. Mr. Pultney came out of his back door and stood watching the man work. Mr. Pultney was wearing raggedy blue bib overalls. Jimmy calls them overhauls, and he isn't kidding. Mr. Pultney took out a hawk-billed linoleum knife and cut a piece of chewing tobacco from the plug in his hand. He said to the man, "You cain't put no fence thar."

The man started talking about set-back lines and ease-ments or something, and pretty soon Mr. Pultney backed off to his own porch like he was getting away from the words he didn't understand. I came out on our back porch to watch the man dig holes with his post-hole digger, and Mr. Pultney called into his house to someone, maybe Jimmy, "There's that damn sissy kid. His daddy cain't even build his own fence." Somebody inside the house laughed, maybe Jimmy.

Jimmy said to me, "You better bring me that arrow, kid. You don't, I'm climbing over there and stomp your ass."

again. Them and their goat and that tired old woman Jimmy calls Mommer and Jimmy's nine brothers and sisters. Dad says at least the rest of the Okies made it to California before they wallowed in again. I don't want to watch Jimmy Pultney cut the chicken's head off, but I know I will. I've watched before.

I'm trying to understand how he can do it. Swing the hatchet down on that neck he makes as long as his own, then squat there holding the chicken by its hind legs. Its wings fly, and its long neck swings and sprays blood all over Jimmy and the chopping block and what little grass the goat left behind.

I hear my dad leave the bathroom. He stops humming and goes into the bedroom to put on his white shirt and his tie. I lift my eyes to the end of our yard, where our grass stops and the wheat field starts. I look on across the wheat field to the silo. It's a mile. I've walked it. We live in a sub-division. At night we can see the lights of Omaha. They remind me of a storm coming. I don't know why. My dad works in the city, in a lawyer's office. This all used to be a farm, but the farmer died and his wife, Mrs. Boatwright, sold the land to the man who built our house, our whole street. The builder went broke, my dad says, after he built our street, and so here we are, my dad says, stuck in the middle of all this wheat like a string of wagons that never made it West. Our wheels fell off, and we're stuck here with the Pultneys.

The hatchet comes down hard and straight, and the chicken's head bounces once on the block, and the white wings beat, and then Jimmy's holding the big white bird out in front of him like he just caught it taking off. The wings

I don't talk like Jimmy. I don't say ass or shit or dam
Sometimes I wish I could, but I don't. If I did, and my da
heard it, he'd spank me with his belt and wash out m
mouth with soap. That's what he said he'd do.

I told Jimmy I was going to break his arrow, but
already knew I wasn't. His eyes knew I wasn't going t
either. And pretty soon, his smile knew. I went as close t
the fence as I could and threw the arrow over. Jimmy waite
'til I was inside my house and then walked over and picke
it up. For an hour, I listened to him shooting it into the doo
of his father's shed. Thunk, thunk, thunk it goes into that
door. And I know his father is going to beat him when he
comes home, and I know Jimmy's not going to cry when his
father stripes him with that big greasy razor strop he uses,
and I know Jimmy's eyes aren't going to change.

I can't go outside because I'm wearing my church
clothes. My pants are gray wool, and they itch. Through the
backdoor screen, I can see Jimmy squatting in front of the
chopping block. He's got the chicken's neck between his
thumb and forefinger, and he's moving his hand up and
down, making the neck longer. There are ten, maybe fifteen
chicken heads lying around that block with their eye
crossed out, and they stink. And that's not all that stink
about the Pultneys. They keep a goat. Mr. Pultney calls he
his lawn mower. I've seen him milk her, pressing his stub
bledy cheek against her side and whispering to her. H
spreads goat doo on the sorry patch where he grows collar
greens.

My dad says the Pultneys are worse than Okie trash. H
says they didn't even have the gumption to get two stat
away from some pig-filthy holler before they squatt

beat and the blood pumps. The neck with no head whips like the mouth of a garden hose when you drop it in the grass. The blood pours, then it's a red mist. I can't see Jimmy's eyes, but I know they didn't change. Small and cold and don't care. I don't know how to kill Jimmy. There's no way to do it and not get my dad's belt. There's no way Jimmy wouldn't kill me if I messed it up.

Jimmy walks to the house swinging the chicken like a bell, and I turn back into my kitchen. Dad fixed me breakfast this morning, and it was bad. He fries the bacon 'til it's black, then he puts my eggs in about two inches of grease, and they come out with hard, brown edges. Sometimes he breaks them. I don't complain about it. Once when I complained, he looked at me for a long time and said, "Son, when I was on Guadalcanal and we got separated from our unit, we ate land crabs. A Jap patrol passed only ten yards from where we were hiding. We could smell the rice and saki on their breath. We had to stick the crabs with our trench knives and pry off their shells and eat them raw. You don't know how lucky you are to have those eggs. Even the way I cook them." And he looked at the far away like he does a lot now, and he said, "And you don't know what those crabs were eating before we ate them."

I stop at the table and pick up half a piece of cold toast and eat it. I drink the rest of my orange juice. My dad's not looking, so I drink the rest of his coffee. It's cold, but it's good to me. It tastes like walnuts and brown sugar, and it makes me feel grown-up. The morning paper is open on my dad's side of the table. The headline says, NIXON ATTACKED IN CARACAS. My dad reads the paper every morning. He holds it up so I can't see his face, and I wait, and after a while he puts it down and tells me something about the news. He says it's educational for us to talk about world affairs. My dad doesn't like Nixon, but he likes Eisenhower. "Son," he tells me, "the president was a great general, and a better one was Doug MacArthur. There never was a general that sold a man's life for more than MacArthur. He made them pay ten times for every dead G.I. You know what I mean?"

I say yes, but I don't. I like to hear my dad talk about the war. He talks about it to me, but he won't to other people. I've heard them ask him. I've heard him say, "Oh, hell, we've all heard the same stories a hundred times. Let's talk about that new kid the Yankees got to replace the Clipper. What's his name? Mantle?"

I go into my dad's bedroom to watch him finish dressing. He smiles and winks at me and says, "Hey, Slugger." He's wearing his gray suit pants and a tie with blue stripes. He sits on the bed and puts on his black Oxfords. He keeps them shiny, like a good Marine. He gets up and touches my head where it still burns from Jimmy Pultney's arrow and walks around to the little table beside the bed where the radio is. He picks up his watch and his wedding ring and puts them on. It's the same watch he had in the war, with a radium dial.

Sometimes when I was little and it rained and hail hit the roof and the radio said tornado warnings, I'd get scared and I'd go into my parents' bedroom and I'd find my dad by his watch glowing in the dark. I'd know his arm was around my mother, and her head was on his chest. I'd come in and stand by the bed, and my dad would be awake, and I'd know he was waiting for me, and he'd say, "What's the matter, Marine? The lightning got you spooked?" I'd try not to cry standing there. And he'd say, "All right, Buddy. Why don't you hop up here? There's always room for one more in this bivouac."

Dad looks at his wedding ring. He turns it on his finger and then looks at the picture of Mom in her kimono on the dresser. Then he looks at the shrine Mom keeps in the corner. It's her household god, she told me. Dad doesn't like it. He says we're Presbyterians, but he lets her keep it. She burns incense on it, and it fills the house with a spicy smell I like. Sometimes she leaves a slice of apple or peach in a little blue dish on the altar. She tells me it makes the god happy. It makes the house a happy place. It gives her and dad a good bedroom. I don't know what she means.

I hear Dad's dreams at night. Sometimes he screams at the Japanese in his dreams. Sometimes he calls out orders and says things aren't going well for the Marines. He sleeps with a bayonet under the pillow, and sometimes he gets up at night and walks around the house holding it in his hand, talking to people who aren't there. I've heard him and Mom arguing some nights after his dreams. Once I came into the bedroom when Dad was at work and Mom was making the bed, and I saw her pick up the bayonet with two fingers like you'd hold a dead snake. She turned to me and said, "This is bad, Travis, *kitanai*. It's got the blood of my people on it. Don't you ever touch it."

My mother is beautiful. She's the most beautiful mother on the block. She looks like the ladies in the magazines, the ladies at church and PTA. Except her face is light brown, and her hair is coal black, and her eyes are turned up at the edges. Once I came into the kitchen after school, and she was drinking something from a white bottle that looked like it might have perfume in it. She told me it was saki. She said, "I love you Travis, and I love you don't look like me."

It made me cry, and then it made my mother cry. I don't know why I cried. I wish I knew. I look mostly like my dad, and he never told me he was glad. My skin is darker than his, but not like Mom's, and I have black hair, and my eyes are brown. They aren't turned up at the edges.

When my mom cried, I said, "I love you, Mom. You're the most beautiful mom in the world." That's the truth, too.

My dad puts on his hat. It makes him look like Superman. He's tall and strong, and his jaw is blue after he shaves, and he walks like I want to walk when I'm a man. Like he knows where he's going and nothing can stop him from getting there. "Come on, Trav, Buddy," he says to me. "Time and tide wait for no man."

two

I hate the hospital. I usually wait in the car. Our car is a black, '54 Chevy. Dad says we're going to get a new Buick Roadmaster when he finishes clerking and gets to be a real lawyer. I don't like our car because it's old and doesn't have a radio. It's hot in the car, and there's nothing to do.

Dad visits Mom once a week, on Saturday afternoon. After he sees her, he always tells me she's getting better and she'll be home soon. Sometimes he smiles when he comes through the big double doors. He walks fast like I know he walked in his uniform when he was a Marine, and he stops in the sun and looks at the parking lot, trying to remember where I'm parked. He puts his hat on and smiles.

Other times, he comes out and stops under the oak tree by the sidewalk, and I see him look at the far away. He takes a deep breath and lights a cigarette and rubs his eyes. He stands there smoking, raising his face to the light that falls through the tree branches. That's when I know I have to be quiet. I can't ask about Mom. I can't ask when she's coming home.

Sometimes my dad talks to me about what he calls her case. He says things about hydrotherapy and insulin shock treatment. I don't understand, and I don't think he's really talking to me. He's talking to himself, and I'm listening in.

One day, I came home from school and found Mom curled up under the kitchen sink. She was holding her knees under her chin and singing to herself, a song in Japanese. I don't think I would have found her until Dad came home from work, except I went for a peanut butter and jelly sandwich and a glass of milk, and I heard the singing. I opened the cabinet door. I don't know, it's crazy, but I thought somebody put the radio under there.

Mom didn't open her eyes when I opened the door. She was lying there with the bottles of Lysol and the Ivory soap flakes all pushed back under the pipes. And she had her little shrine with her. It's blue, and it's made of the same stuff our dinner plates are made of, and it's pretty. She had taken it from the bedroom and put it under the sink.

The worst thing was how she didn't look at me, and how she wouldn't speak English. I didn't know what to do. I thought of calling Mrs. Dietz from down the block. She's the Avon lady. She comes up the street once every two weeks or so and tries to sell my mom some perfume or powder or lipstick. My mom usually makes coffee, and they talk. Mrs. Deitz's husband was in the Pacific, too. He was a Seabee. He built the airfield on Saipan. He has dreams, too, she told my mom. And a collection of Japanese swords and pistols. I asked my mom to let me go see them, but she said no. She said, "That perfume is cheap stuff, Trav. But I'm nice to her. I'm stuck out here with no car and that Mrs. Pultney next door, and Bea Dietz is all I got for grown-up company. But don't you ask her to see those swords. Those are *kegashigoto*, Travis. I don't want you touching them."

I didn't call Mrs. Dietz. I sat on the floor beside the sink and talked to my mom for two hours until my dad came home. She didn't talk to me. She just kept singing in Japanese. I wanted to touch her face. I wanted to touch her eyes and say, "See me. I'm Travis." I wanted to crawl in with her and lie there against her like I used to when I was a little kid.

When Dad came home, he pulled her out, and she fought him. She scratched his face. If he hadn't caught her hands, she would have hurt her eyes. He carried her to their bed and held her down and whispered to her until she pulled her knees up under her chin and started singing again. Then he called the doctor.

I know about hospitals. I had the flu when I was a little kid, and I almost died. I got pneumonia, and it took me six weeks to get over it, and I lost a lot of weight, and I almost died. They put me in a ward with a lot of other kids, and some of them died, so I know what that's like, and I know this is not a regular hospital. It's on the outskirts of Omaha, and there's a big fence around it. You come in through a gate, and a man writes down your license number. I asked Dad why he never lets me go in with him, and he said because it might upset Mom, but I know that isn't true. I know it's because of the people in there. I won't say the word. I hate to even think the word, but at night I lie in bed, and I can't stop it. It comes into my head. *Crazy.* My mom is crazy, and I wonder if I'm going to be crazy someday.

Sometimes I have bad dreams that I'm looking for Mom and can't find her. Sometimes I wake up, and I see the green dial of dad's watch at my bedroom door, and he says, "Trav, buddy, you've been entertaining the bogeyman again. Wake up and get rid of him." And I ask him if I can come to his room, and he says, "No, Buddy. You're too big for that now. You've got to tough it out."

We drive through the gate, and the man writes down our number. For once, Dad finds a parking place under a shady tree, but I know I'm not staying in the car. Dad didn't tell me, I just know. We get out, and he puts his hands on my shoulders. "Listen, Buddy," he says. "You're gonna see some strange things in there. I want you be polite no matter what and don't stare at people. If anybody speaks to you, just answer politely if you think you can, and if you can't, just smile and don't say anything at all. I'll take care of you."

We start walking toward the big double doors, and I think of all the times I've sat in the hot car with nothing to do but stare at those doors and wait for my dad, and now here I am going in, and I'm scared. It's like it was when Jimmy Pultney shot the arrow. My knees are all of a sudden gone, and I feel like I'm going to be crawling soon. I try to take my dad's hand, but he won't let me. We walk a few steps, then he rests his hand on my shoulder. Then he takes it away. "Buck up, old Buck," I hear him say.

The nurse at the desk looks up and says, "Good morning, Mr. Hollister." There's a picture of President Eisenhower on the wall behind her. She sees me and comes around the desk. There's a spool on her belt with big heavy keys on it, and when she leans down, I see she's got a mustache. But her eyes are nice, and she says, "I bet you're Travis. Your momma talks about you all the time." She stands up and looks at my dad. "You're a lucky boy to have such nice parents."

I don't like her telling me that. I know it already, and it's none of her business. She opens her desk drawer and takes out a red lollipop. She bends down, and her breath smells like cigarettes. I look at my dad, and he nods, and I take the candy. I say, "Thank you, ma'am," like Dad taught me. None of my friends at school have to say ma'am and sir, but Dad says we're southerners and we say it. He says my friends are all Yankees and don't know anything about manners.

I'm standing there with the candy in my hand and feeling too hollow inside to put it in my mouth, and the nurse says to my dad, "She's in the day room. I thought the boy would like it better in there." I know the way her voice is. I've heard it before. It's how adults send messages kids don't get. Only sometimes you get them.

There's a door to my right, and from beyond it, I hear somebody moan. It's a long, sad sound, and it falls into my hollow stomach and lies there hurting. It makes my hands go sweaty. The nurse pulls a key from the spool on her belt and unlocks the door beyond the desk. It's like the time I got paddled at school for throwing the chalk up into the ceiling fan. I had to walk down the hall and knock on the assistant principal's door and go in, and there was a witness waiting, Mrs. Tarleton, the third grade teacher, and she's pretty, and I didn't want her to see me cry. I stood outside that door for a long time and couldn't knock until Mr. Beard, the assistant principal, the guy who does all the paddling, opened the door and said, "Travis, are you going to stand out there all day?"

It's just like that now. I don't want to go through that door. Not even to see my mom, and I haven't seen her in a long time. Not even if Dad wants me to see her. But I do. I walk through with my dad, and I hear the key snap back on the nurse's spool, and the door locks behind us, and it smells like pee and Lysol inside.

My mother is pretty and looks like all the ladies in the magazines and at church and at the PTA. She's not tall, but she's slender, and she wears high heels that make her legs pretty and make her taller, and stockings with seams down the back that she keeps straight. She wears dresses that have flowers on them, and she wears lots of slips that make the dresses stand out from her legs and sizzle when she walks. She wears Chanel perfume, and I've watched her get dressed after her bath. She puts a dot of perfume on each wrist and then rubs them together and touches the sides of her neck with her wrists. Then she takes the glass top of the perfume bottle, shaped like a teardrop, and opens her robe and touches it to her chest, down low in the middle, and my neck gets thick then, and I love my mother, and now I see her sitting on a metal chair at a table at the far end of a big room, and her hair isn't curled, it's pulled back straight, and she doesn't have on her red lipstick, and she's wearing a green cotton dress with no belt, and she's holding her hands together tight on the table.

When me and Dad come close, I can see in her eyes she wants to stand up and come to me. She wants to hug me and run away with me, but she knows she can't. Her eyes tell me she knows and she's sorry.

Me and Dad take the two chairs across from her, and he reaches into his pocket and gives my mom a small paper bag. She opens it and takes out some sticks of incense. She smiles and says, "Thank you, Lloyd," and my dad looks at her, and his eyes go big and soft, and I don't know what's happening. Then I know. He's going to cry. My dad, Marine 2nd Lieutenant Lloyd T. Hollister. I can't look at this.

It's like when I walk past my parents' bedroom on Sunday afternoon after church, and the radio is playing softly, and there's a cigarette burning in the ashtray by the bed, and my mom is lying with her head on my dad's chest, and it's what I don't know about them, what they have only for themselves, and I put my eyes down and go by fast, out to the backyard, all the way out to the place where our yard meets the wheat field, and I stand there and stare at the dead farmer's silo a mile away.

My dad takes out his handkerchief, and I look away, and I see there are other people in the room. Crazy people.

A man with no hair and sores on his face sits at a table to my right staring down at a checker board with no pieces on it. He lifts his hand to his face but doesn't touch it. His eyes never leave the board. Behind my mom, there's a couch and two women sit on it. One of them rocks back and forth and hums to herself. I recognize the tune. It's Peggy Lee. It's "Fever." My dad likes that song. When it comes on the radio, he stops and listens. He closes his eyes and taps his fingers on his thigh.

The other woman on the couch is slowly pulling the yarn out of a green sweater she's been knitting. She sees me looking at her, so I smile. She says, "Don't you look at me, you filthy little boy. Don't you dare look at me." She gives me the finger.

I've done something wrong. I try to remember what Dad told me out in the parking lot. *Don't talk. Be polite. I'll take care of you.* But Dad is taking care of himself. He's drying his eyes, and he's looking at Mom, and she's looking at me. "Don't mind her, Travis," my mom says. "She doesn't know what she's saying. She knows you're not a filthy little boy." I just nod. I don't know what I'm allowed to do, to say. I want to go around the table and hug my mother. I know she wants me to, but something's keeping us from it. It's like someone is watching, and we have to sit here like this, like we're sitting in a church pew, my hands in my lap, my dad putting his handkerchief back in his pocket.

My parents talk for a while about the house, my dad's

job, bills that have to be paid, the weather, about me and how I did in school. It's summer now and school's out, but when I was going, I wasn't doing so hot. Not after my mom went to the hospital. They talk like I'm not here, and all the time I look at my mom and think how pretty she is, even without the lipstick and the dress with the slips that sizzle and the stockings with straight seams. How she looks just like the ladies in the magazines and at church and at the PTA except she's Japanese, and her skin is dark, and her eyes are turned up at the edges.

After a while, my dad says it's time to go, and I look at him like he doesn't know what he's doing. How can it be time to go when we haven't done anything? I haven't hugged my mom. She hasn't kissed my eyes like she does before I go to sleep at night. She hasn't told me when she's coming home.

We stand up, and I want to cry or punch something or throw the mean lady's knitting on the sore-faced man's checker board and say, "Why don't you two filthy people play a game of sweater checkers?" I look at my mom and let my eyes ask her. *Please.* She knows what I'm saying. Her eyes are sad, and she shrugs. Her eyes say, "I can't." She looks around at the green walls, and I know now they have eyes and they're watching her, and she has to do what they want or she'll never get out of here. She whispers, "I love you, Travis," and she reaches into her pocket and takes out a wallet and hands it to me. She smiles and says, "I made it for you. I hope you like it. It's for your birthday."

I take the wallet and look at it. It's too early for this. My birthday's in two days. I'm going to be twelve, and I'm going to have a cake, and I'm going to be at home with

Mom and Dad, and there's going to be a lot of presents. The wallet has a picture of Roy Rogers riding Trigger on it. My mom says, "I put that picture on there with an electric wand. I hope it's not too young for you. You're getting to be such a big boy."

She looks at Dad. He looks hard at the far away and says, "Miko, it's not too young for him. He loves Roy Rogers."

I still like Roy, but I'm more interested in creatures now. I saw *Creature from the Black Lagoon* at the Rialto downtown last week, and I liked it a lot. I'd like to swim in a river in South America and find this guy with webbed hands and feet and fight him and drag him up on the bank and put him in a big tank and take him home and keep him in my room. He'd be my creature, and I'd show him to all my friends.

My mom looks at me very carefully now, and I put away the wallet, and I say, "Thanks, Mom. I love my wallet. I really do."

She says, "I want you to be a good boy with Grandpa and Grandma Hollister. Will you do that for Momma?"

I say, "Sure." I want her to hug me. I want us to run away. I'd protect her. I'd take care of her. I'd never say she couldn't have her household god.

My dad puts his hand on my shoulder. We all walk to the door and Dad pushes a button, and we hear the nurse's key in the lock. My mom gets down on her knees in front of me, and she looks into my eyes.

My dad says, "Kiss your mom good-bye, Travis, Buddy." He has his old voice back. I can't see his eyes, but I know they aren't big and soft anymore. I know he didn't like me seeing them that way. I wait for Mom to kiss me.

But she waits for me. It's because we're here. She smiles. I lean toward her, and she smells good, the old way, and I try to kiss her cheek but she stops me. She kisses me on the mouth. It's sweet and slow and soft, and I'm crying like I told myself I'd never do again, and she says, "You're going to love that ride on the airplane, Travis, my good boy. You're going to fly on the wind like the spirits of my ancestors," and then Dad lifts me by the arms, and the door opens, and he pulls me through it, and I don't see much more until we're in the car again.

three

I wake up when the stewardess shakes me. Her name is Wendy, and she smells good like my mom, but she doesn't look like the ladies at church and PTA. She looks like the lady the Creature kidnapped in the Black Lagoon. She's the most beautiful lady I've ever seen that isn't in a magazine or on TV or in the movies. She's my friend. When the plane took off, she let me sit beside her and buckled my seat belt. I was so surprised when we left the ground, I said, "It feels like my stomach's going into my butt," and Wendy giggled and put her finger across her mouth. She gave me a Coke in a paper cup and a Baby Ruth. After I ate the candy and we hit a storm and the plane started to bounce around, I wasn't feeling so hot. Wendy gave me a pill that made my stomach feel better and made me sleepy. She gave it to me with a paper cup full of water, and she leaned down and I smelled her, and she kissed me on the cheek and then rubbed off the lipstick and said, "You'll probably sleep the rest of the way, but don't worry, Gorgeous, I'll wake you up before we land."

I looked at her, and I know I was smiling. I was already feeling warm and my stomach wasn't flopping anymore. I said, "Gorgeous? What does that mean?"

I know what it means, but I wanted her to tell me. She laughed. "It means you're gonna be a heartbreaker some day, Kid. Now go to sleep and dream about the Sugar Plum Fairy."

I said, "I'm too old for that." I yawned.

She said, "Then dream you're Mickey Mantle."

Now Wendy shakes me and says, "Did you hit a home run,

Gorgeous?" and I remember Mickey Mantle, and I'm going to be a heartbreaker, and that must be good because Wendy smiled when she said it. She leans down and says, "That pill really swacked you. Why don't you look out the window? That'll wake you up. We're approaching Panama City."

Wendy has freckles on her nose and red hair pulled back in a bun, and she's wearing a garrison cap. My dad has one. He says the Marines call it a pisscutter. She's wearing a brown skirt that's tight and a white blouse with a brown bow tie and an Eisenhower jacket. She's got a pair of silver wings, and I want her to give them to me, but I know I can't ask.

The man in front of me asks her for a book of matches, and she winks at me and says, "Right away, sir," and goes on up the aisle, and I pull aside the curtain and look out.

I see the ocean for the first time. The land curves down there where it meets the sea, and there's a wide beach the color of wheat, and I can see white waves breaking, and there's even a car on the beach, and I can see people walking near the car, and they look like little bugs. I look back behind us and see how the land curves, and I know from geography class that's what they call the Panhandle, and maybe I can see as far back as where Florida meets Alabama.

I'm not so drowsy anymore. I'm getting excited about my new life. I'm going to live with my grandparents and my Aunt Delia for three months in Florida, and I'm going to get me a boat and go fishing out there in all that blue water and catch marlins and sharks, and maybe a creature. When I come back to the dock, I'm going to hang my big marlin up by his tail and stand next to him with my fishing rod and let people take pictures of me and put them in the newspaper, and I'm going to cut one out and send it to my dad, and he'll be proud.

When we land, it's like my stomach tries to get out through my throat, but I'm ready for it now, and it's kind of fun. We stop at the terminal, and I wait like Wendy told me and watch the passengers go up the aisle. I'm the only kid, and the women look at me, and some of them think it's sad I'm traveling alone, so I look back and let my eyes say, "It's only flying, for criminy sake. What's the big deal?"

When the plane is empty, the captain and the copilot come out of the cockpit door and stretch and smile and look around. Wendy comes back and says, "Time to go, Mr. Mantle."

She takes my hand, and I almost tell her I'm too big for that, but I like her hand. It's soft and cool, and it smells good. We go up the aisle, and the captain bends down and says, "So, what did you think of your first flight, kid?"

And I say, "Neato!" It's all I can think of. I'm looking at the wings on his chest. They're bigger than Wendy's, and they're gold. I can smell cigarettes on his breath, and he uses Mennen's aftershave like my dad. My face is getting red. Wendy says, "What the heck, Bernie, I think 'neato' just about covers it."

The captain smiles and ruffles my hair, and it hurts where Jimmy Pultney's arrow cut me. The captain says, "Yup, 'neato' does it for me, too."

Wendy walks me through the terminal, and we pick up my suitcase, and she takes me to the place where people meet people, and I don't see my Grandma and Grandpa Hollister. I've only seen them once before, when I was a baby. It's a long way from Florida to Omaha, and Dad says

Mom and my grandparents didn't get along all that well, but I know what they look like from the pictures Dad keeps on the bureau in the big bedroom.

Wendy lets go of my hand and looks at her watch. "Gee, Mick, didn't your mom and dad tell them when to meet you?"

She looks around the terminal. It's not as big as the one in Omaha, and there aren't many people now. Through the windows, I can see palm trees. Honest to God palm trees, just like on Arthur Godfrey. It's hot in the terminal, hotter than in Omaha, and I know it's going to be hot outside. And the people sound different. They talk slower, like the farm kids at home, only different. It's more like music. Rock 'n' roll music. Like that Elvis my dad says is a subversive, whatever that means.

Wendy puts her hands on her hips and says, "I got to meet Lucille at 2:30." She looks at me, and I'm not Mick or gorgeous anymore. I'm the kid that's holding things up here. I know the feeling.

Wendy takes me outside, and we look up and down the sidewalk in front of the terminal. It's hotter than I ever felt in Omaha, and the air is full of smells I never smelled before, and I can tell, I don't know how, that I'm smelling the ocean. It's salty and fishy and some other things I can't name. It's exciting, and I'm going to have a boat.

Cars pull up and people get out and hug other people and take their bags, and there's laughing and crying, but there's no Grandma and Grandpa Hollister.

There's sweat on Wendy's forehead, and her eyes look tired red behind the dark makeup. She reaches up and pushes some hair out of her eyes. I pull my hand from hers.

I say, "I can wait here by myself. It's okay. I mean, I won't do anything wrong or anything."

She smiles at me and looks up and down the sidewalk again. "Well...," she says.

I smile at her. I've got to stop being such a kid. I've got to grow up and face things and tough it out like my dad says. I say, "You got to meet Lucille, right?"

She looks at her watch again. "You're such a sweetie, Mick." She kneels and kisses me on the cheek. "Don't talk to any strangers, okay?"

"Sure," I say. Grandma and Grandpa and Aunt Delia are strangers.

Wendy walks a few steps, then turns and looks back at me. She's pretty, and she was my friend, and she said I was gorgeous and a heartbreaker. She waves, and I wave. I'm going to remember the way she smelled and the feel of her lips on my cheek. I watch until she's gone back inside the terminal, then I move my suitcase back into the shade and sit on it and start counting planes that land and take off. A DC-3 takes off, and a Beechcraft Bonanza with a V tail makes a perfect three-point landing.

A man comes by and says, "You okay, Kid?" He's a stranger, but his eyes are all right, so I say, "Yeah, I'm okay. My mom went to make a phone call. I'm waiting out here for my Uncle Fred."

He looks at me a minute, shakes his head, and walks on. I think he knows I'm lying, but maybe not. Maybe I'm good at it.

I count more planes, and a black man comes by in a blue jumpsuit with "Buster" stitched on it in red letters. He stops next to me to light a Camel, and some of the good-smelling smoke drifts across my face. He says, "Hey, Little Guy. Didn' yo folks come for you?" He seems nice, but he's a stranger, and he's black, and I don't know what to say. We don't have black people in Omaha. We've got a few Indians. I've seen them downtown when I go to the YMCA. They drink from a paper bag, and sometimes they stop people and ask for money. Uncle Fred doesn't occur to me this time, so I say, "They're just late. They'll get here, I guess."

I try to look like it's fun sitting on my suitcase in the shade counting planes that land in Panama City. But it's not fun anymore. What if they don't come? What do I do? Where do I stay? In a movie I saw, a stranger rode into town on a horse in a sandstorm, and he broke into the cellar of a house and cut open a can of peaches and ate them and slept on a pile of old saddles and harnesses. I look around and don't see any houses. The airport's out in the country, and the land is hot and green and looks like jungle. There are bare patches of white sand. In a pine tree way off, a big bird, maybe an eagle, sits hunched in the sun.

The black man says to me, "Kid, you go on back inside and ax for the security man. Ax at any them counters. They give you the security man. He call yo folks for you."

I wonder if there will be black people where I'm going. I wonder if I'll get to know any. I wonder if they'll like me. I smile. I don't know what to say. The black man waits a minute. He takes another puff on his Camel, blows on the ash, smiles at me, and walks on down the sidewalk.

That's when I get scared.

four

I go inside, but I don't see the security man. There's nobody at the airline counter. Down the way, there's an old black man with a mop and a bucket, but I can't ask him to call my Grandpa Hollister. I don't know their number. They live in a town called Widow Rock, but I don't know where it is. All I've got is the wallet Mom gave me with Roy Rogers and Trigger on it and the rest of my plane ticket, and a five-dollar bill Dad gave me. Maybe I should walk down the terminal until I find a plane that's leaving and give them my ticket and go back home to Omaha and tell Dad I decided to stay with him. Tell him I'll learn how to cook and stay out of trouble and look after the house when he goes to visit Mom, and I won't kill Jimmy Pultney.

I take out my ticket and look at it, but what if they won't take my ticket now. I've got money. Maybe I should wave at a cab like they do in the movies and stay in a hotel and call Dad and tell him Grandma and Grandpa Hollister don't want me.

I go outside again and look up and down the sidewalk, and I see a big white car coming. It's a Buick Roadmaster, the kind of car Dad wants to buy when he's through clerking and gets to be a real lawyer. There's sun on the windshield, and I can't see who's in the car, but I stand by the curb with my suitcase anyway. The car stops, and the window rolls down, and a big round face looks out. There's a pink handkerchief next to the face, and it's Grandma Hollister. She's crying.

She opens the car door and rushes out at me. She's a big woman, and I know she's going to hug me, and I brace myself. She's got on a black dress with little white dots, and she's got a big chest, and she stoops down and scoops me into her and says, "Oh, child, I was so worried. Your grandpa had an emergency, and then we ran into some road construction, and I just knew you were gonna get snatched by white slavers."

My face is buried between her big old soft chests (Jimmy Pultney calls them titties, but I don't say that word), and she smells like mothballs and the kind of perfume Mrs. Deitz tries to sell my mom, and I'm fighting for air. I know she's got to let me go, but I don't know when. I'm about to put both hands on her and push when she grabs my arms and holds me away from her. "Let me look at you, Child. My Lord, how you've grown!"

I see two legs in black pants and shiny black boots, the kind that go ankle high and zip up the sides, and a voice says, "That's what boys do, Lilah. He was under two years old the last time you saw him. Did you think he wouldn't grow?"

The man laughs, and it's deep and rough like a saw blade getting caught in a board, then breaking free again, and I look up, and it's Grandpa Hollister. He's tall, like my dad, and he looks like my dad, or, I guess like my dad is going to look when I grow up. His black hair is cut so short you can see the white skin on the sides of his head, and his eyes are blue like the ocean when I was way up in the air, and his nose is long and thin, and he's smiling at me, but it's not a smile that says things are funny. It says they're just like he expected them to be.

Grandma Hollister stands up and wipes her wet, red eyes with the pink hanky. I look at the big gold shield painted on the white door of the Buick. It says, Choctawhatchee County

Sheriff. There's an Indian on the shield, and he's holding a book in one hand and one of those scales in the other, the kind you use to weigh things. Grandpa Hollister leans down to take my suitcase, and his black suit coat comes open, and I see the gold badge on his white shirt. I remember what Dad told me about him. "Your grandpa runs that county, Travis. Sure, there are mayors and county commissions and all that, but in those little counties, the sheriff runs things, and if he's a good one, he keeps the lid on things, and if people know what's good for them, they don't cross him. Your grandpa's hard, but he's fair, Travis. He raised me that way, and that's how I'm raising you."

I wonder if Grandpa Hollister is carrying a gun, and if he'll let me shoot it someday. I don't see any gun. He puts my suitcase in the trunk, and I start to get in the back seat, but Grandma Hollister grabs my hand. "Oh no you don't, Little Man. You're sitting right up front between your grandparents. I don't even want you that far away from me. You gave me such a fright."

I'm thinking I didn't give anybody a fright. I'm the one left standing around an empty airport, but I'm not mad. I like Grandma Hollister. She's big and soft, and she likes me. She guides me to the front seat, and Grandpa Hollister says, "Just a minute, Lilah. Didn't the boy forget something?"

"Forget what?" Grandma says.

"His manners."

Grandpa Hollister looks at me out of cold blue eyes and says, "Come around here, Son, and give me a man's handshake and introduce yourself."

So I get loose from Grandma Hollister, and I walk around to his side of the car, and I stand in front of him.

I give him my hand, and I squeeze his as hard as I can like my dad taught me, but it's no contest. My hand is getting crushed, and it hurts enough to make my eyes water, but I say, "Hello, sir. I'm Travis Hollister, your grandson. I'm pleased to meet you, and I hope we're going to get along."

I'm doing real good until I hit the get along part. He doesn't like it, and he gets that look in his eyes my teacher, Mr. Frawley, gets when he says I'm too smart for my own good. (Mr. Frawley's the one who sent me down to get paddled for throwing the chalk into the ceiling fan.) My Grandpa Hollister's eyes get that way, cold and small, and he bends and takes my shoulders in both his hands. He pinches, and it hurts. He says, "You're a good boy, Travis, or so I hear, and you've been raised right by a good man. But you've been raised in the wrong part of the country. We have manners here in the South. Little boys respect their elders. Your grandma and I are going to show you how to do that. Do you understand me?"

He isn't kidding. This isn't funny. His long fingers dig like knives into my shoulders. I nod and say, "Yes, sir, I understand," but I can barely get the words out. He holds me for a while, still looking into my eyes, and I'm thinking about wanting to kill Jimmy Pultney and getting caught by a policeman with eyes like my grandpa's. They see into you. They know what you're thinking. They don't like what you're thinking most of the time. Maybe I'd like to have eyes like that someday.

Grandpa Hollister lets me go, and I get in the front seat, and Grandma Hollister slides in beside me and pushes me up against Grandpa Hollister's leg. She's soft, and he's hard. He's thin and straight, and she's rolly and round. I like her better, but I don't want to look like her.

We pull out of the airport onto a country road, and the tires hum on the asphalt, and the hot air pours in through the windows, and it's got that ocean smell. I look past Grandma Hollister at the tall pines going by and other trees we don't have in Omaha. I can already tell different kinds of palm trees. Tall ones with just a blossom of green at the top, and short, squatty ones with spikes going up their trunks. I want to learn what to call them. I want to know what I'm smelling and seeing, and I look at Grandma Hollister and say, "Am I going to live by the ocean?"

If she says yes, I'm going to ask if I can have a boat, but she just laughs and ripples go through her chest, and she puts her soft hand on my knee and says, "My goodness, Travis, where did you get that idea? Widow Rock isn't on the water." She looks across at Grandpa Hollister.

He's driving with a squint in his eyes and his hands hard on the steering wheel. Grandma Hollister says, "John, how far are we from the water? Tell Travis."

Grandpa Hollister doesn't look at me. He's calculating. We pass a wagon pulled by a horse. The wagon has big wobbly wheels with wooden spokes. A black man stands on the front of the wagon holding the reins in one hand and an RC Cola in the other. When we pass, he lifts the bottle to his mouth and drains it and tosses it into the ditch, and I'm thirsty. Grandpa pulls the Buick back into our lane and says, "We're fifty-two point seven miles from the Panama City limit, I reckon."

I'm disappointed, but I won't show it. I say, "I didn't know they still had horses and wagons like that. Are we gonna see a lot of them?"

My grandpa smiles. It's that smile again. The one that says he knows what you're going to say before you say it.

He says, "Boy, didn't your daddy explain to you the difference between a horse and a mule?"

All I can say is no, he didn't.

Quietly, Grandpa Hollister says, "No *what?*"

I say, "No, sir. Sorry."

Grandma Hollister puts her hand on my knee again. "Don't worry about the ocean, Travis. We'll drive down to see it before you go back home. We'll take a picnic lunch and make a day of it. And we've got a river not three miles from our house. That's where the young people swim. I'll bet your Aunt Delia will take you there if you ask her nicely."

She looks at me, and I smile, and I'm thinking a boat and a river won't be as good as the ocean, but it'll be pretty good. Grandma Hollister says, "Travis, did you know your daddy was quite the hero around these parts?"

She's nice. I'm sure of that now. She's my grandmother, and I'm supposed to love her, and I'm going to try. I say, "You mean in the war, ma'am?"

"Yes, Travis, that, and other things, too. Your daddy was a fine athlete. He still holds the county record for the hundred-yard dash. And he was a very good student. He won the Sons of the Confederacy Award for Citizenship and Scholarship. People around here still remember him as a fine example of young manhood. Small towns don't forget, Travis."

She looks over at Grandpa Hollister. I look, too. It's like looking straight into the sun. "Why, imagine," my Grandma Hollister says, "Lloyd didn't tell the boy about his records and honors."

Grandpa Hollister looks at her, and it's the way my dad looks at the Pultneys' backyard. He says, "Lloyd is modest,

Lilah." He looks at me for the first time since we got in the car. "Hollisters don't crow about their accomplishments, Travis. We let our deeds speak for us. I'm sure you know that from the way your father behaves."

I want to say I know it from my mom, too. I want to tell him I love her, too, and someday I'm going to Japan, and I'm going to meet my Grandpa and Grandma Kobayashi. I want to tell him he should ask me how my mom is doing. I want to tell him my dad never looks at my mom the way he just looked at Grandma Hollister. But I don't. Maybe I will, some of it, later, but not now. I want to get along and make a good impression like my dad told me to. I just say, "Yes, sir."

We ride along, and I watch the speedometer. Grandpa Hollister holds it dead on fifty. It's hot, and the sun makes silver pools on the asphalt road, but we never reach the water. My dad told me it's called a mirage. I like to watch it, but it makes me thirsty. We pass farms, and there are cows and horses, but they're not like the ones in Omaha. They look sick and tired, and they stay in the shade of the trees and stretch their necks and eat the leaves as far up as they can reach.

After a while, we pass people who wave at Grandpa Hollister. The black men take off their hats when we pass. Grandpa Hollister doesn't wave back. He just lifts his long first finger from the steering wheel to each person. We cross over a bridge that says, HIAWASSEE RIVER, and I look down and see the water running fast and brown over slate rocks covered with green moss, but no boats, and then we're gliding past a sign that says, WELCOME TO WIDOW ROCK.

five

We stop at the curb, and Grandma Hollister says, "Well, here we are, Travis. What do you think?"

The house where I'm going to live is on a hill. It's big and white, and it has screened porches in front and back on both floors. There's a vacant lot next door, and on the other side a house that's smaller. I know I'm supposed to like it, and I'm supposed to say so, and I do. "Wow, it's neato." Then I remember and say, "Ma'am." I don't look over at Grandpa Hollister.

We get out, and he gets my suitcase from the trunk, and I look around. There are two big oak trees in the front yard, and two in the back. It's cool under the trees, and I can feel a breeze blowing. The air has that strange good smell, and I wonder if I'm smelling the river. There's a garage beside the house with two doors and the same green tin roof as the house. There's not much grass in the yard, it's mostly just red dirt. We don't have that kind of dirt in Omaha, and I expected sand because this is Florida. The dirt has straight lines in it where somebody raked. The house has columns across the front, upstairs and down, and eight big windows with green shutters. It looks old, and I can smell something cooking, and it smells good.

Out in the backyard, there's a little house with a white door and a green tin roof and a half-moon cut in the door. I look at Grandma Hollister, and say, "What's that, ma'am?"

Grandma Hollister puts her hand to her big chest and blushes. She's got very white skin and a lot of little black dots on her face, moles I guess, and when she blushes, her face gets real red. She says, "Why, Travis, that's the necessary house. Country people call it the outhouse. But don't worry, we've got indoor plumbing. It's just something your grandfather wanted because his family had one. You know, sometimes it's hard for southern people to change."

I still don't know what the little house is for, but I'm going to find out. I'm going to learn a lot of things here. I know that.

Grandpa Hollister carries my suitcase up on the porch and sets it down. He gets back into the Buick and drives it around to the garage and gets out and opens the doors and pulls it into the dark cool in there.

Tires squeal around a corner, and I turn and see a car coming. It's a white '55 Chevy, and I hear the radio playing loud, and I recognize the voice. It's Elvis. He's singing "Heartbreak Hotel." I like his voice. It reminds me of the black man in the airport talking. It reminds me of Wendy saying I'm gonna be a heartbreaker.

The white car with the loud radio comes down the street fast, and it doesn't go on by. It throws up a big cloud of red dust as it pulls into the driveway where Grandpa Hollister is just coming out of the garage. He jumps back as the Chevy rushes past and scrapes to a stop in the garage. I didn't see who was driving, just dark sunglasses and a swing of black hair. The engine rumbles in the dark garage, and Elvis sings about broken hearted lovers. Then the engine stops, and it's quiet again.

I watch Grandpa Hollister. I know he's gonna be mad. I wonder if somebody's gonna be arrested. He's the sheriff. I can see the white car door open in the garage now, and two long, white legs swing out of the car seat. I see two white tennis shoes with pink laces, and then a pair of white shorts and a white blouse and a tennis racket with a green cover. She walks out of the garage and right up to my Grandpa Hollister and goes up on her toes and kisses his cheek. "Hey, Daddy-o," she says, and her voice is music, too. Not like Elvis, but music anyway, and she looks over at Grandma Hollister who's got both hands on her chest now, and the girl says, "Uh-oh. Looks bad. What'd I do now, Mama? Did somebody call in another Widow Rock Gossip Report?"

Grandpa Hollister's eyes change. They look like I never expected them to. They say he doesn't care about the loud radio or the reckless driving. Nobody's gonna get arrested. They say he can't do anything about how he feels right now. Nothing at all. Grandma Hollister says, "Delia, I've told you a hundred times not to charge into the driveway at that dreadnaught speed. You could have run right over little Travis here. You could have gone right through the back wall of my garage."

My Aunt Delia looks at me and smiles, and her smile is like a sunrise over the wheat fields back in Omaha, and then she winks at me, and it's like Wendy, only better, and she says, "Hey there, old Travis. My, aren't you a big boy? And such a pretty one, too. Killer, your pictures don't do you justice. Come here and give your Aunt Delia a big hug."

This isn't going to be like hugging my Grandma Hollister. Suddenly, I'm shy. I don't know what to do. I look at Grandpa Hollister, but he's looking at my Aunt Delia like she can do anything she wants, and his eyes will never again be like they were when he pinched my shoulders and said he was going to raise me southern.

My Aunt Delia sees I'm not moving, and I guess she sees my face is getting red, so she smiles and laughs, and her laugh sounds like I know the water in that river is going to sound splashing over the rocks. She says, "All right then, Killer, I'm gonna run you down and hug you. How 'bout that?"

She bends her knees and does a funny Groucho run at me, and I don't know what to do. I hear Grandma Hollister say, "Oh, Delia, don't frighten the boy. He just got here, and he's got plenty of time to know you're a lunatic."

Delia smiles that smile again. "Look out, ole Trav. Here I come, and I'm a lunatic, and I'm the subject of eighty percent of all Widow Rock Gossip Reports."

I just let her catch me.

I don't move, and she's got me in a tent of her good-smelling black hair and the soft skin of her cheek against mine, and I go soft and strange all over, and I know I'm going to like my Aunt Delia. A lot.

When she lets me go, I don't want her to. I look at her and try to talk, and she says, "Well, Travis, don't you like me? We're gonna spend some time together, Boy, so you better get used to crazy old Delia."

I'm still trying to talk, and she says, "Just like his daddy, old sobersides Lloyd. Too serious to let a girl know where she stands with him."

Finally I get my tongue loose. "I like you, Aunt Delia. I like you fine."

And my Aunt Delia laughs. She throws back her head, and I see her long, pretty throat, and there's a gold cross on a gold chain, and she laughs loud and long like a man. Finally, she says, "Well, I've had compliments, Son. So I'm fine, am I? Well, so are you, Travis old Killer. I can tell we're going to be friends."

She grabs my suitcase, and we go inside, and the house smells good with dinner cooking, and she says, "Come on, Killer, I'll show you your room. You're gonna be right across the hall from crazy Delia." When she calls me Killer and herself crazy, I can hear Grandma Hollister sigh behind me. I follow Delia's long white legs up the stairs.

My room is big, with two windows, and the bed is snug under the slope of the roof. It's a big, high bed made of iron, and Delia says, "Jump up there, Killer, and give it a bounce." I get on the bed, but I don't stand up because I'd hit my head. I just bounce my butt a few times, and the springs squeak, and my Aunt Delia puts her hand to her ear and says, "Hear it? 'Welcome, Killer. Welcome, Killer.' That old bed is glad you're here."

I look at Delia and smile and say, "I'm glad, too."

Delia sits down on the bed beside me, and her eyes go a little funny, and she hugs me again, and there I am for the second time inside that tent of black hair and sweet, scary smell, and her arms are soft-strong around my shoulders, and she says, "I know you've had a hard time, Travis, and I know you miss your mom and even that old sobersides brother of mine, but I'm gonna do my best to make you feel at home here. We're gonna get to know each other just like family should, and maybe when the summer's over your momma will be better, and things will be good for you again at home."

She lets go of me and pushes me away from her and holds my shoulders, and we look at each other, and I know I can trust her. I know I can talk to her. Somehow, I know it. She's the first grown-up, or almost grown-up, I can talk to since my mom. I used to talk to my mom, and she used to understand, and I didn't have to be careful what I said like I do with my dad. If I say the wrong thing with him, he tells me a good Marine doesn't think that way, and I have to remember not to say the thing I said again.

Now I look into my Aunt Delia's eyes. They're soft and blue, and I don't know what to say. My tongue is thick again, and I swallow, and I say, "Thank you, Aunt Delia." She looks at me, and that sunrise smile breaks across her face, and she ruffles my hair, and she says, "You're a poet, Killer. But not of the spoken word."

She starts unpacking my suitcase and putting the clothes in a big chest she calls a high boy, and it's getting dark outside, and we talk about school and how I'm not doing too well, and about Little League and how I'm a pretty good shortstop and our team finished third last summer and how I'm gonna miss playing this summer. And Delia tells me she's got a mitt and a ball, and she knows where she can borrow another one, and she'll take me out for a game of catch and maybe knock me a few grounders and see if I'm really any good at shortstop. I laugh and tell her girls can't throw, and she pulls up the sleeve of her white blouse and makes a muscle for me and says, "You see how hard that is, Boy? Why, I can whip that pill across the infield like old Scooter Rizzuto. It goes so fast you can't even see it."

She makes a few practice throws with no ball, and it's pretty good, actually, but I laugh and hold my nose and say, "You look like an octopus tying his shoes," and I don't know where that came from. It just came. I've never even seen an octopus. She laughs and shakes her fist at me.

She finishes putting my clothes away, and she holds up a pair of my uns and says, "Man, you got some cute little unmentionables, Travis," and I laugh, and I'm not even embarrassed for her to see my uns.

We go downstairs, and the table in the big dining room is set, and I hear someone singing in the kitchen, and I know it's not Grandma Hollister. It's a deep, sweet voice, and the words are beautiful and sorry. "I looked over Jordan and what did I see-eee, comin' fo to carry me hooooome."

Delia stands behind me and says, "Killer, that's Marvadell. She cooks for us. She makes the best spoon bread and biscuits and cheese grits in Choctawhatchee County." She calls out to the kitchen, "Marvadell, come out here and meet old Travis, the lonesome wayfaring stranger from out where the wheat fields grow and the wind blows so hard it snatches a boy's hair right out of his head."

Grandma Hollister comes in, and she's wearing a different dress, loose with flowers on it, and no stockings, and she's wearing slippers with a big yellow flower on each toe, and she says, "Delia, leave Marvadell alone so she can finish dinner. And stop confusing poor Travis." Grandma Hollister looks at me like I'm supposed to agree, and I try to look confused, but I can't. I like being a lonesome wayfaring stranger. I look at my Aunt Delia and try not to laugh.

The singing stops in the kitchen, and a big black face shoves through the door in a cloud of steam. Marvadell's smile is as big and white as her apron, but there's something else in her eyes. Something far away and unreachable like the place in that song, that Jordan. She's got look-over-Jordan eyes, but she wipes her hands on her apron and says, "Please to meet you I'm sure, Travis. I hope you gone like it here."

Delia winks at me and says, "He's sho gone like your cooking, Marvadell. If he doesn't, we'll know he's got a screw loose up there in that cute head of his, and we'll put him on the next plane back to Omaha."

I hear Grandpa Hollister come into the room behind me. The quiet way he walks puts the hair up on the back of my neck. I turn, and he's looking at Delia in that way again, and he says, "Delia, if you don't stop running your mouth at Travis, he's going to think he's landed in Marianna, not Widow Rock."

I look confused, and Delia puts her finger across her mouth and says, "Marianna's the state home for the mentally ill. You know, the crazy folks." Delia sees what happens in my eyes when she says that word, and I guess she remembers about my mom. She says, "Daddy's right. All this Hollister family humor is a little overwhelming. Come on over here and sit with me, and we'll look at the new *Life* magazine until Marvadell serves up."

After dinner, I'm up in my room sitting on the bed. I brought some books, and I'm gonna read one. My Aunt Delia knocks on the door and comes in. She sits on the bed beside me and says, "Travis, I'm sorry about all that crazy talk about crazy. I shouldn't have used that word with you."

"It's all right," I say. Looking into her eyes, it is all right.

She says, "That's good. Words can't hurt you unless you let them. Remember that, okay?"

I tell her I'll remember.

six

It's night and it's raining and I wake up.

I can smell the rain coming through the open window, and I'm going to go find my dad's radium dial shining in the dark, and then I remember it's not Omaha rain. It's Florida rain. I'm in my new home. I can hear the oak trees swishing and groaning outside and see the white curtains swaying wet into the room. Lightning flashes, and I count like my dad taught me—*one-thousand-one, one-thousand-two, one-thousand-three*—then thunder booms three miles away. I get up to close the window, and I'm standing in rainwater.

There's a bathroom out on the landing between my room and my Aunt Delia's. I took my first bath there after dinner (the Florida Hollisters call it supper). They don't have a shower, just a big old tub on feet shaped like bird claws clutching pine cones. I washed and sat in the water until it got cold, and I pulled the plug and watched the last dirt of Omaha go down the drain.

I stand in the doorway of my new bedroom, trying to see my way to the bathroom. I'm going to get a towel and dry the floor. Lightning flashes through the bathroom window, and I can see Delia's bedroom door, and it's open. As I pass, I hear something. At first I think it's just the storm, maybe the oak trees swishing and swaying out in the yard, but then I know it's not. It's Delia. My Aunt Delia. She's crying. I don't know what to do. I hope I don't have to do anything, but I hear her crying. It's like that sound I heard through the locked door in the hospital where my mom is. It's a sad and hurt sound, and it crawls into your heart and makes a home.

I open my Aunt Delia's door a little more and go in. My heart is beating so hard it makes my ears move. I stand in the dark just inside and look for her bed. It's that white thing there under the slope of the roof, and I can see her black hair on the pillow. I don't want to do anything, but I know I can't go. I have to stay here until I know she's all right.

I'm going to say, "Aunt Delia, are you all right?" but before I can, I hear her sob, and then there's a hard catch of breath that says she sees me. She says, "Who's that? Travis? Travis, is that you?"

All I say is, "Yes." Then, "Ma'am."

She clears her throat and sighs, and I hear her move in the bed, and she says, "Come over here, Travis."

I do. I stand by the bed and look down at her. I can't see her face, but I know how it looks. It looks hurt. I can smell her. I can even smell her crying. It's a smell that makes me want to stay and makes me want to run, too. She reaches out and touches my arm and says, "Did the rain scare you?" Her fingers move down to my hand, and the hair stands up on the back of my neck. I shiver and say, "No, ma'am."

My Aunt Delia laughs. It's a sad laugh. "Travis, you can drop all that ma'am crap with me. Just call me Delia. We're gonna be friends, aren't we?"

I tell her yes, I hope so. Then I say, "Delia," and it feels strange because she's so grown up. It feels secret, too, because I know I won't call her that in front of Grandma and Grandpa Hollister.

She says, "You haven't told me what you're doing here."

I say, "I heard you crying. I thought I better see if you needed help."

She doesn't say anything, and I can't see her face, and I'm glad I can't. She might be laughing at me. I hope not. My face gets hot because maybe I've done the wrong thing. Maybe she wasn't crying.

She moves over to the wall and pulls the covers back. "Get in here, Travis. We'll shelter from the storm together. We'll be a couple of wind-blown waifs. How 'bout that?"

I crawl up into the bed. I don't know what waifs is. I lie on my back, but Delia puts her hand on my side and turns my back to her. She pulls me close against her and puts her chin on the top of my head. It feels so good. She's so warm, and I'm in the nest of her smells. I want to stay here forever, and part of me misses my mom so bad, and part of me doesn't want to think about my mom at all.

We lie that way for a while, and the rain beats against the window, and the oak tree hisses and sways, and it lightnings again, and I count inside my head, and the lightning is getting closer. Delia lifts her hand from my side and reaches around me and takes my hand in hers and squeezes it. "You're a gallant man, Travis. Coming in here to comfort old Delia. You've got the instincts of a cavalier."

I don't know what she's talking about, but I know what I want to know. I say, "Delia?" It's hard to say her name even in the dark, but I like it, too. And I say, "*Were* you crying?"

She sighs and her breath is sweet in my hair and around my face. She says, "Yes, Travis, old Killer, I was."

I ask her, "Why were you crying?" and I think of my nights in Omaha lying in my bedroom and listening to my mom and dad talking low and sweet in their bed and the radio playing and Peggy Lee singing, "Fever," and sometimes listening to them whisper hard and raspy when they don't want me to hear, and sometimes, late at night, hearing my dad have his dreams about the war. That's why I want to know what made my Aunt Delia cry.

Delia sighs again, and again it's sweet, but this time I feel her body go hard behind me, and she squeezes my hand so hard it hurts, and then she loosens her fingers, and her body goes soft again, and she says, "For someone lost, Travis. I was crying for someone lost."

"Who?" I say.

"I can't tell you that. I can never tell anyone that," and then she buries her face in the back of my neck, and she cries. Hard. So hard I think even the storm won't cover the sound. So hard the bed shakes, and I imagine Grandpa and Grandma Hollister running up the stairs and finding me in my Aunt Delia's bed, and I wonder what they would do, or if they would do anything, and I wonder if it's wrong for me to be here.

Finally I think it isn't wrong. I'm a cavalier with gallant instincts, and I'm comforting a waif, and there can't be anything wrong with that. I try to turn around and put my arms around her, but she stops me. She holds me hard, and her breath comes so hot and hard against the back of my neck that I can feel her teeth there, and she says, "No, Travis. No. Just let me.... Don't move. This will pass, and..."

Her voice is broken and ragged, and I don't know what to do, but I think I better stay. I better let her ride my back like a boat in a storm. I'm all she's got this night. Maybe this will never happen again. Maybe this is just a storm my Aunt Delia has to get through. I don't think I'll ever understand it. I don't think she'll ever tell me who is lost. I don't think I should ever even ask her.

My Aunt Delia cries and cries. She sobs until my neck is wet, and the shape of her front teeth is pressed into my neck. Sometimes it's almost like she's trying to pull me inside her to stop the crying. I let her do what she wants. I wait. I try not to think about the storm passing over and the sound of her sobbing and the shaking bed waking Grandpa Hollister. And finally, as the rain stops slanting hard, then comes down straight, then just patters in the trees, and then stops and the trees just drip the water left in them, Delia stops sobbing and stops crying, and finally she's breathing soft into the back of my neck, and after a while, maybe she's asleep.

Her breath is long and sweet and slow against the back of my neck, and her arms are loose around me, and I think it's time for me to go back to my bed. It's still dark outside, but I've heard the birds moving in the oak tree, and I know one of them will sing soon, and then the first dawn glow will show at the window.

I try to move, but Delia holds me. She presses her fingers into my chest, and her face against my hair, and she says, "No, Travis. Not yet. Stay with me a little while longer, okay? If you stay, I promise I won't cry anymore."

I try to whisper, "Okay," but nothing comes out, and my voice is stuck from so much worrying, and I clear my throat and softly I say, "I want to stay. I just thought maybe..."

"Good. Good, Travis my old Killer. I'm glad you want to stay. Aren't we a couple of messed up kids?"

I think about it. I guess it's true, and I guess it's good to admit it. As long as I admit it only to my Aunt Delia. I say, "Delia, how come you call me Killer?"

"Geez, Travis, I don't know. I guess it's cause you remind me of Jerry Lee Lewis. That's what they call him. The Killer.

'Cause he plays that killer piano and sings, 'Great Balls of Fire,' and 'Shake, Baby, Shake,' and 'Breathless.'" Delia's arms are around me, and now she shakes me, and the bed squeaks. She giggles in my ear, and I know she's going to be all right. I'm glad I helped her.

I say, "Is he good looking?"

"Who?" Delia asks me.

"That Jerry Lee what's his name."

"He's a dreamboat, Travis. He's a downright dreamboat."

I want to ask if I'm a dreamboat. Wendy said I'm gonna be a heartbreaker some day. I wonder if a dreamboat is a heartbreaker. I don't think I want to be a heartbreaker. Sometimes I think my mom has a broken heart.

I want to ask Delia about my mom. Maybe she knows. Maybe she knows what nobody will tell me. The things grown-ups say over my head. Delia's grown up, but she's not. I'm gonna ask her about my mom, and my dad, too, but not tonight. Some time I'll ask her, and I know she'll tell me if she can. I know I can trust her, and she can trust me.

I wake up with my Aunt Delia against me. I guess it's the birds singing that wake me. Maybe it's the good smell from downstairs. Coffee and eggs and toast. I wake up, and I don't have my back to my Aunt Delia anymore. I'm facing her. I got turned around in the night. And the thing has happened. I don't know how. I don't know what it is, but it isn't the first time. I'm hard. Down there, I'm hard and it feels good, and I'm touching my Aunt Delia. My face gets hot, and my neck gets thick, and I pull away from her slowly, and I hear her moan, "No, don't go," and I know she's not talking to me. There's someone in her dream and she doesn't want him to go. Maybe it's that someone lost she's talking to.

I get up and stand by her bed. I don't want her to see me like this. I give myself a hard pinch, but it doesn't do any good. It's like pinching a rock, and it feels good. I go to the door and look out, and I hear someone coming up the stairs. I know I can't make it to my bedroom without being seen, so I run for the bathroom. I run on tip-toes trying not to make a sound, but the old boards groan and crackle under me. Inside the bathroom, I flush the commode and then run water in the sink. All I'm wearing is my uns, and there's a tent pole sticking out of me, and I don't know how to make it go away.

I hear footsteps out in the hallway, and then my Grandma Hollister calls, "Travis! Breakfast, Honey!" She sounds tired.

I call from inside the bathroom. "I'll be down in a minute."

I can hear her outside the door now, heavy on the old boards. She says, "Do you need anything, Travis, Honey? Is everything all right?"

I don't know what to do. I flush the commode again, and make my voice sound small-boy and say, "I'm okay, I guess. I'll be down in a minute."

She says, "All right, Honey," and I hear her walk away.

I stand in the tub and run cold water on it. After a while, it goes away.

seven

Grandpa Hollister is finishing breakfast when I come down-stairs. He frowns at me over his coffee cup and looks at his watch. He has on the same black pants and white shirt and gold badge he wore to pick me up at the airport, and his black suit coat is folded over a chair. His eyes expect the worst. I stand at the bottom of the stairs and wait. Marvadell comes out of the kitchen and smiles at me. "Sit down, Child, and tell me how you like yo eggs."

I look at Grandpa Hollister, and he nods. I tell Marvadell sunny side up. Grandpa Hollister picks up his newspaper and hides his face like my dad. Marvadell brings my eggs, and they look good, and I say, "Thank you, ma'am," and she smiles and stands over me with her hands on her big hips. There's bacon grease and flour on her apron, and I can smell her perfume and sweat and butter. She smells good. She waits, and I look at her, and finally Grandpa Hollister says, "Eat boy, so Marvadell can go on back to the kitchen and start cleaning up."

Marvadell doesn't look at him, but I see in her eyes how she feels about him. About what he said. There's something hard in there, but it's not hate. It's just who she is and who he is. I know she won't move until I spear an egg, so I take a bite and smile and say, "Wow, ma'am, they're really good. They're as good as my mom makes them." The eggs are good.

Marvadell smiles and looks at Grandpa Hollister and says, "No they ain't, Travis. Nobody cooks for a boy as good as his momma does." She winks at me, or maybe she doesn't, I can't tell, and then she turns and walks into the kitchen. Grandpa Hollister drinks the last of his coffee and says, "Travis, white boys don't call Negro women 'ma'am.' It's the way we do here. You call her Marvadell. You be nice to her like we all do. I don't ever want to hear about you showing her any disrespect, but you don't call her ma'am. That's what you call your Grandma and your Aunt Delia and the other white women you meet here. Do you understand me, Son?"

I don't, but I nod. He doesn't like it, so I nod again and say, "Yes, sir." My eggs are getting cold. I watch him until his eyes are finished with me, and then I get on with breakfast.

Grandpa Hollister stands up and stretches and looks at his watch. "I've got to go to work, Travis." He looks at the stairs. "I don't know what's got into that lazy bones Delia." He looks at me like I might know. I just look back like the lonesome wayfaring stranger Delia said I am. He says, "I suppose she's up there moping. She's a teenager, Travis. Don't ever let it happen to you. Jump right over it and become a grown man. Save yourself a lot of trouble."

I don't know if I should smile. I just say, "Yes, sir."

Grandpa Hollister leaves, and I hear the Buick light up in the garage, and then I hear it whisper slowly down the street.

Marvadell comes out of the kitchen and stands over me looking at my plate. Her face is shiny black, and there's sweat on her temples and on her upper lip, and she's got little brown moles along her hairline. She's the first black lady I've seen close up. She says, "You doan like my grits, Nebraska boy?" She's going to be different with me now that Grandpa Hollister is gone.

I say, "I don't know. I didn't try them yet."

She says, "Well?"

So I scoop a big fork full of the grits and close my eyes and shove them in. I'm ready for the worst, and I'm ready to be polite about it. They're warm and they taste like butter and pepper, and my eyes come open as the smile gets my face. I look at her and nod and spoon in another bite and say, "Eeese griphs are vurr..."

Marvadell says, "Boy, don't you talk to me with your mouth full of food," and she's gone.

I'm finished eating when Grandma Hollister comes out of her bedroom wearing her nightgown. Her hair is up in a plastic shower cap, and she's holding two fingers to her forehead. She looks at me and blinks like she forgot I'm here. "Travis?"

I say, "Good morning, Grandma Hollister."

She smiles a kind of sicky smile and says, "Oh, Travis, your grandma has such a headache this morning. I always get them when the storms come through. The doctor says it's something about the barometric pressure." She gets a little brighter. "Did they teach you anything about weather in school, Travis, Honey?"

I tell her some things I learned about clouds and snow and seasons, and she seems happy with my education so far. I don't want to think about it. It's summer, and a kid has a right to forget what he knows.

Grandma Hollister goes into the kitchen, and I hear her tell Marvadell all she wants is coffee and toast, and I hear Marvadell say, "Humph!" That's all.

I'm out in the front yard, sitting on a root under the oak tree. The ground is soaked from the storm, and there's a bird's nest in a puddle over by the road. A big black cat was eating one of the baby birds when I came out here after breakfast. It made me sick. The mother blue jay tried to kill the cat with her beak. She dove and pecked at him, but he ignored her. He just pulled his ears in close to his head and hunched over and kept eating.

I'm thinking about my dad. I'm wondering what he had for breakfast and what he's doing without me this morning and what my mom is doing in that hospital. I don't even want to think about the food they give her there. When I was in the hospital with the flu and almost died, the food was awful. It makes me sad thinking about the incense my dad gave my mom. I wonder if they let her burn it, and if it makes the pee and Lysol smell go away. I take out my wallet with Roy Rogers and Trigger on it. It feels good in my hands, and I smell it to see if my mom is on it, but it just smells like leather. It's still got the five dollars my dad gave me in it, and I wonder how much a boat costs.

I could put the empty nest back in the tree. Maybe if I climb up and put it on a limb, the mother blue jay will come back and lay more eggs and have some more chicks. She's perched in a tree across the road, watching the nest. She's as sad as I am, I think. The black cat is sitting in a patch of sun on a driveway down the street. I want to go down there and kick him in the head, but I know he just did what cats do, and he'd run before I could land a good kick.

In the backyard, there's more red dirt, and it's shady under the oaks, but the sky is high and white and hot, and I'm sweating. Green vines hang from a big wooden frame in the backyard, and they have grapes on them. I want to taste the grapes, but they don't look ripe. I look at the little house, the one Grandma Hollister said was necessary. I pull open the door and it's dark inside, and it stinks so bad my eyes water, and I can't see why it's necessary. There's a roll of toilet paper stuck on a long nail and a couple of old *Life* magazines beside a board seat with a round hole cut in it. I back off and take a deep breath.

"Exploring, are you?"

I turn, and it's my Aunt Delia. She's wearing jeans, and they're cut off and rolled up above her knees, and she's wearing white socks rolled down and her white tennis shoes with the pink laces. She's got on a white blouse like the one she wore yesterday and lipstick that matches the laces on her tennis shoes. When she bends down to me, the gold cross swings out from her neck.

"Ever seen one of those before?" She means the little house.

I shake my head. I'm remembering last night, the storm, my Aunt Delia crying. All of it. She remembers, too, but she isn't acting like it. She looks happy and fresh except for her eyes. They're a little red and swollen, and they tell me not to mention what we did. She looks up and down the hill through the backyards. I look with her, and I can see two more necessary houses. "Kind of dumb, aren't they?" she says.

I nod. I don't know where this is going.

"Well, Travis old Killer, you're learning about country people. You're learning about the southern branch of the Hollister family."

"What branch am I?" I ask her.

"You're the uprooted midwestern branch. That's what your grandpa says, anyway. He never wanted your daddy to leave Widow Rock." She points at the little house. "Your grandpa comes out here about once a week just to keep in touch with his heritage."

"We don't have those back home."

"Good," says my Aunt Delia. "Would you like to go for a ride with me?"

I've been out in the yard since Grandma Hollister went back to bed with her headache, and all I've seen is a couple of cars go by, and some people wave at the house, and no kids. I was hoping there'd be kids. I say, "Yes."

My Aunt Delia says, "Just yes?"

I say, "I'd like that."

My Aunt Delia takes me for a ride. She says she wants to show me the confines of her prison. She wants me to see how small the town is. We drive down the street where the Hollisters live and turn on another street just like it, and at the bottom of a hill we come to the railroad tracks. There's a gate across the tracks with red reflectors and a big silver weight that raises and lowers it. Down the track, there's a little station, and I can see boxes and crates waiting to be loaded on some brown Seaboard Coastline freight cars. The crates have SIFFORD CONTAINER AND PACKING CO. written on them in big white letters.

We cross the tracks and turn right, and there's a barber shop with a red and white–striped pole that looks like a candy cane, and a drugstore with green glass windows and a big sign on the front door that says, COOL AIR. The blue letters of the sign are dripping with white-painted icicles.

"That's Tolbert's Drugstore," my Aunt Delia says. "That's where the kids all hang out. All ten of them." My Aunt Delia doesn't look at me when she says it, and her voice is bored and maybe sad but not that sad.

She turns on the radio and tunes it, and some scratchy music comes through. "We get the stations from Tallahassee and Birmingham," she says. "Sometimes Jacksonville comes in pretty good. It depends on the weather, I guess." I hear someone singing about being a teenager in love, and I ask, "Is that the Killer?"

My Aunt Delia looks at me, then she throws her head back and shakes her hair. "Oh, you mean Jerry Lee? No, Honey, that's Dion and the Belmonts. They're cool though, don't you think?"

I watch my Aunt Delia. She wants to know if I think Dion and the Belmonts are cool. It's called rock 'n' roll music, and my dad doesn't like it. When Elvis was on Ed Sullivan, before our old Philco broke, my dad turned him off. For a second, I wonder if Aunt Delia is making fun of me, like grown-ups do, but her eyes say she isn't. She wants to know what I think. I say, "Yeah, they're cool, but not as cool as the Killer. When can we hear the Killer?" I like saying that word, "Cool." It reminds me of the sign in the drugstore window. It makes me feel grown up. It makes me like my Aunt Delia more than I already do, and that's a lot.

We listen to the rest of the song, and my Aunt Delia sings along. She's got a pretty voice. "If you want to make me cry, that won't be so hard to do. If you should say good-bye, I'll just go on loving you." I love the dreamy look she gets in her eyes when she listens to the music.

When it's over, a man comes on talking about buying a Ford at some place in Tallahassee, and Aunt Delia's eyes wake up. She says, "We'll hear the Killer soon enough. He's got two songs in the top ten right now."

"That's okay," I say. "Dion's pretty cool."

Aunt Delia looks over at me and smiles. We drive on through the town, past the mercantile, the sheriff's office, an ESSO gas station, a post office with a sign that says, NOTARY, and a doctor's office, and suddenly we're out in the country. We pass houses that look like the ones in town, only there are pens with pigs in them, and big vegetable gardens, and fields of corn and men on tractors in the fields plowing and throwing up curls of red dust behind them. We come to a crossroads and stop. "Well, Killer," my Aunt Delia says, "this is where the citizens of Widow Rock make the big decision. You can turn right, and about a mile down there's a juke joint called Luby's. That's where the bad boys go and some of the bad girls, too, but nobody I know."

She winks at me and smiles, and it's the look she gave Grandpa Hollister when she drove too fast into the garage yesterday, and I thought he was going to be mad. It's a look ladies give men in the movies. It's a look that says they know what the men are thinking, and they don't mind it at all. I don't know. I don't understand it, but I like it when my Aunt Delia looks at me like that.

"Not you," I say. "You'd never go down there."

"No, not me," she says, and smiles again.

I say, "What's juke?"

My Aunt Delia shuts her eyes and thinks about it. Then she opens them and wiggles her shoulders, and it's like she's dancing right in the car, and she says, "You know, it's what you do in juke joints. You juke." And she wiggles some more, and it makes my throat get thick.

I look up the road. "What's in the other direction?"

She says, "The river's down there, Honey. And Widow Rock's down there, the promontory for which our little hamlet is named. I'll tell you the story of Widow Rock, but not right now. I don't want you to be overcome by excitement on your first day."

I think about telling her all I've got to look at most of the time where I live is the miserable Pultneys and a wheat field and a dead farmer's silo. I think about telling her sometimes I stand at the edge of our yard with my back to our house and the miserable Pultneys and just stare at that silo because it's the only thing out there that's not wheat. The only thing that's not flat.

I think about telling her I love the warm air blowing through the windows when we drive together, and the smells of things alive and scary and waiting for me out there. I think about telling her I love the Chevy's red upholstery, and the scratchy, far away music coming from the radio, and the shiny chrome on the front of the radio, and the way her black hair whips around her face in the wind. I think about asking her a lot of questions. Why does Grandma Hollister have headaches, and when is Grandpa Hollister going to smile, and will he ever let me shoot his gun, and what does he do when he goes to work, and are we going to talk about last night? I just say, "I like it here. It's exciting."

My Aunt Delia laughs, and her laugh sounds like I know the water will sound running over those flat stones I saw from the bridge. She says, "You're sweet, Travis. It's sweet of you to say that. But the truth is, Widow Rock is so boring sometimes I think I'm gonna jump out of my skin. I'm gonna get on that highway and just drive 'til I can't drive anymore, and I'm gonna start a new life some place where the music comes from right around the corner and the people don't think it's a matter of honor to shit in their own backyard."

I'm quiet.

My Aunt Delia reaches over and touches my arm. "Oh, Travis, I'm sorry. I've shocked you with my language. Well, don't worry. Nobody heard me but you, and I promise I'll do better. I'll try not to offend your virgin ears. You're my brother's little boy after all."

I don't like it. I turn to her and say, "I'm not a little boy. Today's my birthday, and I'm twelve, and that's not little."

My Aunt Delia looks at me, and her eyes go dark and wide, and she says, "Oh, Travis. Is today really your birthday?"

I nod. Hard. "And I'm not little." I want to say, "I'm cool," but I don't.

For a second, I think my Aunt Delia is going to cry again. But she doesn't. She reaches out and puts her fingers on my cheek. I'm mad, and I should pull away, but I don't. I like how it feels with her fingers there. She says, "That damned Lloyd. It's your birthday and he forgot to let us know."

She takes her hand away from my cheek, and it burns where she touched me, and she looks out across the steering wheel. We're sitting at the crossroads, and the engine is running, and there's no wind blowing through the windows now. In a field across the road, a horse stretches up to pull down a branch from a tired-looking oak tree. It's too far, but the horse keeps reaching. A buzzard circles over the field, riding higher and higher on the wind.

"He's not damned Lloyd," I whisper.

My Aunt Delia says, "I know, Travis. I'm sorry. He's your daddy, and he's got an awful lot on his mind right now."

Then I feel her hand on my cheek again. "Let's go back to the thriving metropolis of Widow Rock," she says. "I've got a surprise for you."

It's her old voice again, low and full of breath and like cool water over rocks.

eight

I've wanted to go in that drugstore ever since I saw the blue words with white ice dripping from them: COOL AIR. I've only been in air-conditioning a couple of times. Once in a drugstore in Omaha, and once in a doctor's office when I was little. It's great. When you walk in, the hair stands up on your arms, and you shiver, and the air smells good, and when you breathe through your mouth, it tastes like peppermint.

Delia parks the white Chevy in front of the drugstore, and there are two other cars, a red Oldsmobile and a white Ford pickup truck. We get out, and she looks at the two cars and winks at me. "Oh-oh, Killer. Look who's here."

I say, "Who?" and she says, "You'll see."

We go in, and it's so cool my teeth hurt, and I like walking in with my Aunt Delia. I like the wavy way she walks and the way everybody looks at us when we come in.

Just inside the door, we stop to look around. There's a counter on one side full of Band-Aid boxes and cans of Barbasol and ladies' perfume and razors and blades. On the other side, there's a soda fountain with red stools and booths with red seats. Where we're standing, there's a cash register and a gun rack with some rifles and shotguns and boxes of shells.

A man in a white apron and a white garrison cap smiles at my Aunt Delia and puts both hands on the marble counter and leans toward us. He says, "Hey there, Miss Delia, what can I do for you today?"

There are two boys in one of the booths, and one of them giggles and makes his voice high, and sings, "Hey there, Miss Delia."

I can feel my Aunt Delia go hard beside me, and she lifts her chin a little, and she's not walking so loose and wavy as we go to the counter.

She slides onto a stool, and pats the one next to her, and I take it. The boy giggles again, and the man across the counter says, "Behave yourself, Sifford, or you'll not be scarfing milkshakes in here for a month."

He looks at Delia and smiles, and she smiles, but her smile is small and thin. She says, "Mr. Tolbert, I want to introduce my nephew, Travis, from Omaha. He's here to spend the summer with us."

Mr. Tolbert has a big, tanned, square face with pale blue eyes and a blue jaw like my dad's. He's got forearms like the business end of a baseball bat, and they've got thick black hair on them. A long scar starts over his left eye and goes up into his hair, and I wonder if it's from the war. He smiles at me, and we shake hands and he says, "You're Lloyd's boy, aren't you?"

I nod and smile and remember to say, "Yes, sir."

Mr. Tolbert looks past me at the front windows where the light comes in through the green glass, and I know he's looking at the far away like my dad does. He says, "Your daddy's one heck of a man, son. I'm proud to have you in my establishment." I don't know what he means. Maybe it's the war, the things my dad won't talk about. Maybe it's the things my Grandma Hollister told me about in the car on the way from the airport. Scholarships and running the hundred so fast.

There's another giggle from the booth behind us, and the boy makes his voice as high as a girl's. "Poor Travis, stuck in Widow Rock for a whole summer. That boy's gone lose his mind."

My Aunt Delia turns around, and I turn, too, and it's fun to spin on the stool, and I look at my Aunt Delia, and she's got that small, tight smile on her face. She says, "Travis, I want you to meet two scoundrel dog boys. That one with the ugly red hair and the big ears is Ronny Bishop. The conceited one with the funny voice is Bickley P. Sifford. Bick for short. He's conceited because he thinks he's cute, and because his daddy owns the box factory and he's accepted to Princeton. But you know what I think, Travis?"

My Aunt Delia stops and looks at me. The two boys watch us, grinning. They look just like my Aunt Delia said. Red hair, big ears. Conceited and cute. But there's more to both of them. The one called Ronny is as big as a man, and his neck fills his button-down shirt collar too tight, and his eyes are small and pale blue and seem to aim at you through the field of freckles on his cheeks. The one called Bick is tall and muscular, too, but he's blond, and at first he reminds me of Tab Hunter. But he's not that cute. There's just something unreal about him, especially sitting across from the other boy. He looks like he knows he could say something that would change everything here. He looks important.

The boys are waiting for me to ask, "What?" I can't see him, but I know Mr. Tolbert is waiting behind the counter, too. So I say, "What?"

My Aunt Delia says, "I think he's going to get up there at Princeton with all the other boys, and their daddies are gonna own even bigger box factories, and they're gonna be even cuter and even more conceited, and our Mr. Bickley P. Sifford is going to have him a comeuppance."

Mr. Tolbert laughs behind me.

The red-haired boy looks at the one called Bickley P. Sifford and waits.

Sifford is wearing a white shirt with a button-down collar, an alligator belt, penny loafers with shiny pennies and fuzzy white socks, and a pair of tight, faded jeans. I wonder if he's cool. I think he is. I wait. His face is getting red, and I know he's trying to think of something to say back to my Aunt Delia. Finally, he smiles, a kind of slow, evil-sneak smile, and I know he's got something in mind. He says, "Delia, I bet you can't spell comeuppance. I'll bet you a ride in my car you can't spell it. Mr. Tolbert's got a dictionary, and after you try, we can look it up and prove I'm right. What you say, Delia? Will you go for a ride with me if I win the bet? Ronny here'll take your nephew home, won't you Ronny?"

Ronny doesn't like it much, but he smiles his own low, sneak-mean smile and says, "Sure. Sure I will, Bick."

I look at my Aunt Delia, and she's thinking about it. I don't want her to go for a ride with Bickley P. Sifford. I don't want to ride home with his red-haired, jug-eared friend, Ronny. I like my Aunt Delia, and I want to stay with her, and it's my birthday, and that's our secret.

My Aunt Delia puts her thumb under her chin and presses it there and makes a face like a little girl and thinks about it. Finally, she says, "You want to complete your list, don't you, Mr. Bickley P. Sifford?"

Sifford looks at her. He knows what she's saying, and he doesn't like it.

"Your list of local girls and rides in your fancy red Oldsmobile. And then you can tell all the conceited sons of box-factory owners at Princeton that you took all the girls of Widow Rock and neighboring boroughs for a ride. That's it, isn't it, Mr. Bickley P. Sifford?"

Sifford's face is as red as his car. Mr. Tolbert is washing glasses behind us. I'm looking at Delia, and it's strange. It's strange because she's saying one thing, but her eyes are saying another. They say she wants to go for a ride with Sifford. And Sifford's eyes say he knows it, and that's why his face is red. I think everybody here knows it, and they all knew it before I did.

Sifford clears his throat, and his voice goes raspy when he says, "I'm starting a new list, and it's gone have just one name on it. Yours. Why don't we ride on out to Widow Rock. It'll be cool out there by the river." He looks at my Aunt Delia long and deep, and his eyes say things that make me look away at the gun rack over the counter. And I want to take down one of those guns and shoot him. I don't look back until I feel my Aunt Delia's hand on my shoulder. She says, "You and your bosom friend Ronny there can put your fancy red Oldsmobile in the back of his truck and ride off together. Me and Travis are on a shopping trip. Today's his birthday, and I'm going to buy him a tennis racket." She looks down at me and smiles. Then she reaches down and runs her hand through my hair.

"How 'bout that, Travis?"

I'm a shortstop, not a tennis player, but I smile big and say, "That's neato, Aunt Delia."

Mr. Tolbert says, "I think we got a few things you can look at, Miss Delia."

Delia spins her stool around to face Mr. Tolbert, and I do too. She says, "First, we're going to get Travis a big fat birthday chocolate malted milk, and then we're going to buy him the best tennis racket in the place."

Again I smile and say, "Thank you, Aunt Delia."

Mr. Tolbert says, "Will that be two malts, Miss Delia?"

My Aunt Delia says yes, and we sit together watching Mr. Tolbert's big hands scoop the ice cream and pour in the chocolate syrup and the little malt balls, and then put the shiny steel container on the little rack with the propeller above it. He pushes a button, and the propeller spins until the chocolate malted swells up to the top. He puts the two malts in front of us, and I hear the two boys slide out of the booth behind us.

Sifford says, "Last chance for that ride, Delia."

My Aunt Delia's voice is mocky and sing-song. "Last chance to learn something about yourself before they teach it to you at Princeton, Bick Sifford."

Sifford laughs, and his friend follows with his own hee-haw. The two stretch and groan and shuffle, but we don't look at them. Before they get to the door, there's a loud rumble and an engine races, then cuts off, and I see Mr. Tolbert's eyes go hard.

I turn and look through the green glass at the front of the drugstore. At the curb, there's a boy in a black leather jacket and loose jeans and black engineer boots getting out of a midnight-blue street rod. Sifford and Bishop stop at the front door and watch him. Sifford looks back at us and says, "Hey, Delia, maybe you want to go for a ride with old Duck's Ass out there. How 'bout that?"

Mr. Tolbert says, hard, "Sifford, you know I don't tolerate language in my store."

Sifford says, "Sorry, Mr. Tolbert," but he doesn't mean it. Then he says, "See you around, Delia. We got all summer for that ride," and it sounds like Jimmy Pultney telling me he's going to climb over that fence and stomp my ass if I don't give back his arrow. Delia says to her malted milk, "See you, Ronny."

The two boys go out and stand on the sidewalk watching the boy in the leather jacket. The midnight-blue rod has cool red flames painted on its sides. The flames swell up from the engine like it's on fire. It has moon disks and Lakes Pipes too. When I grow up, I'm going to have a car like that.

The boy in the black leather jacket stops in front of Sifford and Bishop, and they say something to him, and he says something back, and Mr. Tolbert takes off his apron fast and goes around the counter. He's got his hand on the front door when Sifford and Bishop look in at him and smile and get into the red Olds and the Ford pickup and drive off. Mr. Tolbert sighs and comes back to the counter. He leans on it and says, "Miss Delia, I don't know what gets into those boys, do you?"

My Aunt Delia says, "Often as not, conceit gets into them, and moonshine whiskey." She looks at Mr. Tolbert, and he sighs again and shakes his head and starts washing glasses.

Outside, the boy with the black leather jacket is working on his engine. He's got the hood open and he's leaning in, and the engine's running, and he's making it rev and come back down with a loud pop-pop-pop. He leans back and stretches, and the sides of his jacket fly out like black wings, and he looks up at the sun, and I can see the sweat on his pale cheeks and forehead.

My Aunt Delia says, "Turn around Travis and stop staring."

nine

I like the way the tennis racket feels in my hand. It's got a tan leather grip and shiny varnish, and the strings are tight and white, and it says, T.A.D. across the bottom. My Aunt Delia says that stands for Thomas A. Davis, but the kids just call it a Tad racket. She says she's going to teach me to play tennis, and we're going to play a lot, and by the end of the summer I'll be as good as Pancho Gonzales.

Delia takes a twenty and a ten out of her pocket and puts them down by the cash register, and Mr. Tolbert says, "How 'bout some balls, Miss Delia?" And my Aunt Delia says, "Why not? Travis is starting a new year of his life today. We might as well start out with fresh ones." Mr. Tolbert reaches under the counter and brings up a red can that says Spalding. It has a key on top like a can of tuna.

My Aunt Delia waits for her change, but she's watching the boy outside working on his car. He's got long black hair, and there's a lot of oil on it, and it's combed back like Elvis. He closes the hood and looks at the window, and I wonder if he can see us standing here. My Aunt Delia counts her change and says, "I got enough for one more malt, Travis. What do you say?"

I look at her and at Mr. Tolbert, and he smiles, and I say, "Sure, if you'll share it with me." Delia puts her hand on the top of my head. "Travis, that's sweet, but I don't want any more." She touches her middle. "As my grandmother used to say, 'I have had a sufficiency.'" Mr. Tolbert laughs. I guess he remembers my Aunt Delia's grandmother.

We sit on our stools again, and the bell at the front door rings, and I know the boy in the black leather jacket is here. His thick boots bark and scuff on the floor, and I hear him slide into the booth where Sifford and Bishop sat. I spin around and look. He takes a pack of Camels and a silver Zippo lighter from his jacket pocket and starts tapping the lighter on the table. Delia doesn't turn around, but she doesn't tell me to mind my business. I like watching the boy. He's big and his big hands are greasy. He's got a silver ring with a red jewel on his right middle finger, and he's wearing a white T-shirt under the jacket and his silver dog tags hang outside his shirt.

Mr. Tolbert puts another malted in front of me and says, "There you go, Travis." I turn around and look at my Aunt Delia, and she's got that small tight smile on her face again, and I wonder if she's thinking about Sifford.

The Zippo keeps tapping on the table, and Mr. Tolbert says, "Griner, what can I do for you?" Mr. Tolbert's voice is too loud. He sounds like my dad when I'm getting on his nerves. The boy in the black leather jacket says, "Jack, I'm sitting here waiting for you to bring me an ashtray."

Mr. Tolbert bites his jaw down hard and says, "Griner, I've told you you can't smoke in here, and I've told you not to call me Jack."

Griner looks at Mr. Tolbert for a long time, and a drop of sweat comes out of his shiny black hair and rolls down his forehead. He ignores it and says, "Everybody smokes in here, Mr. Tolbert, and I seen you come round that counter quick as a monkey and bring them ashtrays. If them boys that just left out of here wanted to smoke, you'd sure-God bring them ashtrays."

Mr. Tolbert says, "Griner, you are sorely trying my patience."

Griner shakes a cigarette out of the Camel pack and lights it and draws in a big chest full of smoke and blows it at Mr. Tolbert. He says, "I'm just as good as any customer that comes in here." He pulls out his wallet and takes out a five-dollar bill and slaps it on the table top. "I got money to spend just like them rich boys."

Mr. Tolbert bites his jaw and slowly shakes his head. "Griner, you'll be legal to smoke in here when you're twenty-one. Now put out that cigarette."

Griner takes another big puff and huffs it out and smiles. He pulls up his leg and puts the thick sole of his engineer boot on the red upholstery and sticks the cigarette in where he's rolled up his jeans. It hisses, and a puff of smoke rises from the burnt cloth. He smiles bigger and says to Mr. Tolbert, "Now we're legal. How 'bout you bring me a co-cola there, Jack?"

Mr. Tolbert looks at my Aunt Delia, and his eyes tell all about his patience. He fills a glass with ice and Coca-Cola and just leaves it at the end of the counter. He turns his back and starts washing glasses. Griner looks at the Coke on the counter and then at Mr. Tolbert's back. He shrugs and comes over to get his Coke. He puts a quarter on the counter and picks up the Coke and catches me looking at him. At first I think he doesn't like it, but then I see he does. He winks at me and says, "What's shakin', Buddy?"

My Aunt Delia spins on her stool. "Kenny Griner, you leave him alone."

Griner smiles and raises both his hands and the jacket spreads again like the wings of that big buzzard I saw circling over the pasture when Aunt Delia and me were driving in her white Chevy. Griner says, "I ain't doing nothing, Miss Delia. All I done was say hello to the boy."

My Aunt Delia looks at him for a while, and he keeps smiling at her, and she says, "Well, all right then," and turns around to face the soda fountain.

Griner goes back to his booth and sips the Coke and says, "News gets around fast in a small town."

My Aunt Delia turns around again, and there's something scared in her eyes. Something I've never seen before. "News about what, Kenny? Did you set a new speed record from here to nowhere and back?" She's smiling, but her eyes are holding Griner's, and they've still got that scared thing in them.

Griner shrugs again. "Naw, I already hold that record. I'm talking about Mr. Flatland there. Him being in town for the summer an' all." I look at my Aunt Delia. I don't know how I'm supposed to act. She's not scared anymore.

She gives Griner a tired look and says, "Last time I looked, Kenny, I didn't see any mountains around here."

"We got hills though," Griner says, "out there north of town, and we got the rock. Good old Widow Rock. Now that's pretty high, ain't it. Out where that boy comes from it's as flat as your momma's ironing board and just as hot."

My Aunt Delia says, "When's the last time you were in Nebraska, Kenny?"

Griner looks hurts. He takes out another cigarette and flips open the Zippo, but before his thumb scratches the lighter, he looks over at Mr. Tolbert and just holds the cigarette in his mouth. He says, "I know about Nebraska. I read about it in a book one time." Griner reaches into the pocket of his black leather jacket and pulls out a paperback book and puts it on the table. On the cover, there's a picture of a boy on a motorcycle. He's wearing a jacket like Griner's and a leather hat with a pair of silver wings on the front. He's leaning over the handlebars and looking off down the road. Griner says, "See, I read a lot, Miss Delia. Just 'cause I ain't still swallowing the crap they dish out in that high school don't mean I don't read."

My Aunt Delia looks at Griner now, and her eyes say she's sorry. She says, "I wish you hadn't quit school, Kenny. You didn't have to quit."

Griner looks out the front window, squinting at the sun, at the cool blue and flaming red street rod out there at the curb. He looks back at my Aunt Delia and says, "I didn't have to stay either. That's one thing they couldn't make me do."

My Aunt Delia shakes her head and slides down from her stool. My malted is only half-finished, but I've had enough. My stomach's not that big. She says, "Come on, Travis." I'm standing beside her. Griner's looking at his book now, pretending to read with that cold cigarette hanging from his mouth. My Aunt Delia says, "Kenny, what are you gonna do with yourself? You can't just stay around here and work in that box factory and fiddle with that stupid car for the rest of your life." Now she sounds angry, but I know she's not angry at Griner. Not exactly.

Griner pulls his eyes out of his book. "Why can't I, Miss Delia? A lot of folks do, folks that don't live over on Bedford Street or out to Pleasant Hills with your friend Sifford."

Bedford Street is where I live now.

My Aunt Delia says, "Bick's my friend, Kenny, and so are you, or at least you used to be. I care about what happens to both of you."

"Don't worry about me," Griner says. He taps his book with his greasy finger. He lifts the finger to his forehead and touches it there. "I'm getting an education. Worry about Sifford if you want to worry. He'd like it if you did that."

My Aunt Delia says, "If I worried about Bick, he'd just take it as a compliment. It's you I'm worried about."

"Like I told you," Griner says, "don't worry about me. School ain't the only way to be a success in life."

My Aunt Delia shakes her head once, slow, then turns to Mr. Tolbert behind the counter. She says, "Thank you, Mr. Tolbert. We'll be in again real soon."

Mr. Tolbert smiles at my Aunt Delia and says, "Say hello to your daddy for me." At that, Griner grunts and then laughs. "Me too," he says.

My Aunt Delia looks at Griner one more time, and I can't tell what she's thinking. She lifts her chin a little, and we walk out together.

ten

We drive through town, and it's quiet, and the heat wiggles over the asphalt, and all the people we pass wave to my Aunt Delia. She waves back, and sometimes she calls, "Hey there!" through the open window. We drive to a park, and there's a white church with a tall steeple at one end, and across the road from the church there's a statue of a soldier leaning on a long rifle. At the other end of the park there's a tennis court made of red clay with white chalk lines and a net that's kind of droopy. There are oak trees on both sides of the court and green benches under the oaks so you can rest after you play. Two girls are playing tennis when we drive up and stop in the red dirt parking lot. My Aunt Delia turns off the engine, but she leaves the radio on. It's Dion and the Belmonts again: "Why must I be a teenager in love?" One of the girls hits the ball into the net, and they both laugh. Then they turn and wave at my Aunt Delia.

"Hey, Delia!"

My Aunt Delia leans out the window and calls out, "Hey, Caroline! Hey, Beulah!" She pulls her head back in and says, "Aren't they a couple of toads, Killer?"

I can't help it. I laugh real hard.

We watch the two girls play for a while, and we listen to the radio. I'm waiting for Jerry Lee to come on, but he doesn't. Finally, the two girls finish. I can't tell who wins. I don't think they care. They walk over to Delia's window and lean in, and the blonde one says, "Hey, who's the good-looking guy?"

My Aunt Delia says, "This is my nephew, Travis, from Omaha. He's spending the summer with us so he can learn how the gracious life is lived."

The two girls giggle. The brown-haired one leans in and says, "Don't let old Delia here get you in any trouble, Travis. She's known for that around here." The two girls giggle again and they look at Delia, and she looks back at them, and it's like they all know something they're not telling. I don't know what to say, so I just smile. I'm glad my Aunt Delia doesn't giggle.

It's hot, and the two girls have sweat on their faces and dark wet patches on their white blouses. When they lean into the car, I can smell perfume and girl sweat mixed together, and it's better than either one by itself, and it goes with the song on the radio: "Tell Laura I love her. Tell Laura not to cry. My love for her will never die."

Delia and the two girls talk for a while, and I listen to the radio and hold my new tennis racket on my lap and run my fingers over the strings and wonder what it's gonna be like when I hit a ball. Finally, the two girls push away from Delia's window and walk over to a brown Ford and drive away. Delia looks over at me and flutters her eyelashes in a funny way she has. "Beulah's a great big pain in the butt. Her daddy preaches in that church right over there, and she thinks she's got to be the baddest girl in town. Caroline's okay, I guess, but she only knows three words, and two of them are 'boy.'"

Before we go out on the court, my Aunt Delia kneels in front of me and rolls up my jeans and looks at my shoes. I'm wearing the summer sandals my mom always gets for me. I hate them. I always ask my dad for combat boots, but he never lets me have them. My Aunt Delia says, "Killer, I don't think these are quite right for tennis. You'll have to play barefoot." I take off my sandals and my white socks, and we go out on the court. "What do I do?" I say. I like the way my feet feel on the hot red clay.

My Aunt Delia says, "Just be a good shortstop. That's a start."

We hit the ball back and forth, and she's good at it, and I'm not. Most of mine go into the net or out into the park or just into the back fence. Delia doesn't care if I'm any good. She laughs and runs after my bad balls and hits them back to me, and, once in a while, she gives me a tennis tip. "Keep your eye on it, Killer, just like it's a baseball and you're Mickey Mantle." "Follow through there, Killer, don't hack at it. You're not chopping cotton."

After a while I get the hang of it a little. I like playing, and I'm thinking maybe by the end of the summer I'll be as good as my Aunt Delia, and then after that I'll go on and beat Pancho Gonzales. I hit one out into the grass under the oak, and I'm waiting for Delia to go get it, and I hear loud music behind me, and I turn, and there's the red Oldsmobile, and there's Bick Sifford sitting in it watching me. The radio is loud: "Come on over baby, we got chicken in the barn. Ain't fakin'. Whole lot of shakin' going on."

I turn back, and my Aunt Delia's standing beside me, and she puts the ball in my hand and says, "That's him, Killer. That's Jerry Lee Lewis, your namesake."

The song is jumpy and silly and I like it. I can't figure out the words—they're goofy—but I like the sound. It makes me want to shake and jump. Jerry Lee sings some, and sometimes he just whoops and hollers. Sifford's arm rests on the windowsill of the red Oldsmobile, and he pats his hand along with the tune. "Shake, Baby, shake."

Aunt Delia puts her tennis racket in my hand and says, "Travis, do me a favor and sit down for a minute while Aunt Delia talks to her friend."

Before I say it's okay, she turns me and points over my shoulder at the green bench in the shade and gives me a little push. Then she's walking over to Sifford's car.

I don't want to go sit in the shade. All of a sudden I feel mad, crazy mad. It's like that song. I don't know what it means. I don't know how I really feel, but it's got me, and it won't let go. I want to turn around and shout, "No," to my Aunt Delia. I want to go over and sink my teeth into Sifford's arm, but that would be a girl thing, so I think of myself going over there and telling him to get out of that car and I'm going to stomp his ass. I want to be in a fight. I want to be a teenager in love, but I know I'm not. I don't know what I am. Jerry Lee sings, "Easy now. Shake it one time for me," and I sit on the bench and watch my Aunt Delia stand at Sifford's window and lean in.

They talk and their voices are quiet, but words blow over to me on the wind: "dance" and "summer" and "maybe later" and "why not?" I don't know. I don't get much. I match the two tennis rackets together and put them on my lap and lay the three balls on top of them and invent a game about making the balls sit still in the middle. Three balls touching, not moving. Then I try to move the rackets so that one ball goes to the edge and two stay in the middle. I look up at the hot high white sky. I look up into the oak tree—no squirrels or birds. I look at my feet. The red dust is all the way up my ankles to my jeans.

I wait three songs, and after a while I'm getting sleepy in the heat, and I see my Aunt Delia lean over and put her head almost in the window, and I like the way her long legs look in the sun, and how she goes up on one toe and swings her heel from side to side. I like the way her black hair fans down the back of her white blouse, and I like the dark wet spot in the middle of her back. I can see her brassiere through the wet spot, and I like that. I can see Sifford's arm close to her face, and see his lips moving and the way his eyes are when he talks to my Aunt Delia, and I know he's trying to get her to do something, but I don't know what.

Once, he stops patting his hand with the music, and he reaches up to where my Aunt Delia's arm rests on the roof of the car, and he touches her, and they stop talking. Then she steps back, and his hand falls back to the windowsill.

The radio keeps going: "I'm just a lonely boy."

And: "Personality. Smile and personality."

And: "Alley-oop, oop. Oop. Oop-oop."

After Sifford touches my Aunt Delia's arm, I know she's going to stop talking to him. I don't know how I know, but I know. She looks over at me, smiles and waves, and takes another step back from the car. Sifford tries to open the door, but my Aunt Delia reaches out and pushes it shut, and he laughs. After a while, he starts the engine and drives away. My Aunt Delia watches the red Oldsmobile until it's out of sight around the corner by the church. Then she walks over to where I'm sitting on the green bench.

"Hey, Killer, you want to play some more tennis? You're getting pretty good at it."

I look away at the church, the trees. Everything looks stooped and bent in the sun. I say, "No."

My Aunt Delia sits down beside me. "Are you mad at old Delia?"

I don't say anything.

She says, "I'm sorry I left you alone, but it wasn't all that long, and Bick and I had some things to talk about."

"What?" I ask her. I turn and look at her, and her eyes are sleepy and warm, and I know she's still thinking about Sifford.

She says, "Oh, secret things. Grown-up things."

"You can tell me," I say. I remember the storm and how the rain came in my window, and how I went to get the towel and heard my Aunt Delia crying and what we did then. I remember how I woke up that morning. I keep my eyes on hers, cool and quiet. Two little red spots start in her cheeks. She looks away.

"No, I can't."

"You can," I say.

She pushes at the grass with her white tennis shoe. There's red dust up the sides and on the pink laces. Her white legs are getting red from the sun. She says, "Maybe I can, someday. Maybe I will. Because I like you, Killer." She puts her arm across my shoulders and squeezes me hard. "But not now. Not today."

My Aunt Delia stands up. "Let's go on home and see what Marvadell's got cooking for lunch, what do you say, Killer?"

I stand up too. "Neato," I say. Then I say, "Grandpa Hollister told me not to say ma'am to Marvadell. Is that right, Aunt Delia?"

My Aunt Delia thinks about it. She looks up at the sun, and over at the white church, and at the soldier leaning on the long rifle. She says, "That's right, honey, but not because you don't respect her. It would just...it would make Marvadell uncomfortable."

I don't understand, but I say, "Okay, Aunt Delia."

She smiles and says, "Killer, I told you to call me Delia. If you don't, I'm going to start calling you Nephew Travis. You wouldn't like that, would you?"

I say I guess not, and we walk to the car, and my Aunt Delia starts the Chevy and turns on the radio. She backs out of the red-dirt parking lot and turns toward the house on Bedford Street, and I look over to my right, into the dark shade under the trees, and I see red flames on midnight-blue metal. As we go around the corner, I see black leather through a gap in the branches and a puff of cigarette smoke, and I wonder how long he's been there. I wonder if he saw me playing tennis with my Aunt Delia, then her talking to Bick Sifford and me sitting alone on the bench.

eleven

It's night, and my Aunt Delia and me are sitting out on the porch. My Grandma Hollister calls the porch the gallery. She calls the one upstairs the upper gallery. My Aunt Delia says Grandma Hollister puts on airs and tries to keep up with the ladies in town who have money. She says a sheriff's wife has social position without money, and that's what gives my Grandma Hollister headaches. Marvadell made banana ice cream, and Aunt Delia and me are eating two big bowls. Grandpa Hollister is inside reading the paper from Panama City. We can see his head through the window screen. Grandma Hollister is down at the Presbyterian Church singing at choir practice. Sometimes when the wind blows this way, we can hear the choir.

I like sitting out here at night with my Aunt Delia. It's cooler than inside, and some nights the wind brings the smell of the ocean, and it makes me think of my boat. Some nights the stars are as bright as rock candy sprinkled on dark blue paper, and my Aunt Delia says that's one of the good things about living in the country. You can see the sky at night.

"When are we going to the ocean, Aunt Delia?"

"It's Delia, honey."

I look at the window screen. Grandpa Hollister isn't listening. "Okay," I say, "Delia. When are we going to the ocean?" It still feels funny calling her Delia, but it feels good, too.

She says, "I don't know, Travis. But don't you worry. We'll go some time. We've got the whole summer ahead of us."

"Am I gonna get to swim and catch fish?" I don't dare ask about the boat. Not yet.

"You're gonna get to swim and *try* to catch fish. It's a matter of some skill, you know."

I like the way my Aunt Delia talks to me. She doesn't make things simple because I'm a kid. I lower my voice and ask her, "Delia, why were you crying the other night?"

She looks at the window screen, sharp, then puts her finger across her lips and shakes her head. "Not now, Honey. I told you I can't talk about that."

We sit for a while in the quiet. I hear a whippoorwill cry. "To-whit, to-whee, to-whit, to-whee." I look at my Aunt Delia and she smiles at me, sorry, like we have a sad secret together. We hear a rumble and a radio playing far away, getting closer, then a pop-pop-pop, and I know who it is.

Griner's street rod comes around the corner and idles slowly up our street. I look over at my Aunt Delia. She puts down her bowl of ice cream, and her hand goes to her hair and then to the gold cross at her neck. I don't know what's in her eyes now. I don't know if Griner's gonna stop and talk to us. It's Bobby Darin coming from the radio: "Dream lover, where are you, with a love oh so true."

My Aunt Delia whispers, "Don't stare, Killer. He's just a big showoff."

The hotrod with the red flames coming out of the engine passes under the street light up the block, and I can see Griner's pale face and his slick black hair and his leather jacket.

"Delia, what's he doing here?"

My Aunt Delia jumps. I don't know how Grandpa Hollister moves so quiet. I don't know how he got out here through the screen door without me hearing him. He puts on his steel-rimmed glasses and watches as Griner's rod goes by. Griner looks over and sees him, and the look on Griner's face doesn't change. It's a smile my dad calls insolent.

Grandpa Hollister says, "Delia?"

My Aunt Delia twists the cross at her throat, and I remember what she said about this town. How it makes her want to jump out of her skin. She looks up at Grandpa Hollister and says, "He's driving, Daddy. It's a small town. He's bound to take our street some time."

Griner's rod makes the corner and backs down, pop-pop-pop. Grandpa Hollister says to himself, not to me or my Aunt Delia, "Those pipes are illegal in this county. That boy's gone push me too far one of these days."

My Aunt Delia looks up at him, and her eyes are scared. "Daddy, it's just a car for crying out loud. What's the big deal?"

Grandpa Hollister watches the place where Griner's rod disappeared into the dark. "To me, Delia," he says, "the law is a big deal." His voice is soft, but it's colder than the ice cream in my bowl.

My Aunt Delia and me are on an errand for Grandma Hollister. We get out of the white Chevy and walk down the main street of Widow Rock, and we pass an alley, and there's smelly water running down the alley, and halfway down there's a red neon sign that says, WHISKEY, and a man is leaning up against the wall. He's got a greasy hat pulled down over his face, and he's holding a brown paper bag. My Aunt Delia reaches down and takes my hand and pulls me close. "Come on, Killer, walk a little faster."

We get down the sidewalk some more and someone calls, "Hey, Delia. You there! Delia Hollister!" My Aunt Delia stops, and we turn around.

It's the man. He's got his hat pushed up now, and I can see his long, gray face and that he didn't shave. He takes a drink from the paper bag, and his eyes are all wrong. I know he's drunk, but it's not funny drunk like I've seen in the movies. This is mean whiskey. The man says, "Who's that with you there, Miss Delia?"

My Aunt Delia sighs and says, "You know very well who it is, Mr. Latimer."

The man throws back his head and laughs, but it's a nasty laugh, and he says, "Oh, it's *Mr.* Latimer is it? Ain't that sweet. Sweet little Delia Hollister and her half-nigger nephew." The man takes another drink from the paper bag. He's got greasy sweat on his face, and his pants are dirty around the pockets, and one of his shoes has been cut with a knife so his toe can stick out of it. He's not wearing any socks. My Aunt Delia squeezes my hand hard. She says, "Mr. Latimer, you better go on now and leave us alone."

The man smiles mean again, and squats down. He rocks back and almost falls over. He leans against the hot brick wall and puts the bottle in the paper bag down beside his knee. He says, "Little half-nigger boy, come over here. Let me get a look at them eyes. I want to see if you got your mommer's Jap eyes. You shore got her brown skin, ain't you?" He holds out his hands to me, and his eyes tell me to come.

I don't. I look up at my Aunt Delia. If he tries to hurt her, I'll kill him. I'll kick that bottle against the wall and take up a piece of glass and cut his eyes.

My Aunt Delia pulls me away with her. She says over her shoulder, "Mr. Latimer, I'm not going to tell my father about this."

The man shouts after us. "Boy, your daddy was Mr. God High Everything around here, an' he went off just like I did to fight them damn little Jap monkeys, an' damn if he didn't come back wiff a Jap wife and a half-Jap kid." I look back, as we turn the corner. The man falls over into the alley and knocks over the bottle, and it spills under his leg. The last I see, he's trying to get up, and he can't, and his pants are covered with whiskey.

My Aunt Delia pulls me down the block to the Curl Up and Dye Beauty Parlor. We go in and get a bottle of rinse for Grandma Hollister, and then we get in the white Chevy and we drive. We go fast, out to the country, to the road where Delia said there's a decision to make, and this time we turn downhill into the dark pines. After a while, I can smell the river.

We turn onto a sand road, and then onto another one so narrow that tree branches brush the car. We stop in a wide place with tire tracks in the sand where people have come in cars. In front of us, a path leads into the woods. My Aunt Delia shuts off the engine and turns to me and pulls her legs up on the seat and hugs her knees. "Are you okay, Killer?"

"Sure," I say. "How about you?"

She nods. I think I can see tears starting in her eyes, then I don't know. Maybe not. She doesn't say anything, so I say, "I wasn't going to let him hurt you."

She smiles, sad, and says, "I know, Killer. I wasn't worried."

I say, "How come he called me a...you know?"

"That's right," my Aunt Delia says, "don't say it. If we say that word, we become like him. All the people like that."

"Why?" I ask her. I want to know.

"Because he's ignorant, that's why."

"It's because I'm half-Japanese, and he thinks that's the same as Negro?"

My Aunt Delia nods. She waits. I say, "Delia, do you know what's wrong with my mom?"

My Aunt Delia looks at me for a long time. She hugs her knees tight and closes her eyes, and when she opens them, she says, "Probably people like Mr. Latimer, Travis. That's probably what's wrong with her. That and she misses her family."

I know she means my mom's family in Japan. My Grandma and Grandpa Kobayashi, but I still don't like it. "I'm her family," I say. "Me and dad are."

My Aunt Delia says, "Maybe she needs more than that. Like I needed you the other night in the storm, and you might need me some time."

I just nod. I have to think about it. I say, "What's wrong with him, that Mr. Latimer? Why does he hate me?"

My Aunt Delia shakes her head and looks out the window at the trees. It's quiet and hot, and I can smell pine cones, and there's no wind. I can smell the river, too, and I know it's close, and I want to see it. She says, "He was in a place called Bataan, Travis. And the Japanese put him in a prison camp, and a lot of bad things happened to him there. He hasn't done much since he got back but drink whiskey and bother people."

"Did he really know my dad?"

"Everybody knew your dad, Travis."

"Were they friends?"

My Aunt Delia nods and hugs her knees. "They played football and baseball together. All the men around here did. Mr. Tolbert, too."

I think about it. I don't like Mr. Latimer, but I'm not going to hate him like I thought I was. I don't want to hate anybody here. As long as he doesn't hurt my Aunt Delia, I won't do anything. I say, "Does he hate my dad now?"

My Aunt Delia says, "No, honey, I don't think so. I think he's just confused and drunk and full of what's hurting him."

I ask my Aunt Delia if we can go to the river, but she says no, not today. We've got to get that bottle of rinse home to Grandma Hollister.

We're sitting in the third pew on the right in the white church across the park from the red-clay tennis court. Beulah Laidlaw's father is preaching about the parable of the prodigal son. He's a tall, fat man with gray hair and a red face, and he's wearing a black robe, and he's telling us about this boy who runs off and spends all of his dad's money and gets drunk. When he tell us that the boy "consorts with women of ill fame," it gets quieter in the church, and some of the women reach up and touch the gold crosses at their necks. I don't know. Maybe it means women like the one who got kidnapped by the Creature from the Black Lagoon. Women who look at you like they know what you're thinking. The boy finally ends up eating with pigs, and he gets sick of it and comes home, and his dad hugs him and takes him back. His dad has a big dinner for him, and everybody celebrates but his other brother. The other brother is mad because he stayed home and worked hard and didn't get drunk or spend money or consort. The point of it all, according to the Reverend Laidlaw, is forgiveness. We have to care more and worry more about the ones that stumble and wander than about the ones that stay put and do things right.

I'm thinking about Mr. Latimer and what he said about me and about my mom and dad. I'm thinking about the Japanese and what they did to him, and I'm as confused as all get out.

I'm sitting between Grandpa Hollister and my Aunt Delia. Grandpa Hollister has on his same black suit and white shirt, and a blue and red bow tie. Only it's not the same suit. I know now he's got three of them, all the same. Grandma Hollister has on the black dress with the little white dots on it that she wore to pick me up at the airport in Panama City, but she's up in the choir loft, wearing a white robe, and I can see the sweat on her forehead and under her chin, and I know she's miserable, and it's gonna give her a headache. She's smiling her miserable-but-not-letting-on smile.

My Aunt Delia's got on her white Sunday dress. It's made of raw silk, she told me, and it has a crinkly feel to it, and I like the way she looks in it. She's got her black hair up on the back of her head with combs, and her neck is as long as my whole face. She doesn't look at the Reverend Laidlaw. She looks at the big wooden cross behind him and the stained glass window that says INRI. Or she looks at Beulah and Caroline Huff. They sing in the choir along with Grandma. Sometimes when the Reverend Laidlaw gets real worked up over the prodigal son, I can see Beulah roll her eyes, and I know my Aunt Delia's got that look on her face she gets when she and Beulah and Caroline Huff talk about how provincial Widow Rock is. And I know I better not look at my Aunt Delia, or I'll start laughing or something. Grandpa Hollister is watching. Sometimes I think he can see what's going on behind him.

The Reverend Laidlaw finishes his sermon, and the choir stands up to sing, "He Leadeth Me," and we all stand up and sing with them. I hold the hymn book, and Grandpa and my Aunt Delia lean over me and sing with me, and I like their voices, and I like looking at the women in the choir loft. They look like angels. They're the same women I see on the streets of Widow Rock, and in the stores, and some of them are not very pretty, but in their white robes and singing like that, they're pretty, and their voices and ours out here in the pews are so loud I bet they can hear us all the way to Panama City.

But we're not as loud as the Baptists.

All afternoon it's cloudy, and then a big blue storm rolls up out of the Gulf of Mexico, and I'm sitting on the porch after dinner eating Marvadell's ice cream with my Aunt Delia. I know she's not happy. I ask her, and she says, "I'm just moody sometimes, Killer. It's the female prerogative. Don't you know that?"

I say, "Do boys get pre...pre..."

"Prerogatives. Yes they do, Killer. Boys get to be mean and jealous and stubborn, and they think they get to tell girls what to do, and they think they get to run around acting like jackasses and scoundrel dogs, and girls are supposed to stay home and sit with their knees together and do needlepoint or something. Until the boys come calling, that is."

"I don't want any of those pre...prerogatives."

"Good, Killer. I knew you'd say that."

But I know my Aunt Delia isn't just moody, she's unhappy, and there's a storm coming.

Late at night, the rain comes. First there's a rush of cool air through my window, and I'm lying outside the covers, and it feels good on my legs and chest. Then I can smell the air from way up high, and it smells like it does out in Omaha before the tornadoes come, and then it starts to rain. Big drops, and they hit my window with a sound like Marvadell smacking pie dough with her rolling pin. Then the trees begin to lash, and the limbs start to push each other around, and the birds complain in their nests, and I know I have to go to my Aunt Delia's room.

I get up and close my window and go outside into the hallway. I can see through the bathroom doorway and out the bathroom window into the moving trees. I walk down the hallway quiet and careful and stand outside my Aunt Delia's doorway. Her door isn't open this time, and I think maybe she's all right, and I should go back to my room. But I can't go back. I have to go into my Aunt Delia's room. I don't know why. I just have to. She might need me.

I don't knock. Someone might hear. I just open the door, and I can see her bed there under the slope of the roof. It's like a white boat floating on a sea of moving leaves and branches. I can see her head on the pillow, her black hair spread out. I don't hear her crying. I think she's all right. I turn to go.

"Come here, Killer."

I walk over and stand beside her bed. She reaches out and touches my arm like she did before. She says, "Are you okay? Did the rain scare you?"

I say, "No. I'm not scared."

My Aunt Delia doesn't say anything. She just lies there on her side, and I can hear her breathing, and she's touching my arm with her fingers. Then she says, "Did you come in here because you thought I'd be sad?"

I say, "Yes."

My Aunt Delia says, "I'm okay tonight, Killer. I'm just a little sad. The rain, it makes me sad."

I say, "I'm glad you're okay, Delia."

We wait for a while, and the storm gets bigger outside, and I wonder if it's going to tear shingles from the roof or blow the glass out of my Aunt Delia's window. Delia whispers, "It's really rough out there, isn't it, Killer?"

I say, "Yes."

She throws back the covers, and her good smell pours across my face in the still room. She says, "Why don't you get in here with me for a while, Killer? If the house blows down, we'll help each other crawl out of the wreckage."

I say okay. I climb into my Aunt Delia's bed. I turn my back to her like I did before, and she rests her chin on the top of my head, and I can feel she's not wearing her nightgown. I guess it's too hot for that. I can feel her chests pressing against my back, and it makes my breath come quick. My Aunt Delia says, "How's that Killer? You okay?"

I say, "Yes," and I think my voice sounds funny.

My Aunt Delia says, "Let's go to sleep now, okay?"

I say, "Delia, did something bad happen to you when there was a storm?"

My Aunt Delia doesn't say anything for a while, then she says, "Let's go to sleep, Killer, okay?"

I say, "Okay."

It's a long time before I can go to sleep. I get that way again, down there. It feels good, and I wonder if it's wrong. I wonder if I'm turning into the prodigal son. I can feel my Aunt Delia's breathing going long and slow, and I know she's asleep. I hope she's not sad anymore. I hope she has good dreams. I hold myself down there. I wonder if I'm going to dream about my Aunt Delia. It's a long time before I fall asleep.

JULY

You shake my nerves and you rattle my brain.
Too much love drives a man insane.
You broke my will. What a Thrill!
Goodness, gracious! Great balls of fire!

GREAT BALLS OF FIRE
—Music and Lyrics by Jerry Lee Lewis
—Recorded by Jerry Lee Lewis

twelve

It's night and I'm sitting in the back seat of the white Chevy and my Aunt Delia and Caroline Huff and Beulah Laidlaw are all crammed together in the front. My Aunt Delia's driving fast. The disk jockey says, "That was Duane Eddy and his twangin' guitar. And now, here's the latest from Little Anthony and The Imperials." A high voice like a girl's starts singing, "You don't remember me, but I remember you. It was not so long ago, you broke my heart in two."

I like driving at night. The air blowing in the windows is cool, and it smells different because the things that come out at night are calling to you. And the music seems to come from out there in the night, from the wind and the moon, not the radio. Little Anthony sings, "If we could start anew, I wouldn't hesitate. I'd gladly take you back, and tempt the hand of fate." Caroline Huff says, "That little nigger boy can sho sing. I read where they just stand around on the street corners up there in Philadelphia and practice the doo-wop. Can you believe that?"

Beulah Laidlaw says, "Any little nigger boy stood around singing on some corner in Widow Rock, Delia's daddy would snatch him bald-headed."

My Aunt Delia pushes down on the accelerator and slowly shakes her head. "Will you two not be such rednecks in front of Travis? He's not used to your kind of stupidity."

Caroline giggles and twists around on the seat and looks back at me. Her blonde pony tail bounces over the back of the seat. I want to reach out and touch it. She says, "Sorry about your virgin ears, Travis."

Beulah Laidlaw says, "Thank God for Travis."

Caroline says, "Amen to that."

When they want to go out at night, they tell their parents it's all right because Delia Hollister is bringing Travis along. Tonight, we're supposed to go to the Baptist youth group over in Warrington. Warrington's the rival high school, but it's summer now, so the kids from Widow Rock and the kids from Warrington take turns going to youth groups. They're supposed to talk about Jesus and being a teenager and the problems of growing up too fast. I know we're going to drive around until ten o'clock looking for other kids who skipped the youth group. Most nights, we find them. My Aunt Delia and Caroline and Beulah call it, "Seeing who's there." It's one of their jokes: "Why don't we go on down to Tolbert's and see who's there." There's always somebody. There's nothing else to do.

Beulah Laidlaw looks back at me. "You wouldn't ever tell on us, would you, Travis? I mean, I want you to know you'll go to hell if you do. Little boys who break promises go to hell when they die, and sometimes God doesn't even wait to let them grow up before he sends them there." She tries to give me a grown-up, parent look, but it doesn't work. She's just Beulah Laidlaw. My Aunt Delia says she's got hot pants. My Aunt Delia says she's boy crazy. I say, "Unh-uh, I won't tell." I mean it for my Aunt Delia. I want her to know she can trust me.

Beulah and Caroline giggle again. "Will you listen at that boy," Caroline says, "he's been here a month, and he sounds like they found him under a collard leaf."

I don't sound like Omaha anymore. I can't help it. My Aunt Delia laughs at me sometimes, too. She says, "Killer, when you go home, they gone put your picture in the paper and ask for somebody to come an' claim this poor lost little southern boy." She's just kidding me. I like the way I sound. I like to sound like other people.

We pass Luby's Roadhouse, and my Aunt Delia slows way down, and for a second I can hear the juke box. Beulah and Caroline don't recognize any cars in the parking lot.

"Farmers," Beulah says.

"No," Caroline says, "worse. Farm equipment salesmen."

We go on down the road in the dark, and the country night pours in the windows, and I lean back as far as I can and look at the stars through the back window. I can smell the perfume and the shampoo from the front seat and hear them talking. Sometimes they whisper and spell things like, "m-a-k-i-n-g o-u-t," and I pretend I don't know what's going on. The truth is, sometimes I don't, but I'm getting an education.

We come to the outskirts of Warrington, and it looks like the outskirts of Widow Rock, only it's got more hills and it's in the opposite direction from the river. Warrington's got a Dairy Queen, and we stop for Cokes and french fries, then we cruise past the Baptist church. "There's Ronny Bishop's truck," Beulah says. She runs her fingers through her brown hair and gives it a flip.

Caroline pokes my Aunt Delia in the ribs and says, "I don't see Bick's Oldsmobile. I don't see it anywhere."

My Aunt Delia says, "The whereabouts of Bick Sifford's Oldsmobile is a matter of no importance to me, Caroline Huff."

We turn around at the end of the block and slide by the church again. Some kids I don't know are getting out of a car. Caroline and Beulah scrunch down in the seat as we pass. They giggle together. My Aunt Delia says, "You can get up now." They push back up, still giggling. Beulah Laidlaw says, "Let's stop. I want to see Ronny Bishop. He's cool."

Caroline Huff looks across my Aunt Delia at the front of the church. Lights come on in the basement recreation room where the youth group meets. A young couple named the Dagles lead the youth group. Mr. Dagle is a lawyer, and his wife teaches English at Warrington High School. He's good looking, and she's pretty, and most of the kids think they're pretty cool, and they listen when the Dagles talk about how Jesus doesn't want them to grow up too fast.

My Aunt Delia says, "Ronny Bishop sticks his fingers in his shoes and then smells them."

Caroline says, "EEEE-EEWW!"

Beulah says, "Delia, you're just jealous because Ronny likes me better than you."

My Aunt Delia says, "No, seriously, I watched him do it in Algebra II. He sticks them way down in there when he thinks nobody's looking, and then he pulls them out and pretends he's resting his chin on his hand and thinking about a quadratic equation. Then he gives them a real good sniff."

Beulah says, "Poop on you, Delia Hollister. I still think he's cool."

"Well," my Aunt Delia says, "he's got hot feet."

I can't help it. It makes me laugh.

We drive out of Warrington. We're in the country again, and I think: so much for Jesus and growing up too fast. We're on our way to see who's there. After a couple of miles, we pass Luby's again, and up ahead a big car slips out from under a tree by the roadside and turns on a flashing red light, and then we hear the moan of a siren. "Uh-oh," says Caroline, "somebody's gonna get it."

Beulah says, "Some John Deere salesman had too much kickapoo juice at Luby's."

My Aunt Delia goes stiff and quiet, and I lean forward and look at her hands on the steering wheel. They're hard and white in the light from the dashboard.

Caroline says, "Stand on it, Delia. I want to see what's going on."

My Aunt Delia speeds up, and after a while we start to catch up with the police car, and then he stops, and we see he's got somebody pulled over. "It's a long way from US 90," Beulah says. "I don't know what the road patrol's doing way out here."

"That's not the road patrol," my Aunt Delia says. Her voice is different now. It's not her night voice. It's not dreamy and slow and ready to joke or sing with the radio. She stops about a hundred yards behind the two cars and turns off her lights. "That's my daddy," she says.

Beulah says, "I wonder who he's got."

Caroline says, "Let's go see."

My Aunt Delia says, "We can't. We're in Warrington talking about growing up too fast."

We sit that way for a while. The radio plays "Stagger Lee." We see Grandpa Hollister get out of his car and walk into his own headlights, but we can't see the other car or who's in it. "It's probably some flatland tourist," Beulah says.

We've got hills around here, so we call people from further south flatlanders. I don't think our hills are big enough for that, but I don't say much about it. Caroline says, "Yeah, looking for the moon over Miami." We wait.

Beulah says, "We left Warrington because the discussion was boring and we wanted to get home before curfew."

My Aunt Delia says, "Oh Beulah, use your brain. The discussion's just getting started."

I can see Grandpa Hollister standing in the high beams, then leaning down over the car. Then he does something fast. I've never seen him move fast, and before I can say anything, my Aunt Delia turns on her headlights, and we speed, then she slows down. As we slide past the two cars, I see red flames on midnight-blue metal and Griner's black leather jacket. Grandpa Hollister's got something in his hand. He swings it down hard. His hand comes up again and stops. His head turns to us so fast you can't see him do it. My Aunt Delia grinds the Chevy into reverse and stops in the middle of the road. It's hot without the air blowing in, and I can hear three engines running, and smell the cattle in the field across the road from us, and I see Grandpa Hollister shove something black into his pocket.

Kenny Griner is face down on the wet grass in front of Grandpa Hollister. He tries to get up. He makes it to his hands and knees, but he falls again. I hear him groan. I look at Beulah and Caroline, and they've both got their hands over their mouths. My Aunt Delia leans out the window and looks at Grandpa Hollister. He looks at her, and it's like the first day I came when my Aunt Delia drove into the garage too fast, and I thought he'd be mad at her. He isn't mad. I can't see his face very well, but I know he isn't mad. He bends over and takes Griner by the two wings of his leather jacket and picks him up and sits him on the running board of the street rod. Griner's face is down in the dark, but he lifts it, and blood runs from above his eye down to his cheek. It drips from his chin onto his white T-shirt. Griner takes his cigarettes from his jacket and tries to light one, but his hands are shaking, and he smears blood on the Camel pack and the Zippo. Finally, he just lays the whole mess down on the running board and stares at it. Then he looks at us. And he smiles. He says, "Hello, Miss Delia."

Caroline Huff whispers, "I think I'm gonna be sick."

My Aunt Delia says, "Hey there, Kenny. Looks like you had an accident."

She doesn't sound like herself. She sounds grown up and like a kid at the same time, and I know she's talking to Grandpa Hollister not Griner.

My Grandpa Hollister says, "His head hit the steering wheel. I've told him not to drive so fast out here. This road is tricky at night." Grandpa Hollister comes over and stands at my Aunt Delia's window. He bends down, and I stick my head out the back window. A braided leather thong dangles from a fat lump in his hip pocket. He says, "Caroline, Beulah, let this be a lesson to you. Driving fast on this road at night is dangerous."

Both Beulah and Caroline yes sir him.

Grandpa Hollister stands up, steps back, and looks at his watch. Then he looks at my Aunt Delia. She says, "Daddy, do you need any help? Is there anything we can do for Kenny?"

Griner is still smiling at my Aunt Delia, but his hands tremble harder. Grandpa Hollister shakes his head. "You girls go along now, hear?"

We pull away, and I watch through the back window. Griner looks after us like we're the whole world slipping away from him. He gets smaller and smaller there in the circle of car light, and the last I see is my Grandpa bending down to him again and Griner looking up into his face.

We drive back to Widow Rock, and nobody talks. The radio plays "Whole lot of shakin' goin' on," and nobody shakes. I'm the Killer, and I don't shake, but I'm thinking about Griner's hands.

thirteen

My Aunt Delia is out on a date with Bick Sifford.

Bick Sifford's father is throwing a big dinner dance for their twentieth wedding anniversary. Grandma Hollister is all excited about it. She fussed around the house all day like she was going out and not my Aunt Delia. Before he went off to work this morning, Grandpa Hollister threw the newspaper on the dining room floor and said, "Calm down, Lilah, or you'll be in bed for a week with a migraine."

Marvadell wouldn't serve my Aunt Delia any cheese grits with her scrambled eggs. She said, "Girl, you eat one mo bite, and you gone look like you swallowed a honeydew melon in that party dress of yours." My Aunt Delia said, "I wish you all would quit fussing. The only reason I'm going is to see Bick Sifford's house. I might as well investigate the local mansion before he disappears off to Princeton."

Caroline Huff's daddy is a vice president at the box factory. Her parents are invited, but Caroline doesn't have a date. She says there's no suitable boy within a forty-mile radius. Beulah Laidlaw is in bed sick because Ronny Bishop didn't ask her. He went off to a golf camp in Atlanta for a week instead.

Grandpa Hollister put on his black coat when he heard Bick's Oldsmobile in the driveway. Grandma Hollister wore her church dress and her pearls. Marvadell usually goes home at six o'clock, but Grandma Hollister made her stay late and make lemonade and oatmeal cookies.

Bick sat on the sofa and Marvadell served him cookies and lemonade on a silver tray. He held a glass of lemonade in his hand. He picked up one cookie and put it back on the silver tray. Marvadell peeked out the kitchen door. "Humph!"

Grandpa Hollister said, "Bick, be sure and tell your father I said congratulations on the anniversary," and Grandma Hollister hovered around like a big, overfed pea-hen, touching the pearls at her neck and asking Bick if he'd like more lemonade. Bick said, "No, ma'am, but it sure is good." He looked at his watch and then at the stairs.

I sat by the fireplace reading *Life*. I wanted to turn on the TV, but Grandma Hollister said that would be vulgar. Bick Sifford looked over at me and winked, and said, "How's it going, Trav, Buddy? You getting used to life in Widow Rock?"

I didn't say anything. Grandpa Hollister cleared his throat and rattled his newspaper. Grandma Hollister said, "Why Travis, where are your manners? Bick asked you a question." So I said, "I'm getting better than used to it. I like it a lot." *I just don't like you, you possum-faced snot.* I smiled, and Bick smiled back like we were two big buddies and we had some big secret.

Finally, my Aunt Delia came down. She looked so beau-tiful in her white party dress and her makeup, and I could have killed Bick Sifford. He got up and ran his hands down the front of his white coat. He couldn't think of anything to say. He just looked at my Aunt Delia, then at Grandma and Grandpa Hollister, then he lowered his eyes like he was get-ting away with something.

Grandma Hollister's eyes got red and wet, and she came over and stood in front of my Aunt Delia and picked a piece of lint off the front of her dress that wasn't even there, and whispered, "My lovely Delia." Then she looked at Bick and said, "My, but you two are a handsome couple. Aren't they, John?"

Grandpa Hollister lowered his newspaper and looked at my Aunt Delia and Bick, and for once his eyes didn't expect the worst. He said, "They sure are."

Bick Sifford cleared his throat and looked at his watch. "Well, I guess it's time we..."

I wanted to walk over and kick him in his ass. He didn't even tell my Aunt Delia how pretty she looked.

In my dream, I walk into my mom and dad's bedroom. My mom is kneeling at her shrine lighting incense and speaking Japanese. When she hears me behind her, she turns and says, "Travis, you mustn't tell your dad you saw me do this. Promise me you won't." And then I'm in church with Caroline Huff and Beulah Laidlaw. It's night but a bright light shines through the stained glass window and throws the shadow of the cross on the floor in front of me. Beulah says, "Remember, Travis, little boys who break promises go to hell." And then I'm in my Widow Rock bedroom, and it's storming outside, and I go to my Aunt Delia's bed, and she wakes up, but she won't take me in with her. She sends me away, but first she says, "I'm in hell, Travis. I'm in hell. You have to leave me here alone."

I have to put my feet on the floor and feel the Florida pine and smell the linseed oil and the old musty wallpaper before I'm sure I'm awake. I lie there shivering and trying to figure out the dream. I've been missing my mom and dad a lot and trying not to worry about them. And trying not to have these dreams at night. I've been wondering why my dad hasn't called me. When he didn't call on my birthday, my Aunt Delia said it would be our secret that my birthday came. She said not to tell Grandma and Grandpa Hollister the tennis racquet was my birthday gift because they'd be embarrassed. I miss my mom, and my Aunt Delia is off at the party with Bick Sifford.

It's not cold, but I'm still shaking from my dream. I don't know what hell is. I'm not sure there even is one, but I know you have to die to find out, and I sure don't want to do that. I don't hear anyone awake downstairs. The clock says it's after midnight. My Grandma Hollister always goes to bed at ten. So does my Grandpa unless he's out lawing around. Then he comes in at all hours. You never know when to expect him. I wonder what he does out there at night in a place as quiet as Widow Rock. I'm shaking.

It's earlier in Omaha than here, and I can picture my dad sitting at the kitchen table working with his law books and papers. He's still got his suit pants and white shirt on from work, but his tie is thrown over the back of his chair, and there's a cup of coffee and a pack of cigarettes on the table in front of him. He puts his pencil down and rubs his eyes, and then lights a cigarette, and I wonder if he's thinking about my mom. I wonder if he can't work anymore because he's thinking about her. I wonder if he wants to go to that hospital and run away with her and bring her here and get me to run away, too. All of a sudden I have to talk to him.

It's dark downstairs, but I know my way around. I stand at the bottom of the stairs, and I can smell the ham and biscuits from dinner. Marvadell leaves the biscuits under a cloth on the kitchen counter. I could go have one with butter and blackberry jam. I can hear Grandma Hollister breathing from her and Grandpa's bedroom. Sometimes she snorts in the middle of a breath, and it wakes her up, and she says, "What? What?" and then she goes back to sleep. I can see some of the yard and the street through the front windows. It's quiet, and the moonlight glitters where it strikes the dew.

The phone is on a table in the foyer. There's a hall seat next to it. I stand there in the dark with my hand on the cold black phone wondering what to do. I've never called long distance before. I've only used the phone when my dad let me say hello to my mom at the hospital. I know my number at home.

There's a buzz when I pick up the phone. I'm supposed to dial, but I can't see the numbers in the dark. I dial anyway, and nothing happens. I hang up. My hands are sweating. I dial again, and nothing happens. I'm about to put the phone down when a lady says, "Your number, please?"

I know my number, but I don't say it. I don't say anything. She says, "Sheriff Hollister, is that you? What can I do for you, sir?"

The back door opens, and I crouch down with the phone in my hand. I'm afraid to hang it up because it's gonna make noise. The lady keeps talking, and her voice is like a wasp flying around me. Grandpa Hollister comes through the kitchen door. He lifts his hand to his mouth, and I know he's got one of Marvadell's biscuits. The phone in my hand is heavy, and my hand is sweating, and the lady keeps asking if she can help the sheriff. Then she says from far away, "Is everything all right there, Sheriff?"

I stand up slowly to put the phone in its cradle. I know it's going to make a click, but I've got to stop her talking. Grandpa Hollister lifts the biscuit for another bite, then he lowers it and looks at the foyer where I'm hiding. He stands very still for a second, and Grandma Hollister snorts and says, "What?" and I try to put the phone in its cradle, but it slips from my wet fingers and lands with a "Clack!" Grandpa Hollister hears me. He stands stiff still in the dark, listening, then he shakes his head and takes another bite of biscuit.

He walks straight toward me, all the way to the foyer, and I'm crouching in the dark between the hall seat and the umbrella stand beside the front door. He stands there in the dark looking out through the little window in the front door, then he turns his back to me and bends down to the secretary.

I crouch, trying not to breathe, but I'm shaking again like in my dream. I don't know what Grandpa Hollister will do if he catches me here. I don't know what I'll say to him. I'm afraid I might lie, and then he'll send me away to reform school. I'm afraid the lady on the phone will tell him I called. I'm afraid I'll never see my mom and dad again. I hear him unlock the secretary and pull down the breakfront. He steps back, and his black boots stop one inch from my bare toes where I'm hunkered down in the dark.

He empties his pockets, and I know the sounds. His wallet, then his keys hit the breakfront, then I hear a heavy sound I don't know. I lean to the right, and I see it in a splinter of moonlight through the window. It's the braided thong from out there on the highway the night Kenny Griner had his accident. Only it wasn't an accident, because I see what's attached to the leather thong. It's a club, some kind of club. It's leather, too, and it's shaped like a big teardrop. It's not a billy stick. That's made of wood and wouldn't fit in anybody's pocket. I've never seen one like this, but I know what it is, and I know what happened to Kenny Griner's eye. I remember my Grandpa Hollister saying, "That boy's going to push me too far."

My Grandpa Hollister locks the secretary and stands straight and stretches, and I pull my toes back so he doesn't step on them. He turns and tries the door latch to see if it's locked, then he walks back into the living room. He stops to eat the rest of the biscuit. I hear a snort and then, "What? What?" Grandpa Hollister shakes his head and goes into the bedroom. I hear him undressing, and after a while I hear the bedsprings. I sneak to the foot of the stairs. I wait a minute there. Then I tip-toe up the ends of the risers so they won't squeak.

fourteen

When Bick Sifford's Oldsmobile whispers in at one o'clock, I get up and look out. I can see the driveway from my bedroom window. Bick turns off the engine, and I see the sleeve of his white dinner jacket and then the glow of the cigarette lighter as he brings it to his face. Smoke drifts like words from his window up to mine. I can't see my Aunt Delia. I wonder if she had fun at the dance. I wonder if seeing Bick Sifford's big house was worth going there. I don't think she told the truth about why she wanted to go. I remember the park and how Bick Sifford reached up and touched her arm just like she touches mine sometimes when I come into her room at night. I remember how she pulled away from him and how she waited a while before she did it. I watch them. Bick drops his hand out the window and flicks the ashes from his cigarette.

After a while, Bick Sifford gets out of the Oldsmobile and opens my Aunt Delia's door and walks her to the front porch where I can't see them. I lie in bed listening. I think about sneaking down again to see what they're doing, but Grandpa Hollister might catch me. He might be down there himself in the dark looking through the front door at my Aunt Delia and Bick Sifford.

After a while, I fall asleep, but I wake up when my Aunt Delia tip-toes down the hallway. Her light comes on, and I get up and go stand outside her door and listen. The radio comes on soft like it does when she's thinking or she's sad. She's humming low with the radio. It's Del Shannon's "Runaway": "As I walk along, I wonder, what went wrong with our love, a love that was so strong." When I knock, she says, "Come in, Killer."

She's sitting at the vanity table in her white party dress, but she doesn't look as pretty as when she left. Her hair is messed and tangled, and her makeup is mostly gone. She's got dark places under her eyes that make her look sad. She says, "Killer, did I wake you up? I'm sorry. I tried to be quiet."

I say, "You didn't wake me up." There are so many things I want to tell her. There are so many questions I want to ask her. She looks at the clock in her radio. "It's awfully late for you to be up. Is anything wrong?"

"I can stay up as late as you can." I don't know why I said it. I just did.

She turns back to the mirror. She gives herself a look in it like she wonders who she is. She says, "Okay, Killer. Stay up as late as you like. I'm tired, and I'm going to bed. Before you start your all-night vigil, help me get out of this dress." She reaches back and pulls her hair out of the way. "Just start the zipper for me, Killer."

I pull the zipper down a little, and she pulls it the rest of the way. She stands up and shakes herself like she's dancing, like she's doing the shake, baby, shake. The dress slips down in a pile around her feet, and she side-steps out of it. She's in her bra and underpants. I turn and start to walk out again. She laughs. "Hey, Killer, it's all right. Come on back. All my vital parts are covered." My neck is thick, and I can feel the two red spots growing in my cheeks. I swallow and turn around and walk toward her. She picks up the dress and turns to the closet, and I try not to look, but I can't help it. I love the way her waist goes in, and her hips go out. I love the two dimples below her hip bones. I love how I can see her backbone. She hangs up the dress and turns, and I see the dark shadow between her legs through the white cloth of her underpants. For a second, I can't see at all, and my throat is so thick I can't breathe. Then I see a red scratch. It's about five inches long, and it goes across the top of her chest and into her armpit.

She sits at the vanity, and her long black hair pours down her back, and it shines bright. She hands me a brush over her shoulder. "If you're gonna be here, you might as well brush me some." I like the way she looks at herself in the mirror, knowing everything about her own face and seeing it for the first time. I like how she approves and disapproves. I think she's the most beautiful girl in the world. I can see her chests in the mirror, but I try not to look.

I take the brush and start pulling it through her hair. I pull it real slow and try not to hurt her.

She turns to me. "So, Killer, do you think old Aunt Delia is pretty tonight?"

My face is hot. I look into her eyes and clear my throat and say, "I think you're prettier than the lady in the Black Lagoon."

She laughs for a long time. She laughs until she gets tears in her eyes, and she wipes them with a tissue, and she says, "I saw that movie. She is pretty. Prettier than me."

I say, "What's that, Delia?"

She says, "What do you mean, Killer?" She doesn't look at me.

I point at her chest. It's a raw red line just above her bra and into her armpit. She touches the scrape with her fingers and says, "Oh, that. It's just a scratch. Don't worry about it."

I say, "Did Bick Sifford do that?"

My Aunt Delia looks surprised. Then she looks sad. She hugs herself like she's cold, and she gets up and goes to the closet and puts on her bathrobe and sits on the bed and says, "Come over here, Killer." I do and she takes me by the shoulders and says, "I'm going to tell you something, but it has to be our secret. You can't share it with anybody, okay?"

I nod.

She says, "Bick Sifford likes me. He likes me a lot. Oh, he acts stupid like all boys do, and sometimes stupider than most, but he likes me a lot, and he wants me to like him. And I would. I'd like him if I could. But I can't."

I want to know why she can't like Bick Sifford, but I don't want to ask. I don't want her to like him. "Did he hurt you?" I ask.

She frowns and looks at me for a while. "Yes, Killer, he did, but it's nothing for you to worry about. It's just a little bitty hurt, and he didn't mean to do it."

The Creature from the Black Lagoon had webbed hands and feet and big claws, and he caught the lady and took her under water. He never scratched her like that. I say, "Did he grab you?"

My Aunt Delia lets go of my arms and pulls her legs up on the bed and lays her head on the pillow. She says, "Killer, go turn off the lights." I do, and she calls me over to the bed again. She pats the place beside her and says, "Climb up here, and let's talk."

We're lying on our backs staring at the ceiling in the dark. The house is quiet, but the radio is playing soft. The disk jockey says, "This is for all you late-night lovers out there in radio land, and especially for the last of you crazy jalopy jockeys trying to get little Suzie home before Mom and Dad lock the front door." The song is one I haven't heard before: "Wake Up, Little Suzie." I like it. I like lying here next to my Aunt Delia in the dark with the radio playing and the trees moving slowly in the wind outside.

My Aunt Delia says, "Killer, how much do you know about boys and girls?"

I guess I have to be honest. "Not much."

She says, "That's what I thought," and her voice changes, and I know she's smiling in the dark. She doesn't say anything for a while, and we listen to the radio. "The movie's over. It's four o'clock, and we're in trouble deep. Wake up, little Susie. We gotta go home." My Aunt Delia sighs, and says, "Bick Sifford did grab me, Killer. We danced and it was hot, so we went for a walk out in the garden, and there was a big ole moon, and we stopped under a magnolia tree, and he grabbed me. Bick's what Beulah and Caroline call a foreigner."

"A foreigner?" I don't get it. I thought Bick Sifford was born right here in Choctawhatchee County. He sure talks like it.

My Aunt Delia says, "He's got Russian hands and Roman fingers. That's what they'd say, Killer. Do you understand?"

I don't, not exactly, but I say I do because I want her to keep telling me about boys and girls. "He grabbed you, and he hurt you?" I ask.

She says, "He just got a little excited. We both did. But it's not anything for you to worry about. It's not going to happen again. I can't get excited like that anymore, so I'm not going to."

"Are you going out with Bick Sifford anymore?"

"No, Honey. Not if I can help it. And he'll go off to

Princeton at the end of the summer, and there won't be any excitement for a long time after that."

"How come?"

"Because Bick's gonna meet a lot of rich girls from Vassar and Bryn Mawr, and he's gonna forget about ole Delia Hollister back here in one-horse Widow Rock."

I don't get it. I don't see how anybody could forget my Aunt Delia. I know I never will. I say, "Is he a dreamboat?"

My Aunt Delia sighs, and her arm rises up like a long white snake in the dark, and she reaches toward the window, and she drags one fingernail down the window screen, and it makes a long tearing sound. She says, "Yes, Killer, he is, but he's not my dreamboat."

"Who's your dreamboat?"

"You are, Killer." And she reaches over and tickles my side in the dark, and we both laugh, and she holds her hand over my mouth so nobody will hear, and then we're quiet for a while, and I say, "Am I really your dreamboat, Delia?"

She says, "Of course you are, Killer. Didn't I just say so?" Her voice is slow and dreamy, and she'll fall asleep soon, and I know I'm not staying with her tonight. She wants to be alone. I wanted to tell her about my dream and going downstairs to call my dad and the leather-covered club and Kenny Griner's eye, but it'll have to wait now. I push up and sit on the edge of the bed.

"Are you going, Killer?" She wants me to go. "Good night, sleep tight."

"Aunt Delia, what's hell?"

"Why Killer, what a question!" She pushes up on her elbow and rubs her eyes. She looks at me for a while, and I'm glad she can't see my face. She says, "That's complicated, Killer. We'll have to save that one for another time, okay?"

"Okay," I say, "but just tell me this. Is there really a hell?"

My Aunt Delia falls back and stares up at the ceiling again. She thinks about it. Finally, she says, "I don't know, Killer, but if there is, sometimes I think it must be a lot like Widow Rock."

I don't know what to think now. I like Widow Rock. I like it better than Omaha. My Aunt Delia's here. She can tell I'm confused. She sighs and says, "Never mind, Killer. I was just making a joke. We'll talk about it later, okay."

I say, "Okay." I go to the door and stop and look back.

My Aunt Delia says, "'Night, Dreamboat."

In my bed, I can hear the radio in her room. It's gonna play all night and make it hard for me to sleep. I'm gonna lie here for a long time and think of all those boys like Bick Sifford out there in all those cars like boats drifting along the night highways, going home with girls like my Aunt Delia. Floating home so there won't be trouble deep.

fifteen

I wake up and my Aunt Delia is standing over my bed. She smiles and holds her finger across her lips and says, "Shhhh." I sit up and rub my eyes and don't say anything. She leans down close to my ear and whispers, "Let's say we're sick and skip church, okay?"

I whisper, "Sure." Then, "What's wrong with us?"

My Aunt Delia tilts her head to the side and thinks. Then she whispers, "Oh, I don't know. Maybe I ate some bad shrimp at the Sifford's anniversary soiree, and I brought one home and gave it to you, and it gave us a tummyache."

"Okay," I say. "I got a stomachache." I hold my stomach and groan.

My Aunt Delia watches me groan and stretch my face out of shape with the pain. She whispers, "Don't overdo it, Killer. Don't win the Academy Award. We want a little religious freedom, not a trip to the hospital."

So I add a little courage to the pain. My Aunt Delia watches and then gives me the thumbs-up. "Great. That's just right. I'm gonna go arrange things for us."

I lie there looking at the ceiling and listening to the jays and mockingbirds in the big oak tree outside my window. When I hear Grandma Hollister's footsteps on the stairs, I start my stomachache. She comes in and sits on my bedside. She's got on her flowered housecoat and her hair is up in curlers. She's got on too much perfume, so it's not hard to act sick. She leans down and kisses my cheek and says, "Does my Travis have the misery? I don't know what got into your Aunt Delia, feeding a little boy shrimp after midnight. Would you like a dose of Pepto Bismol?"

I don't know what Pepto Bismol is. We don't use it in Omaha. I look at her and groan, then smile some courage and say, "No, ma'am. I think I'd just like to lie here for a while and see if I feel better." I tilt my head in the general direction of the bathroom. "I think I might need to..." My Grandma Hollister understands. She says, "You poor, sweet thing. I suppose you'll be all right here 'til we get back from church. If you're not better then, we'll take you to see Dr. Cohen."

I'm hoping this thing doesn't get out of hand. I got enough doctors when I was a little kid and had the flu and almost died. I hate shots. Every time you go to the doctor, even if you're not sick, they say, "This boy needs a booster shot." Why do they always have to boost you? And why do they always stick you in the heiny? I don't mind it in the arm, but in the heiny hurts, and it's embarrassing, too.

I say to Grandma Hollister, "I'll be okay. I just need to be close to the..." She nods, feels my forehead, kisses my cheek, and says, "I'm going to worry all through church." She goes to the door. She says, "Bringing bad shrimp into my house after midnight. It gives me a histamine headache." She touches her forehead and goes to my Aunt Delia's room, and I hear them talking. I wait and don't groan and doze a little and wake up and don't hear much until Grandpa Hollister pulls the Buick Roadmaster out of the garage, and they drive away.

Then my Aunt Delia's bare feet pound the pine boards, and she flies through the air and lands on my bed. "Whoopee, I'm sounding the all clear. We got religious freedom, now let's do something with it."

We drive downtown, but we don't dare go past the Presbyterian church. We pass the Baptist Church, and I can hear them singing. They sing louder than we do. I say to my Aunt Delia, "How come we aren't Baptists?"

She squints at me. "The questions you ask, Killer." The radio is playing church music. You get preaching, too, and sometimes it's funny, especially from Del Rio, Texas. Me and my Aunt Delia listen to it and laugh. My Aunt Delia says, "We aren't Baptists because they have something called an altar call."

"What's an altar call?"

"That's when the end of the service comes, and the preacher calls for all the sinners in the congregation to come forward and kneel at the altar and dedicate themselves to Jesus. The choir sings, 'Just As I Am,' and the people sit there, and it's hot, and they're all hoping they don't have to go down and dedicate themselves 'cause they've all done it before, and they're all pretty well dedicated, and they've seen all their neighbors get the fit of righteousness and stagger down the aisle and fall on their knees and let the preacher lay on his hands. So they sit there, and it gets hotter, and the choir sings, 'Just as I am, I come to thee.'"

My Aunt Delia sings the words. She's got a pretty voice, and it's a pretty song, but she's making fun of it a little. She stops singing and says, "The choir sings lower and lower and slower and slower, and it gets quieter and quieter in the church, and the preacher is sweating so hard he might just boil down to bone and gristle in a black coat, and his eyes look so hurt 'cause nobody's getting the fit, and I swear, Killer, it's a battle of wills. There's all these people in the church, all of them just as dedicated as they can be and just as saved as a whole boxcar of peppermint Lifesavers, and they don't want to get up in front of all their neighbors and go down that aisle and fall on their knees and rededicate. 'Cause rededicating means maybe you've done something to undedicate yourself, and nobody wants anybody in a small town to know the freshness is out of their dedication.

"So the battle of wills wears on, and the choir sings, and they're all sweating, and everybody's fanning with those fans that advertise some funeral home, and it gets past noon, and the Sunday roast is roasting back home and stomachs are rumbling, and kids are fidgeting, and the choir isn't even singing anymore. They're just swaying and humming. Things are so bad, the choir can't even sing the words anymore. Finally, the preacher wins. Some poor soul, somebody's crazy Aunt Bewhooziz, or unmarried sister Towhatziz gets up and gives a sob, and wails out her secret sin, and wobbles on down to the front and kneels, and the preacher lays on his hands and thanks his Jesus, and the choir sings real loud, "I come, I come," and everybody's happy because the roast isn't gone be as tough as shoe leather."

I say, "I'm glad we're not Baptists."

"Hallelujah to that, Killer. And here's to religious freedom."

We drive down Main Street and it's deserted. Tolbert's Drugstore is closed. Mr. Tolbert's a Baptist, but my Aunt Delia says he isn't iron-clad because he sells Cokes and coffee and lets people dance to the jukebox. We pass the Mercantile and the Curl Up and Dye Beauty Parlor and come to a little white house with a sign that says, DR. D. COHEN, M.D. Two cars are parked in front, and one of them has a snake climbing up a cross on the tag. My Aunt Delia pulls in and stops.

I wonder what's going on. I thought we were just play-ing sick to get religious freedom. I hope I'm not getting a booster shot or something. Once when my dad took me to the dentist, he didn't tell me until we were in the parking lot. I asked him why he told me we were going out for cigarettes. He said, "It's just a lot less trouble this way, Travis. You'll know what I mean when you get kids of your own." I didn't like it. I look over at my Aunt Delia and I'm wondering if she tricked me. She smiles, but she looks serious. She says, "Come on, Killer. I want you to meet a friend of mine."

Inside there's a waiting room with chairs and copies of *Life* and *Look* and *Time*. There's a tank with some tired-looking goldfish and an office with a frosted glass window, and there's a door. My Aunt Delia walks through the door, down a narrow hallway with rooms on both sides, and, at the end, we come to another office, and there's a man in a brown suit with a bald head and wire-rimmed glasses. His face is gray, not tanned like most of the men in Widow Rock, and he looks tired, and he's writing. He looks up when my Aunt Delia sticks her head in.

"Hello, Dr. Cohen. Is Mrs. Cohen around? I saw her car out front."

The man pushes his glasses up his nose and blinks at us. He doesn't smile. He holds his fountain pen an inch above the paper on his desk. The nib is perfectly still. "Hello, Delia." He looks at me and nods.

I say, "Hello, sir."

His eyes go back to Delia, and they're doctor's eyes. He says, "She's back in the storeroom taking inventory. Go on back if you want to."

My Aunt Delia smiles and says thanks, and I think she

likes the man, but it's hard to tell. He's got lots of books in the little office, and colored pictures of body parts on the walls, and a glass case with metal and rubber instruments in it. He holds his pen above the paper and doesn't look down until we walk away.

I follow my Aunt Delia to the storeroom. It's dark inside, but I can see rows of shelves with boxes and bottles on them. It smells like medicine. My Aunt Delia says, "Mrs. Cohen, it's me, Delia Hollister."

I hear an "Oooh!" from inside like somebody's startled, then a woman comes out of the dim. She's tall and thin, and she has a narrow face and lots of thick brown hair. She's wearing wire-rimmed glasses, too, and a white blouse, and she's the first grown woman I've seen in Widow Rock in pants. She's holding a clipboard and a pencil. It's dark and hot inside the storeroom, and the woman steps out into the hallway and stands in front of my Aunt Delia.

My Aunt Delia says, "I saw your car, so I thought I'd drop in and say hey."

Mrs. Cohen smiles at my Aunt Delia and then looks at me.

My Aunt Delia says, "This is my nephew, Travis, from Omaha."

Mrs. Cohen offers me her hand, and I take it. It's cool and dry and strong. She says, "Yes, I heard about Travis. How do you like it here, Travis?"

"It's kind of small, but it's neat," I say.

My Aunt Delia and Mrs. Cohen look at each other, and their eyes pass a message I'm not supposed to get.

Mrs. Cohen puts the clipboard down and says, "Why don't you two come to the house for some iced tea?"

My Aunt Delia takes a step back. "Oh, no thanks," she says, "we don't want to bother you. I just wanted you to meet Travis and all. It's been a while since I've seen you."

Mrs. Cohen takes off her glasses and rubs her eyes. She calls down the hallway, "David, I'm going to the house for a moment with Delia and Travis."

"All right, Susannah."

Outside, we walk across a raked red-dirt yard to the back door of a bigger house. We go through the kitchen and into the living room, and everything's clean, and a shelf of books covers one whole wall. Mrs. Cohen takes down a book. She turns to my Aunt Delia. "Did you finish the Wharton?"

My Aunt Delia says, "Not yet. I'm about halfway through it. I like it a lot."

Mrs. Cohen hands my Aunt Delia the book. "Try this one next. If you like the Wharton, you'll like it, too."

My Aunt Delia takes the book. The cover has a man and a woman on it. He's holding her in his arms. I can't make out the title, but I can see who wrote it: Mary McCarthy. My Aunt Delia says, "Thanks, Susannah. I don't know what I'd do without you."

Mrs. Cohen gets a mother look in her eyes. She takes a step toward my Aunt Delia, then she looks down at me. She says, "Travis, will you do me a favor?" I look at my Aunt Delia, and she nods.

I say, "Yes, ma'am."

Mrs. Cohen smiles and says, "Go back into the kitchen and bring me the cookie jar from the countertop."

As soon as I leave the room, they start whispering. I know I'm not supposed to come back. I know it's not the cookie jar they want. The cookie jar is in the shape of the

Quaker Oats man, and his black top hat is the lid. I open it and look in at the chocolate chip cookies. They look fresh and smell good. I can hear my Aunt Delia and Mrs. Cohen whispering in the other room. It sounds like the squirrels running through the leaves in the rain gutter above my bedroom window. It sounds like the wind in the trees before it storms. It sounds like my parents arguing behind their bedroom door at night. Only I don't think they're arguing, Mrs. Cohen and my Aunt Delia. I stay in the kitchen until Mrs. Cohen calls, "Travis, did you find that cookie jar?" Then I call, "Yes, ma'am, I'm coming."

sixteen

We're going to the river. I've got six cookies in a paper napkin in my lap, and we're going to have a picnic. The sky is clear and blue, and it's starting to get hot, but the wind is cool blowing in the windows. My Aunt Delia drives fast like she always does. The radio's playing gospel music: "I went to the garden alone, when the dew was on the roses." She says, "Did you like Mrs. Cohen?"

I know she wants me to, so I say, "Yes."

She says, "So do I."

I say, "How come they don't go to church?"

My Aunt Delia looks over at me quick, then she smiles and says, "Travis, the Cohens are Jews. Jews go to what's called a synagogue, and they go on Saturday."

I say, "We read about the Jews in church, right?"

My Aunt Delia says, "That's right, Travis."

I've already heard a lot of stories. The Jews are the people who fought the battles in the Bible. They got stuck in Egypt and got out again. They got the commandments. David slew Goliath. Slew means kill. The prodigal son went away and consorted and came back, and they celebrated. But I didn't think there were any Jews left. I thought they were all gone like the Omaha Indians.

My Aunt Delia says, "I'm glad you got a chance to meet Susannah. She's been good to me." Her eyes go dark blue and sad, and she looks away, out the window at the corn fields and the tobacco patches with the beds of new seedlings. Most people think Florida is just beaches and oranges, but Florida is corn and tobacco and cattle, too.

Caroline Huff and Beulah Laidlaw call it Lower Alabama.

We take the same turn-off we took the day Mr. Latimer called me a half-nigger, and we park in the same place, and I can smell the river. It smells spicy, but not like salt and pepper. It's a spice that grows wild where water runs. It smells like the air when you go outside in the morning after a rain storm. It smells like fish, but it's a wild, living smell, not like the fish on your dinner plate. My Aunt Delia says, "Come on, Killer, let's go see the local attraction."

We take the path through the woods, and, after a while, I can hear it, too. It's not a roar or a splash, it's a kind of pressure in your ears like when you have a cold, or when you hold a big conch shell to your ear and listen to the ocean trapped inside. As we go, the sound gets louder, and the path tilts uphill, and it's not easy walking. There are rocks and roots, and there's slippery green moss on the rocks. The sound gets louder, and the smell gets stronger, and then we break through the trees into a big wall of sunlight.

We step out onto a shelf of white rock as big as the sanctuary of the Presbyterian church. The rock slopes away to my left and climbs to my right, and across the emptiness there's the other side of the gorge, another white stone shelf, only it looks thin because it's so far away. My Aunt Delia takes my hand, and we step to the edge and look down. The sides of the cliff are white and brown, stained by the dark water that's been cutting down through the stone forever. At the bottom of the gorge, the river runs fast over brown rocks and green moss, with curls and crests of foamy white.

My Aunt Delia says, "Isn't it pretty?"

I nod, and she tells me about how the river comes down out of Alabama and flows all the way to the ocean. How it's been here since the first people lived here, and how it's eaten down through the rock—she calls it limestone—until it made this gorge. She tells me how the people came from the state university and climbed down into the gorge and found flint tools and arrowheads that belonged to people who lived here thousands of years ago. And then she tells me why this place is called Widow Rock.

"It goes all the way back to Civil War, Killer. There was a woman who lived near the river, a farmer's wife, and her husband was a soldier in the Confederate army. Do you know what that means?"

I say yes. We studied it in history.

"Anyway, this woman, her name was Mary Gray, or Cray, nobody knows for sure, she waited all through the war for her husband to come home, and he wrote her letters, and he fought in a lot of big and bloody battles, and she got letters from him all the way through to the end. She waited and she prayed for him to come home, and she kept the farm going—those were terrible times for people around here, Killer—and finally she heard from a man, a soldier who had fought with her husband, that he had been captured by the Yankees and put in a prison 'til the war ended, and then they let him out."

My Aunt Delia is still holding my hand, and I don't mind because there's nobody here but us, and we're standing close to the edge of the cliff, and I won't let her fall. I look up at her eyes, and I can see she's gone far away, back to the time when the woman waited for her husband to come home from the war.

"This man who had fought with her husband, who said he was a friend of her husband, told Mary Cray her husband didn't want to come home to her. He said her husband had been let out of the prison and had gone off to start a new life somewhere else. He said her husband had gone to Birmingham or Atlanta to find another wife and have another family.

"Mary Cray told the man he must be mistaken. If her husband had not come home, he could only be dead. Either he had been killed in battle or he had died in the Yankee prison. A lot of men did, Killer. They died of disease and starvation in those terrible prisons. But the man kept at her and kept at her. He wouldn't leave Mary Cray alone. He said her husband was alive, and he could prove it. He said her husband had a young, pretty wife and new children, and he was never coming home.

"Mary Cray called the man a liar. She said her husband was dead, and from that day on, she wore black, and she demanded to be called the Widow Cray. People saw her walking in the woods at night wearing her black widow's dress and a long, black veil. Some people said she was a witch. Some said she was just crazy. Some said the man who kept at her had some grudge against her husband from the war. Some said he wanted Mary Cray to be his wife, and he knew she'd never take another man unless she came to hate her husband. Mary Cray appealed to the government for information about her husband, but the authorities couldn't tell her what became of him. Some people say she traveled to Atlanta and Birmingham looking for him. Others say she never did that because she couldn't believe he was alive and had not come home to her.

"One night she came to the place where we're standing, Killer, and she threw herself into the gorge. They found her down there on the rocks in her black dress and her long black veil, and that's why they call this place Widow Rock. There wasn't much of a town here when Mary Cray killed herself. But the railroad got built and some houses and stores took hold for the railroad workers and their families, and after fifty years, there was a town, and they called it Widow Rock."

I look up at my Aunt Delia. Her eyes are dark, and she looks out into the emptiness, and I know she's not here. She's back in the time of Mary Cray and seeing Mary Cray standing here, and then seeing her gone from here, her body floating down on the wings of that black veil, floating down like a big dying bird.

My Aunt Delia says, "I used to come here alone a lot, but I don't anymore. I used to stand here and wonder what thoughts were in Mary Cray's mind the night she died, how she could do it, just fling herself off into the dark nothing like that. I don't come here alone anymore, Killer. It's better to come with a friend."

I say, "Wow," and it's a stupid thing to say, but I want my Aunt Delia's eyes to come back to me. I don't like what she's saying, and I want to be her friend. We're standing close to the edge, and the wind pushing up from the gorge is cool with that river spice, and it makes me dizzy. I pull my Aunt Delia's hand, and she looks down and says, "What? Oh, Killer. You're right. Let's sit in the sun and enjoy our religious freedom."

We back away from the cliff and sit on the warm white rock. There's a place almost like a chair in the rock, and we sit in it and lean back and let the sun hit our faces. We can feel the cool air from the gorge and the cool shade from the trees behind us. My Aunt Delia pulls her white blouse out of her jeans and tucks it up under her bra. She unzips her jeans and rolls them down so that her belly button shows. She says, "Killer, take off your shirt, and let's work on our tans."

I do. It feels good. But I'm already dark, and I don't know if I should get any darker in Widow Rock.

I decide it's time to ask some questions. I take a deep breath of that river spice and blow it out and close my eyes and say, "Delia, how come Grandma Hollister gets her headaches?"

My Aunt Delia's voice is sleepy-dreamy, and I know she doesn't mind my asking. She says, "I don't know, Killer. It's just a lady thing. A lot of the ladies her age get them. They get what they call 'the vapors.' She'd never say so, but I think it's because she doesn't have anything much to do but sing in the choir and serve on church committees and keep up what she imagines is her social position. She wasn't always like that. She was slim as a girl, and she used to ride horses and go hunting with the men. She came from a wealthy family up in Alabama, and they were country people, and they rode and hunted and had a lot of land, and your grandma had servants, and I guess she feels like she married down to Daddy. I think she's just disappointed with life, Killer, and she can't admit it to herself, so she has headaches instead. But she's a good person. She's been a good mother to me in most ways, and I love her. When I was your age, she and I had a lot of fun."

I knew that. The love part, not the other stuff. I say, "She's good to me, too, only she wears so much perfume I hate when she hugs me."

My Aunt Delia laughs. Her laugh is dreamy-sleepy, too.

She says, "Promise not to tell her that, okay?"

It's okay. I say, "Delia, does Grandpa Hollister have a gun?"

"Sure, Killer. He's got a .38 caliber revolver. He keeps it locked in a fishing tackle box in the trunk of his car. I bet you'd like to see it."

"I sure would."

"I bet you'd like him to let you shoot it."

I say I'd like that, too. I try not to show how excited I am. Sometimes when a kid does that, it works against his plan. My Aunt Delia says, "All you boys are alike. I don't know why you love guns so much."

It feels good that she didn't say little boys.

I say, "How come Grandpa Hollister keeps his gun in the trunk? Doesn't he ever need it?"

My Aunt Delia says, "Killer, if a sheriff in a county like this needed to have his gun on him all the time, he'd consider himself a complete failure. It isn't guns that keep order around here. It's history. It's just doing things the way they've always been done."

There's a scrape of boot on rock and, "Well, looka there. If it ain't Miss Delia Hollister and her flatland nephew."

My Aunt Delia jumps beside me, and her hands go to her clothes, the white blouse down from her bra, the denim rolled up over her belly button. I stand up between her and Kenny Griner.

seventeen

Griner just stands there grinning with his hands shoved into the pockets of his greasy jeans. He's got on the leather jacket and he lifts one of his boots and scuffs it again, hard, on the white rock. It leaves a black mark. He's got a big, red bruise above his right eye. I can see black thread in the middle of it. I count the stitches, six, and he sees me doing it, and he takes his hand out of his pocket and touches the red welt. There's crusty black blood where the skin is pulled together with thread.

Behind me, my Aunt Delia says, "Kenny Griner, you scared the hell out of me. You shouldn't sneak up on people like that."

Griner shrugs and goes out to the edge of the cliff and looks down. He turns back to us and says, "Same old Widow Rock. Except it ain't the same with you here, Miss Delia."

"Don't *Miss* me, Kenny. I don't like it when you *Miss* me."

Griner looks at me, then at my Aunt Delia. His eyes get small. "What *was* you two doing when I come up on you, Miss Delia? Look like you were nearbout naked. How old you say that boy is?"

My Aunt Delia's cheeks get the two red spots, and the spots start to grow. She says, "We were just sunbathing as you very well know. And if you start talking ugly, Travis and I will leave."

"Aww, don't leave," Griner says. He scuffs the rock again with his big-heeled boot. He shoots both hands out straight, and the wings of his leather jacket spread like he might take off and soar over the gorge. He says, "It's lonely enough up here on a Sunday morning." He squints over at me and my Aunt Delia. "Hey, why ain't you two in church? Shouldn't you be praise-the-Lording and amening with all them other good citizens?" Griner throws his hands out again and the leather wings flap. I see a brown bottle in his hip pocket. It's like the one Mr. Latimer had, only smaller. And now I see that Griner's eyes are like Mr. Latimer's were that day in the alley.

I guess my Aunt Delia sees it, too. She says, "Why, Kenny, you've been drinking. Damn if you ain't got three sheets to the wind on a Sunday morning."

Griner's eyes get small, and he raises a hand to shade them. He peers under it at my Aunt Delia. He says, "I ain't been drinking."

My Aunt Delia nods her head very slowly. "And I'm your fairy godmother. Look out or I'll sprinkle you with pixie dust."

She looks at the empty nothing out there over the river and then closes her eyes and leans her head back in the sunlight. She takes a deep breath and lets it out with a sigh and says, "Kenny, why don't you take off that jacket. It's dead summer, and you're sweating like a field hand." She opens one eye and looks over at Griner. He's looking out into all that nothing, pretending he doesn't hear her. My Aunt Delia's voice is sleepy-dreamy again. She says, "Oh, well, I guess that jacket's your Marlon Brando disguise, and you just can't be seen without it. Not even up here on Widow Rock with old Travis and me."

"Damn you, Delia." Griner is still looking out over the gorge, but his voice is smaller now, and I know his throat is getting thick.

My Aunt Delia says, "You can't damn me, Kenny. Only God can do that."

Griner turns and looks at me, and I know how he feels. My Aunt Delia takes away all his words. She knows what he's thinking, too. His shoulders go down flat, and he shrugs and takes off the jacket and folds it and lays it on the rock at his feet. He doesn't like me seeing him do it. My Aunt Delia isn't even watching. She's got her eyes closed again and that sun smile on her face.

Griner reaches back to his hip pocket and takes out the bottle and tilts back his head, and bubbles rise up the neck of the bottle. My Aunt Delia doesn't see it. I wonder what she's going to do when she opens her eyes and sees him drinking. Griner lowers the bottle and looks at me, and his eyes are big and wet with the sting of what he swallowed. My dad let me taste his beer once, and I know what it's like. It's cold, but it burns all the way down, and it makes your nose itch and your eyes get big.

My Aunt Delia says, "Bring that over here, Kenny. Or are you gonna pig it all yourself."

Griner walks over and looks down at her. The bottle hangs from his hand, and she lifts her hand up and just holds it there. She doesn't open her eyes. The bottle's six inches from her hand and Griner whispers, "Damn it," and leans down and guides it into her fingers. She takes it, wipes off the mouth, and says, "Thanks, Kenny old buddy. You're not a pig after all."

Griner turns and looks at the river. My Aunt Delia raises the bottle to her lips and lets the brown liquid slip into her mouth. I watch close to see how much she takes. She takes a lot. She holds it in her mouth, then swallows, then smiles and holds the bottle out to me. "Give this back to Mr. Griner, will you, Travis?" She still hasn't opened her eyes.

I take the bottle from her and sniff it. Even that makes my eyes water a little. It smells like the rubbing alcohol they put in your ears after you swim at camp. It smells like something burning, too, like smoke. I like the way it smells.

My Aunt Delia says, "That was good. I thank you, Kenny." Then she says to me, all sleepy-dreamy, "Travis, we just toasted religious freedom in Widow Rock."

I say, "I didn't get to toast."

My Aunt Delia says, "You got to sniff. I heard you. Sniffing's good enough for a guy your age." I like it she called me a guy. I look over at Griner like a guy, and he looks back at me and shakes his head.

My Aunt Delia says, "Kenny, religious freedom's my excuse, what's yours?"

Griner puts his hand to his split-open head and says, "Pain's mine. Your daddy hit me in the head with that knuckle-duster of his the other night."

My Aunt Delia pushes herself up hard, and her eyes open so quick I can almost hear them snap. She says, "My daddy what?"

"Hit me," Griner says. "See?" He leans down, and the split-open welt in his forehead looks like a ripe plum bursting in the sun. My Aunt Delia looks at it. "You had an accident, Kenny, just like Daddy said. You were driving that stupid car of yours too fast, and you went off the road, and you hit your head on the steering wheel."

Griner says, "Dumb little Delia Hollister. She just don't know how it is."

My Aunt Delia says, "Oh, I know how it is, Kenny Griner. Boys lie and girls listen. They listen 'til they're sick to death of it." She looks out over the gorge. "Why, this place is named for a woman who got sick to death of it."

Griner's voice is low and quiet. "I ain't lying, Delia. He hit me. And it didn't have nothing to do with my driving. Not driving on *that* road anyway."

"What do you mean, Kenny Griner? What are you insinuating?"

"Never mind," Griner says. He turns his back and goes out to the very edge of the cliff and stands there in the sun. He's got on a white T-shirt, and there are sweaty spots under the arms, and he's got a pack of Camels rolled up in one white sleeve, and his arm muscles are big and bunchy. There's a tattoo on his other arm muscle. I can't see all of it, but some of it's a girl in a grass skirt doing the hula. He's got long, oily black hair so far down the back of his neck it soaks the collar of his T-shirt. I remember Bick Sifford calling him Duck's Ass in Tolbert's Drugstore. I look at the hair now to see if it really looks like a duck's back. It does.

My Aunt Delia says, "Kenny, I'm waiting."

Then we hear a car door shut down below, and then voices, and my Aunt Delia says, "Well, Kenny, sounds like the whole town's coming out this morning."

Griner looks at the opening in the trees that leads to the path we took to come up here. "Some of your rich shit friends, I guess."

I don't like him talking that way in front of her, even if she says the same words herself sometimes. But I don't know what to do about it. It seems like up here on Widow Rock things are different. People come here to do things they wouldn't do back in town. I like it, but it scares me, too.

We hear another door slam and more voices. I recognize Caroline Huff's voice, or maybe it's Beulah Laidlaw. It's one of them giggling. Griner raises the bottle to my Aunt Delia. "I guess I won't stick around for the rich folks' party." He takes a long drink, and his eyes get that sudden crazy light in them, and I hear Bick Sifford call from down below, "Delia! Delia Hollister, are you up there?"

Griner rares back and throws the bottle as far as he can out over the gorge. It almost makes the other side. I picture it splashing that other white rock shelf with dark glass stars, but it hits the cliff below the shelf. It breaks with a muffled pop, and the pieces rain down into the brown water.

I hear the voices again, and I look at the opening in the woods that leads to the path. When I look back at Griner, he's got his black leather jacket in his hand. He smiles at me, and it's a smile I don't like. He doesn't take the path we took. He steps into the trees on the downstream rocky cliff. My Aunt Delia says, "Be careful, Kenny. It's slippery that way."

eighteen

My Aunt Delia and me wait and listen to the voices. As they get closer, she reaches into her jeans and takes out a pack of Spearmint gum and puts a piece in her mouth. She winks at me. "Don't want booze on my breath," she says. She offers me a piece, and I take it. She tucks her shirt back in and buttons her jeans. We sit on the rock like before, and she closes her eyes and lifts her face to the sun. I listen to the voices.

I know them all but one. There's Bick Sifford and Ronny Bishop and Beulah Laidlaw and Caroline Huff, and there's another one. A boy. I hear Bick Sifford say, "I know she's up there. Ain't but one white Chevy around here, and it belongs to Delia Hollister."

"Why didn't she answer you, then?" It's the new boy's voice. Bick Sifford doesn't say anything.

We wait and the kids come through the clearing and out onto Widow Rock. It's a big place, but it looks crowded with all of them here. My Aunt Delia doesn't move when they come up. She just sits beside me with her face to the sun. Caroline Huff says, "Hey, Delia. We missed you in church."

Beulah Laidlaw says, "Yeah, Delia. Your mama said you were under the weather." When Beulah says, "under the weather," she imitates my Grandma Hollister's voice, kind of high and out of breath. Everybody laughs.

My Aunt Delia doesn't open her eyes. She says, "I *was* enjoying the weather. It's so nice up here."

Bick Sifford and Ronny Bishop walk over to the edge of the cliff. Ronny takes a pack of Salems from his pocket, and

Bick leans over while Ronny tries to keep a match going in the cool wind that blows up from the river. The new boy stands by himself behind Beulah and Caroline. He looks like he doesn't care if anybody notices him or not. He's wearing cool clothes, like Ronny and Bick wear, only better. His penny loafers shine like a wet bird, and the copper pennies in them look brand new. He's wearing a blue shirt with a button-down collar and tan pants with a sharp crease and an alligator belt. He's got brown hair in a crew cut and patches of freckles under both cheeks, and his teeth are white between his thin lips. His face is long and narrow like a preacher's. He watches Caroline and Beulah talk to my Aunt Delia, and she still hasn't opened her eyes.

Ronny and Bick get the cigarettes lit, and they stand there in the cool wind smoking. They take little puffs and hold the cigarettes out in front of them and turn their hands over and admire their fingernails. They knock their hips out to the side and flick the ashes from the cigarettes. Ronny flicks his so hard the whole red coal at the end falls on the ground. He looks over at the girls and whispers, "Shit," and bends down and sticks the coal back into the end of the cigarette. Bick Sifford laughs and says, "Smooth move, Ronny."

Beulah Laidlaw says, "Hey Delia, we want you to meet Quig Knowles. He's Bick's cousin from Birmingham."

My Aunt Delia says, "Quig? What's a Quig?"

Beulah looks at Caroline, and their mouths get small and tight. They don't like the way my Aunt Delia's acting. They want her to jump up and get all flittery like they are about Bick Sifford's cousin Quig from Birmingham. My Aunt Delia's eyes roll open like two grouchy cats waking up, and she looks out at Ronny and Bick smoking on the edge of the cliff, and then over at Caroline and Beulah. "Where's this Quig?" she says. "I ain't never seen a Quig before."

Quig Knowles steps up between Caroline and Beulah and says, "Hey, Delia. I heard a lot about you from Bick and his friends here. Sounds like you know how to have a good time."

My Aunt Delia shades her eyes and looks up at Quig Knowles. She says, "Not like they do in Birmingham. I hear they have a *big time* in Birmingham." She looks at me. I don't know what's going on, so I just look back at her. She winks at me and says, "I bet you have a big time in Birmingham, Quig. You better not hang around Widow Rock too long. You'll forget how."

Caroline and Beulah giggle, and Bick Sifford comes over from the edge of the cliff and says, "I told Quig if he'd come down and visit, we'd raise some hell. All we did so far is get stuck going to church." He stands over my Aunt Delia with the cigarette smoke burning up his arm. "And you skipped it, Delia. You're supposed to be home in bed with some lady complaint."

Caroline slaps Bick on the arm, and the cigarette showers sparks, and Beulah says, "Oh Bick, don't be ugly." Bick laughs and rubs his arm, and Beulah giggles, and my Aunt Delia gets up and dusts off the back of her jeans. I stand up too. My Aunt Delia says, "Well, this is it. This is what we call a good time in good ole Widow Rock. Anybody bring a radio?"

Beulah reaches into her bag and takes out a little transistor radio and tunes it to Birmingham and sets in on the rock where we were sitting. Up here on the high ground, the songs come in strong. The Shirelles are singing, "My Guy."

My Aunt Delia goes out and stands by the edge of the cliff and starts to move with the music. She slides her hips and dips and rolls her head, and her black hair swings around her face. It's slow and sleepy, and the boys' eyes change watching her. After a minute, Caroline and Beulah go out there and start dancing, too, and they aren't as good as my Aunt Delia is. Caroline's okay, but Beulah's kind of stiff like she's watching herself in a mirror. The three boys stand together, and Ronny gets out the pack of Salems, and they light up again. My dad says menthol cigarettes are for women. The boys want to dance, but they're too embarrassed. I would be, too. I'd rather strike out with two down in the ninth inning and the bases loaded than dance. The boys watch for a while, and Bick Sifford says something low behind his hand when he raises the cigarette to his mouth, and the other two laugh. Finally, Quig Knowles says, "Aww, what the hell," and goes out to the edge of the cliff and starts dancing.

He looks stupid doing it, and his face gets red, but he's out there, and I know Ronny and Bick wish he'd stayed with them. They smoke and watch. Quig dances with all of the girls for a while. They're all out there, and from where I'm sitting on my Aunt Delia's rock, it looks like they could take one step the wrong way and they'd be dancing on air. They're all moving kind of loose and crazy to the music, and then Quig Knowles isn't dancing with three girls. He's dancing with just one, and it's my Aunt Delia. He faces her, and each time she tries to slide back to Beulah and Caroline, he steps over in her way. He moves her off from the others, and they dance that way for a while.

Caroline and Beulah don't like it. They look at each

other like they do when my Aunt Delia drives too fast or changes their plans without telling them or tells them to stop biting their nails. Beulah says, "Come on, you two. Dance with us." Ronny and Bick look down at their penny loafers. Then they look back up at the white sky, and Ronny blows a smoke ring. Bick says, "It's too hot to dance. Let's go over to Warrington. I know a guy who'll sell us some shine. We'll come back here and have a real party."

The radio plays a slow song, "Sleep Walk." It's all guitars, no words, but it makes even me want to get up and move. Quig Knowles takes my Aunt Delia by her waist and her hand and pulls her close to him. They dance that way for a while. Caroline and Beulah stop dancing. I guess they'd look silly dancing to a slow song together. Caroline looks over at Bick and Ronny. "What a couple of dorks," she says. "Yeah," Beulah says. Then Quig Knowles leans his head toward my Aunt Delia and tries to kiss her. She says, "Wait a minute, Buddy," and pushes him hard, and he stumbles backward to the edge of the cliff. He waves his arms in wild circles trying to get his balance, and his face goes as white as the rock he's trying to get a purchase on, and then he gets his balance and jumps away from the edge.

Caroline and Beulah both stand with their hands over their mouths and they're both white as rock, too. "Damn, girl!" Quig Knowles says. "Are you trying to kill somebody?"

My Aunt Delia looks at him. Her eyes are cold. "Maybe. Are you trying to kiss somebody?"

"Shit," Bick Sifford says. "Let's get out of here. It's too hot up here. Let's drive to Panama City and find some air-conditioning somewhere."

Beulah says, "Yeah, let's go."

And Caroline says, "Yeah, I'm for that."

But Quig Knowles comes over and bums a cigarette from Ronny Bishop and says, "Naw, let's stay here for a while. I like it here. I want to talk to Delia." His hands shake when he pulls the cigarette out of the pack. His face is still a little pale. I think of what it would be like to fall. I think of the widow in her black veil floating down in the moonlight. I wonder if she screamed as she went down. I wonder what was in her mind.

Quig Knowles says, "I think I know you, Delia."

"Sure you know me," my Aunt Delia says. "You just tried to kiss me. You have to know a girl pretty well to do that."

Quig Knowles shakes his head. He takes a big puff on the Salem. He knows how to smoke better than Bick and Ronny. He smokes like my dad, pulling hard and closing his eyes when the smoke is way down in there. He says, "No, I mean I think I heard about you. You ever meet a guy named Morgan Conway?"

My Aunt Delia closes her eyes and tilts her head to the side and says, "Let me think. Morgan Conway. Morgan Conway. Nope. It doesn't ring a bell."

But something's wrong. When she opens her eyes and looks at Quig Knowles, she slips her hands into her pockets because they're shaking. I look at the others. They see it, too. Maybe not Bick or Ronny, but Caroline and Beulah. Caroline gets still and small, and Beulah buttons the top button on her blouse. They're not thinking about Panama city and air-conditioning anymore. They want to stay and hear this. Quig Knowles walks out to the edge of the gorge and looks down. "Man, it's a long way down there. Anybody ever fall off this damn rock?" He looks at Bick and Ronny. They both grin and shrug. Ronny says, "Some ole girl a long time ago. The widow of Widow Rock. At least that's what I heard."

Quig Knowles looks down into the gorge again, takes a puff from his cigarette, flicks it out into the empty nothing, and says, "Man, that's a long way down." He turns and looks at my Aunt Delia. "This guy, Morgan Conway, and I go to school together."

Beulah pipes in, "Quig goes to the Masterson Academy. Lah-dee-dah."

Caroline says, "I don't know what he's doing out here in the piney woods with us common folks."

Maybe they're trying to change the subject. Quig Knowles doesn't even look at them. "Anyway," he says, "this guy Morg, he's a pretty cool guy, and he told me he met a girl named Delia last summer when he was a senate page in Tallahassee. He said she was some hot babe. He said she came from around here." Quig Knowles looks at my Aunt Delia like she's supposed to prove she's not some hot babe.

She smiles at him, and the two red dots get bigger on her cheeks, and her mouth is small and tight. She says, "Now I know what a Quig is." She walks over to me and holds out her hand, and I take it. She says, "Come on, Travis, let's go. We got to get our tummyaches back home."

We walk past Caroline and Beulah, and they look at my Aunt Delia like they don't want her to leave them alone here. We walk past Bick and Ronny, and Ronny looks down at his loafers, and Bick smiles at my Aunt Delia, and I can't tell what his eyes mean. Behind us, out on the edge, Quig Knowles says, "Ole Morg said it was just like baseball with that ole girl Delia. He said it was first base, second base, third base, and then, what do you know, home run. All the way around the bases with ole Delia. That's what Morg said."

Caroline says, "Bick, tell your friend to stop that ugly talk."

Beulah doesn't say anything. I don't care if Caroline is dumb as dirt and her butt wiggles like a duck when she walks, I'm always going to like her.

We're in the trees, and then we're on the path, and it's slippery, and we have to be careful. My Aunt Delia says, "Take your time, Killer. We're not in any hurry," but she's the one pulling me by the hand. She's the one going fast. I can hear Beulah's radio playing back there on the rock. It's Del Shannon again, "As I walk along, I wonder, what went wrong with our love, a love that was so strong."

nineteen

My Aunt Delia drives fast and looks at the road, not at me. I know she's mad, and I don't think I should talk. Not yet. She doesn't even turn on the radio.

At home, Grandma Hollister asks where we've been. My Aunt Delia says we got to feeling better, so we went for a ride to cool off. Grandma Hollister wants to ask more questions, but she sees my Aunt Delia's mad. They stand on the front porch looking at each other, and my Aunt Delia's eyes are small and dark and cold. Finally, Grandma Hollister touches her throat and then the damp hair at her temple and says, "It *is* stifling. And there won't be any relief until October." She looks up at the sky. It's clear and white. She says, "I wish it would rain."

My Aunt Delia says, "I'm going up to my room," and she does. I'm on the porch with my Grandma Hollister. Grandpa Hollister is out doing the law. Grandma Hollister puts her hand on my forehead. "Are you feeling better, Travis, Honey?"

I say, "Yes, ma'am."

She looks at the screen door. My Aunt Delia's radio comes on upstairs. I can't tell what the song is. Grandma Hollister says, "What's wrong with your Aunt Delia, Honey?"

I say, "I don't know. Nothing, I guess."

Grandma Hollister says, "Did something happen on your ride?"

I just shrug. I say, "No, ma'am. We just rode around to cool off a little."

Grandma Hollister looks worried, and I feel sorry for her,

but I can't tell her anything. She looks at the screen door again, touches her temple, and I see a drop of glow in the wispy hair in front of her ear. Grandma Hollister says horses sweat, men perspire, and ladies glow. She says, "I've got to go talk to Marvadell about the shopping. Can you find something to do, Travis?"

I say, "Sure." Then, "Yes, ma'am."

I go up to my room and get my John R. Tunis novel. I'm reading the one about the catcher now. There's a book about every guy on a major league baseball team. I started with the shortstop because that's what I am. I've read the pitcher, the first baseman, and now I'm reading the catcher. It's pretty good, but it's hot up here under the roof. If you lie by the window and hold yourself still, it's not so bad. I can hear the radio playing in my Aunt Delia's room. It's the Killer: "You shake my nerves and you rattle my brain. Too much love drives a man insane. You broke my will. What a thrill! Goodness, gracious! Great balls of fire!" I wonder what she's doing in there. I want to go see her. I want to ask questions, but I think maybe she wants to be alone.

It's too hot, and I don't want my Aunt Delia to be mad. I want her to be happy. I try to read, but the words don't mean much to me, and after a while I start wondering if she's mad at me. It's driving me nuts wondering that, so I get up and walk down to the bathroom and pretend to go. I flush the toilet, and then I stand outside my Aunt Delia's door. All I can hear is the radio. It's Little Anthony again. "If we could start anew, I wouldn't hesitate. I'd gladly take you back, and tempt the hand of fate."

I stand and listen. Little Anthony's voice can get inside you.

"If you're gonna stand out there listening, Killer, you might as well come in." She sounds mad, but not at me.

I go in, and she's lying on the bed over by the window. She's got her white blouse on, but her blue jeans are on the floor in front of me. She's got one arm thrown across her eyes, and she's pulled the gold cross up from her neck. She's twisting it with her fingers. "What did Mama ask you, Killer?"

"Just if anything happened."

"What did you tell her?"

"Nothing."

"Nothing?"

"I mean, I said nothing happened. We just went for a ride to cool off. Just like you told her."

My Aunt Delia laughs. It's a quiet laugh, and it's no fun, and she keeps her arm over her eyes. She lets the cross fall beside her neck. She says, "You're a good liar, Killer. Not as good as me, but getting better all the time. Lying is one of life's essential skills."

My dad told me not to lie. He says always tell the truth and live with the consequences of what you do. I don't like my Aunt Delia saying I'm a good liar, but I want her to like me. Her long legs seem to float above the white bedspread, and I see how her stomach in her underpants rises and falls as she breathes. I hear the breath coming and going through her nose, and I see how her black hair fans across the pillow. I feel the thing sudden hard and hot in my chest, and I don't know what it is, but I know I'd do anything for her. It doesn't matter what, I'd do it. I've never felt this way before. It's good, but it's hard. It's going to be hard to carry, but I know I have to do it. For my Aunt Delia.

I stand by her bed, and she reaches her hand out to me, the one that held the gold cross. I take her hand, and she says, "You're a good boy, Killer. You're good to me. It means a lot to have you here right now."

"I'm not a boy. I'm just a guy."

She doesn't laugh. I'm glad. She just says, "Okay. I won't call you that again. You'll just be my own special Killer. How 'bout that?"

"Okay," I say. Her hand is warm in mine, and she squeezes my fingers, and I squeeze back. I say, "What did that boy mean, that Quig Knowles? What did he mean about you and baseball?"

She sighs, and then blows her breath out hot and hard on my hand. It smells good, like Spearmint gum and whiskey and her own secret spirit. I lean closer and watch her face. I like it that her eyes are covered. We can talk. "Tell me," I say. I say it soft, almost a whisper. I squeeze her hand.

She sighs again, long and hard and hot, and I know she's going to. She says, "All right, Killer, I'm gonna tell you. Not all of it, but some of it. Only, you've got to promise not to tell anybody. Okay?"

I wish she hadn't said it. I say, "I already said I wouldn't."

She says, "I know. But I had to ask. You can't tell a person your secrets without getting a promise in return. That's just how it is. Secrets are worth something."

I say, "Okay." I know she's right.

My Aunt Delia keeps her arm over her eyes. I know it helps, and my hand helps, too. I want to get into bed with her and listen, but she doesn't move over. She doesn't pat the place beside her, so I just stand by the bed and listen.

She says, "I did know Morgan Conway. I met him last summer when I went to Girls' State."

"What's girls' state?"

"Oh, it's nothing, Killer, just some meetings in the state capitol. They pick one girl from each high school—you're supposed to be interested in public service—and they send you off to Tallahassee for a week, and you act like politicians for a while, and the whole thing is organized by a bunch of boozed-up VFW wives. It's silly, really, but I did meet Morgan Conway there. He was a senate page, just like that ass, Quig Knowles, said."

I don't get girls' state, not exactly, and I sure don't know what a senate page is—it can't be a page in a book—but I don't care. That's not the story.

My Aunt Delia says, "Anyway, me and some other girls snuck out one night and met some guys, and this Morgan Conway was one of them. He was a cool guy, and I liked him, and after a while, we were going out together without the other kids. You don't know what love is, Killer, but that's what happened with Morgan and me. We fell in love. I've never felt that way about anybody before, and I never will again. I guess that's why we did some things we shouldn't have done. Because I loved him so much. We talked about all the things we were going to do together. We talked about getting married. We made promises..."

She squeezes my hand hard, and her arm is pressed down hard over her eyes, and I squeeze back and listen as her breathing gets shorter and rougher. "Did you tell secrets?" I ask. I believe what she told me about secrets and promises.

She says, "Yes, Killer, we did, but I guess there was one secret I didn't know about Morgan Conway. If he told Quig

Knowles about me, there was one great big secret I didn't know."

The first tear squeezes out from under her arm and leaves a silver trail down her cheek. It rolls slow at first then fast and splashes on the pillow and turns the white cloth gray. All I can do is squeeze her hand and listen. I don't know what to say. I might say the wrong thing. She might send me away.

She says, "I came home after that time with Morgan and we wrote to each other for a while, but then some things happened, things I can't tell you about, and I couldn't write him after that, and Susannah Cohen helped me. If it hadn't been for Susannah, I'd be dead now. I truly believe that."

"Did she give you books to read?"

"Yes, Killer, and she did some other things for me, too."

I want to know the other things, and I don't want to know them. Knowing things is hard. It makes you older. I try to think what happened. I know I can't ask her. She'd tell if she wanted me to know. I wonder if Grandpa Hollister found out about her sneaking out at night with Morgan Conway. Another tear slips from under her arm and splashes the pillow. It makes the gray place bigger. She says, "When the summer was over, Morgan went off to the Masterson Academy in Birmingham. I guess he really does know that shitty Quig Knowles. Excuse me, Killer. Your virgin ears."

"That's all right. I've heard that word a lot, I guess."

"You shouldn't hear me say it."

"Do you still want to see Morgan Conway? Are you gonna write him anymore?" I hope she says no. I don't know why, I just do.

She says, "No," and the hard breathing turns into sobbing, and it's loud now, and I know Grandma Hollister's gonna hear, so I let go of my Aunt Delia's hand and turn up the radio. The radio's too loud, and my Grandma Hollister might come to the bottom of the stairs and call up, "Turn that infernal thing down, will you please, Delia?" especially if she's got a headache, but I have to take the chance. I can't let her hear my Aunt Delia crying.

I come back to the bed and take her hand again, and my Aunt Delia says, "No. I can't ever see him again," and she's crying hard, and I think this is it. This is what she cries about at night when it storms. This is why she said someone was lost. It's Morgan Conway. He's lost, and she'll never find him, and that's why she cries and needs me sometimes at night. I stand by the bed holding her hand while she sobs, and the radio gives us the Drifters: "But don't forget who's taking you home and in whose arms you're gonna be. Oh, darling, save the last dance for me."

Finally, she lets go of my hand and turns her face to the wall. I stand there wondering what to do, and the sobs get quieter and turn into hard breathing and then softer breathing, and then my Aunt Delia says, "Thanks, Killer. You're so good to me, but I need to be alone now. Okay?"

"Sure," I say. "Okay."

I go over and turn the radio back down. It's Maurice Williams and the Zodiacs now, "Oh, won't you stay, just a little bit longer." I stand there listening, trying to understand. I know they're called love songs, but they're all about pain. I think Bick Sifford loves my Aunt Delia, and maybe Kenny Griner does, too, and both of them act like jerks, and it looks like they're in pain. My Aunt Delia loves a guy named Morgan

Conway, and I guess he doesn't love her anymore, and she cries at night when it storms. I don't know what books to read or who to talk to so I can understand love. I just know I have to understand it. I just know I've got it inside me now, and it's a big hot hard thing in my chest, and it's hard to carry.

I know I can't talk to my Aunt Delia about it. It's the one thing I can't tell her. That I love her now not as my aunt but like they love in the songs. I wonder if she understands love. Maybe nobody does. Maybe you just have to listen to the radio until the right song comes on, the one that tells you what to do.

I watch my Aunt Delia's back for a while, and her white legs float on the white bedspread, and her black hair fans across the pillow, over the gray place where her tears landed. I can't hear her breathing now, but I know she's almost asleep. I know if she talked to me now, her voice would be all sleepy-dreamy. And I know I can't wait any longer. I have to tell her. "Delia," I say, "what Kenny Griner said is true."

She whispers, "What do you mean, Killer? Said about what?"

"About Grandpa hitting him and cutting his eye."

She's quiet for a while, thinking, I guess. Then she says, "I know, Killer."

"You knew it that night, didn't you? When Grandpa said Kenny had an accident."

"Yes, Killer, I knew it. How did you know it?"

"I saw the thing he did it with. The thing Kenny Griner called his knuckle-duster. It has a long leather thong on it, and it was sticking out of his pocket, and last night I was down-stairs when Grandpa came in, and I saw him take it out of his pocket and lock it in the secretary by the front door."

"What were you doing downstairs when Daddy came in?"

I don't know if I should tell her. I don't know what she'll think about it. I have to tell her because she tells me her secrets. "Promise not to tell anyone?"

My Aunt Delia says, "Yes. I promise."

"Grandma was asleep. It was earlier in Omaha. I was gonna call my dad, but I didn't know how. Some lady came on the line and asked if I was the sheriff."

My Aunt Delia sighs, and her voice is sleepy-dreamy. "That's right. Your daddy hasn't called you. My perfect brother Lloyd hasn't called his son, and you've been here six weeks. We'll have to see about that, won't we."

I say, "Don't see about it. I didn't tell you so you'd see about it. It's a secret."

She says, "All right, Killer. If that's what you want, I won't see about it."

I go over and touch her hair. It feels soft, and it smells like shampoo and like the wind that blows up from the river. I say, "See you in a little while, okay?"

She says, "Okay, Killer." I can barely hear the words.

I go to my room and lie on the bed and leave the door open so the radio can get in. I listen because I want to know. I want to be awake when the right song comes. The one that tells the truth about love.

twenty

In the late afternoon, my Aunt Delia comes downstairs and says, "Come on, Killer. Let's go for a ride."

We drive around town some, and then go to the tennis court. There's nobody there, and we don't feel like playing. It's too hot. We drive by Tolbert's, and the COOL AIR sign is dripping with ice, but Mr. Tolbert's a Baptist, and he doesn't open on Sunday afternoon. We drive to Warrington and get Cokes and french fries at the Dairy Queen. We pass some kids from Warrington who know my Aunt Delia. She waves, and they wave. We drive back toward Widow Rock, past Luby's Roadhouse, and past the place where Grandpa Hollister pulled Kenny Griner over and busted his eye.

"Where is everybody?" I say.

My Aunt Delia says, "They're all inside being very still so they don't melt in this heat. The country people are reading the Bible and hoping the animals don't kick up any dust and make them do something about it, and the town people are all lying down in dark rooms."

"What are the kids doing?"

"Now that's an interesting question, Killer. Ronny Bishop lives out on a cattle ranch, and his mama and daddy aren't all that churchy, so they might be sitting out under the oak trees sipping iced tea and talking about rainfall and summer forage for the cattle. Ronny might be doing it with them, practicing to be his daddy, or he might be out riding his horse. He's got a pretty Appaloosa gelding, and he goes out riding in the woods. Sometimes he takes a shotgun with him and shoots quail from the saddle.

"Bick Sifford will be sitting out by the pool with his mother, flexing his muscles and talking about going to Princeton. She'll be drinking a Manhattan and making a list of the things he's gonna need. She'll have the Manhattan in a tall iced tea glass with a lemon peel in it, and the only way you'll know it's not tea is her nose runs when she drinks. She'll be writing down all the shirts and sweaters and shoes Bick's gonna need to look as cool as all the other factory owners' sons at Princeton, and she won't forget the Harris Tweed overcoats, and the leather-bound, gold-edged stationary set so he can write to his mama once a week.

"Bick's daddy will be inside working on some reports from the factory, and he'll have a glass of bourbon on a coaster on the desk beside the papers, and every once in a while he'll lift his head and take a sip and look out the window at Bick and his mother, and he'll think how proud he is of young Bickie boy for getting into Princeton, and how, one day, his boy's gonna take over the business.

"Caroline Huff's sitting with her mama beside their pool. And it's a lot smaller than Bick's pool, because a box-factory vice president is not allowed to have a pool as big as the owner's. Caroline's mama's a country girl, and she has to drink at company functions, but she doesn't really like the taste. She puckers up and squints every time she takes a sip of her scotch sour, so today, she's drinking a Coke and doing needlepoint, and poor Caroline is out there in her bathing suit scratching her arms and drinking Coke, too, and worrying about the Coke giving her pimples, and she's studying biology or algebra so she won't flunk and have to repeat a year and never get into Sophie Newcomb.

"And then there's Beulah Laidlaw. Poor Beulah, she's got it worst of all. She's the preacher's daughter, so she has to do church all day Sunday, and Wednesday nights, too. She's like me—social position and no money. Sometimes she even has to eat lunch with her mama and daddy at the homes of the deacons and elders of the church. Her mother calls it 'eating the crust of humility,' and Beulah says it's a colossal bore sitting there in your white dress and pinchy patent leather pumps eating greasy fried chicken and talking about the sorry state of Christendom when you know Caroline Huff's sitting by her smaller-than-the-owner's pool, and Delia Hollister is out riding around in her souped-up Chevy with her handsome nephew, Travis."

"Does she really say that about me being handsome?"

"No, Killer. That's what they call poetic license. I was telling a story and I used some poetic license on you."

"You're a good storyteller."

"Why, thank you, Killer. It's a southern trait, like eating grits and shouting, 'Fawther, I who was lost now am found.'"

"Did you get it from Grandpa and Grandma Hollister?"

"No, Honey. I got it from the atmosphere. It's just in the air."

"Is the car really souped up?"

"No, but it runs good, and it's pretty, don't you think?

We come to the crossroads, the decision place, and my Aunt Delia stops and looks up at the white, hot sky, at the stunned-looking horses in the farmer's field, at the road that goes back to Widow Rock, and the road that goes to the river.

She says, "Come on, Killer, we don't have a pool, but we're going swimming."

We drive to the river, but we don't go the way we did before. We cross over a bridge and take a road that leads to the riverbank below the gorge. My Aunt Delia says there's a place where you can climb down to the bank, and it's sandy, not rocky, and you can swim. We leave the white Chevy in the woods and walk along a path to the river. It's hot under the pines and oaks, and the land slopes toward the rushing sound of the water, and there's that smell again, that spicy smell I like. Along the sandy riverbank you can see where the river tears into the roots of big trees and the roots stick out into the air like arms of bone reaching for the water.

The water is dark, and it runs over a sandbar that catches the sunlight like the back of a big white fish resting in the shallows. I take off my sandals and wade out, and it's cold, and I look back upriver. I can see the gorge and the white shelf of Widow Rock where we went this morning for religious freedom.

"What do you think, Killer?"

I look back at my Aunt Delia. She looks happy. She doesn't look mad or scared like she did up on Widow Rock when Quig Knowles said that about baseball and Morgan Conway. We can't hear anything but the river running over the sandbar and out in the middle, dividing itself around some big rocks, and it sounds like I knew it would. Like my Aunt Delia's voice. All of her voices. I can hear her laughing, and crying, too, and I can hear her sharp voice when she's telling Carolyn and Beulah not to be so stupid, and even the voice she uses singing with the radio.

I like it here, and I tell her that. We don't have a smell like this in Omaha. The closest we get is after the rain beats down the wheat, and the sun comes out and steam rises from the wheat. It's kind of the same smell, but it's not the same. The river looks dirty, but I know it's not, because it smells clean. "How come it's brown?" I ask my Aunt Delia.

She looks out at the river and squints. The sunlight hits her face like it did up on Widow Rock, and it makes her look like a statue, a girl made of white stone, perfectly still in the light. She says, "They say it's because of tannic acid, Killer. You know, from the cypress bark and the leaves and branches that fall into the river. Don't worry, it's clean."

I scoop up a handful, and it's not brown in my hand. It's clear. I'm not worried. I'm happy here. I don't think about sad things here, not even my mom in that hospital and my dad not calling. I say, "Are there any fish?"

"Oh, yeah," my Aunt Delia says. "Sunfish and crappie and warmouth and large mouth bass and mud fish, and even alligator gar. They're the ones with the long bodies like a cigar and the long snouts with all the ugly teeth. But they don't hurt anybody. They just look like they would."

I roll up my jeans and wade in deeper, and my Aunt Delia says, "Can you swim, Travis?"

I say, "Sure." I learned at the YMCA.

My Aunt Delia smiles. "I just wanted to make sure."

I don't see how we're gonna swim. We don't have bathing suits. I say, "Are we gonna go back and get our suits?"

My Aunt Delia smiles and winks. "Nope, we already got them. We're gonna swim in our birthday suits."

She watches me. I watch her. I don't know if she's kidding. Finally, she says, "Are you shocked, Killer?"

I say, "Nope. I'm not shocked. I just never..."

She says, "You just never a lot of things you're gonna

do this summer, and one of them is the fine old southern art of skinny-dipping."

She turns and starts walking downstream. Over her shoulder she says, "I'm going down there to that clump of driftwood and shuck my duds. You take off yours and jump in. When I call, 'Yoo-hoo, Killer!' you turn and look upstream at Widow Rock, and I'll come and jump in. Okay?"

I say, "Okay," and my throat is thick, and the thing, the hot heavy thing in my chest is starting. My Aunt Delia turns to look back at me. She smiles, and her smile is careful, and she says, "Is it okay, Killer? Really?"

I say, "Sure." I smile. I'm trying to remember if I ever took off my clothes outside before. We've got pictures of my bare butt at a picnic, and my mom putting a diaper on me, but that was when I was little. I think about what it'll be like to feel the sun on my thing, and to feel the cool water running between my legs without any bathing suit there.

When my Aunt Delia is out of sight behind the driftwood, I stand watching for a while. I see her hand come up and hang her white blouse on a limb. I wait, and her hand comes up again and hangs her jeans. I think of going down there. Of seeing her. I wonder what she'd do. I wonder if she'd be mad. I wonder what she'd look like. Then I think I'd better get naked and get in the water before she comes back.

I take off my clothes and pile them on a bed of pine needles on the bank, and then I wade into the river. I stop when the water is up to my knees, and I turn toward the hot sun, and it feels good on my bare skin, and it feels good on my thing, and I know the thing is going to happen if I don't get into the water, so I jump in the rest of the way, and it's so cold it stops my breathing, and I sink down until my feet hit the sandy bottom, and I can feel the river pick me up and carry me slowly down toward my Aunt Delia. I kick off the bottom and swim two strokes back to the sandbar and crouch there with the river flowing between my legs. I look across the river, up at Widow Rock. From down here, it's just a thin line of white stone, but it looks warm, and it's so high up. The tops of the trees sway in the wind. "Yoo-hoo, Killer? Are you in the water?"

"I'm in," I call, but I don't know if she hears me.

She doesn't say anything, but I know she's coming. I could turn and see her, but I won't. She wouldn't like that. I hear her bare feet slapping the sand, and it reminds me of her feet slapping the old pine boards of the hallway between our rooms, and then I hear a splash and a gasp, "My Gawwd, it's cold," and then I feel her arm brush mine, and she says, "So, Killer, how do you like our old river?"

We're shy and don't say anything for a while. She moves her arm away from mine, and I can feel her crouching there beside me on the sandbar. After a space, she says, "When you get used to the cold, it feels so good."

I say, "I wish we could stay here all day."

My Aunt Delia says, "Come on, let's see who can swim fastest."

She pushes off downstream, and her white shoulders plow the brown water, and her arms churn, and her black hair twists and flows behind her. It's so pretty I forget to swim, and then I remember and take off. I bury my face in the cold and churn my arms, and after a while I can see her feet rippling and kicking in front of me. I don't have to let her win. She'd win anyway.

She stops swimming and stands in the neck-deep river, and I come up beside her and stand, too. We're breathing hard, and leaning back against the current, and on the bank near us is the white tangle of bony driftwood where my Aunt Delia's clothes hang white and blue in the sun. I see her tennis shoes with the pink laces—she calls them tenny pumps—resting on a tree root reaching out from the bank. I'm breathing hard, but I say, "I love it. I love your old river."

My Aunt Delia laughs. "Good ole Killer. You got a natural aptitude for the good life in Widow Rock. You like tennis, you like to drive around at night..."

"And see who's there," I say.

She laughs, "...and you like to swim, and you can even put up with Beulah and Caroline."

I want to say I don't like Bick Sifford, but I don't. I want to say I don't like Kenny Griner, and I hate Quig Knowles, but I don't. I don't want to spoil things.

My Aunt Delia says, "Come on, Killer, let's push our way back to the sandbar and bask a while."

I don't know what bask means, but I'm gonna find out. We walk upstream against the current. It's harder than it looks when you're standing on the bank. The river is cold heavy against your chest and legs, but if you lean forward, you can push through it. It takes us a while to get back to the sandbar. It's white in the sun, and the brown water breaks over the bar in a little wave. We stop, and my Aunt Delia kneels on the sand. Then she turns her back to the current and sits down, and I do, too. The water covers everything but our heads, and we sit there with our feet digging into the sand and pushing back into the body of the river. My Aunt Delia reaches down and digs up a handful of sand and lets it go, and it ripples between her fingers like milk going into a cup of coffee. She says, "I love it here. It's so peaceful. And when you think the summer's never gonna be over and the heat's never gonna stop, you can come here and get cool for a while."

"Have you been here...like this before?"

She knows what I mean. Naked. She raises her head and looks off where the river curves and disappears into a valley of cypress trees. My Aunt Delia says, "Of course I have, Killer. I told you it's the fine old southern art of skinny-dipping. You don't perfect an art without lots of practice."

"Who did you come here with?"

"Beulah, of course, and Caroline, but she just sat on the bank watching and telling us someone was gonna come along in a johnboat any minute, some redneck out setting a trotline for catfish, and we were gonna get caught with our..." She looks over at me. "Well, you know what I mean."

"Did you come here with anybody else?"

"My goodness, Killer, aren't you curious."

She leans back and closes her eyes and lets her hair down into the river, and when she does, her chests come up, and I look over and see them. They're white, and the nipples are the same color as the pebbles in the river bed below Widow Rock. I've never seen anything like them before, and it seems right for me to see them now. It's the time. My Aunt Delia pulls her hair out of the water and swings it over her shoulder, and it touches my face like a paintbrush dipped in cold water. She says, "Since we tell each other our secrets, I'll confess. I've been here a couple of times at night with Beulah and Ronny and Bick. The boys took off their clothes right here where you did, and Beulah and me went down the bank like I just did."

"Was it fun?"

"Sure it was fun. We romped around and splashed each other, and there was no moon that night, and then we got out and drove over to Warrington for Cokes and fries at the Dairy Queen."

I lean my head back in the sun and think about it. I wish she didn't like Bick Sifford. I wish I knew why she does. I wish I hadn't asked who she came here with before.

My Aunt Delia says, "Sometimes when you sit here, the little sunfish nibble your toes. They like moles, too. Beulah has moles on her back, and they bite them. It scares the crap out of her." She reaches over and tickles my side and laughs. It makes me laugh, and it feels good, and I want to tickle her back, but I don't.

She pushes off from the sandbar and wades out toward the deeper water, and I go out there with her. The bottom is sandy, and it slopes away toward the middle of the river. Even when you can swim, it's a scary feeling. The current tries to push us down river. My Aunt Delia says, "How much do you weigh, Killer?"

I say, "I don't know, about a hundred, I guess."

She says, "Come over here."

I do, and she picks me up and holds me in her arms. I can feel her chests against my side hot in the cool river. I rest my head on her arm and my legs across her other arm. She says, "You're light in the water."

"So are you," I say. I don't know what to do or what to say. I know she can look down and see my thing if she wants to, but she doesn't. She looks into my eyes. I'm afraid her chests against my side are gonna make the thing happen, even in the cold river. I look into her eyes, and she says, "Rock-a-bye, Travis, in the treetop," and she starts to turn us around, and she rocks me up and down, and her eyes are closed. I want to close mine, but I can't. I have to see her face. She turns me around and around slowly, and we move downstream, and she sings, "When the wind blows, the cradle will rock. When the bough breaks, the cradle will fall, and down will come Travis, cradle and all."

She opens her eyes and leans down, and I see her lips coming. She kisses me on the forehead, like my mom used to do when she tucked me in at night. It feels warm, and her breath smells like Spearmint and her secrets. Then she bends and lets me go, down into the river. My feet hit the sand, and my Aunt Delia says, "See, the cradle didn't fall. It doesn't always fall."

She looks up at the high white sky. I look up there, too. It's like looking up from the bottom of a green canyon. The green tree tops sway in the wind. She says, "I guess the wind didn't blow hard enough today."

My Aunt Delia starts floating downstream to the place where her clothes are hanging. Over her shoulder, she calls, "Killer, Honey, go on and get dressed, okay?"

I try to say, "Okay," but my throat is too thick and nothing comes out. I turn and push against the river. I can't tell her my secret.

twenty-one

Me and my Aunt Delia drive out on a country road, and she says, "Killer, come over here and sit on my lap."

I do, and her breath is warm on my neck, and her lap is soft under me, and her arms curve around me to the steering wheel. She says, "Can you reach the pedals?" Fats Domino is coming from the radio: "I found my thrill, on blueberry hill. On blueberry hill, where I found you."

I look down between our legs at the three pedals. I know one's the gas, and one's the brake, but I don't know what the other one is. I stretch my legs out, and I can just reach them. My Aunt Delia says, "Okay, good. Now, that one on the outside is called the clutch. It engages and disengages the gears that make the car go. First thing we're gonna do is practice with the clutch."

My Aunt Delia puts her foot on the gas, and the engine goes faster, and she says, "Okay, Killer, push in the clutch. I'm gonna put her in first gear. When I tell you, start letting it out real slow."

I do it like she says, and I'm looking off down the hot, white road with that glimmering water far off you never reach. The oak trees grow close to the road, and their branches lean over and almost touch, and my hands are on the steering wheel real hard right next to my Aunt Delia's. I let the clutch out, and the Chevy bucks and bucks, and then the engine quits. I say, "Did I hurt it?"

My Aunt Delia laughs. "Naw, don't worry. Everybody does that when they first start out. You can't hurt this ole tank." She turns the key, and I smell gas, and she says,

"Don't steer. I'm doing that. You're gonna learn one thing at a time, and the first thing is how to use the clutch. When you get that down, then we'll let you steer."

I work at it for a while, and it gets easier. Sometimes I grind the gears, and my Aunt Delia laughs and yells out the window, "Grind me pound!" The road is straight and narrow and hot, and the sky is white, and the fields on both sides are green and empty except for a few cattle. We pass houses, and some are empty with gray clapboard sides and falling-down rusted tin roofs and old cars and tractors with dog fennel and broom sage growing up around them. When a car finally comes along, my Aunt Delia says, "Put in the clutch, Killer," and I do, and we pull over until it goes whistling past.

Finally, she lets me steer and do the pedals. I can't go over thirty, and I can't make a turn, and if anybody comes along, I have to pull over. I drive like that for a while with her breath warm on my cheek, and her lap soft under me, and I say, "This is really neato. I thought you had to be six-teen to drive."

We pass a field, and there's a man on a tractor mowing hay. White birds follow behind him using their curved red beaks to spear the mice and bugs that live under the tall grass. My Aunt Delia says, "City kids don't drive 'til they're sixteen, but country kids start early. You look out in these fields, and you'll see boys and some girls not ten years old driving tractors and combines. They aren't doing it for fun, they have to do it. I was driving when I was your age."

"Did Grandpa Hollister teach you?"

"Not hardly, Travis boy. That just wouldn't do, not even in Widow Rock. I learned from Caroline's older brother. He was a wild boy when he lived here, and he used to take me and Caroline out and teach us." My Aunt Delia looks out at the fields. She looks as far as she can at the hazy green line where the long field rises into the sky. "There's just not enough to do in a place like this. Kids have to do things as soon as they can. You'd go crazy if you didn't."

I don't like that word, crazy, but I don't say anything. I'm glad to be here with my Aunt Delia. Driving is about the most fun thing I've ever done. I say, "When can I drive by myself?"

My Aunt Delia leans to the side and makes big eyes at me. "Whoa, there, Killer. You're getting way ahead of yourself. You and me can do this, but that's all, and don't you mention it to anybody, okay."

"Sure," I say. "Okay."

I'm in the kitchen with Marvadell. Aunt Delia's off in Panama City at the dentist. Grandma Hollister says she's not gonna feel good when she gets back, so I have to leave her alone. "My," she says, "you two sure have hit it off well. I've never seen an aunt spend so much time with her nephew."

I don't know what to say, so I just say, "Yes, ma'am," and smile big.

I like Marvadell, but, mostly, she doesn't like anybody in her kitchen. When Grandma Hollister comes in and stands over by the back screen door and says, "Why, Marvadell, isn't that a pretty handbag. Did you get that here in town?" or she says, "Now don't put too much salt in the gravy, Marvadell," Marvadell just nods her head hard and pounds the biscuit dough and says, "Yes'um," and "Noam," until

Grandma Hollister clears her throat and touches the glow at her temple and says, "My, it is hot today, isn't it?" and goes on out of the kitchen.

When I come in, Marvadell looks over at me and says, "Humph," like she wonders what rascality I'm just fresh coming from. She told me once she thinks little boys are devils, and they grow up to be mens, and then they turn into dogs. She says, "Little boys is okay 'til they gets they man hair."

When she said that, I told her that devils have horns and dogs have tails, and it didn't make any sense to me. I told her she should say men, not mens, because mens made the word plural twice, and she hit the biscuit dough so hard a cloud of flour flew up around it, and she said, "Boy, don't you c'rect my speakin. My speakin be mine, and yours be yours, and you ain't old enough yet, ner smart enough yet to c'rect yo elders."

At first I didn't think she was really mad, but then I saw it in her eyes, and I knew I better say I'm sorry. I did, and she just said, "Humph," and slapped the dough, and I started slipping out quiet when she said, "They's a piece of that peach pie I made fo supper yesterday left in the pantry. I give it to you wiff a glass of buttermilk if you want."

I stopped slipping out quiet and said, "Thank you, Marvadell. That would be real cool."

Marvadell rolled her eyes and hit the dough and said, "Now they got you talking like that Miss Delia and her friends."

I'm watching Marvadell make blackberry jam. She gathers the wild berries out in the country where she lives and brings them here. She boils them with sugar in a big pot, and she heats big bars of wax to seal the Mason jars, and she pours the hot jam into the scalded jars and then pours the wax on top, and the whole kitchen gets like an oven, and the windows get misty and run, and sweat runs out of Marvadell's hair and wets her blouse all the way to her apron ties.

I'm watching, and once in a while she lets me get something for her, and sometimes she closes her eyes and sings about heaven. We hear a knock at the back door, and a black man comes in before Marvadell tells him to. He looks at Marvadell, and she looks at him, and then he looks over at me. I don't like his eyes on me. He looks at me the way Mr. Pultney looks at his goat. Marvadell says, "Eddie, what you doin' here?"

The man says, "That ain't no way to talk to me, Mama."

I stand by the kitchen door so I can leave quick, but I don't leave. The man walks over to the counter by the bread basket where Marvadell always puts her purse. He's got on tight black pants and a purple shirt with a zipper all the way up the front, and it has yellow pockets. The shirt's made of something that shines like the skin of a chameleon lizard. We got lizards all over the place out in the yard. They do push-ups and change colors when they move from place to place. When I'm bored, sometimes I go out and catch them and hold them and let them bite the ends of my fingers. It doesn't hurt, and I like to look inside their mouths. You have to be careful, though, because their tails come off real easy.

The black man, Eddie, Marvadell's son, is wearing a white straw hat with a purple band. He's got on black shoes with pointy toes, and his black socks have a purple line up each side. He's got a pack of Kents in his shirt pocket and scars on the backs of his hands. He smiles, but there's no fun in his eyes. He picks up Marvadell's purse and opens it and reaches inside. His scarred right hand comes out with some of Marvadell's money. I can't tell how much. He puts it in his pocket, smiles that goat smile at me, and turns back to Marvadell.

She's standing with her hands on her hips. She's got hot wax on her hands, and I guess it doesn't hurt her. The wax is gray on her shiny black skin. She just watches Eddie. She doesn't say anything. He walks across the kitchen and out the back screen door. I follow him.

Marvadell says, "Travis, you come back here," but I don't. I go out on the back porch and watch him walk toward the backyard. He hears me and stops. He turns and looks at me standing up here on the back porch. I know Marvadell's inside watching. He says, "Come'ere, kid."

I come down the steps and stand in front of him. He's tall, and he smells like cigarettes and whiskey and Old Spice aftershave. He says, "I'm gone show you something."

He reaches into his pocket and takes out something shiny black I've never seen before, and he pushes a button on it, and a blade jumps out. It's a knife with a blade that jumps out when he pushes a button, and when it flicks out with a little click, it scares me, and I jump back a step. Eddie takes that step away from me. He stands close to me, and he holds the knife down low between us, and he says, "Look at this, little white boy. You know what I do with this?"

My throat is dry, and my lips are cold. I can't take my eyes from the knife in his scarred black hand.

Eddie just stands there holding it. He doesn't say any more. He lets me look at it for a while, then he turns and starts walking through our backyard, past the privy toward the woods.

"Eddie, what are you doing here?"

I turn quick, and it's my Grandpa Hollister. He's halfway around the house, and he's wearing his black suit and his black ankle boots and his black bow tie. He's got some papers in his hand. I never heard him coming. I don't think Eddie did either. Eddie stops with his back to my Grandpa Hollister. He doesn't turn, and he doesn't say anything.

My Grandpa Hollister says, "Eddie, what were you saying to Travis? I want to know."

I hear the screen door squeak, and I hear the spring that closes it stretch and groan, and I hear Marvadell's heavy feet on the back porch steps. She comes down and stands beside me, and I feel her hand on my shoulder. Grandpa Hollister says, "Eddie, I'm not gone ask you again."

Eddie doesn't turn, and I look up at Marvadell. She's not watching Eddie. She's watching my Grandpa Hollister. She says, "Mr. Hollister?"

My Grandpa Hollister says, "Marvadell, I'm talking to Eddie." He doesn't look at her.

Marvadell says, "Mr. Hollister, *sir?*"

My Grandpa Hollister clenches his jaw, and I see his fingers tighten on the papers, and I hear them squeak in his hand, and I think the ink's gonna bleed from them. I look at Marvadell's eyes, and I don't know what they're saying. She holds her head higher than usual, and her back is stick straight. She's picking wax off one of her hands with the fingers of the other. She says it again, "Mr. Hollister?"

My Grandpa Hollister looks at her now. His jaw is clenched white. He looks at Marvadell, and she looks back at him, and then he looks at me. Then he looks down. He moves his right foot. His jaw goes loose. It goes from white to red, and he says, "All right, Eddie."

Eddie's still standing with his back to us. His shoulders roll, and he starts walking toward the woods again. He never looks back. He walks real loose, almost like he's dancing. Almost like my Aunt Delia and Caroline and Beulah up on Widow Rock that time with Bick and Ronny and Quig Knowles. We all watch until Eddie disappears into the woods. Marvadell lowers her head and wipes her hands on her apron. She turns and walks back into the kitchen.

My Grandpa Hollister waits until the screen door closes, then he says, "Travis, come here."

I go over to him. "What was Eddie saying to you, Travis? Why was he here just now?"

I look up into his police eyes. I can't lie to him without his knowing it. I remember my Aunt Delia telling me I'm a good liar, and it's one of life's essential skills. I know I've got to lie to him, even if he doesn't believe me. For Marvadell.

I say, "Sir, he came to borrow some money from Marvadell. She gave him some." I look around the yard. My mind is moving like a slow train on the tracks that go through town. I don't know what to say next. I see the grape arbor over next to the privy. The grapes hang thick and black. Marvadell's gonna make jam from them soon. I say, "He asked me if the grapes were ripe. He asked me if I've eaten any of them yet."

"Are you sure that's all he said?"

"Yes, sir. I'm sure."

My Grandpa Hollister looks at the back door. We can hear Marvadell singing. She's singing louder than usual. "Hush, little baby don't you cry. You know your momma's bound to die. All my trials, Lord. Soon be over." Grandpa Hollister looks down at me again. "All right, Travis. You go along now."

I don't think he believes me. I think he knows. He turns and walks back around to the front of the house with the papers in his hand. After a while, I hear him start the Buick Roadmaster in the garage. He backs out and whispers off down the street.

twenty-two

It's Wednesday night, and Beulah's at church. Caroline's gone on vacation to Yellowstone with her family. She's gonna see Old Faithful. She's gonna send me a postcard. Me and my Aunt Delia are at the Dairy Queen in Warrington getting Cokes and french fries. We drive on through Warrington and then turn around and drive back. My Aunt Delia says, "Same old Warrington." She looks at the Coke in her lap. "Same old Coke and fries." The radio is playing The Drifters' "Under the Boardwalk." I like the Coke and french fries. Back in Omaha, I don't get to go out like this at night.

We drive back toward Widow Rock, and when we pass Luby's Roadhouse, my Aunt Delia slows down and says, "Whoa now, son. Look at that."

I look, but I don't see anything. She points, and I see Ronny Bishop's white pickup truck way at the back of the parking lot. My Aunt Delia pulls in, and we stop next to the red neon sign that blinks on and off: WHISKEY. DANCING. WHISKEY. DANCING. We can hear the jukebox booming inside and people laughing. It's hillbilly music. My Aunt Delia and Beulah and Caroline call it shit-kicker music. They don't like it, except for Patsy Cline. They like rock 'n' roll.

My Aunt Delia pulls around back, as far from Ronny's truck as we can get. We don't see anybody in the truck. We wait, and a man comes out the back door of Luby's. When he opens the door, the music jumps out with him loud, then it stops when the door closes. He's wearing a white cowboy hat, jeans, and a blue western shirt with pearl buttons. He's holding a brown paper bag. He stops and looks around the parking lot. That's when Ronny and Bick stick their heads up.

They jump out of Ronny's pickup and walk over to the man. Bick takes out his wallet and gives the man some money, and the man hands Bick the bag. The man gets into an old Hudson and drives away. We watch his red taillights disappear off toward Warrington. Bick and Ronny throw back their heads and whoop at the moon, then they jog-trot back to the truck.

Ronny drives the white pickup out to the county hardroad, and my Aunt Delia says, "Come on, Killer, let's give 'em a scare." She pulls out, and we follow the pickup back toward Widow Rock. About a mile from Luby's, she charges up close behind the pickup and starts blinking her brights on and off. The pickup slows down. It goes slower and slower, and then the brown bag flies out Ronny's window into the ditch. We go another half mile, and the pickup pulls over. My Aunt Delia pulls alongside and leans out the window. "What you boys got in that car?"

I can see Bick's face. First he's scared, then he's angry. Ronny leans over and looks at us. "Shit, Delia," he says, "I thought it was your daddy."

My Aunt Delia says, "You're dumb, Ronny. My daddy has red lights."

Bick's not saying anything. His face is stuck angry.

My Aunt Delia says, "What was that I saw flying out your window, Ronny?"

Ronny says, "Why don't you go back and see."

Bick just looks at my Aunt Delia and shakes his head.

She says, "You go back and get it. If it's not broken, bring it to Widow Rock." She gives the Chevy hard gas, and the tires burn, and we're gone. I look back, and the pickup pulls out and turns around, and Bick and Ronny go back to look for the thing they threw out the window.

It's exciting going to Widow Rock at night. We leave the Chevy and the pickup down below and climb up by the light of the moon. Sometimes we slip, and Ronny falls once and says, "Shit fire!" and my Aunt Delia says, "Ronny, if you can do that, light our way."

Bick takes out his cigarette lighter, and the flame shows us the way until the lighter gets too hot to hold anymore. It takes a long time. When we come out on the big shelf of rock, it's a creamy white in the moonlight, and the gorge is just that empty nothing, a lake of cool black air out there above the river. We can smell and hear the river, but when I take little half steps out to the edge of the cliff and look down, all I see is dark. My stomach drops like when I took off in the airplane.

We stand looking at the moon and listening to the river below. The trees behind us rub and fuss in the wind, and my Aunt Delia says, "I wish we had Beulah's radio." Bick reaches into his back pocket and pulls out the brown paper bag. "We got this. No thanks to you, Delia."

My Aunt Delia says, "Well, what do you know? It didn't break."

She walks over and takes the bag from Bick and rolls the paper down, and I see the whiskey bottle. She wads the paper bag and wings it out over the gorge. When she pulls out the cork, it makes a little pop, and she wipes her palm across the mouth and takes a drink. "Cheap whiskey," she says, and hands it back to Bick.

He laughs, and it sounds hard. He says, "You wouldn't know Rebel Yell from panther piss, Delia Hollister."

My Aunt Delia tilts her head to the side and watches him from one eye. "Mr. Sophisticated. His daddy gives him one drink every Saturday night to train him for Princeton."

Bick shakes his head again and raises the bottle and drinks. Ronny says, "Come on, Bick, give me a bite of that. We wouldn't have it if I didn't have friends in low places."

My Aunt Delia looks over at me. "Travis, have you ever seen two bigger jerks in your life?" She's smiling, and her face is white in the moonlight, and her eyes look like they've got stars in them. I say, "I guess not." I look at Ronny and Bick, but they don't look at me.

Bick goes out to the edge of the cliff and lights a Salem. My Aunt Delia puts her finger across her lips and says, "Travis, Bick's gonna have a coughing fit."

Ronny puts the bottle down on the rock where my Aunt Delia and me sat the first time we came up here. He reaches into his back pocket and takes something out, something dark and gleaming. He says, "Hey, Travis, Boy, look what I got."

I look, but I can't tell what it is. I go over close. It's a pistol. He holds it out to me, and before anybody can stop me, I take it, and it's so heavy my hand falls a foot before I catch it. I've never held a real one before, only toys, and I can't believe how heavy it is. Behind me, my Aunt Delia's voice is slow, careful, and angry. "You fool, Ronny, why did you bring that up here?"

Ronny looks up at the moon. "I don't know. Snakes, I guess." He and Bick laugh.

I turn with the pistol in my hand. My Aunt Delia stands with her hands on her hips looking at Ronny. The moon's behind her, so I can't see her face, but I know she's mad at him and maybe at me.

Ronny says, "Relax, Delia. You know how kids love guns. I thought me and Travis here would do some target shooting tonight. I bet he'd like that, wouldn't you, Travis?"

There's nothing in the world I'd like more, but I don't say so. I keep my voice quiet and say, "I guess so. Is it okay, Aunt Delia? I'll be careful. I promise."

Ronny looks over at Bick. "What do you think, Bick? Should me and old Travis go down and do some target shooting?"

Bick turns from the edge of the cliff with the red glow of the cigarette hanging from his lips. He says, "Every boy loves a little target shooting. I don't see how it can hurt anything."

My Aunt Delia says, "Travis, I don't like the way you're holding that thing. Point it at the ground."

My face burns hot in the night air. I didn't know I was pointing the pistol at her. I know better than that. I point it straight down. She comes over and says, "Check and see if it's loaded." I look up at Ronny, and he nods, and I find the catch that releases the roller that holds the bullets. It flops open against my palm, and I can see six bright brass circles with dark little eyes in their centers. I say, "Yes, ma'am. It's loaded."

My Aunt Delia says, "Ronny, unload that thing right now."

Ronny takes the pistol from me. He pours the bullets into his hand.

My Aunt Delia looks over at Bick. He's standing with his back to us looking at the moon. I can see a halo of cigarette smoke around his head. The wind pulls the smoke out toward the empty nothing. My Aunt Delia says, "Now don't you reload that pistol until you're all the way down to the bottom. And be careful." She looks at Ronny. "You hear me, Ronny?"

Ronny looks at her and smiles. He takes a big drink of whiskey from the bottle and puts it down on the rock. "I hear you, Delia."

Ronny turns on the pickup's headlights. He gets some Coke and 7-Up bottles out of the truckbed and sets them up on stumps and in the crotches of pine saplings. He hands me the pistol. "All right, Travis, Boy," he says, "light 'em up."

The bottles glitter in the headlights. The dew is coming down, and the trees are starting to drip. The bed of pine needles under my feet is wet. The pistol is cold and heavy in my hand. I hand it back to Ronny. "You better go first."

Ronny laughs. It's more of a giggle, and I know if I saw his eyes they'd look like Mr. Latimer's eyes when he called me a half-nigger. Ronny says, "S'matter kid, you scared to cap an old Coke bottle?" He takes the pistol and holds it down low between us. I hear him cock the hammer. He says, "This here's a double-action piece, Travis, Boy. You don't have to cock it, but you'll get more accuracy if you do."

Ronny turns to the side, aims the pistol straight-armed, and closes one eye. The 7-Up bottle disappears before the bang hits my ears like a hand slapping my head. It makes me yell, and I jump back a step from Ronny. Pieces of glass rain down through the dripping trees. There's a little ring of smoke around Ronny, and it smells strong, and like nothing I've ever smelled before. I like the smell. He's holding the pistol down by his leg again and looking at me. "Travis, I bleeve you just squealed like a girl. Ain't you ever heard a gun go off before?"

I say no, but I can't hear my own voice. The bang hurt my ears or something. I look up at Ronny and say, "Now it's my turn," and hold out my hand. Ronny laughs. "You sure you want to? I don't want to let no girl shoot my pistol, now." I stand there with my hand out, and for some reason I'm remembering how Ronny and Bick Sifford looked at each other when Ronny said he'd take me down here to shoot, and how Bick said, "I don't see how it can hurt anything," and then he turned away to the gorge.

Ronny hands me the pistol, and this time I push my hand up so he can't tell it's heavy for me. I lower it to my knee and cock it with my thumb, and my hand is sweating. I'm afraid my thumb's gonna slip off the hammer and the pistol's gonna shoot my foot. But I feel it cock, and I raise it and hold it out straight toward the Coke bottle in the crotch of a little cypress about twenty feet away. Ronny says, "Now line up that little notch with the sight at the end of the barrel."

I'm not listening to him. I'm trying to remember my Aunt Delia's eyes when she looked at Bick Sifford. When she looked at him just before she said I could come down here.

I guide the pistol back and forth until the white letters that spell, "Coca-Cola" come into the sight, and then I pull the trigger and the bang is not so loud this time, but the pistol jumps in my hand, and the shock of it goes all the way back to my shoulder, and it's like Jimmy Pultney hit me in the arm with his fist.

I open my eyes, and the Coke bottle is gone, and Ronny Bishop says, "Damn Kid, you got some beginner's luck." I turn to look at him, but he's looking down at the gun. I look down too, and I'm pointing it at his stomach. He reaches out and slowly puts his hand over the barrel.

"Take your finger off the trigger, Travis."

I do.

He takes the gun from me by the barrel. He says, "What did your Aunt Delia tell you about pointing guns at people?"

I don't say anything. I just nod. I'm thinking about my Aunt Delia and Bick Sifford up there on Widow Rock. I'm thinking about how she came home with that scratch on her chest. I'm thinking about how he touched her arm at the tennis court and how she let him do it for a while before she pulled away.

Ronny Bishop takes the pistol and walks over and puts it on the hood of the pickup. He says, "Travis, I got to go take a leak. Wait here for me and don't touch that piece 'til I get back, okay?"

He walks off into the bushes singing, "Hard-Headed Woman." It's Elvis's new song. It's a hit. They're playing it every half hour, all day long on the Birmingham and Jacksonville stations.

When Ronny's gone into the bushes, I turn and run for the path that goes up to Widow Rock.

twenty-three

When I come to the top of the hill where the path isn't steep anymore, I stop running. I'm out of breath. I rub my knee where I scraped it on a root and try to hear over the sound of my breathing. I don't hear anything, so I go closer. Through the ragged opening in the trees, I can see a space of white stone in the moonlight. I can feel the cool air from the river on my face. Then I hear them. Bick Sifford says, "Come on, Delia. Please, Delia," and his voice sounds like the Reverend Laidlaw's voice when he closes his eyes at the end of the sermon, asking Jesus for something. Something he really wants. Something we're all supposed to want. It makes the hair go up on the back of my neck.

I listen for my Aunt Delia's voice, and I hear hard breathing, and I can't tell whose, and then she says, "Stop it, Bick. I want you to stop it."

I come out onto the white rock shelf and see them lying where my Aunt Delia and me sat in the sun that first day we came here. Bick's on top of her, and I can see him holding her wrist with his left hand and touching her with his right. My Aunt Delia's got her left arm around his neck, and he's got his leg between hers. I stop ten feet from them, and she says, "I mean it, Bick. I want you to stop."

I reach down and feel at my feet. I find a piece of loose rock, and I wing it side-arm right into the middle of Bick Sifford's back. Bick Sifford squeals, "Oww! Shit! What's that?" He rolls off my Aunt Delia, and she turns away from me and pulls her jeans up and her white blouse down.

Bick Sifford jumps up and faces me. He pulls up his zipper and takes a step toward me. He says, "Get out of here, you little turd."

My Aunt Delia sits up, but I can't see her face because Bick's in the way. Bick Sifford takes another step toward me and stamps his foot like he's trying to scare a cat. His bare foot slaps on the white rock. "Get!" he says. "I mean it."

I stand my ground. I say, "You were hurting her. I saw you."

Bick says, "You sneaky little shit. Standing over there in the trees watching us? Where's Ronny, anyway? Did you shoot him?"

I say, "You leave her alone." I want to say, you rich boy Princeton shit turd. I want to say all the words Jimmy Pultney says that I don't say. I just say it again, "Leave her alone."

Bick says, "I'm not gonna tell you again, Travis. Get out of here. Me and Delia want to be alone." His face is big and white and jaw-clenched, and his hands are tight fists at his sides.

From behind his legs, I hear my Aunt Delia say, "Stay, Killer." She sounds tired. She sounds sad. She gets up and tucks in her blouse and runs her fingers through her black hair, twice on both sides. I'm glad I can't see her eyes very much. I'm afraid they look like they do at night when it storms and I come into her bedroom. She walks around Bick and comes to me. She says, "Bick, you leave Travis alone." She takes my hand and pulls me toward the opening in the trees. I can hear Ronny calling out to me down there, "Travis! Hey, Travis, Boy!"

My Aunt Delia and I pass through the tree door, and I hear Bick Sifford behind us, "Goddamn cock-teasing bitch," and I let go of my Aunt Delia's hand, and I start back fast.

I'm gonna hit him. I'm gonna find a big rock and hit him in the throat. I'm gonna stomp his ass. My Aunt Delia catches me by the shirttail. I pull, but she holds on, and then I stop seeing the hole in the trees through my white rage. It goes buttery moonlight yellow again, and I hear her behind me saying, "Come on, Killer. You don't need to do that. You've done enough already. Let's just get out of here."

We pass Ronny on the way down. He's slipping and falling and fighting the whiskey as much as the rocks and roots and the dark. He looks up and sees us coming and says, "What the...?" and we pass him fast, and my Aunt Delia doesn't say anything. Behind us I hear him call out, "Bick? Hey Bick, you up there?"

My Aunt Delia drives to Dr. Cohen's office and parks where we can't be seen from the main street of Widow Rock. There are no lights on in the doctor's office. There are lights in the doctor's house, and we see Mrs. Cohen come into the kitchen and get something from the refrigerator and then go out again. "Are we going in?" I say.

My Aunt Delia says, "No, Killer. We're just gonna sit here. I feel safe here."

I say, "You're safe with me, Delia."

She looks at me and smiles her sad smile. She reaches over and touches my face and pushes the hair out of my eyes. "I know, Killer. You're sweet. You did the sweetest thing for me tonight."

I want to tell her I'll stomp his ass. One way or another I'll do it. But I don't say it. She doesn't want to hear that now. We sit for a while in the dark car with the windows open and the warm air full of my Aunt Delia's perfume and the spicy smell of the river and her secret skin. She says,

"We forgot to turn on the radio."

She reaches over and turns it on low, and the light comes on inside the radio, and I see that the back of her hand is scraped from fighting Bick Sifford. The song comes out slow and sad: "Tonight the light of love is in your eyes, but will you love me tomorrow?" My Aunt Delia leans her head back on the seat and listens. When the song is over, she says, "He's going to talk about me now, Killer."

I don't know what she means. I know it's Bick, but I don't know what she means about talk. She says, "My reputation is shot now," and I remember the song "Wake Up, Little Suzie." "The movie's over. It's four o'clock, and we're in trouble deep."

"What's he gonna say?" I ask. "You didn't do anything."

Her head is still back on the seat. She's staring at the gray cloth that lines the roof of the Chevy. She says, "You don't know how it is in a town like this, Killer. It doesn't matter if you did anything. If they start to talk about you, there's nothing you can do to stop it. They can make your life hell."

I don't know what to say. I'm thinking about the joke we played on Bick and Ronny. About how they threw the bottle out the window and then had to go back for it. I'm thinking it made them mad, and that's why Bick Sifford did that to my Aunt Delia. But then I know that's not it. He did it because he had to. Because he's Bick Sifford, and his daddy owns the box factory, and he's going to Princeton, and my Aunt Delia's the prettiest girl in Choctawhatchee County. I say, "Are you gonna tell Grandpa Hollister?"

She looks over at me like I'm crazy. She shakes her head and leans back again and stares up at the gray lining, and I wonder if she's thinking about Kenny Griner's eye. I think about the braided leather thong that disappears into Grandpa Hollister's pocket. I think about Bick Sifford with his eye busted like that. I say, "Are you gonna leave town?"

She gives me that same look again, and says, "No, Honey. I'm stuck here until I graduate from high school."

We listen to the radio for a while and watch the Cohens' house. Nobody comes into the kitchen. Mrs. Cohen's cookies were good. There's a light on in the living room, and I remember all those books. Grandma and Grandpa Hollister just have the Bible and *Life*, *Look*, and *Time*. They've got the newspaper from Panama City and *Reader's Digest*. The radio plays Dion and the Belmonts: "Stay away from runaround Sue." Some headlights come around the corner and stop. When they start moving again, I reach over and turn our radio off. But we keep hearing the same song, and I know it's Ronny and Bick in Ronny's pickup. We hear the rest of "Runaround Sue" as they go down to the traffic light in front of Tolbert's Rexall and then move on. My Aunt Delia hugs herself and says, "I'm scared, Killer. I'm scared of what's gonna happen now. I don't want them to talk about me."

"Don't worry. It's gonna be all right." I want to say I won't let him hurt her, but I can't stop anybody from talking.

My Aunt Delia doesn't look over at me again. She just watches the light in Mrs. Cohen's kitchen window and listens to the radio. Jerry Lee, the Killer, comes on. It's "Breathless." I listen close because it's my name. Maybe he'll tell me what to do now. He sings it like he's whispering to someone in the dark. "My heart goes round and round, my love comes a tumbling down. You leave me breathless. I shake all over, and you know why. I'm sure it's love, Honey, that's no lie. 'Cause when you call my name, you know I burn like wood in flame. You leave me breathless. Come on baby now don't be shy, this love was meant for you and I. Wind, rain, sleet, or snow. I'm gonna be wherever you go. You leave me breathless."

My Aunt Delia always closes her eyes and swings her shoulders to the Killer, but now she doesn't. So I say, "We'll just stay away from them. We don't have to see Bick and Ronny."

My Aunt Delia laughs, but there's no fun in it. She says, "We have to see them. That's what you do in Widow Rock. You go see who's there."

One day after supper, I'm in my room reading John R. Tunis. My Aunt Delia's in the bathroom getting ready to go out with Beulah. I hear the phone ring, and then my Grandma Hollister comes to the bottom of the stairs and calls up, "Travis, come on down, Honey. It's your dad on the phone."

I just keep reading. I don't want to talk to him. I don't know why. She calls me again, and I don't answer. She says, "Just a minute, John. I'll go up and get him." I hear her coming up the stairs, and I hide behind the book. I'd go out the window, but there's no way down. I'd go out the window in my Aunt Delia's room, but my Grandma Hollister would see me. I hear her footsteps out in the hall.

"Travis, did you hear me call you? Are you asleep already?"

She opens my door, and I hide behind the book. She says, "Travis?"

"I don't want to talk to him."

I hear her breathing. The words in front of my face run down the page and spill their ink. She comes into the room and sits on the bed. She reaches out and pushes my book down. She wipes my face with her fingers. "Honey, your daddy loves you. I know he does. He loves you very much. He didn't call before because it's hard for him."

"It's hard for me, too."

"I know that, Honey. He should have called before now, but I want you to go down and talk to him, and I want you to be a big boy and not upset him. Will you try, Travis?" Her face looks tired. She looks like she's gonna cry. She's squinting like she's got a headache. She loves my dad and me, too.

"What's the matter, Mother?"

My Aunt Delia stands at the door. She's in her bathrobe, and her hair is wet, and she doesn't have any makeup on. She's beautiful, and I want to run away with her. My Grandma Hollister says, "Lloyd's on the phone, and Travis won't go down and talk to him."

My Aunt Delia comes in and sits on the other side of my bed. "Why, Travis, you're crying."

"I didn't want to," I say. I promised myself I wouldn't cry anymore. I just didn't think my dad would call.

My Aunt Delia hugs me. "I know, Honey. I know. But you have to talk to your daddy. Think how he'll feel if you don't."

"I don't care how he feels. He doesn't care how I feel."

My Grandma Hollister says, "That's not true, Travis. You know it isn't." She sighs, and I know she's gonna tell me something she doesn't want to. I hope it's not about my mom. She says, "Your daddy's just...he's just one of those men who can't admit it when things hurt them. And it hurt him to have to send you here, and right now things with your mother are very hard for him. The important thing is that he wants to talk to you. Can't you go down and talk to him?"

I look at my Aunt Delia. She nods. She smiles. I'd do anything for her.

"Hello, Dad."

"Hello there, Marine. How are you doing?"

"Fine, sir."

"Are they taking good care of you? Are you eating plenty of Marvadell's good cooking?"

"Yes, sir."

"Grandma says you and Aunt Delia are big friends. I'm glad to hear that, Son. I always wanted you to get to know my family."

"Yes, sir."

I hear my dad sigh, or maybe he's taking a puff on a cigarette. If he is, it's a big one, and he draws the smoke way down into his chest and blows it out hard. He says, "I went to see your mom today, Travis. She's fine. She's getting better. She wanted me to tell you how much she loves you and how much she misses you."

I want to tear the phone out of the wall. I want to take the black cord that connects the part you hold to your ear to the part you dial and wrap it around my neck. I want to run away with my Aunt Delia. I want my mom.

"I miss her too, sir."

"Well, they've sure got you sirring down there in Widow Rock, don't they, Travis?"

"Yes, sir."

"All right, Son. You take care, and try not to worry about things. We're gonna be all right."

"Yes, sir."
"Put Grandpa Hollister back on, will you, Son?"
"Yes, sir."

AUGUST

Got to get to dancin', get my hat off the rack.
I got the boogie-woogie like a knife in the back.
Come on baby, got nothin' to lose.
Won't you let me take you on a sea cruise.

SEA CRUISE
—Music and lyrics by Huey Smith
—Recorded by Frankie Ford

twenty-four

Bick Sifford's been calling every day.

He calls in the morning after my Aunt Delia wakes up and at night when he knows she'll be home. At first my Aunt Delia told Grandma Hollister she didn't want to talk to him. Grandma Hollister got her headache look and went back to the phone and told Bick my Aunt Delia was indisposed. Then she came up to my Aunt Delia's room and said, "But why, Honey? I thought you liked Bick."

My Aunt Delia just said she didn't know why. She said maybe she was bored with him. Maybe she just thought Bick Sifford was a drip. When she said that, Grandma Hollister got even more worried and went to her room to lie down in the dark. After that, my Aunt Delia had to talk to Bick. I'd hear her say, *Yes*, and, *No*, and, *Yes, I know*, and, *Sorry, but I can't do that*, and then she'd get off real fast. She never laughed when she talked to him.

About a week after the night Ronny let me shoot his pistol and I hit Bick with a rock, a big box of flowers came to the house. There's no flower shop in Widow Rock or Warrington. They came all the way from Panama City, and they were as big as our dining-room table, and that's where my Aunt Delia left them. She wouldn't take them up to her room. A card came with the flowers. It was made of pink parchment paper, and the gold lettering on it said, "Sorry, Friend, if I've offended you." My Grandma Hollister got to it first, and after that, she took my Aunt Delia for a walk to the park, and they talked. When they came back, my Aunt Delia went up to her room and turned on the radio low, and I knocked on the door.

"What did she say?" I asked her.

She was sitting at her vanity table looking at herself in the mirror. The radio was playing, "Dream Lover." My Aunt Delia said, "She wanted to know why Bick sent the flowers."

"What did you say?"

"I lied, of course. I told her Bick said I was fat and I should dye my hair blonde like Sandra Dee and quit playing so much tennis like a tomboy. I told her I think Bick's a stuck-up poothead, and I can't wait 'til he goes to Princeton."

"Did she believe you?"

"Probably not."

"What are you gonna do now?"

She peered into the mirror like she was looking through a window at some other girl. She reached up and pulled the corners of her eyes to the side until they looked like my mother's eyes. She gathered her black hair on top of her head with both hands and tilted her head to the side. She let her hair fall and picked up a brush and held it out to me. I walked over and started to brush. I like the way her hair smells when I brush it. I like the way it shines. I like the way it flows through my fingers like black water.

She said, "I'm gonna stay away from him 'til he leaves, and then I'm gonna forget about him. And you're gonna help me stay away from him, Killer."

I brushed her hair. I said, "Okay."

When we go out, we go with Beulah if we can. We can't wait for Caroline to get home from Yellowstone. We go to the youth group in Warrington, and all the girls like me. Mr. and Mrs. Dagel think I'm too young to be talking about growing up too fast, but my Aunt Delia asked them if I could stay, and they said yes. At the meetings, I sit between Beulah and my Aunt Delia, and we listen to Mr. Dagle talk about how a man has to master his impulses so that he can have a deeper and more fulfilling relationship later on with the woman he loves. Mrs. Dagle smiles and looks at him like she wants to put vanilla frosting on him and eat him up. So do most of the girls. My Aunt Delia looks over at Beulah and sticks her finger down her throat, and Beulah looks at the ceiling to keep from laughing.

All of the girls at the youth group think I'm cute. When we take a break and drink red punch and eat cookies Mrs. Dagle baked, they run their hands through my hair and feel the muscle in my arm and even kiss me on the cheek and whisper, "Travis, you're growing up way too fast." I like it, but I don't like it as much as I like being with my Aunt Delia.

Bick and Ronny come to the youth group, too. They sit in the back, and Bick looks quiet and sad, and when he thinks my Aunt Delia is looking at him, he makes big sad cow eyes and shapes the words, "I'm sorry," with his mouth.

When he looks at me, his eyes say he'd kill me if he thought he could get away with it. I'd do the same to him, and he knows it.

We don't stay out as late as we used to. If we go somewhere and Ronny and Bick show up, we leave. A couple of times we're driving, and we see headlights behind us, and we know it's Ronny and Bick. We stop, and they stop behind us. We start, and they start again. They don't get too close. They don't blink their lights. They don't do anything bad. They just follow us.

Last night I was up late reading, and I heard a car pull into the driveway. I thought it was Grandpa Hollister, but I went to the window anyway. It was Bick Sifford's red Oldsmobile. I looked at the clock. It was one in the morning. I went down the hall to my Aunt Delia's room. She had the radio on low, but it was dark, and I knew by her breathing she was asleep.

I went back to my bedroom window and watched Bick sit in the car with the radio playing low. Cigarette smoke drifted out the open widow and into the oak tree above the driveway. Sometimes he put his hand out the window and flicked the ash, and I could see the sparks fall. It was two-thirty when he started the Oldsmobile and drove away. I was as tired as the night I stayed up waiting to catch Santa Claus.

Me and my Aunt Delia go down to the ESSO station to get the white Chevy's oil changed. The station's on the main drag across from Dr. Cohen's office. It's really just a white shack with a tar-paper roof. On one side, a shed supported by four cypress poles covers the grease rack. There's a big red soda machine in front of the station. We stop there for Cokes when Tolbert's Rexall is closed. Old Mr. Dameron runs the station. He's got three fingers gone from his left hand, and he wears bib overalls and thick, steel-toed shoes, and the grease is worked so hard into the creases in his skin it won't ever come out.

My Aunt Delia says she wonders what it's like for his wife lying in bed with a man who smells like a lube job. She says she wonders if everything in Mr. Dameron's house has grease on it. I say, "The salt shaker," and she laughs. I say,

"His tooth brush," and she laughs. I say, "The toilet seat," and she really laughs. She says, "The Holy Bible," and I laugh. Then she says, "Especially the Last Supper," and we both laugh like crazy.

We pull in under the shade of the shed roof, and Mr. Dameron comes out of the little office dragging a red rag from his hip pocket. He leans down to my Aunt Delia's window scrubbing his hands on the rag. "Aft'noon, Miss Delia. What can I do for you?"

My Aunt Delia says, "Hey, Mr. Dameron. Daddy says it's time to change the oil in this old wreck."

Mr. Dameron leans back and looks at the Chevy like he can see right through the hood to the oil. He nods. Yes, we need a change. He wipes his forehead with the greasy red rag and says, "All right, Miss Delia. Pull her in there."

We pull into the cool shade of the grease rack, and Mr. Dameron's giving my Aunt Delia hand signals to go right and left and stop. We get out and stand beside the car, and Mr. Dameron call outs, "Hey you, Kenny. Come in here, will you?"

I look through the back door of the shed into the alley, and there's red flame on midnight-blue metal and a slice of chrome moon disc. Kenny Griner comes through the door. He's wiping his hands on a rag and saying, "Mr. Dameron, I..." He sees my Aunt Delia. He stops and squints in the shade. My Aunt Delia says, "Hey, Kenny. How are you?"

Griner doesn't say anything. He just pulls his mouth to one side and hoods his eyes and looks up at the ceiling where a bunch of fan belts and hoses hang in the dusty dark. My Aunt Delia walks over and stands in front of him and looks at his forehead. The stitches are out now, but you can see the six little puckers where the skin is cinched together like the mouth of a change purse. It's not blue and red anymore, it's just red. When Griner sees her looking, he lifts his hand to touch the scar, then lets it drop to his side. My Aunt Delia says, "Looks like you won the badge of honor for bad driving, Kenny."

We all know Grandpa Hollister hit him.

Griner looks at her and shakes his head. He looks over at Mr. Dameron who says, "Kenny, can you change Miss Delia's oil. She takes the thirty-weight, I bleeve."

Griner's wearing a blue denim jumpsuit with an AC Spark Plugs badge sewed over his heart. "Kenny" is stitched in red on the other side. He's not covered with grease, just a few smudges here and there. His hair gleams with Brylcream. He looks at my Aunt Delia, then at me, then at the Chevy, and says, "Yeah, I guess I got time."

"All right then, Miss Delia, we'll get her done for you." Mr. Dameron walks out of the dark shed toward the office.

We're alone with Griner. He turns his back to us and pretends to look for something in a greasy old cabinet covered with broken parts and tools. He doesn't find what he isn't looking for, and I hear him give a big breath and mutter, "Damn." He turns back, red-faced, and kneels and pulls the big forks of the grease rack out and positions them under the car. I squat and watch. He goes over to the wall and flips a switch. Out in the alley, a small engine starts. He looks at me and says, "You got to build up the pressure in the tank before the rack'll lift the car."

I nod.

Griner goes to some shelves and pulls down a blue oil filter and shows it to me. He doesn't say anything, so I don't either. My Aunt Delia stands very straight in the space between the Chevy and the wall. Her purse is crushed under her folded arms, and she watches us with her I'm-not-falling-for-this smile.

Griner shows me a tool with a handle at one end and a wide metal band at the other. "You wrap this around the filter, and it locks tight, and then you twist and the filter comes off." I nod. The little motor is chuff-chuffing outside, and pressure hisses into the tank by the grease rack. Kenny Griner squats and looks at the glass face of the gauge. "You got to check the pressure," he says to me.

I nod. I say, "How high does it have to go?"

"Sixty pounds ought to do it," he says.

My Aunt Delia steps up behind him and bends and does something quick. I can't see what.

Griner jumps and reaches behind him. He stands up and looks at her, and his face is even redder. She opens the book she snatched from his back pocket. It's a paperback, *The Subterraneans*. She flips some pages, reads what's on the back. "Wowie-Zowie!" she says. "Kenny, you're Widow Rock's very own beatnik?"

Kenny Griner holds out his hand for the book. He says, "I might be. You don't know what I am."

She holds the book out to him, and her face changes. She's not kidding him anymore. "I might know," she says. It's almost a whisper.

He takes the book, and she turns and walks to the mouth of the shed and lifts her face to the sun. Griner stuffs the book back into his hip pocket.

With her back to us, hugging herself, my Aunt Delia says, "I don't see why we can't be friends, Kenny. I didn't hit you in the head."

Griner doesn't say anything. He just pulls the lever that lifts the grease rack. There's a lot of hissing and groaning, and it's neat to see the Chevy rise off the concrete and see what's underneath a car. When it's up all the way, and it's quiet again, my Aunt Delia says, "Kenny, did you hear me?"

Griner says, "I heard you." He walks under the car, and I go with him. He says, "Travis, you got to be careful under here. You don't want anything falling on you or dripping in your eye, okay?"

I nod. Under here, in the heat from the engine, he has to bend his head a little not to bump it, and I can smell his aftershave, and he doesn't seem so tough. I think we could just be two guys.

My Aunt Delia says, "Kenny?"

Griner keeps working. He doesn't turn and look at her. He loosens a nut, and the oil pours out black and hot into a big bowl on a high stand. I like the smell, like burnt coffee. Griner waits with the wrench in one hand and the nut in the other. Oil from the nut runs down his first finger and drips onto the floor. He says, "I don't want to be your *friend*, Delia. You know that."

My Aunt Delia doesn't say anything.

Griner says, "*Don't* you, Delia?"

My Aunt Delia still has her back to us. She doesn't say anything.

Griner says, "Delia?" His voice is soft and low, and the oil drips from his finger onto the floor. The last of the oil flows from the hole under the engine, and then it starts to drip.

My Aunt Delia says, "Killer, I'm gonna get a Coke. You want one, too?"

"Sure," I say.

When she's gone, Griner turns and looks at the place where she was standing. His face is red, and his eyes are strange. He looks down at me and then looks away quick. He puts the nut back in the hole and loosens the old filter and spins it off.

After a space, my Aunt Delia comes back with three Cokes. She hands me one and puts the other on the floor next to Griner's foot. She stands close to us now and watches Griner work. She looks happy, and I don't know why. I'm not sure what just happened, but something did. I drink my Coke and my Aunt Delia drinks hers. Griner just leaves his on the floor.

When he turns to get the new filter, my Aunt Delia says, "I brought you a Coke, Kenny."

They look at each other for the first time.

And it's the first time.

twenty-five

We hear tires chirp, and Bick Sifford's red Oldsmobile stops behind my Aunt Delia's white Chevy. Bick and Ronny get out and shade their eyes staring in at the three of us. They see Griner tightening the new oil filter and wiping the old oil from around the place where it fits. They see the Coke on the floor by his foot. Griner wipes his hands on the rag, reaches down, and picks up the Coke. He takes a sip, looks at my Aunt Delia, then turns to face Bick and Ronny.

I watch Bick's face. I remember his moony eyes from the back of the Baptist recreation room in Warrington. Bick looks at Delia, then at Griner, and his jaw tightens. His shoulders fall, and he shoves his hands into the pockets of his white slacks and looks down at his penny loafers.

Bick and Ronny look at each other, and Ronny says, "Hey Bick, how 'bout a Coke?"

Bick nods, and they walk over to the front of the station. We hear them put money in the machine, and it goes chunka-chunk. They come back carrying Cokes, Ronny leading, and walk right up to the grease rack. Ronny stands next to Kenny Griner. The white Chevy hangs above Ronny's head, and he reaches up one hand and steadies on it. He looks underneath. "You get that filter on good and tight, Boxie?" he says to Griner.

Griner doesn't say anything, but his eyes go tight and his jaw seizes. *Boxie's* what some people around here call the box-factory workers. Ronny goes under the car. He grabs the oil filter, and I see the muscles bunch in his forearm and his knuckles go white. The filter moves about a half turn.

"Wut'n tight enough, Boxie." Ronny turns to my Aunt Delia. "It's all right now, Delia. I fixed it for you."

My Aunt Delia doesn't say anything to Ronny. She just looks at Bick. Bick gives her a pleady look, shoves his hands farther down into his pockets, and shuffles his loafers on the greasy floor.

Griner goes over to the bench, puts down the Coke, and picks up the tool he used on the filter. He goes under the Chevy and loosens the filter a half turn. "You get her too tight," he says to Ronny, "and the seal'll crimp, and she'll leak." Griner's face is pale. His fists are rocks. Ronny says, "Don't you smart mouth me, you duck's ass trash."

Griner drops the tool and goes for him, but my Aunt Delia jumps between them. I've never seen her move so fast, not even on the tennis court. Her back's against Ronny's chest, and her chest is pressed to Griner's. They feel her between them and stop. She squirms sideways between them and puts a hand on both their chests and pushes them apart.

She turns to Ronny. "Don't you talk that way to him. You're not your daddy yet. And he'd whip your ass if he knew you were going around town calling people trash."

Ronny's face is as red as the heart of a watermelon. His red hair seems alight with his anger. He says, "Nobody's gone whip my ass."

Griner says, "We'll see about that."

My Aunt Delia says, "Shut up, Kenny."

She looks at Bick. He's got his hands out of his pockets, and they're fists, but he doesn't know what to do with them. She says, "Bick, do something useful and get Ronny out of here."

Bick looks at her. He's got his trouble in his eyes. If he was a kid, I'd say he was about to cry. He says, "Come on, Ronny. Let's get out of here."

My Aunt Delia gives Ronny another push, and he stops leaning into her hand. He steps back. Bick comes close and grabs Ronny's shoulder. Ronny shrugs off his hand and says, "Let go of me, damn it."

Bick steps back and raises his hands. "Okay, okay." He looks at the white sunlight at the front of the shed. He says, "Old man Dameron's gonna come out here."

Ronny looks at him, and then over at Griner. "I'll whup both their asses."

Griner laughs at him. He says, "An old man's about your speed."

Bick says, "Ronny, come *on*."

I can see Ronny's not gonna fight Griner. He's just got to talk 'til he can leave.

Ronny says, "You're my speed, Boxie. Any time, any place."

My Aunt Delia says, "Thank you, Bick."

Bick Sifford looks at her. He doesn't know what she's doing. She steps out from between Ronny and Griner and goes over to Bick. She takes his arm and pulls him over toward the red Oldsmobile. She guides him to the car door, and I hear her say, "Thanks for the flowers. That was sweet."

Griner looks over at her. He watches her and Bick, and his eyes go sick and tired, and he looks up at the dark, cob-webby ceiling where the fan belts and the hoses hang, and he shakes his head. He goes over to the bench and tosses the Coke into a crate full of empty oil cans. It foams and spills. When he passes Ronny, their shoulders bump. Ronny's fists whiten, but he doesn't do anything. Griner walks out through the back door. The street rod starts up with a whine, and then backs down with a pop-pop-pop. Then I hear it spray gravel as Griner takes off.

When we get out of town, my Aunt Delia lets me drive, and I think we're just going nowhere, but then she starts giving me directions. "Turn at that next rusty mailbox, Killer. Slow down to twenty and take that fork to the right."

I've learned to turn pretty well now, and I've got my speed up to fifty on a good flat straightaway. I asked my Aunt Delia if I could take the car out alone, but she said, "Not hardly, Killer. You might get the Widow Rock wanderlust and never come back."

I drive, and she gives me directions, and finally I ask, "Where are we going?"

She just says, "Never mind."

We pass Ronny Bishop's cattle ranch. Hundreds of white-faced Hereford cattle graze in the fields, and the fences are sturdy cypress, and the house is white with green shutters like ours, only bigger. It's surrounded by sheds and pens, and I can see the new green paint of a John Deere tractor in one of the sheds. Ronny's white Ford truck is parked in the yard near the back door, and there's a new blue Cadillac and an old red Ford. There is a silo at the back of the big lot, but it's not as big as the one I see from my backyard in Omaha. The cattle all face the same way, into the south wind, and some of them look up as we pass.

We come to an old field with rusted-down fences and broken salt licks and toppled troughs, and my Aunt Delia says, "Turn right and stop by that old house there."

From the road you'd think the old farm house was empty. The tin roof is rusted dark brown and twisted up by a big wind along one eave. Screens hang in tatters from the windows. The red-brick chimney has a big crack in it somebody tried to patch with fresh mortar. There's an old barn out back with an oak tree in front of it. A beat-up blue Plymouth is parked under the tree. The engine is pulled out of the Plymouth, and it hangs in the air from a greasy block and tackle chained up in the oak.

We stop in front of the house next to some fresh car tracks in the red dirt, and my Aunt Delia says, "Wait here, Killer. I won't be long."

She gets out, and I get out, too. She says, "I want you to wait here for me."

I just shake my head. I'm not letting her go in there alone.

We go up on the porch, and some of the boards are rotten, and they bow under our feet. My Aunt Delia knocks, and there's nothing, and she knocks again, and we hear, "Hold on a minute." I don't recognize the voice.

A boy comes to the door. He's blond, and his eyes are milky blue, and he's wearing dirty jeans and tucking in a brown work shirt with SIFFORD CONTAINER AND PACKING CO. stitched across the heart. He squints at us and yawns and says, "Yeah?" Then he says, "Oh, hey, Delia."

My Aunt Delia says, "Hey, Randle. Is Kenny here?"

The blond boy scratches his face, and I hear the whiskers rasp in his hand, and I wish I had them. He says, "Naw, he went over to Warrington to get some parts for the rod." The boy looks at me, and I smile at him, but not big. He says, "Hey." And I say, "Hey." My Aunt Delia says, "Randle this is Travis, my nephew."

Randle says, "Yeah, I heard about Travis." Then he says, "You want to come in for a Coke or anything?"

My Aunt Delia thinks about it. Her face is strange. She looks lost but happy. She looks like she's been here before and never seen anything like this place. She looks like she might run away any second and might move in. She says, "Thank you, Randle, that would be nice."

We go in, and Randle walks barefoot to the kitchen and gets us Cokes. It's not so bad inside. The floor is bare pine, but it's rubbed with linseed oil, and there's a clean hooked rug on it, and the fireplace is swept, and there's a big picture of a racing car tacked on the wall over it. My Aunt Delia takes her Coke from Randle, and so do I. She sips and says, "Thanks. That's good on a hot day."

I say, "Thanks."

Randle lifts his half-tucked-in shirttail and scratches his stomach. He says, "It's been a long time since I seen you, Delia. You been okay?"

"I been fine, Randle." She shrugs. "You know."

We stand there. They don't know what to say. Finally, Randle says, "I bleeve Kenny'll be back in about a half hour if you want to wait."

My Aunt Delia says, "No, no we better not wait. Is that Kenny's room?" She's looking through the open door of a bedroom. Randle says, "Uh, yeah." He sips his Coke and scratches with the other hand. He lifts the cold Coke and holds it to his forehead. My Aunt Delia goes into the bedroom, and I follow.

The bed is narrow and neatly made. Car posters cover the walls. There's a small bookcase with about thirty books in it, mostly paperbacks. Over on the dresser top, there's some silver jewelry and a comb and a big bottle of Vitalis.

There's a mirror above the dresser. On the table beside the bed there's an old windup alarm clock. Beside it, there's a picture of my Aunt Delia in a cheap wooden frame. It's a picture somebody cut out of a newspaper. There's a line of print under it: "Widow Rock Teen Goes to Girls' State."

My Aunt Delia goes over and picks it up. She looks at the picture, and her face goes soft, and a little smile comes to her lips, but it flies as quickly as it lit. She puts the picture down exactly where it was, and we walk back into the living room. She says, "Randle, you don't need to tell Kenny I was here. It wasn't anything important."

Randle looks confused. His face reddens, and a cluster of pimples on his right cheek comes on like a light. He says, "All right, Delia."

I know he's going to tell Griner. So does my Aunt Delia.

We walk to the door, and my Aunt Delia says, "Randle, it was good to see you again. And thanks for the Coke."

"Yeah," I say, "thanks." I finish mine and put it down on the table by the sofa. My Aunt Delia doesn't finish hers.

We go outside, and I know my Aunt Delia's gonna drive. She pulls out slow, and we keep on going away from town, out into the country. She turns on the radio, and we listen for a while, then I reach over and turn it down and say, "How come we went there?"

She doesn't look at me. She looks off down the road and says, "I needed to see where he lives."

I say, "Why?"

"I don't know. I just needed to."

I say, "Are they poor?"

She looks over at me and smiles. She says, "Yeah, but they don't mind. They're just boys. They work on their cars and drink beer when they can get it, and they don't have anybody to nag them about cleaning up the place. They're in heaven. They'll care about it later, but they don't now. They don't see into the future too well, boys don't."

"Not even Bick."

She looks off down the road. It's hot and the asphalt is white and the mirages dance out there, and it's water we'll never reach. She says, "Bick's different. He listens to his daddy, and his daddy tells him all about the future. You don't go to Princeton unless you care a lot about the future."

twenty-six

It's August and I'm bored. Beulah says it's hotter than a whore's dream. Caroline's back from vacation, but the four of us don't go out as much as we used to. My Aunt Delia's staying away from Bick. When he calls, she's not rude and she doesn't hang up, but she doesn't say much. Mostly she listens and looks at me and shakes her head or makes a smirk. She covers the phone and whispers, "What a dork." Sometimes I ask her what he's saying, but she won't tell me. She just says, "He's putting the moves on me, Killer. You know."

I don't know, not really, but I don't tell her that. I wish I could put the moves on. If I'm a dreamboat and a heart-breaker and a Killer, I should be able to do it, but I don't know how. Sometimes I think the answer's in the songs. It's the crazy stuff you hear like, "A wigglin' walk and a gigglin' talk, make the world go round." It's, "I'm a lonely frog." And it's, "Be my guest, you got nothin to lose, won't you let me take you on a sea cruise?"

I listen to the radio playing low and watch my Aunt Delia's face when she talks to Bick on the phone, and I know she likes him. Not all the way, but she likes him. He's got something she wants. He's in her mind, and she can't get him out. It's like that voice I heard moaning from behind the locked door in the hospital where my mom is. I still hear that voice. It lay down inside me and made a home. Bick's voice is like that for my Aunt Delia. Or maybe I'm just going crazy with the heat.

Sometimes Caroline and Beulah come over, and the four

of us listen to the radio, and they do each other's hair all different ways and try on my Aunt Delia's clothes and makeup and talk about their friends. Some of them are kids I know from the youth group in Warrington. They drink Cokes and talk about what they're gonna do when school starts. Caroline says she loves summer. She doesn't want school to ever start. My Aunt Delia looks at her and then at me and then out at the oak trees so still in the heat. She says, "I can't wait for summer to be over. Certain people will be gone then, and life'll be a lot easier."

Caroline and Beulah look over at me quick. They think maybe she means me leaving. But I just look out the window at the oaks and remember how the limbs fussed and rubbed against each other in the storm. I know who she means.

We haven't seen Kenny Griner since that day at Mr. Dameron's ESSO station, but sometimes at night I hear his car go by. I know the sounds of his engine now even if it doesn't back down with a pop-pop-pop. Sometimes I hear him in my sleep, and I get up and look out, and there's midnight-blue metal and red flame and moon discs under the streetlight at the corner. Other times, I don't make it to the window in time, and I go back to bed and lie there wondering what he's thinking. I wonder if he thinks some night my Aunt Delia will be out there waiting for him, and she'll get in the car, and they'll run away together.

I'm gonna get my boat, sort of.

I told my Aunt Delia I wanted one. I told her about flying over the ocean and looking down at sand like wheat and water as blue as the china my mom brought from Japan, and about how I decided I was going to have a boat and go out and catch marlin and big sharks and maybe a creature. I asked her how much a boat would cost. She said she didn't know, but she thought it would be a lot. Then she said, "Come on, Killer, I got an idea," and we went out and got into the Chevy.

It's called The Johnny Barnes Fish Camp. It's on the river, about three miles down from Widow Rock. My Aunt Delia parks the Chevy against a white-painted cypress log, and we walk into a little shack with BAIT painted on the front in white letters. Underneath, in smaller letters, it says, NIGHT CRAWLERS, WORMS, CRICKETS. The shack is right on the river bank, and there's a dock, and I can see six dark green boats with outboard motors tied up in a row.

It's dark inside the shack, and every spot has something sitting on it or hanging from it. There are rods and reels, cane poles, bins of hooks and sinkers and bobbers and plugs. There are nets and blue lanterns and seat cushions and red gas tanks and straw hats and sandwiches and boiled peanuts. There's a big red cooler full of iced drinks. In the back, there's an old stone horse trough with two window screens on top of it. From inside it, I can hear crickets chirping. They're bait.

An old man sits behind the counter reading a gun magazine. He's wearing a khaki shirt and a green eyeshade, and a bare light bulb hangs above his head. When we come in, he looks up and smiles. "Hey, Miss Delia. You goin' fishin'?"

My Aunt Delia says, "Hey, Mr. Barnes. This is my nephew Travis from Omaha. He's spending the summer with us."

Mr. Barnes looks down at me. "Travis."

"Hey, sir."

Mr. Barnes's left earlobe is split in two. He sees me looking at it and reaches up and divides the two parts. "Travis," he says, "I was fishing with a man one day, and he was throwing a top-water plug for bass, and he got a little lengthy with his backstroke and stuck a treble-hook in my ear." He twiddles the two parts of his earlobe with his finger and smiles at me. "But that wudn't the bad part. The bad part was when he made his cast." He laughs and lets me think about it.

I say, "I bet that hurt, sir."

"Not as bad as his head after I got through with him."

My Aunt Delia says, "What you asking to rent a boat, Mr. Barnes?"

Mr. Barnes says, "All day with gas, five dollars. Back before dark."

My Aunt Delia reaches into her jeans and pulls out a ten-dollar bill.

My Aunt Delia steers us upriver. She sits facing me with her arm over the tiller of the five-horse kicker. The motor is loud, but I'm used to it now. I like the way it smells and the way the blue smoke floats over the water behind us and the way the brown water boils white as we cut through it. At first it was strange in the boat, the way it moved under me. My Aunt Delia could see I was worried. She said, "Just sit in the middle facing me, and that'll keep us balanced. The worst that can happen is we fall in and have to swim."

Now I'm used to it, and I'm sitting up on the seat instead of down in the bottom. Away from the fish camp, the river is wild. The banks are steep and rocky, and we see cooters slipping into the water from logs and rocks ahead of us.

Birds roost in the tall cypresses along the bank, and my Aunt Delia says, "Look, Travis, there's an osprey. People around here call them fish hawks. And that bird with the big black wings is an anhinga. Some people call them snake birds because they swim underwater and they wiggle like a snake."

I like the way the wind cools my face as we move, and the way it lifts my Aunt Delia's black hair from the shoulders of her white blouse. We slow down and idle along the bank, moving from one patch of shade to another.

Then I see the big tangle of white driftwood, and beyond it, the sandbar glimmering under the coffee-colored water. I say, "Is this the place where we...?"

My Aunt Delia smiles and nods. "What do you say, Killer? You want to pull in and perfect the fine old southern art of skinny-dipping?"

I nod and smile, and my throat gets thick thinking about it.

My Aunt Delia points the boat at a sandy place on the bank below the driftwood, and she says, "Move back toward me, Travis." I crawl along the bottom of the boat toward her and crouch at her feet. She says, "We need the weight back here so we can slide her up on the sand." We hit with a crunch and a gritty slide, and my Aunt Delia cuts the motor, and it coughs and dies in a cloud of blue smoke.

We do it like we did before. I strip and fold my clothes, and my Aunt Delia goes down to the driftwood to undress. I watch her hand rise up white with her white blouse and hang it, and then again with her bra, then her jeans. I turn away and look up river toward the white shelf of Widow Rock. I touch my thick throat and take a deep breath and let it out and feel the thing heavy and hurting and wonderful in my chest. I love her.

I'm only twelve, but I'm a teenager in love.

My Aunt Delia shouts, "Yoo-hoo, I'm coming, Killer," and I dive into the river, keeping my face to Widow Rock. I go under the cold coffee dark, and the cold makes my chest seize, and I open my eyes and hold my hands in front of me like two white fish. I surface and swim upstream to get warm. When I turn, my Aunt Delia is sitting on the sandbar with her back to me. She hugs herself in the cold, but she says, "Ooh, isn't it delicious, Killer. I wish this river ran through my room at night, and I could just roll off the bed and flop around in it a while."

I drift down and sit beside her on the sandbar, and we let our arms point downstream in the current and wiggle them like snakes. We kick off and race again, and she beats me again, and I like watching her white shoulders ploughing and her black hair fanning over them. We walk back pushing against the current and sit on the sandbar again, and I say, "Do you like Bick Sifford?"

She hugs herself and looks downstream. I don't look at her face. She lets out a shivery sigh and says, "I told you I do, remember? The night I came home from the party." I look over at the place on her chest. The scratch Bick gave her is almost gone. There's a faint red line in the white skin. I wonder if the trace will always be there. I wonder if he marked her. I say, "Yeah, you told me."

She says, "I'm confused, Killer. I want to like a lot of people. I want to do a lot of things, a lot of things you wouldn't understand. I like him, and I don't like him. He's so...*young.*"

I have to say it. "I don't want you to like him." I try to make my voice sound old, but it comes out young.

My Aunt Delia looks over at me. She stops hugging

herself and puts her arm around my shoulders. It's warm on my back, but it makes me shiver. She says, "I know, Killer. I know."

I say, "Remember when you asked me what I know about boys and girls, and I said I didn't know anything, and you told me about how you and Bick got excited under the magnolia tree, and you weren't going to get excited anymore like that, and you were waiting for him to go to Princeton?"

She says, "I remember." Her voice is small, and her chin is down almost to the water, and it's like she's whispering to the river. I don't know what to say now. I want to tell her I'm excited. I'm a teenager in love. Her arm is around my shoulders, and she gives me a squeeze, and her side is warm against my side in the cold river. She says, "Travis what is it you want to ask me?"

I say, "Tell me where babies come from."

I don't know where the question came from. I didn't think it was there. It wasn't what I wanted to ask. But now I know I had to ask it. Because it's what everybody knows, and I don't know. It's what Bick and my Aunt Delia and Caroline and Beulah and Ronny know. It's what my parents whisper about when I walk past their bedroom door on Sunday afternoons and my mom has her head on my dad's chest, and the radio is playing Peggy Lee and "Fever."

My Aunt Delia doesn't say anything, and I can't look at her. I can feel my face is red. Finally, she sighs and says, "Poor Killer. Things are so confusing, aren't they?"

I say, "Yeah," and it barely comes out.

She says, "Well, we're all confused. Remember that, Killer. No matter how old you get, or how much you know, you're still gonna be confused. That's just...life."

I wait, and she sighs again, and says, "Where do you think they come from?"

I can't tell her what I think. One boy at school said he thought babies came from kissing. Another boy said he thought if you were in a room with a girl and you farted she could have a baby. One of the boys used to live on a farm, and he told us what he thought. He tried to show us what horses and pigs did, but we didn't believe him. I can't tell my Aunt Delia. I just say, "I don't know."

She takes me by the shoulders and turns me toward her. I look into her eyes, and they're like two cats watching me out of the dark, and I can't keep my eyes on them, so I look at the green wall of trees behind her. I hear the river moving around us and rubbing along the bank and rustling the tree limbs that dip down low. My Aunt Delia pulls me closer to her, and I can feel her chests touching me, our nipples brushing together. She reaches down and takes my hand and says, "Touch me, down here." She pulls my hand down and under until my chin is in the water and she's looking up at the sky. She turns my hand upward and fits it between her legs. She says, "Here. They come from here, Killer."

She holds my hand to her, pushing upward, and then she lets go and puts her hand on my shoulder again. My eyes are closed, and I'm dizzy, and I'm seeing her in her underpants the night she came home from the dance at Bick's house, and I'm seeing her dark shadow through the white cotton cloth, and I'm feeling in the cold river the hot place where the dark color is her hair, and it's stiff and coarse, and she's warm and open, and I wonder if the river's flowing into her. I hold my hand against that warm open and close my eyes tight and feel my thing growing hard as the bone in my arm. My Aunt Delia rests her chin on my head and whispers, "Do you see, Killer?"

I'm dizzy. I can't think. I want to stay with her like this forever. I find my voice way down in the hollow bottom of me and say, "No."

My Aunt Delia's hand moves, and I feel her fingers close around my hot, hard thing. She says, "Now do you see?"

My hand is on her, and hers is on me, and I see. I know how it happens now. I can't talk, I just nod under her chin, and I hear her sigh, and I don't want us to move. Ever. I put my arm around her and pull her toward me, and I feel us touching chest to chest, nipple to nipple, my hips against her thighs, our hands where they are, and then I hear it. My Aunt Delia hears it, too.

A sound from the trees along the bank.

A voice, laughter.

My Aunt Delia goes stiff in my arms. She pushes me away hard, and the cold river flows between us.

twenty-seven

My Aunt Delia whispers, harsh, "Get dressed!"

She turns and swims downriver as fast as she can, and before I can get out of the water, I see her run up the bank, all the long white length of her, and disappear behind the driftwood clump.

I swim to the bank and run to my clothes. I'm pulling on my uns when I hear it, "Pop-Pop-Pop!" The sound comes from out there in the woods where my Aunt Delia parked the white Chevy the first time we came here. I get my jeans and T-shirt on and look downriver. My Aunt Delia's already in the boat, and her wet hair is squeezed into a rope that hangs down one side of her face and pours water onto her white blouse. She turns to the woods, listens, calls to me, "Hurry, up, Travis!"

I run down to her and push the boat off the sand and wade in and jump aboard. We make a lazy turn, floating down with the current. My Aunt Delia kneels in the back of the boat, pulling on the cord that starts the outboard. She pulls and pulls, and mutters, "Shit!" She pulls, and finally it hacks and stutters and then roars, and she throttles it back and throws us into a turn so tight it sprawls me down in the bottom of the boat.

When she straightens us out, we're reared up and going as fast as we can, and our bow is splitting the river and sending out a long, wide V that washes up on the banks behind us. I look at her and smile and try to get her to smile back, but she doesn't. She bites her thumbnail and feels for the cross at her throat, and a dead sick look comes into her eyes when she knows the cross is not there. After that, she bites her thumb again and scrunches down small in the middle of the seat, and we speed on down the river without saying anything.

We drive way out into the country to an old roadside park. There's a rotting picnic table and a rusted-out barbecue grill, and nobody comes here anymore. A Highway Department sign says, NO DUMPING. The sign's full of bullet holes. My Aunt Delia pulls us under the shade of a big oak and turns on the radio. The song is "Summertime Blues," and she whispers, "Shit," and changes the station from Tallahassee to Birmingham. Birmingham is playing, "Goin' to the chapel, and we're gonna get married. Goin' to the chapel of love." She leaves it there, but turns it down low.

I don't know if we're gonna talk or just sit here. Either one is all right with me. I can't get my mind off what I learned about men and women. I can't stop looking at my hand, the one that fit perfectly between my Aunt Delia's legs. Finally, she says, "Did you hear it?"

I nod.

She throws her head back against the seat and rests her arm across her eyes and says, "Oh, God." It sounds like a curse, not a prayer.

We sit for a while, and the radio plays soft, and the songs come and go, and I know they can't tell me the truth about love. Not the truth I learned in the river. You can't put that truth on the radio. I say, "He won't tell."

My Aunt Delia tears her arm from her eyes and looks at me like the fish hawk I saw perched in the cypress by the river bank. "He'll tell," she says, harsh, cold. "He's a boy. They always tell."

I turn away and look out at the rotting picnic table and the rusted grill. "I'm a boy," I say. It's so low I don't know if she can hear me above the radio. "I won't ever tell," I say.

I sit there listening to my own heart rattle like rain on the roof. I feel her hand on my shoulder, light, then gone. She whispers, "I know, Killer. I believe you."

When we get home, my Aunt Delia puts the white Chevy in the garage, and we go upstairs. Halfway up, we hear Grandma Hollister say, "Why Delia, look at you. You're all wet."

My Aunt Delia says, "Travis fell in the river, and I pulled him out." She says it without looking back. She keeps climbing the stairs. My Grandma Hollister says, "My goodness! Travis, are you all right? Delia, I hope you aren't letting that boy do anything dangerous at the river. You can swim, can't you, Travis?"

I stop and look back. Grandma Hollister stands there with her hand at her neck twisting her strand of pearls. I say, "Yes, ma'am, I can swim." I start to tell her not to worry, but my Aunt Delia says, "It's all right, Mother. Come on Travis." She pulls me by the sleeve of my wet shirt.

Grandma Hollister says, "Delia, come down here. I want to talk to you."

My Aunt Delia says, "Mother, I've got a headache," and keeps on walking.

Grandma Hollister doesn't say anything more, but I know she doesn't like it. When we get to the top of the stairs, I hear her walking toward the kitchen.

In my Aunt Delia's room I sit on the bed, and she sits at the vanity with her back to me. I can see her face in the mirror, and she can see mine. She says, "We have to talk."

"Sure," I say.

She says, "Did you see anybody? My back was to the bank. You were facing that way. Did you see anybody?"

I was facing the bank, but my head was under her chin. My eyes were closed, and I was in a place I never wanted to leave. How could I see anybody? I say, "No."

"Tell me what you heard."

"It was somebody laughing, maybe."

"Maybe?"

"I think it was somebody laughing."

She lifts her chin and looks at herself in the mirror, and it's like the night she came home from Bick's party, only worse. She's looking in a window at somebody she doesn't know, and now it's somebody she doesn't want to know. Somebody she doesn't like. She says, "That's what I heard, too." She lowers her head and whispers, "Damn it. Damn it to hell."

I say, "Don't worry. It's gonna be all right."

She turns so fast on the chair that it twists the rug under her. "Don't say that." Her eyes are flame, and her voice is ice. "You don't know that, and you shouldn't say it. Say things that are true. Isn't that the way we are?"

I look into the heat of her eyes. I know she's right. I know I shouldn't have said it. I nod. "What are we gonna do?"

She watches me, and finally she smiles. It's a smile I've seen before. It scares me, and I like it. Then I remember where I've seen it. It's Grandpa Hollister's smile. She says, "I don't know. We can't do anything yet. We have to wait and see what happens. We have to wait and see what he does."

"You mean, Griner?"

"If it was Griner."

"It was his car."

I'm the one who wakes up nights hearing that car go by. I'm the one who hears that engine backing down, Pop-Pop-Pop, in my dreams.

My Aunt Delia closes her eyes and says, "Yeah, it was his car."

She turns on the radio. It's Tallahassee. The Killer singing, "You shake my nerves, and you rattle my brains. Too much love drives a man insane. You broke my will. What a thrill. Goodness, gracious! Great balls of fire!"

My Aunt Delia lies on her bed. She puts her arm over her eyes, and her fingers drop to the side of her neck, and they try to find the gold cross. When they know it's not there, her hand seizes into a quick white fist.

I say, "Did it come off when you were swimming?"

"No," she says. "I think he took it. I hung it on the driftwood with my clothes. He must have been hiding down there for a while, and he took it."

It makes my stomach drop like it did on the plane. It makes my knees so weak I'm glad I'm sitting down. It makes my eyes so small I'm seeing my Aunt Delia like she's on the other side of a keyhole. And then it makes me mad.

A week goes by, and we stay close to home. Bick doesn't call, and we don't know why. My Aunt Delia thinks maybe he's out of town. Caroline and Beulah come over, and my Aunt Delia asks if they've seen Bick. Caroline says sure they've seen him. She says her and Beulah go see who's there, and he's there, just like always.

"We haven't seen much of *you*, though," Caroline says.

Beulah says, "What's the matter, Delia? You say Bick's a dork, and now you're all curious about him."

My Aunt Delia gives Beulah a look that could burn through a manhole cover. It's like a death ray. She says, "I'm not *all* curious about him. I just asked if you'd seen him around."

"All right," says Beulah. "I don't know what you're getting so pissy about."

My Aunt Delia picks up Beulah's tenny pumps from where she shucked them off over by the door. She shoves them into Beulah's middle. "Go home, Beulah."

Beulah gasps. "Well, I never! Come on, Caroline." Her chin quivers.

Caroline gets up blinking like she's trying to find her way out of a dark room. She looks at Beulah and my Aunt Delia. "You two need to cool off."

My Aunt Delia turns to the window. "Good-bye, Caroline."

We're supposed to be at the Baptist Youth Group in Warrington, but we go back to the river to look for the gold cross. My Aunt Delia thinks maybe she shook it off on the bank when she was putting on her clothes so fast. She says it's a long shot, but maybe we'll find it. She sneaks a flashlight from Grandpa Hollister's car, and we drive out there. It's creepy in the woods at night, and there's a cloud of mist snaking up and down the river, and my Aunt Delia sends me back to the path halfway between the car and the bank. She says, "Stay there, Killer, and keep watch. I'll go look for the cross."

I want to go with her, but I don't say so. I do what she tells me. I'm scared for her, and I'm just plain scared, but I don't say so. I stand in the path for a while, then I move into the woods and stand with the dew dripping on me and skeeters whining around my head until I see her flashlight beam come back along the path. "Did you find it?"

"No," is all she says.

The next day my Aunt Delia and me are in the living room playing *Monopoly*. I've got Boardwalk and Park Place, and she has the whole side from New York Avenue to St. Charles Place. My Grandma Hollister comes in the front door. She stops in the foyer and heaves a sigh because it's so hot outside. She's wearing her white organdy dress with the black belt and a string of coral beads. She's wearing her black and white spectator pumps and carrying her matching handbag. It's her church committee outfit.

She looks worried. She says, "Delia, I just talked to Mrs. Dagle at the Tri Delta chapter meeting, and she happened to mention that they missed you at the youth group the other night."

My Aunt Delia looks up with the dice in her hand. She's about to throw, and she doesn't want to land on my property. Her eyes jump with fear, then she covers herself with a stretch of her arms and a yawn. She puts down the dice and says, "Well, she was right. I wasn't there. Travis and me went out driving around."

My Grandma Hollister says, "Travis, come with me." She turns and walks into her bedroom. She leaves the door open for me. I look at my Aunt Delia. I can feel my stomach filling up with cold. My Aunt Delia looks at me hard and draws a finger across her lips, and I get up and go into my Grandma Hollister's bedroom.

She's sitting on the bed. Her white gloves are folded on her handbag on the bed beside her. Her hands are clasped and her mouth is tight. She looks determined, but she's no match for my Aunt Delia. I know that. Then I see Grandpa Hollister sitting at the little desk in the corner by the window. It's where he does his accounts. I didn't even know he was home.

My Grandma Hollister reaches out and pulls me close by the shoulders. When she looks into my eyes, I see worry and hurt. I still like her, but she's weak, and I'm not going to be like that. She says, "Travis, where did you and Aunt Delia go last night when you didn't go to the youth group?"

I look into her eyes. It surprises me that my hands don't sweat, and I'm looking at her so straight, even with Grandpa Hollister over in the corner working on his sheriff papers. I say, "We just went out driving around."

Grandma Hollister screws her eyes down tighter and grips my shoulders harder. "*Where* did you drive to, Travis? You must have gone somewhere."

I smile. I shrug. "We went to the Dairy Queen in Warrington. We had Cokes and french fries and listened to the radio."

My Grandpa Hollister clears his throat and leans back in his chair. I look over at him. He's not looking at me, but he's listening. I say, "We sat there for a long time just listening to the songs on the radio. We like to do that."

My mind storms, then clears, and I see the last time we went to Warrington. We sat in the Dairy Queen parking lot and listened to the radio. Kids from around the county came in their cars, and we said hey to them. This funny song came on the radio for the first time: "Purple People Eater." It made us laugh.

My Grandma Hollister holds my shoulders tight. "Travis, are you telling me the truth?"

When she says "truth," Grandpa Hollister looks over at me. She's never asked me a question like this before. I don't like it, but I smile and say, "Yes, ma'am."

She takes me by the hand and walks me back to the living room where my Aunt Delia sits at the table counting her *Monopoly* money. My Aunt Delia looks up and smiles. My Grandma Hollister says, "Delia, come with me."

My Aunt Delia looks at me, and then at Grandma Hollister standing with her hands on her hips by the bedroom doorway. I look into my Aunt Delia's eyes, and I sing: "One eye, one horn, flying purple people eater." I sing it low, under my breath. My back's to Grandma Hollister, and I wink at my Aunt Delia. She looks confused. She doesn't get it. We hold our eyes together for as long as we can, and I'm sending her thought letters about the Dairy Queen in Warrington. Cokes, french fries, and purple people eaters. She gets up and goes into the bedroom.

The door closes, and I wait. I count my money and arrange my deeds. I rub my hands together because they're sweating now. The cold in my stomach moves down into my legs.

Five minutes later, the door opens, and my Aunt Delia comes out smiling. My Grandma Hollister doesn't come out. My Aunt Delia and me play for a while longer, then she stretches and yawns and says, "I'm tired, Travis. I think I'll go up and take a snooze, okay?"

I say, "Okay," and she leaves. I wait a while, then go up, too.

When I come in, she's sitting on her bed with her knees up under her chin. She tightens her jaw, tilts her head to the side, and says, "You're a good guy, Killer. You saved our butts." We're like two soldiers after a battle.

"Did you get it?" I ask her.

"I got it," she says.

"The Dairy Queen?"

"The Dairy Queen. We had french fries and Cokes and listened to the radio."

She holds out her hand to me, and I take it. We shake, and I know it's a bargain. We lie together from now on.

My Aunt Delia and Caroline and Beulah make up on the phone. My Aunt Delia apologizes and says it was just the heat and the boredom and the long summer. They come over, and we sit up in my Aunt Delia's room listening to the radio. I see how glad they are to be here, and I know they need my Aunt Delia more than she needs them. I know they're not real without her, just like I'm not now. So much of what I know and what I am now is because of her.

We listen to the radio, and they talk about who's cool and who's not, and what Elvis is doing in the Army, and finally the talk runs down, and Caroline says, "Let's go to Tolbert's and see who's there."

I know my Aunt Delia doesn't want to go, but she can't let them know.

twenty-eight

Three cars are parked at the curb in front of Tolbert's—Bick's red Oldsmobile, Ronny's white Ford pickup, and Griner's midnight-blue street rod. We pull up behind the rod, and Caroline shapes her bangs with her fingers, and Beulah picks some lipstick from the corner of her mouth with her little fingernail. They both look at the cool green windows trying to see who's inside. I look over at my Aunt Delia. Her face is as pale as it was in the moonlight the night we went up to Widow Rock and I chunked Bick with a rock. Her hand shakes when she takes the key from the ignition and shoves it in her jeans.

The jukebox is playing inside. It's the Everly Brothers, "Walk right back to me this minute. Bring your love to me, don't send it. I'm so lonesome every day." Mr. Tolbert's at the cash register selling a can of Prince Albert to a farmer in a khaki shirt and green galluses. Ronny and Bick sit in a booth. Griner's in another as far from them as he can get. He's got a cup of coffee in front of him and his face in a paperback book. Bick and Ronny are halfway through two large Cokes. Two women I recognize from church sit in a booth closer to Bick and Ronny than to Griner. They lean across the table, talking over two lemonades. We all walk through the cold, peppermint-tasting air to the fountain and take stools and dangle our feet into the room.

Everybody says, "Hey," except Griner, but we don't sound the same. We sound like we're all suddenly strangers. Bick doesn't look at my Aunt Delia. He just stares at his Coke like he's never seen one before. The jukebox stops playing, and Ronny says, "I been feeding that thing for an hour. Somebody cough up a quarter." He's smiling, but it's his mean smile. Beulah and Caroline look at each other and raise their chins a little higher. Beulah always says girls don't put money in the jukebox when there are boys around.

Ronny says, "Hey, Kenny, whyn't you shuck a quarter out of those greasy Levi's."

Griner doesn't look up. He just keeps reading, but his jaw grinds, and the muscle jumps. Ronny says to all of us, "Ole Kenny'll listen all day, but he won't pay. I guess he figures he's entitled."

One of the grown ladies looks over and says, "You can leave it quiet in here, and we won't mind."

The other one nods like she does in church when the preacher says something particularly scriptural. They lean together and go back to talking.

Mr. Tolbert calls from the front. "I'll be with ya'll in a minute."

My Aunt Delia gets up and goes over to the jukebox. She stands there sorting change in her hand and pretending to read the numbers and letters. It's all wrong. The stiff way she moves, the way she holds her head down between her shoulders, the way she studies what we all memorized a long time ago. She feeds the slot and punches in three songs.

The bell at the front rings as the farmer leaves. Mr. Tolbert walks over and takes our orders. I get a shake and Beulah, Caroline, and my Aunt Delia get Cokes. We turn back around and dangle our legs. The jukebox plays Pat Boone: "My lonely heart aches with every wave that breaks over love letters in the sand."

Ronny looks over at us and says, "Ole Travis and his harem. Hey, Travis Buddy, you mind if I dance with one of your girlfriends?"

I don't know what to say. I can feel the red start in my cheeks. Ronny gets up and holds out his hand to Beulah, and she slides off the stool, and they start slow-dancing in the small space between the counter and the booths. The two women watch Beulah and Ronny pressing close together, Beulah's hips slipping from side to side and Ronny's butt muscular in his tight jeans. They finish their lemonades and leave, whispering.

Ronny lifts his chin from the top of Beulah's head where he's left a dent in her hair spray and says, "Hey, Delia, dance with Bick. He's too shy to ask you."

Bick lifts his Coke and taps it twice on the table. He doesn't look at my Aunt Delia. She closes her eyes, then she slides off her stool and goes over to him and holds out her hand. Griner lowers the book to watch them. He looks like a man who hasn't eaten for a week standing outside the window of a restaurant in the rain. Bick looks up at my Aunt Delia, and I can't tell what's in his eyes. It's nothing I've seen there before. He takes her hand before he stands up, and she leans back and pulls him out of the booth, and they dance the rest of Pat Boone.

The next song's a slow one, too, and that's strange. My Aunt Delia usually mixes in the jumpy ones. It's "The Sea of Love." Bick holds her, but not too close, and they move around in lazy circles, sometimes bumping into Ronny and Beulah, sometimes just standing in one place and swaying from side to side. I look at Griner and catch him peeking over his book at them dancing. I think he might do something.

He might do it right now. I remember the laugh from the riverbank.

My Aunt Delia still isn't moving right. She dances like the floor's shifting under her. I remember her swimming, turning and curling in the water like she lived there. Like a water animal. When I think of the river, my throat gets thick, and my mouth gets dry, and I turn to the counter and take a sip of my shake. When I turn back, the song's over. Bick sits down, facing us now and looking straight at my Aunt Delia. I still can't tell what's in his eyes. It's not the same old sorry I saw coming from the back of the room at the Baptist Youth Group. He's past sorry now and into something else, and it makes me want to leave. It makes the hair come up on the back of my neck.

The next song is Buddy Holly, "True Love Ways." It's slow, too, and Ronny dances it with Caroline. When they finish, he goes over to the booth, picks up his Coke, and finishes it. He says, "Come on, Bick, let's go."

Beulah says, "Hey, you guys, stay a while."

Caroline says, "Yeah, where you goin', anyway?"

Bick stands up and looks at my Aunt Delia. She doesn't want to look back, but she has to. Their eyes are like a match and dry grass. Then Bick and Ronny walk out.

Griner lowers the book to watch them leave. He looks at my Aunt Delia. She looks at him like she's been waiting for this, like it's the thing she had to do since we heard that laughter come from the riverbank and Griner's engine winding down. She swallows and says, "Kenny, would you like to dance with me? I'll put another quarter in."

Griner looks at her for a long time. His face is pale, and I think of him in the shadows of the grease rack and working the graveyard shift out at the box factory and working on engines in the old barn behind that falling-down house in the country. He seems like something from the night, the shade, not the sun. He says, "Delia, you know I don't dance."

She pushes off from the stool and goes over to him in that stiff, strange way. Caroline and Beulah put their Cokes down. Beulah puts her hand over her mouth. Mr. Tolbert stops washing glasses to watch. My Aunt Delia stands in front of Griner and holds out her hand. She says, "Come on, Kenny, dance with me. It's time you learned. I'll teach you."

Griner looks at her, then down at his book, then back up. Her hand hangs in the air between them, and I hope I'm the only one who sees it trembling. My Aunt Delia says, "I'll teach you, Kenny."

Griner looks at the green windows. Ronny's truck and Bick's red Oldsmobile are gone from the curb now. He looks back at my Aunt Delia. "You already had your dance for the day. You don't need one with me." He looks back down at the book. He pretends he's reading, but his eyes aren't taking the print.

Mr. Tolbert says, "Kenny, be a gentleman and dance like she asked you."

Griner doesn't say anything.

My Aunt Delia lets her hand drop. She walks straight to the front door, and we all get up and follow her. Behind us, Mr. Tolbert mutters, "Man didn't turn a lady down like that, not in my day."

My Aunt Delia hits the door with the heel of her hand, and the bell rings.

Outside in the sudden heat, she stops and looks over at Griner's street rod. I see her chin go up and her legs stiffen, then she walks to the rod and bends down into it.

Caroline and Beulah come out behind me, and Beulah says, "Delia, what are you doing *now*?"

Caroline laughs her mean laugh. "Take his keys, Delia. If he won't dance, let him walk."

My Aunt Delia walks back to her side of the white Chevy. I get in the back like always, and Beulah and Caroline stuff themselves into the front with my Aunt Delia. We pull away from the curb, and my Aunt Delia throws her right arm over the back of the seat, steering with her left. Her hand is a white fist in front of me. The fist opens, and the gold cross falls out of it into my lap.

twenty-nine

"It was hanging from his rearview mirror," my Aunt Delia says.

We're sitting on her bed up under the slope of the roof. She's got her legs crossed and I have too, and we've got the window open between us. Below in the backyard, the grapes in the arbor are black ripe, and the birds are at them. Marvadell comes out the back door with a broom. "Shoo, shoo, you scounrel thieves!"

The blue jays and sparrows scatter away, but they'll come back. They always do. The black cat that ate the baby birds my first morning here sits in the tall grass over by the privy. He switches his tail and watches the birds. There's a cool breeze high in the oaks, and sometimes my Aunt Delia leans toward the window screen as we talk, and she lifts her hair away from her neck to let the air at it.

She says, "Did he put it there so I'd see it and take it, or was he just going to keep it and ride around town letting everybody see?" She puts her hand to the gold cross at her neck. She's wearing it again. She asked me if she should, and I said yes. Anything else would look funny.

I say, "It could be either one."

Her eyes watch me for answers because I'm a boy, and she thinks I know how boys think, but I'm thinking about Griner. What he's like, what he's really like. Back home in Omaha, when we saw guys like Griner in leather jackets and ducktail haircuts, my dad told me they were hoods and greasers and drugstore cowboys. He said they were punks, and they acted tough but they were no match for a Marine hand to hand. He said the country was going to hell, and it was going there on the back of a Harley Davidson driven by some punk who thought he was James Dean. But I don't think Griner's like that. At least I didn't until he spied on us at the river and stole my Aunt Delia's necklace.

I liked the way he showed me things under the grease rack. How the pump fills the tank with air to lift the rack. How to take out the old oil and put the filter on. Maybe I'll work on cars someday. I like the way Griner reads books in front of people and doesn't care what they think about it. The doctor's wife gives my Aunt Delia books, and she hides them in the top of her closet in a hat box with her picture albums because Grandma Hollister would be scandalized if she saw them. I think they must be books about men and women. I think my Aunt Delia and Griner are more alike than her and Bick, even though Griner's poor, and Bick's rich and his family name is written with ours on the pedestal of the Confederate monument down at the park.

"Which one, Travis?"

My Aunt Delia shows me impatient eyes. She wants me to tell her what a boy would do. A boy like Griner.

I say, "I don't know. I wish he put it there for you to take."

My Aunt Delia's mouth twists like she just bit into a sour apple. She says, "Wish in one hand and poop in the other and see which piles up faster."

It's funny, and any other time I'd laugh.

She says, "Do you think anybody saw me take it?"

I say, "Naw." I'm pretty sure, too. Nobody passed by on the street. The two ladies who left Tolbert's turned the other way. Beulah and Caroline were behind me coming out the door. Neither of them has the self-control to see something and not talk about it.

I say, "What are you gonna do now?"

She says, "I'm not gonna do anything, Killer. I'm gonna wait and see what he does."

I say, "Griner doesn't talk to anybody you know." But I'm hoping again, and her hard eyes say she knows it.

She shakes her head. "Word gets around. Somebody talks to somebody, and he talks to somebody else. Pretty soon the highest is hearing from the lowest through the people in the middle. It happens by little steps."

"What does he *want*?" I ask.

We look at each other, and I wish I hadn't said it. We both know what he wants. He wants my Aunt Delia. I remember Griner spying over the book in his hands, watching her dance with Bick. I remember the eyes of a hungry man standing in the rain. It didn't look like a mean hunger, but what do I know about that? I'm not a man yet, and I've only been hungry for a little while.

And I wish I hadn't asked the question. I look at my Aunt Delia, and she leans to the cool air coming through the window screen, and she lifts the black hair from her long white neck. Her hand trembles, and I know we're scared but we're not gonna show it. It's like we've been told we're sick. We have to live with this and it's gonna take a long time to get well.

Lightning strikes close, and I wake up. I'm sweating, even in the cool wind that blows in with the rain. When my head clears of dreams of home, I know there's a storm. It's another black howler boiling up out of the Gulf of Mexico sixty miles south. Marvadell told me they'll come all summer, but some summers are worse. She said, "The Lord be punishing his servant's iniquity. He be sendin' the high wind and the hard water and fire from the sky to knock down the bad man's house. The house built on the soft sand."

I asked her if she meant our house. Grandpa Hollister's house. She just looked at me and smiled and started singing one of her over Jordan songs, "Deep River."

I get up and close the windows so the rain won't come in and then lie down again in the still, close air. I could go to my Aunt Delia's room. She might be crying. I know she might need me, but I'm scared. I'm not scared of the storm. I'm scared of what we might do now. I'm scared, but I want to know what the next thing is, the next thing we might do. It's that way with knowing. You can't stop once you start, and I guess you start the second your eyes open in your mom's arms in a hospital bed. Maybe you start before that, lying under her heart in the cradle of her bone, in the warm bath of her blood. The preachers don't say it, and no book I've read yet tells me, but I know curiosity is heaven and hell.

I lie in the dark with the storm blowing and shoving the trees around outside, and I can't decide. I can't make myself get up and go. Then I hear a soft sound, and I turn and see the white shape of my Aunt Delia's nightgown at my bedroom door. She stops there and watches my bed. I could pretend I'm asleep, but I don't. I move over to the window. I throw back the covers for her. She crosses to me, moving the still air and bringing me the smell of her hair and her skin. She lies down beside me with her back to the door, and I turn to the window, and she pulls me to her chest. She reaches around me and puts her hand on my arm. We lie that way for a while, and then I reach back and feel the tears on her cheeks.

She kisses my fingers and moves her face down to my ear, and I turn my head to her mouth. She whispers, "Listen, and I'll tell the rest of it."

Her voice is breaking a little, and I can tell she's pulling the words up from a long way deep, from the deepest secret place. I press my ear against her mouth. I whisper, "Okay."

She whispers, "Because I have to tell somebody, and it has to be somebody I trust, somebody who knows me, and now you're the only one." She stops, and her breathing goes quick and ragged, and she whispers, "But you don't have to, Killer. You don't have to listen. I'll go if you want me to."

I move my ear against her mouth. I whisper, "I want to."

So we lie that way, our heads together, her mouth to my ear, and she tells me.

"Remember what Quig Knowles said about me and Morgan Conway?"

I nod. Her whisper makes the hair behind my ear buzz, and the gold cross around her neck pricks me. When I nod, she squeezes my arm with her hand.

She says, "And I told you Susannah Cohen helped me?"

I nod. The storm outside is rising. The lightning is coming closer. When it hits earth, the sudden light shows me the window and the trees lashing and heaving.

My Aunt Delia says, "And I told you something happened, and I couldn't ever write or talk to Morgan again?"

I nod.

She says, "Remember what we said about secrets?"

I remember. *When you tell someone a secret, you earn a promise from them. Secrets are worth something.* I nod again. I don't want to talk. I just want to lie here and listen in the warm of her body with this window between us and the storm.

She says, "I never felt anything like it before, Killer. I've read about drug addicts and how they crave the drug or they'll die. That's the way I felt about Morgan, and that's the way he said he felt about me. We met one night when a bunch of us girls snuck out, and some boys did, too. They were all senate pages. One of the boys had some whiskey, and we passed it around, and I ended up in the corner of a cloak room with Morgan. It was dark, and there was a lot of whispering and giggling, and then it got quiet, and we knew what the people around us were doing, and then he kissed me. From the first taste of his mouth, I knew I had to have him. I had to have him always."

She pulls her mouth back from my ear and buries her face in the back of my neck, and the gold cross sticks me hard. Lightning touches earth somewhere out on the edge of town near the river, and across the street a limb breaks and I hear it fall with a crack and a thump. Rain runs hard in the gutters along the roof like the blood of this old house, pumping hard as it fights the storm.

My Aunt Delia trembles and puts her mouth back to my ear and says, "After that, we snuck out alone, just the two of us. We had to find places, and it wasn't easy. We spent a night in a trailer full of old newspapers that had been collected for a paper mill. We spent a night in a senator's office after Morgan crawled in through the transom and unlocked the door for me. And we didn't just kiss, Killer. We did the things men and women do, and finally, we did what I showed you in the river."

I nod. I think of my Aunt Delia and me in the river. What she showed me and how it felt, and how it feels now to know. I can't help hating that she learned it first with him. I want to turn and say I hate it, but I know I can't. It happened before she knew me. I'd erase him from her mind if I could, but you can't do that. Part of knowing is knowing that, and it's part of hell, not heaven.

She says, "We were only together two weeks, but it was our story, and it had to have the right ending, and we both knew it, and the ending came one night in the senator's office when we did what I showed you in the river. We made love, and it was my first time and his, too, and I loved him more than anything in the world that night, and the next day we had to say good-bye.

"We'd planned to meet, but at the last minute Morgan learned his parents were in town. It was a surprise for him. They'd come to take him home with them on the train. He couldn't get a message to me about leaving early, so I went to the place where we'd agreed to meet and say good-bye, and I waited, and he didn't come. At the last minute, he'd left a note for me with another boy. The note said he'd write, and it gave his address.

"I came home to Widow Rock, and we wrote to each other for a while. We wrote promises and told secrets, and planned to meet again, and then the thing happened." My Aunt Delia squeezes my arm tight and digs her nails into me so hard I think I'll bleed. She presses her mouth hard to my ear and says, "I learned I had a baby inside me. Morgan and me had made a baby.

"I wrote to him and told him. I asked him to tell me what to do. I don't know what I wanted, but I wanted him to do something. More than anything, I wanted him to say he loved me. I kept writing, but I never heard from him again. I didn't know what to do then, and that's when Susannah helped me.

"I don't know why we talked the first time. I didn't really know her. We'd passed on the street and said hey and talked about how hot it was and when fall would finally come. But one day I was in Tolbert's, and she was, too, and we both had books with us. I was reading something dumb by Frances Keyes, and she saw it and came over to my booth and sat down, and we talked about reading for a while, and then she got this really impatient look on her face and said, 'Delia, by all accounts you're an intelligent girl. Why don't you read something a little more serious?' And she showed me her book. It was a novel by Edna Ferber. I took it from her and read a few lines, just wherever the book fell open. And I could see it was different from anything I'd read before. And then I looked up at her, and I just started crying. I didn't know why. I still don't know exactly why. I must have seen something in her eyes. Maybe I saw that she wasn't from here. That she just wasn't from Widow Rock, and she'd understand I was a stranger, too.

"When she saw me crying, she got this very severe look on her face and stood up. I thought she was angry with me. I thought she was about to leave. But she said, 'Come on, Delia. Take a walk with me. We have to talk.'

"I told her everything, Killer. All about Morgan and the baby and when I finished, the first thing she said to me was, 'Well, you've got to stop writing him. That's the first thing you've got to do. It's clear he doesn't care, and the more you write, the more you put yourself in his hands.'

"I didn't know what she meant. I still wasn't sure until Quig Knowles came to town. Even after Morgan cut himself off from me, I didn't believe he'd talk about me.

"Susannah told me there were just two things I could do, and that she could help me with only one of them. The first was tell my parents and let them do with me and the baby what they wanted to do. The other was go with her to a friend in Jacksonville. She said this friend could take care of me.

"I didn't think about it very much then. I was so confused. I agreed to go with her. One Saturday afternoon, I told Mama and Daddy I was going to Panama City, and I drove out of town and met Susannah, and we hid my car and drove to Jacksonville in hers. All the way we talked about books and reading, and she told me about a woman named Margaret Sanger who was a pioneer in women's rights. She said Margaret Sanger was a saint to modern women. I listened, but I don't know how much I heard. It was more important to me then that I was with Susannah and that she liked me and believed I could do what I wanted, not what my parents wanted me to do.

"In Jacksonville, she took me to the home of her friend. He was a doctor who had known her husband in medical school. I can't tell you his name because he never told me. He talked to me for a while, then he left me alone and talked to Susannah. I sat with a door between me and them and listened to them raise their voices. I don't know what they argued about. I thought about what the doctor had told me. There were risks. They were not all physical. I would worry about what we were going to do. It would plague my mind. He asked me several times if I was sure. All I could think then was that I had to get Morgan Conway out of me. I had to lose the part of me that was him, that had trusted him. And I could never tell my parents. They'd never understand. They'd think it was about them, not about me. They'd think about Widow Rock and what I had done to their place.

"So I said yes, and the man took me to his office. It was empty, and we went in the back way. He did things to me while Susannah held my hand. He gave me a drug to take my mind away, and I didn't think of anything until I was halfway back to Widow Rock and the pain started. Susannah gave me some pills she'd taken from the store-room at her husband's office, and told me what would happen next, and how I'd feel, and told me what was normal and what was not. And I got in my car where we had hidden it, and I drove the rest of the way back to Widow Rock and told my parents I'd had a fine time in Panama City. I told them the water was lovely, and the gulls were gray and white with pink beaks, and they swung on the wind, and dove down and took french fries from my hand while I walked on the beach. Then I went up to my room and slept for two days.

"When Mama came to my room worried, I told her I was just very tired. When the sheets were stained, I washed them in the bathroom sink and dried them with a towel. And I got better, and nobody ever knew..."

Behind me, she shudders. She squeezes my arm hard again, and digs her nails in. Her voice comes back smaller, colder, and it sounds strange like a voice from a radio playing in another room. "...But, Killer, when it storms, I can't help it. I'm afraid. I cry for someone lost.

"I asked Susannah about it the day we went to see her. The day she sent you to the kitchen for cookies. She told me there was a storm while I was lying on the doctor's table in Jacksonville. She said it was violent, and water flew straight against the windows, and the lights went out for a few minutes, and the doctor couldn't use his instruments. She said I didn't notice it. I was asleep and smiling through the whole thing. She didn't see how I could know there was a storm."

She pulls her lips back from my ear, and I can feel her breathing change, and I know that a cold, tired spirit has come out of her, and I know it's the spirit of her trouble. I know she'll be better, because now the spirit is mine, too. She's told me, and she's better now. But I have to ask one more question.

I say, "It's Morgan Conway you cry for? He's the one lost?"

She says, "No, Killer, it's not him. When the storms come, I cry for my baby. I know he's out there somewhere on the storm. He's flying the wind and fighting the rain, and he's trying to get back to me, and he can't find the way, and I can't find the words to call him home to me."

"It's only a dream," I say, and I feel her sigh against my neck. It's a stupid thing I said, but I don't know how to help. The storm is climbing the highest place. The wind screams like mad dogs, and the rain pounds the window like fists that rattle the panes in their moldings. I look out at the black, the wet, the confusion of the trees, and I wish I knew the secret words to call a baby home.

And I remember what my mother said when she knew I would fly south to my father's family. "You'll fly on the wind like the spirits of my ancestors." I wonder if my mother's pain comes because she can't call her people home to rest. Because they're lost out there on the wind. I can't think of the words to bring my Aunt Delia's baby home, so I reach back and put my hand on her face, and I draw her tears down her cheeks and hold them in my hand.

thirty

The next day it's hot, and the ground steams from the rain, and the sun burns water from the street in shimmering waves. My Aunt Delia sleeps late. I go to her room and look at her. She's lying with her face to the window, and her arm over her eyes. The radio is playing soft the way she likes it late at night.

I go downstairs for breakfast. Grandma and Grandpa Hollister are already eating. They look angry. Marvadell brings my eggs, and she looks angry, too. Grandpa tells me he's tired of me coming down late for breakfast. Why can't I get up on time and not put the household into such an uproar? He says I'm starting to act just like Delia, like a teenager. Grandma puts her fork down hard and tells him not to be so harsh with me. I'm just a boy, she says, and I deserve a little rest and some fun in the summer. I'll be leaving soon. I'll be going back to school. Marvadell lets the kitchen door swing shut, and we hear, "Humph!"

Grandpa wipes his mouth with his napkin. He looks at me and then mops his forehead with it, too. I know Grandma doesn't like that. She thinks he's crude and not as good as the men in her family. I know he thinks the men in her family are all drunkards and wasters even if they went to Vanderbilt University. Grandpa Hollister's eyes tell me he's thinking about me leaving soon. He throws his napkin in his plate and goes to the hall secretary. He unlocks it, takes out his sheriff things, and leaves by the front door.

Grandma comes around and stands behind me. She puts her hands on my shoulders and leans down and says, "I'm sorry, Travis. We shouldn't have scenes at breakfast. It gets the day off to a sad start. It's the heat. And we've had so many storms this summer. Don't worry about it."

All I can say is, "Yes, ma'am. I won't worry."

But the day is already started wrong. Outside, the steam rising from the ground makes me feel like I'm swimming in hot water. I go to the backyard and shoo the birds and eat some grapes. They're sweet and ripe. Eddie, Marvadell's son, comes out of the woods at the back of our lot. He sees me and stops his strutting walk. He stands there watching me in his purple pants and pointy black shoes. He smiles and puts his hand in his pocket, feeling his push-button knife.

I go to the front yard to leave him room to visit Marvadell and get her money. After I hear the backdoor bang shut, I go to the side of the house and look up at my Aunt Delia's open window. I can hear the radio playing faint, and I know she's still asleep. I walk down to the park and look at what the rain did to the tennis court. The clay is washed all the way out into the grass near the Confederate monument. The white chalk lines are gone. The net is wet and steaming like everything else.

Some green shingles are missing from the roof of the Presbyterian Church across the street. The whole town looks tired and beaten down. Times like this I wish there were kids around so I could make friends. But I know it's too late for that. Even if there were kids, I'm leaving too soon to get to know them. And I'm my Aunt Delia's best friend now, and that's taking up most of my time.

I walk back to our house looking at the sky. A strange, gray-yellow light glows from behind the clouds. My dad says it's the light you see before a tornado comes. But that was in Omaha. I don't know what that light means here in Widow Rock. People are staying indoors, away from the steamy heat. As far as I can see, there are no cars and no people. I wonder if it's gonna rain again.

When I walk into our driveway, I see a cigarette butt over by my Aunt Delia's car. I go over and look at it. It's wet but not falling apart. Somebody dropped it last night after the rain stopped. I don't know when it stopped, but I know it was late, late at night. I look into my Aunt Delia's white Chevy, and there's something lying on the seat. My heart starts to rattle even before my eyes are sure what it is. I open the car door a few inches and look back at the house. Nobody. I open the door all the way. It's a small white envelope. I don't know why it scares me so much.

I try to tell myself it's my Aunt Delia's. She left it there. But she hasn't been in her car since we got out of it together yesterday. Someone put the envelope there last night while my Aunt Delia and me were sleeping in my bed. Someone who smokes. I know it's trouble, and I know I have to take it to her.

My Aunt Delia doesn't wake up easy mornings after it storms. I go to her bedside and lay my hand gently on her hair. I stroke her black hair, and she sighs, and it's almost like a cat purring, and then her eyes come open, and I like it that she meets me with a smile. But then her mouth pinches, and her eyes go hard, and she says, "Something's wrong."

She sits up fast, and my hand falls from her hair, and I show her the envelope. "I found it in your car. Somebody must've put it in there last night."

She blinks and takes the envelope and holds it to her chest, but she doesn't open it. She rubs some sleep from her eyes with her free hand and pulls her legs up under her. She looks at me hard and says, "Tell me again where you found it."

I tell her. She puts the envelope down on the bed and her eyes are bright awake. She looks like she did the day she drove the boat down the river, like she's looking off into the distance for what might come around the bend. "All right," she says, "open it."

I do. There's a piece of notebook paper inside, the kind kids use in school. The words are written in pencil. It's a boy's handwriting. The note says,

> Delia,
> Meet me tonight behind the gas station, 9:00. I'll be waiting in my car. Don't bring the little boy you like so much. Come or the whole town will know how you like to swim.

There's no name at the bottom.

"It's him," my Aunt Delia says.

"Yeah." My mouth is dry. I can see her trying to swallow and the next word sticking in her throat.

"What do you think he wants?"

She gives me a look I've never seen from her before. It's the look a dog gives you after you kick it. It's the look Marvadell had on her face when Eddie walked into her kitchen and took the money from her purse. I look away at the window.

She says, "What do you *think* he wants?" Her voice is so low I can hardly hear it. It's like she's talking to herself. "He wants *me*. He wants me to...do it with him. If I do, then he'll keep his filthy mouth shut."

We talk about it for an hour, until we have to go down

for lunch. We talk until Marvadell comes to the bottom of the stairs and hollers up, "You chirrins come on down here an' eat! Don't make me wait fo you!"

I ask her what she's going to do, and she says she doesn't know. I don't want her to go. I don't say it yet, but she knows I don't, and she knows why, I guess. I keep trying to think about what's best for her and not for me. I keep asking her what she's going to do, but she keeps talking about him.

"I just didn't think he was like that," she says. She looks at me like I can tell her what he's like. Because I'm a guy.

She says, "Under all that tough guy, greaser attitude, I thought he was good. I thought he was just somebody people didn't understand."

I want to say I know how he could want her so much. Enough to make him do this thing. How he could get so confused wanting her, he'd hurt her to get what he wants. But I can't tell her that.

I say, "Well he's not who you thought he was." I pick up the note from the bedspread where it lies between our knees. I say, "*Here's* who he is."

She turns to the window and looks at the trees. Even when it's hot and still, they move. If you really listen, you hear it. The branches and the leaves fidget and fuss and rub together because they're still growing. For a while, we listen to the oak tree talk.

Finally, she says, "I have to go. Maybe I can talk to him. Make him see what he's doing."

"You can't go." Now I've said it, what she knew I'd say. She looks at me. Her love for me is in her eyes, but it's there only a second. I see it change to pity, then to anger. She says, "Killer, you just don't know how it is for me. You don't know what my life will be like here if he tells about me and you."

"What if you go with him, and he tells about that, too?"

Her eyes tell me she's thought about it. She says, "I'll just have to take that chance."

Then she says the thing I hate. "If he likes me enough, maybe he'll do what I want." She looks straight into my eyes, and her voice goes low and sweet as she says it, and I know she's not just talking to me. She's practicing for him.

I can see she wants to stop talking now. I say it quick. "I'll go with you. Let me go with you. If I go, maybe he won't..."

She smiles slow and sorry. "I can't do that, Killer. You know it wouldn't work." She goes over to the vanity and sits down and looks at herself in the mirror. She turns up the radio a little, and it's Jerry Lee singing, "Breathless." She says to the mirror, "But I can't do it without your help. You've got to help me tonight, Killer."

That's when I think the awful thing. Maybe she wants to go with him. Maybe a part of her wants to go. I love her. I'm her only friend. She held me in the river. She let me touch her. She showed me what love is. I have to say yes. I have to say I'll help. "Okay," I say, and Marvadell calls up from the foot of the stairs, "You chirrins come on down here an' eat!"

The rest of the day goes by like the week before Christmas. I keep watching the clock and trying to think of something new to say, something so she won't go, but my Aunt Delia's eyes are shut to me. They say she's made up her mind. She's looking at the far away now, past tonight. She's trying to see how things will be for her after she meets him tonight.

All day the thing is big inside my chest. It's the true

thing I have for my Aunt Delia. We listen to the radio in her room. We don't talk much, but the radio talks to me about love. Birmingham and Tallahassee play the songs that say they understand who I am and how I feel.

At eight-thirty, we walk downstairs like we planned. We stop in the living room where Grandpa Hollister sits with his newspaper like a curtain across his face, and Grandma Hollister watches Ed Sullivan. We look at *Life* for a while like we always do, and then my Aunt Delia stretches and yawns and says, "I'm bored. Travis, let's you and me drive over to Warrington for Cokes." She always says it this way. Then she waits to see what they say. It's her way of asking without asking. We wait. Grandpa Hollister rattles his paper and clears his throat, and Grandma Hollister laughs at some Hungarian unicyclists balancing dinner plates from broom handles on their chins. We walk slowly to the front door. When my Aunt Delia opens it, Grandma Hollister calls, "You two be careful and come home at a reasonable hour."

My Aunt Delia calls over her shoulder, "All right, Mama."

We have a plan.

My Aunt Delia drives the white Chevy to the place behind Dr. Cohen's house and parks it. She leaves the keys in the ignition so the radio can play for me. She says, "You'll be all right here, Killer. If anybody comes, just turn off the radio and hunker down in the seat. I'll get back here no later than eleven."

She gets out and stands in the moonlight outside the window. She leans in, and her hair falls around her face, and I smell the shampoo and perfume I like so much. The moon behind her makes a glow around her face, a halo, and I think: Night Angel. The halo makes it hard to see her eyes. Her skin is white, and she's wearing the dark red lipstick she only puts on after we leave the house. Her white blouse has a Peter Pan collar and no sleeves. She's wearing her faded jeans and her white tenny pumps. She looks prettier to me than she's ever looked before.

I can't help it. I say, "Please let me go with you." I lean close and smell her hair.

She shakes her head, and I'm glad I can't see her eyes. She says, "What would you do with me tonight, Killer? Think about it. What would you do?"

I want to ask again, but I don't. I want to say please again, but I don't.

She reaches in and puts her hand on my cheek, and her fingers burn my face with the names of our secrets. She strokes me and leans in and gives me a kiss. She says, "Thanks for covering for me, Killer. You're a great guy." Then she's gone, and I'm sitting with the taste of her lips on mine and the radio playing, "Save the Last Dance for Me."

thirty-one

I think of her walking to meet him. It's only three blocks down and one block over. I think of him sitting there in the alley behind the grease rack in his street rod with the midnight-blue paint and red flames coming from the engine. Lakes Pipes and the moon discs gleaming in the moonlight. I see him in his leather jacket, and his white T-shirt and the ducktail haircut and the scar above his eye. I wonder if he's doing this to her because Grandpa Hollister hit him. I wonder if it's his way of getting revenge.

I think of him taking out the silver Zippo lighter as he sits there waiting for my Aunt Delia. I see him light the cigarette and throw his head back and draw a big chestful of smoke and blow it out into the still night air.

And then it comes to me.

The cigarette on the driveway this morning had a filter. Kenny Griner smokes unfiltered Camels. I lean forward and turn the key, and the starter whines, and the white Chevy comes to life around me. I reach down and pull the lever that moves the seat forward and strain my legs down to the pedals. I turn on the lights and put the Chevy in reverse and back out of our hiding place behind Dr. Cohen's house. I'm driving slow on the empty streets, past the parked cars and the houses with open windows and flickering screens where Ed Sullivan is saying goodnight to America.

I keep the speed down to twenty. Three blocks down and one block over.

I turn into the alley behind Mr. Dameron's ESSO station, and all I see is the shut door at the back of the grease rack and moonlight on a stack of empty oil cans. I sit there with the engine idling and the radio telling me, "No muscle-bound man can take my hand from my guy. There's not a man today who can take me away from my guy." I don't know what to do. I don't know where they are. I try to think, but my mind is whirring like the big Westinghouse mixer Marvadell uses to make frosting, and the things in the mixer are pictures of my Aunt Delia with Griner. I rub my eyes with the heel of my hand, and my mind goes still, and I try to get a message from my Aunt Delia about where she is. But nothing comes. I hit the steering wheel with my fists, and then the radio says, "Under the boardwalk, down by the sea. On a blanket with my baby, is where I'll be." And I get it. There's only one place they could go.

I know I can't go the way they went. I have to go the other way, the way me and my Aunt Delia went when she took me swimming. I've never driven at night, and it's scary. The headlights bore down the county hardroad, and the broken white line rushes at me, and the wind pours through my window with all the wild smells of the country night. The white faces of cows are sudden and then gone as my lights sweep the fields, and I hope there won't be any people. Everybody in this county knows my Aunt Delia's white Chevy, and all the kids are out driving at night, going to see who's there.

I cross the bridge and take the narrow hardroad that runs with the river a few miles, then I turn again on the two-rut track with the weeds growing up tall between my wheels and lashing underneath the Chevy. Night bugs zip through my lights like tracer bullets I've seen in war movies, and a red fox runs ahead of me for twenty yards, then stops to watch me pass. I find the place where me and my Aunt Delia parked. I kill the Chevy's engine and leave the keys in the switch. I run to the river. Standing on the bank with my shoes sinking into the wet sand, I see the white clot of drift-wood downstream in the moonlight. I take off my shoes and socks and wade out and look back upstream at Widow Rock. It's white and dreamy in the moonlight, and I can see some-thing, something up there. I stare hard at it. I try to make my eyes reach long and bore through the dark, and maybe I see something move. I can't tell. It's too far and too high. I know what I have to do now. All the way out here in the car, driving with my hands claw-tight on the steering wheel, I've been thinking about it.

I take off the rest of my clothes and pile them on top of my shoes and step into the river to my waist. It's colder than in the daytime, and the sand slips away downstream as my feet sink in, and I can feel the riverbed sloping out to the deep water. The river pulls at me. It wants to take me downstream, all the way down to the Johnny Barnes Fish Camp where me and my Aunt Delia rented the boat. It wants to take me all the way to the Gulf of Mexico. I lean down and push off and swim hard in the cold. I swim as hard as I can to get warm and to reach the far bank without landing too far downstream.

It's a long, cold swim, and out in the middle of the river, my mind tells me there's no other side. It whispers to me as I churn and kick and open my eyes to the dark sky when I breathe. It says I'll just swim on forever, and then my arms and legs will seize, and my breath won't come anymore. It whispers I'll sink, and no one will ever know what happened to me. My arms and legs get thick and slow, and my stom-ach goes sick, and my mind mixes pictures of Griner and my

Aunt Delia naked together up on Widow Rock, and then I see my body blue and scraped and limp washing up on a beach somewhere along the coast where the river ends.

I know it's panic. I know I can't give in to it. There is no river without two banks. I keep swimming, pulling my head up every two strokes and sucking in cold, river-smelling air, and my mind goes dark, and I'm only legs and arms beating water, and finally trees lean out over me with moonlight silver on their leaves, and my fingers claw sand, and I lie full flat naked, retching for air on the river bank.

When my breath comes back, and my legs warm, and the cramp in my stomach eases, I walk back upriver, looking across for the white driftwood clot. I walk maybe a hundred yards, picking my way along in the shallows careful of the rocks and the claw hands of tree roots reaching out from the bank. I see the driftwood clot like bleached and tangled bone across the river. In the moonlight, it looks like the skeleton of some huge beast that died and rotted huddled there against the bank. It tells me where I am.

There's a way up somewhere. I know it because Griner came down this way the first time my Aunt Delia took me to Widow Rock. After he drank whiskey and gave my Aunt Delia some, and me a sniff, and we heard Bick and Ronny and Quig Knowles and Beulah and Caroline calling from below to my Aunt Delia, Griner stepped into the trees heading downstream. My Aunt Delia said, "Careful, Kenny. It's slippery that way."

I know I'm only a hundred yards downstream from the rock, and I know there's a way up.

I turn into the woods feeling with my hands. I'm a naked boy in the woods at night, and the vines and branches claw and catch at me. I stumble and cover my eyes and my parts and keep pushing ahead looking for the path. Fifty yards into the woods I stop and grind my teeth in rage and stop my mouth from howling in it, too. I turn back toward the river, going upstream. I promise myself I'll find it. It has to be here. I'll step out into a clearing and see the path snaking into the trees, rising with the land up to the bluff. It has to be here.

I'm about halfway back to the river when I fall and cover my eyes and slide on my butt down a bare clay ditch-bank into a culvert of roots and rocks. My feet stop me hard at the bottom, and I know they're cut. I get to my hands and knees and look up. A silver line of moonlight falls through the trees. I've found it.

From here on, I have to be quiet. I go up on all fours. I'm an animal now, climbing four-legged, nose to the ground, smelling my way up the rocky, rooty track to the top of Widow Rock. My breathing is hard and fast but silent, my bleeding feet make no sound as they find their holds on the soft clay, the rock, the bark. I see where the trees open at the top. I see the moonlight bright, glancing from white limestone. I slow and creep. At the top, at the tree door, I rise to my feet and become a human boy again, but a mad boy, and resolute. Yes, that's it: resolute.

I see them lying out on the rock, their bodies glowing in the white moonlight. They've made a bed of their clothes. He's on top of her and moving. I can see the muscles of his arms taut and wet with sweat as he holds himself up over her, his head hanging and buried in her hair. I can see her throat white and her head thrown back. I can see her knees rise and her heels dig into the rock, and his legs taut and straight as his feet push behind her heels. I can hear him breathing hard and ragged, and worst of all I hear her moan. I wish it were the moan of her sorrow, her abuse, her cry for someone lost, but it's the moan of her pleasure, and though I've never heard the sound before, I know its name.

My rage comes white hot and as loud in my head as the storms outside my window at night. I walk out onto the rock on feet that have grown fur and claws. I feel the cool wind on my naked skin. I stand there with my fists knotted at my sides. My feet grip stone still hot from the sun. I wait, the last of my boy giving way to the wild thing that swam the river and climbed the bluff, and then I howl rage to the moon. I scream the name of wild, outrageous insult to the moon, and then I run.

Ten strides to go, but they're ten miles. It's a year, and it's over in an eyeblink. As I near, I see him crouch between her legs and see him rise. I see him shove his hands out to defend. I see her push back from under him, crabbing back with the shape of her moan still on her lips. I don't look at his face, I look at my target. It's his bare middle, white and muscled in the moonlight. That's where I hit him, and I hear the breath go out of his body, and the hitting takes my breath, too. I'm lying face down on the rock, my eyes banged shut. I open them, and he's doing his tightrope walk out on the edge, and it's not until I hear my Aunt Delia scream, "Bick! No!" that I look at his face.

He doesn't speak as he goes over. He doesn't cry out, and his eyes say only that he's trying hard to stay with us. I close my eyes and see the Widow's black veil spreading out into all that nothing. I see the wings of a big dying bird in its last clumsy mating with earth. I don't hear him hit. I don't know if he splashes or lands blunt. I push over onto my back and look up at stars and moon. I feel the cool wind from the river on my hot skin, and I know I'm not sorry.

thirty-two

Everything is quiet. My mind holds no pictures. I'm only the animal boy with bleeding feet and cool, windy skin, and I know for the first time the still, empty feeling of a thing finally and completely done. I want this moment to last forever, but I know it won't. Nothing does.

I roll and look at Delia. She's standing now, looking out at the edge. She holds her face in her hands, and she tries to get her breath. She starts toward the edge, and her eyes, dead in the moonlight, call me back to the world I left for the wild. I get up and stand in her way. She tries to shoulder around me, and I wrap my arms around her naked waist. She tries harder, and I push her back. "No," I say, "don't look. It's too far down. It's too dark to see." But it's not her looking I'm worried about. I remember when she told me, "I don't come up here alone anymore." I didn't know what she meant then, but I know now.

She fights me hard. She kicks and hits at me, but I move her back. I push her to the rock where we sat the first day, and I sit her down. "Listen," I say, but she shakes her head and covers her ears. She moans. I say it again, "Listen, we've got to get out of here. Somebody might come."

She looks at me for the first time. Her eyes are blurry, and her face is slack like it is when she sleeps. She whispers, "Nobody comes up here at night. The path's too hard at night. That's how we knew we'd be safe."

She's not making sense, but I want her to talk. Anything but the moan. Screaming his name again. Better the blurry eyes and the sleeping face. I say, "We've got to get out of here right now. Put your clothes on." I tug at her hands to pull her up, but she won't move. She looks at me again, and her eyes go sharp and hot. She says, "Travis, why did you do it? Why?"

"He was hurting you."

I know it's true, and I know it's not. And I know most things are that way now. I know what I have to live with.

She shakes her head. "I never thought...I never thought you'd do it."

I look at her. My eyes say there's nothing I wouldn't do for her. The thing in my chest is big now, an unbearable weight I know I'll always carry. The night is a big radio, and the songs are all playing in my head, and they all say you do anything for the one you love. My eyes try to say all this, but it's dark, and the moon's at my back, and I don't know what she can see. I say, "I'd do anything for you, Delia. You know that."

I pull her hands again, and she gets up, and her shoulders fall like she's run a long race and she's tired. She stands in front of me, and I take her hand and lead her over to her clothes. They're all mixed with Bick's, and I can smell him and her on them as I kneel and pick up her bra and underpants, her jeans, blouse, and socks. Her tenny pumps are under Bick's shirt with his penny loafers. Their shoes were her pillow.

I stand up with her clothes in my hands and turn to her. I say, "Go over there and get dressed." I point to the seat in the rock.

My mind is telling me now about the things I didn't plan. She can't swim the river in her clothes. Should I turn and tell her not to get dressed? That I'll carry her clothes down with me? I'll swim across the river with them held high in one hand? I can't swim the river with her clothes and keep them dry. I barely made it fanning with both arms. She'll have to get dressed and go down and wait for me by Bick's car. We'll just have to hope no one comes.

I turn, and she's standing by the rock seat with her clothes bundled in her hands. She's so pretty even now. Looking at her stops my planning mind and makes the thing in my chest too big to hold. I drag a big breath and stagger drunk and wait 'til the hum in my heart for her stops, and I say, "Delia, go ahead and put them on. Do you want me to help you?"

Her eyes snap to me sudden and cold. "No," she says. "I don't need your help. I don't need you anymore."

I know why she's saying it. I know it's not true. I watch until she leans to fit her chests into her bra, and then I turn back to the bed of Bick's clothes. I think: *What did Bick do? What did he do here in the middle of the night? Alone.*

I hear a scrape of shoe and feel a rush of air, and Delia passes me running for the edge. I think she'll go over, but she stops, and I hear her fingernails scratch rock as she claws Bick's clothes up into her arms. She raises them above her head to throw them after him, but I'm there behind her. I seize her arms and twist the clothes from her hands and drop them where they were. She turns and stares at me with crazy eyes, and I say, "Listen to me. He was *alone*. Don't you see? He was here alone."

Her eyes close, open. "Alone," she says.

I push her away, back toward the rock seat.

I turn to the edge again and think, *What did Bick do? What did he do here alone in the middle of the night?*

Nothing comes to me. All I know is Delia wasn't here. I kneel and gather Bick's clothes, and I start to fold them. I don't know why, but I do. I fold the shirt that smells of sweat and aftershave and Delia's secret skin. I fold the pants, the socks, and the underwear. I put the pile of clothes on top of the shoes. I look at them. There's something wrong.

I move the underwear to the bottom of the pile. That's how he'd do it. I stand and look at the clothes, at the edge, the dark well of night out there over the river, and I think about what Bick Sifford did here by himself.

After a while, I'm Bick, and I'm doing what he did. He came because it's beautiful up here at night. It's cool, and even though this town is in a lonely country, there aren't so many good places to be alone. And so Bick came here, and he thought about being a boy again, and he thought about the way it feels to be naked in the wild night under the moon, and he took off his clothes and stood here feeling how good it is, and then he went out to the edge. He stood out there drunk with the wind and the cool and the stars high and bright, and he looked down into the well of nothing, and it called to him...and he slipped. He slipped and fell into the river.

That's it, and it will have to do.

I turn back to Delia. Dressed, she stands there looking at me. I tell her, "I put the car where we parked when we went skinny-dipping. I swam across. I have to go back and get the car. Can you get down the hill and wait for me by Bick's car?"

She just looks at me. For the first time, I get scared. What if she runs away? What if she wanders into the woods? What if she won't move and they find her here in the morning when they come looking for Bick? And the worst thing: What if she tells? I'm bigger than I was an hour ago, a lot bigger, but I can't fight her down this hill. I go and stand in front of her and take her hands. She tries to pull them away, but I hold them. I know I have to take her to her fear before she'll move. I say, "Delia, we've got to go right now. If someone finds us here, we'll go to jail. They'll put us in the electric chair."

I don't really know what the electric chair is, but I've heard about it. I've seen the men in movies walk down the long, dark hallway with the priest whispering beside them and the guards watching to see if they'll go like men or boys.

She looks at me, and her eyes open wide, and the fear pours into them. She says, "All right, Travis. I'll meet you down at Bick's car." She shivers and hugs herself, and with that hug, she's the old Delia again. The one who knows the secrets. She whispers, "But hurry. Promise me you'll hurry."

I nod. I'll never break a promise to Delia.

The river's not so bad this time. I don't fight the water. For every yard I make across, it takes me three yards downstream, but I don't worry. I let the river take me. I swim when I can and rest when I have to. The cold water feels good on my bleeding feet. When I find the bank, I walk back up in the shallows looking for the dead beast's white bones. When I see them, I know it's only twenty yards to my clothes. I don't dress. I can't explain wet clothes. The air will dry me. I run through the woods to the white Chevy. I stand beside it, all dry but my hair, and put on my clothes.

There's dew on Bick's car when I stop beside it. Delia steps out of the dew-dripping woods into my headlight beams. She gets in on the passenger side, but I get out and come around to her window. "Slide over," I say. "You've got to drive. Everything's got to look like normal."

She slides over and backs us up, and we pull out onto the red clay track that leads to the county hardroad and freedom. My heart is rattling like nuts and bolts in a coffee can because we've made it through the hard part now. A few more minutes and everything will be all right.

We come to the place where we turn onto the hardroad, and I whisper, "Stop. Turn off the lights." She stops. She looks at me, confused. I lunge across her lap and slam the light switch into the dash with the heel of my hand. Grandpa Hollister's white Buick Roadmaster stops at a cross-roads two hundred yards down to our right. He sits there, idling in the moonlight, and I can see the gray fog of his exhaust crawl under the car on the night wind and become solid in his headlight beams. He sits for a long time, and I know he's looking both ways up and down the road, look-ing for the trouble he always expects. I hope the hope of heaven and hell that the palmetto scrub along this cow track rises high enough to keep us hidden from him.

His exhaust pumps gray fog, and he turns right, away from us, and when his taillights are tiny red points in the night, Delia turns onto the hardroad.

At the decision place, Delia starts to turn toward home. I reach over and straighten the wheel. "No, we've got to go to Warrington. We've got to get Cokes and fries and sit there like we said we would. Everything has to be like we said."

She looks at me, and her eyes send me letters of misery and love, and she pushes the accelerator down, and we head for Warrington.

thirty-three

Some high school boys from Warrington find Bick Sifford's abandoned car. The next day when they read in the paper that Bick's father reported him missing, they tell their parents what they saw. Sheriff Hollister goes out to the foot of the bluff and examines the car. The keys are in the ignition. He drives the red Oldsmobile back to town and parks it, locked, in front of his office across from the barber shop.

The town knows all this. People walk past the red Oldsmobile and stop and stare. They talk about Bick's disappearance in Tolbert's, and they talk about it at the Baptist and the Presbyterian churches. They talk about it in the barber shop and at the Curl Up and Dye Beauty Parlor. People who never speak to each other stop and talk about it on the street. People who never even talk, talk about it.

Some say Bick was kidnapped for ransom. Some say he went lunatic on bad moonshine and ran away. These say he'll show up in a day or two awfully damned embarrassed and very glad to be leaving soon for Princeton.

Most say he's in the river. Some of these say he'll never be found. Others say the river only gives up its dead after three days, and that's when Bick will be found. His body will rise, they say. Bodies always do.

Some of the older men talk about other times and other drownings. How the bodies look, white and bloated and gnawed by snapping turtles and alligator gar, when they finally rise. They tell stories of men dragging the river with grappling hooks and divers going down to look for the drowned. Mothers cry and tell about sons lost in car crashes and in farm accidents and to any old scratch or bug in the days before the wonder drugs were invented. For the town, it's a time of inward sight and reconciliation. It's a fine time for the preachers.

The Baptists have altar call, and their preacher says it's time for a revival, a good-old-fashioned tent meeting with pitch-pine flares and gospel music and marathon preaching. He says it's time to bring back the old-time religion. He says the disappearance of the fine young son of the town's most prominent citizen is a sign. He doesn't read the sign, but the town knows it's not a good one.

At the Presbyterian church, the Reverend Laidlaw preaches love and loss and the tragedy of youth cut down in its prime. He preaches how brief and meaningless is this life compared to the majesty and beauty of the next. He closes with a reading from Isaiah, about the green grass of morning cut down by the hard blade of the midday sun, and there is no man or woman under the stifling arch of his sanctuary whose eye is dry.

Sheriff Hollister is a man of few words, but says he is pressing his investigation. He leads a group of volunteers to the foot of the bluff. They spread out in a long line and climb to Widow Rock looking for any sign of what happened that night. They find nothing. After that, the sheriff says he'll drag the river and canvas the entire county. Bick's father gives the box factory a holiday and organizes his own search. He and two hundred factory workers search the hills and bluffs and comb the woods on both sides of the river. At sunset, exhausted, they quit as planned and congregate at the foot of Widow Rock. Men bring forward spent shotgun shells, tatters of clothing, pieces of soaked illegible paper, and there is one ancient New York Yankees baseball cap. Mr. Sifford extends heartfelt thanks, promises bonuses, and sends his men home.

On the morning of the third day, it rains. It's a steady, soaking rain, and the town sees it, too, as a sign. On the afternoon of the third day, Mr. Sifford demands to have his son's car back. He wants it examined by experts from Tallahassee. Sheriff Hollister refuses. He says the car may be evidence in a crime, and it's his right to keep it until such time as he, and anyone else he chooses to ask, have properly examined it. The town knows all this, and the town isn't surprised.

At sundown on the third day, a man returns from fishing in a rented boat. The fisherman, a veteran of two wars the newspapers say, lives in Milton, downriver from Widow Rock. Walking the dock past rows of tethered boats to return his red gas can and oars to Mr. Johnny Barnes, the veteran notices something odd floating in the shallows, wedged between a piling and the bow of a boat. The body is naked, bloated, and white, and there is no recognizable face, though the funerary arts will provide one later. The veteran is shocked but does the right thing, helping Mr. Johnny Barnes pull the body out and wrap it in a tarpaulin. And so, Bick Sifford is found.

The town knows all this only hours after it happens. The town knows that the damage to Bick Sifford's handsome face, most likely from his fall from Widow Rock, is so ghastly that anything the snapping turtles and the alligator gar have done is not immediately apparent. Widow Rock has no mortuary, so the body is taken to the one in Warrington.

This is what is known: at eight-thirty on the last night of his life, Bick Sifford told his parents he was going for a drive with Ronny Bishop. Ronny Bishop said he didn't hear from Bick that night. They had no plans for a ride, though it would not have been unusual for Bick to drop by anyway. No one has come forward to say that he or she saw Bick Sifford between the times when he left home and when he was found in the river.

The town has a great many things to say about all of this. The moonshine theorists maintain that Bick was drunk when he fell from Widow Rock. Those who are for kidnapping say that desperate men waylaid Bick, then panicked and threw him from the rock before they fled the scene. When the talk comes to the fact of Bick Sifford's nakedness, voices are lowered. The people of Widow Rock do not ordinarily speak of such things. Who does? Such things may be the dark side of love, and though many must know them, their names are rarely spoken aloud.

But a naked body in the river forces Sheriff Hollister to speak. For the first time, he tells of finding Bick Sifford's clothes the same day he brought in the red Oldsmobile. He says he found them neatly folded there on the white limestone in the morning sunshine.

Me and Delia have things to talk about.

We've laid low.

The night Bick died, we had french fries and Cokes at the Dairy Queen in Warrington. Kids from around the county came and went while we were there. We smiled and waved and called out, "Hey, ya'll!" We listened to the radio, and Delia drummed her fingers on the steering wheel and didn't eat or drink and didn't look at me.

When we came in that night at ten-thirty, Grandpa Hollister was still out patrolling, but Grandma Hollister was in the living room asleep with her needlepoint in her lap.

She said, "What? What?" when we came tiptoeing through. She woke up, and we said, "Hey," and told her we had a good time. We were all asleep when Grandpa Hollister finally came home.

Since then, the hardest part has been listening to the town talk. We've had to be curious with everyone else, we've had to ask questions with them, and we've had to make our eyes big with surprise when things were revealed about Bick. Mostly we've stayed home, up in our rooms, me reading and Delia listening to the radio or reading one of the books the doctor's wife gave her. When Caroline or Beulah calls, Delia talks but says she doesn't want them to come over. She says she's upset about Bick. I don't think they're suspicious, but I'm worried about her. She isn't acting right.

I go into her room and check on her sometimes, and she just looks at me and looks away. Sometimes she smiles and nods, telling me everything's fine, but I can see in her eyes it's not. I don't know what she'll do. I'm afraid mostly for her, but some for me, too. I lie in bed with a book on my chest hoping Bick's death will pass like a storm in the night, leaving limbs down and shingles blown away, but Widow Rock mostly the same.

On the second day after Bick rises, I find Delia in her room staring at herself in the vanity mirror. It's not like before, a girl looking through a window at a girl she doesn't know, maybe doesn't like. She's a girl staring into nothing. I stand behind her with my hands on her shoulders. I touch her hair and say, "Please, Delia, talk to me."

She's says, "I am talking to you."

I say, "We have to go over this. I have to know everything you know, or I can't protect us."

She turns in the chair and looks deep into my eyes, see-ing things in me neither of us knew were there. Her eyes burn me, and I blink. She gets up and goes tired and slow to the bed, and we sit facing each other with our legs crossed.

I reach out and put my hand on her knee, and she looks at my hand. She doesn't care if it's there or not. I say, "Tell me what Bick said before I got there."

"He said he loved me." She stares at my hand as she talks. "He said he had to show me, and this was the only way he could do it."

"No, I mean about what he knew. About us."

She looks at the window, the oaks move, rubbing, fussing in the light wind, the birds are irritable in the heat. She says, "It was him watching us at the river, not Kenny. Bick left my gold cross on Kenny's mirror. When Bick got to Tolbert's, Kenny and Ronny were already inside, so he walked over and hung it there. I asked him why. He said he was angry about the way I acted with Kenny at the gas station. Getting him a Coke and all. He said what he did was stupid, and he was sorry."

"What about spying on us at the river? Was he sorry about that, too?"

She says, "He told me he was just out driving and decided to go to the place where we skinny-dipped that time, him and me and Ronny and Beulah. He didn't know we were there. But when he saw us, he couldn't leave."

She pulls her eyes from the window, and looks at me. "He said I was so beautiful, he couldn't leave."

"You were so beautiful he laughed?"

"He said he cried. He said maybe it sounded like laughing to us, but he was crying. He couldn't stop it when he saw what we did together."

"So he wrote you that note about the way you like to swim because he loved you?"

She looks away from me again. Her chin drops and her voice goes low and cold. "I told you he said he loved me. It hurt him that we did those things. He wrote the note so I'd come with him and he'd warn me not to do those things again. It was all for my own good, he said."

I want to change her mind, tell her how Bick really was, but I can't. Not yet. I want to make her happy again, but I can't. Maybe later, but not now. Now I need to know things. I say, "But we heard it. We heard Griner's engine. There's no other one like that around here."

She looks at me.

"We heard it, didn't we?"

I have to ask. If a laugh was crying, then maybe hate is love, and I didn't hear Griner's engine.

Delia says, "Yes, we heard it."

Bick's body is taken to Tallahassee in a refrigerated truck. The autopsy is done by a doctor at the university hospital. It shows that Bick Sifford died of massive cranial trauma. There is no water in his lungs. There is no alcohol in his blood. There is no other substance in his body that arouses suspicion. There are no wounds that might have occurred before the head injury. The doctor's report confirms what was apparent: Bick Sifford died of an eighty foot fall from Widow Rock into the Hiawassee River. The town knows all this.

And the town knows that Mr. and Mrs. Sifford are inconsolable in their grief and suspicious of these findings. That Bick's father has been to see Sheriff Hollister many times in his office to ask about developments in the case. The Siffords and the town want to know what Bick was doing up on Widow Rock alone at night. They want to know why he took off his clothes and piled them neatly on the limestone. But there seems to be no way to know, and so the rumors and the theories are tried and touted, and as quickly as they arise, they die.

Some say Bick went there to meet a girl, some say a married woman, some say a man. Some say that standing on the street of Widow Rock right now there is someone who knows what happened to Bick Sifford. One or two of the talkers, country people fond of the old sayings, remember this one: murder will out. They say the person who met Bick Sifford up there, or who was supposed to go and didn't, or who met him and did him in, will not be able to keep this thing hidden. They say murder will sing from the house or the heart of the guilty party. It always does.

One day, Mr. Latimer, the town drunk, stumbles from the alley where he sits in the shade drinking cheap whiskey from a paper bag. He looks up the street at the red Oldsmobile parked in front of the sheriff's office. He looks at the small gathering of people who never seem to tire of staring at Bick Sifford's car and talking about it. He scratches himself and looks up at the sun and blinks, and then he says, "Aw, hell. That boy just wanted to feel the night wind on his dick. Don't you people know that?" When the crowd of shocked citizens stops talking and stares at him, Mr. Latimer crows, "And he ain't the only one!" This is another theory for the town to consider.

A day comes when the town knows Bick's story is almost over. Mr. and Mrs. Sifford will never be satisfied with the town's theories of what happened to their son. If they have a theory of their own, they will never tell it. They will never forgive the sheriff for not proving that someone else acted in the story. They know a boy like Bick could not die alone in the middle of the night on Widow Rock. He could not die of a joke or a slip or some sorry jape.

The town is concerned with its own feelings. The town knows that feelings rise to a taut, trembling pitch when a funeral comes, and after that will come an awful trough of nothing. Widow Rock will go back to its old grievances and its old monotony and its simple hope.

thirty-four

The funeral will be too big for the Presbyterian Church. The Baptists offer their sanctuary, but it's not much bigger. The two preachers decide to hold the service in the Warrington High School gym.

I sit with Grandma and Grandpa Hollister and Delia in a row of folding chairs about halfway down the aisle on the right. I'm sitting between Grandpa and Delia. He arranged us this way. He's been watching us.

A lot of people are watching him. Some watch like they think he should have solved the case of Bick. Some look at him like they're glad he's sheriff and they're not. They watch me and Delia and Grandma Hollister, too. Some of them know that Bick and Delia went to the Sifford's anniversary dinner dance together, and some remember Bick and Delia talking and dancing at Tolbert's. They're waiting to see if she cries. We sit and watch the people arrive, and I try to take Delia's hand, but she won't let me.

There must be five hundred people here. Everybody's dressed for church. Both high school football teams are here, sitting together, all the boys with their crew cuts and thick necks sweating into the collars of their white shirts. Ronny Bishop sits with the Widow Rock team. Many of the mothers are sniffling already. They're going to cry hard in a little while. Some are not sniffling, and they won't cry, but they hold their children close to them. Their eyes are fierce and vigilant. They say the world is a dangerous place if the richest man's son can die for no reason.

The fathers sit stiff and dignified, but they look a little

lost. They look at the wives who sniffle and the ones who hug their children close, and they don't know what to do. They're just here, buried, like the foundation of all this. A funeral is no place for men.

When the Siffords walk in with Caroline Huff's parents, the towns of Warrington and Widow Rock hold their breath. Mr. Sifford is tall and military and fierce in his black suit. He looks like he'll fight anybody right now who says a bad thing about Bick. Mrs. Sifford's eyes are lost in dark holes above her sunken cheeks. When she stops to enter the first row, she sags against her husband, and he steadies her. When she looks up suddenly into his eyes, the whole gym exhales, and that's when the women who are sniffling begin to cry hard.

I try again to take Delia's hand, but she won't let me. People are watching her, and I know they want to see her cry. They want her to cry the right way, like a girl who's lost a friend, like a girl who has no idea what to do with death, like a girl who's scared of life now that she's seen it end. They don't want her to cry like she loved Bick Sifford. She can't do that. Cry like a lover.

I look over at her. Her eyes are frozen dumb, stunned. I watch Caroline Huff's father put his hand on the small of her mother's back and guide her into the first row after the Siffords. When the four are seated, the organ music begins, and Mrs. Clements, a Baptist lady who works at the Curl Up and Dye, rises in a black choir robe and sings, "When This Weary Life Is Over." She has a beautiful voice, high but full of a throbbing fullness, and the towns of Warrington and Widow Rock listen carefully, feeling every note. When she finishes, some of the men reach up and snap tears from their cheeks with quick fingers or stare up with bewildered eyes at the gymnastic equipment tied to the rafters.

Two mortuary men in black suits wheel in the casket. They center it below the platform decorated with black cloth and pots of white lilies of the valley. They turn at attention and face the people, then walk off together. The Reverend Laidlaw stands and offers the invocation, and then he starts to preach. I don't listen to the words, I reach again for Delia's hand. This time she lets me take it.

I hold it hard, and I can feel Grandpa Hollister on my other side. He can't see it, he doesn't look, but he knows I'm holding her hand.

As the preaching goes on, and the gym gets hotter, and the Reverend Laidlaw gives way to the Baptist minister, Mr. Simmons, Delia doesn't cry. Some of the women around us have spied on her. They've raised their programs to their mouths and pretended to cough, and they've looked. They've lifted their wet-wrung handkerchiefs to their eyes, and they've looked. So I curve my thumb and dig my nail into the soft skin between Delia's thumb and forefinger. I drive it as hard as I can, and I feel her tremble beside me, and I hear her breathing bump and swerve, and then there's an animal sound from her chest, and she pitches forward, and puts her face in her right hand, and the sobs full of her soul pour out.

Grandpa Hollister leans across me and puts his hand on her back. His face is red, and his hand hovers over her for a second like she's too hot to touch or he doesn't know the best place for his hand to light. He doesn't look at me. I lean back and let him comfort her. The women around us stare openly now, and I see how they approve and how the pieces of the story have all come together.

When Grandma and Grandpa Hollister are asleep downstairs, I get up and go to Delia's room. I stand outside her door and listen, but I don't hear anything. The house is strangely quiet. I've never heard the oak trees so still. I think the whole town is silent in its forgetting and its return to the old life. I open Delia's door and go in and stand in the dark to let her see me. In the white bed against the window under the slope of the roof, her black hair fans across the pillow, her white legs lie long and straight, and her arm is thrown across her eyes. I go to the vanity and turn on the radio soft. It's Tallahassee: "When the night has come, and the land is dark, and the moon is the only light we'll see. No I won't be afraid, no I won't be afraid. Just as long as you stand, stand by me." I wait for Delia to hear it, to move, to know I'm here, but she doesn't. She's still. I move to her bedside and stand by her.

I don't know what to say, what to do. The music doesn't tell me. Not exactly. I wait and watch her. The funeral's over, Bick is gone, his parents are sad but quiet, the town is still tonight, but I know there's danger. I have to save us.

She knows I'm here, but she doesn't speak. She doesn't pat the bed beside her and move over. I wish there was a storm, something to make her need me. I wish she'd cry. The song's over, and the DJ comes on talking about lovers and midnight and how it is out there on the roads and at the drive-ins and the burger joints, Little Suzie and Handsome Johnny doing what the night calls them to do. What nothing and no one on Earth can keep them from doing because they're young and they're in love in America.

I close my eyes and listen to what's inside my head for Delia. The words form, and I open my eyes. "I did it for you, Delia."

I wait in fear and hope. My knees are water, and my mouth is dry. I know this could be the end. She could send me away. There could be nothing for us until I go back to Omaha and start school. Nothing but Aunt Delia and Nephew Travis.

As I watch, dizzy in the smell that rises from her in the dark, her long white arm moves from across her eyes, and her hand reaches out to me. She rests her fingers on my side just above my uns, and I bite my lower lip to keep from speaking how it feels to me. She turns her face to me and says, "I know, Travis. I know. I've been thinking about it. I'm sorry for the way I've been."

Her voice is so slow and tired. I can barely hear the words, but her fingers dig into my side and pull me toward the bed, and my knees are so weak I almost fall on her. The big, good thing in my chest swells into my neck and takes my head so I can't say anything. I can't answer her.

I put my hands on her face. I touch her eyes lightly and listen. She says, "I can't say I'm glad for what you did, but I know why you did it, and I know you love me." Her breath comes hard and sudden. "And I know I love you."

I don't want to talk about Bick, not now, but I have to say one thing. "He wasn't ever going to leave you alone. He wanted to own you. I couldn't let him do that."

She sighs, and I see her white face move from side to side in the black cradle of her hair. "I know, Travis. I know."

And I know we can never be like we were. She'll never think of me the same way. What I've done makes me different in her eyes. She'll never call me Killer again, and I'll never think of her as my Aunt Delia. But I know she loves me. She can still do that even though I've been the animal boy who climbed the rock four-legged and pushed Bick over.

I whisper, "Move over." She does, and I slide onto the warm spread beside her. We have to be careful because there's no rain to cover our sounds, and the radio is only playing soft, and the night outside is as still as the hour before morning. She turns her back to me, and I press to her long warm length and put my arm around her. She takes my hand to her mouth and kisses it. I shiver, and my thing gets hard, and I have to press against her. She lets go of my hand, and it falls to her neck, and I feel the gold cross there. I move my hand to her chest and let my fingertips circle her nipple. It grows like I've just grown. She sighs, and then her breath comes ragged and hard and so does mine, and I press my hard thing against her.

I say, "Turn over."

She whispers, harsh, "No, I can't."

But her breathing is harder still, and she's moving against me down there now, and my hand presses the soft grace of her chest.

I say, "Yes you can. Turn over." My voice is hard, urgent, but now I'm calm inside. I know it has to happen now. Nothing can stop this.

I move my hand from her chest, and she gives me a little cry of regret, and I take her shoulder and pull her to me. She turns a little and then all the way. As she turns, I move aside for her and feel her knee move against mine, opening. I rise over her and then settle between her legs. I rest above her on my elbows and let my lips brush her nipples. She gives me a trembling gasp of breath, stiffens, then moves her legs apart. It has to happen now. You don't return from where we're going. You're there forever.

For a second, I see her and Bick as I saw them when the wild boy climbed the bluff and came through the tree door: two white, sweat-slick bodies moving together on the moonlit rock. I don't want to see them. I blink to make it go away. I want us to be the discoverers of this thing.

I let my hips fall and push, and I feel her rise up to me. I try to see her eyes in the dark, but there's a blind, hot necessity, and we're moving. It's crazy and happy at once, and the storms that come at night to shake this old house are nothing like our two bodies in this wild hurricane no one can see or hear but us.

I don't know how long we sleep. It's a sleep I've never known before. It's like the hand of God reached down and took my mind. And when the rock hits the window, I don't know what's happening, only that something's wrong. It's hard for me to wake, and harder for Delia. I squeeze her shoulder until she rises with a gasp and a dance of legs and arms. I sweep aside her black hair and whisper rough in her ear, "Someone's down there." I stab my finger at the window.

She babbles from the remnant of her sleep. "Someone? He's...?"

I shake her shoulder and push her toward the window. "Look out there," I say. "Quick."

I can't look out. No one can know I'm here.

She shivers, pulls the sheet to her chest, and leans to the window. I want to peek over her shoulder, but I don't dare. Just as her face comes to the pane, another pebble strikes. It's as loud as a shot from Ronny Bishop's pistol, but I know it's only a tap in the still night.

I hear Delia whisper, "Jesus Christ, it's Kenny Griner."

Her hand reaches back to freeze me where I am, then she raises the window sash. Her black hair flairs out in the breeze that rushes in. She shakes her head hard, and I know she means no more rocks. She doesn't speak. If he speaks, I don't hear it. After a space, she eases the sash down and rests her head back on the pillow next to mine. "He wants me to come down."

"Are we going?"

"I have to. I want you to stay here. It's too dangerous for both of us to go down. They might hear us."

I don't say it, but it's more dangerous for her if I don't go down. She gets up to dress, and I go to my room for clothes. When I hear her out in the hall, I come out and stand in front of her until she knows she can't talk me out of it.

We go down so slow sometimes I think daylight will find us frozen on the stairs. We keep to the sides of the old groany risers, and when we finally make it to the kitchen, we stand for a long time at Marvadell's squeaky screen door. Finally, I whisper in her ear, "Don't open it. Make him come up on the back porch."

Delia leans to the rusty screen. "Kenny! Kenny, come up here!"

I stand behind her on watery legs with the hair humming on the back of my neck. I send my spirit to the side of Grandpa Hollister's bed with a message of long, deep sleep.

Delia throws her whisper out another time into the night, and then, peeking over her shoulder, I see the bib of Griner's white T-shirt between black jacket wings. His big boots thud on the old porch boards, and I can feel Delia wince with each footfall. He stops three feet from the screen and whispers, "Delia? Is that you?"

I almost laugh out loud. Anybody but us and he'd be dead now.

Delia whispers, "It's me, Kenny. What do you want?"

"Look at me," he whispers back. "Can you see me?"

Delia turns and looks back into the dark house, at the door that separates the kitchen from the dining room. I can feel her anger now. "Kenny, what are you *doing* here this time of night?"

Even whispering, Griner's voice holds the mulish weight of his place in life. He says, "I want you to look at me, Delia."

Delia says, "All right, Kenny. Come closer, into the light."

Griner's big boots slide forward, and his face looms visible, and we hear a scratch, and then the blue flame of his Zippo lighter is bright between us. And there it is above his other eye, a big ragged cut with new black stitches. It looks like the first one, only this time the eye below the cut is swollen like a ripe plumb and black as one, too.

Delia says, "My God, Kenny, what happened?"

Sullen, Griner says, "You know what happened."

Delia is quiet. I reach up and put my hand on her back. When she gets it, I feel something in her break. "*Daddy* did that to you?"

Griner's boots scrape the old boards. The heavy flaps of the leather jacket crackle as he swings his arms out like a bird trying to take off. "Your daddy thinks I killed Bick Sifford. He stopped me out on the road near my house and put me in his car for an *interview*." Griner's voice is louder, and Delia's skin tells my hand she can't take much more of this. Through my fingers I pass my thoughts to her: *Send him away. Get rid of him.*

Griner says, "Your daddy heard from Ronny Bishop that me and Bick had words down at Dameron's ESSO that day we was all there. I told him the words was mostly between me and Ronny, and he says, 'Don't you sass me, boy,' and he slaps me with that crime tool of his."

Standing in the dark behind Delia, I see Griner reach up and touch his split-open head.

Delia says, "Kenny, we can't talk about this now."

Griner says, "I didn't come to talk about it. I came to ask you to meet me somewhere."

"But, what do you want?"

"You to get your daddy off me, that's what I want."

Griner goes stock stiff and takes a step back. "Who's there?" he whispers.

Delia says, "Kenny, I..."

"It's that boy, ain't it? He's there with you, ain't he?"

Delia's shoulders fall, and I step up beside her. I don't say anything.

Griner steps forward again and peers at me. "You two," he says, "always together. Bick said he wondered about you two."

My knees are water, and I can still taste Delia's kisses sweet in my dry mouth. I can feel her fear swelling beside me. I can't touch her or he'll see.

She says, "*Bick* said? *What* did Bick say? When did you talk to him?"

Griner steps away again, his boot dragging loud. "Never mind that. Meet me tomorrow out at the river. There's a place where people go to swim. You can get close in your car if you take the Old Wilson Road. Just park and walk to the river and look for a big pile of driftwood. Come tomorrow at three o'clock."

Delia says, "Kenny, I..."

But Griner's already gone. I see his black shape move past the grape arbor and make for the path into the woods that Eddie takes when he comes for Marvadell's money.

thirty-five

The next day at two-thirty we say we're going for a drive.

Grandma and Grandpa Hollister want us to stay home. Delia asks why, and they just say they think it's best. Delia says we've been cooped up all day, and we need to get out of the house. We can't sit around and mope about Bick forever. She says the whole town's like a cemetery. She says I'll be leaving soon, and we want to have some fun before I go. Finally, they let us go, but Grandpa Hollister comes out and stands on the porch to watch us drive away. He's never done that before.

We don't say much on the way. We don't plan, because we don't know what Griner wants. I remember him watching Delia dance with Bick, and how his eyes changed when she asked him to dance and he refused. First the hunger, then the pride. I remember him under the grease rack, his quick, sure hands moving the tools. That day I liked him, and he liked me. Delia liked him, too. She brought him a Coke, but even I knew the town would never let them be together. I wish Griner hadn't come to Delia's window last night. I wish he'd put what he wants and what he knows in that street rod of his and drive as fast as he can out of Widow Rock.

We park where we did the first time we went swimming. We walk to the river and sit on the driftwood with the big white bones of the beast clutching all around us. We don't even look back upstream at the white shelf of Widow Rock. Delia tells me about the flood six years ago. It raised the river two hundred yards beyond its banks and dragged this big tangle of pine stumps and branches here. I tell her it's not driftwood. It's the body of a monster that lived centuries ago, and the river is just slicing away earth and bringing the bones to the light. She laughs and says, "Travis, you've got some imagination."

She winks at me, and for a second I see again the old, crazy, happy Delia. My Aunt Delia. The one I met the first day when she chased me with her knees bent like Groucho Marx and said she'd hug me whether I wanted to or not. I smile at her and then look up at the sky and get dizzy for a second thinking about how far we've come since that day, and whether I'd go back if I could.

Kenny Griner steps out of the woods above us. He stands there for a second like a big black and white bird, and then he slides in his heavy boots down the steep bank to the wet sand where we're sitting. Delia looks at him, and her eyes go small and tight taking in the plum-blue bruise above his eye.

Griner stands looking at the river with his hands on his hips. He's sweating from his walk, but he's got the leather jacket on. I see a paperback book in his hip pocket when he bends over to pick up a pebble. He skims the pebble across the brown water and says to Delia, "I wanted you to come alone."

Delia closes her eyes and shakes her head. "I get in trouble when I go places without Travis." She opens her eyes and looks up at the sky. She says, "Anyway, Mama and Daddy been keeping me home since the funeral."

Griner looks down and stubs the sand with his boot. "Ole Bick's got the whole town in an uproar, don't he? Anything happened to a guy like me, nobody'd notice. You and your girlfriends'd still be riding around all hours looking for boys."

"Is that what we do?" Delia's eyes fire up, and just as quickly cool.

Griner looks at her. "That's what you do, but that ain't all." His eyes slide over to me, then up and down the riverbank. I can see he's scared of the place where this might take him.

Delia shoves her hands into the pockets of her jeans. She's lost weight since Bick died. Her eyes are a darker, colder blue, and they hide a little now in the hollows above her perfect cheeks. She looks more beautiful than ever to me. She stands in front of Griner and says, "All right, Kenny, get to the point. What did Bick say to you?"

Griner's eyes get big, and his smile's a fake. He says, "Bick Sifford? Did he say something to me?"

Delia shoos away his words with a flip of her hand. She says it slowly. "Last night. On my back porch. You said Bick talked about Travis and me."

She doesn't look at me, but Griner does. I try to make my eyes like Delia's—small and cold. I know what she's thinking. *We both heard it. Here in this river, we heard Kenny Griner's engine whining, then winding down with a Pop, Pop, Pop.*

Griner's eyes go shy. He says, "I don't want to talk about that. I want your daddy off my ass."

Delia says, "I don't tell my daddy what to do, Kenny Griner."

"You can damn well tell him I didn't do anything to Bick Sifford. You can tell him he can't hang Bick on me just to get Mr. Sifford off his back."

"How can I tell him that? I don't know what you did."

"You know I didn't kill Bick."

"How do I know that?"

Griner turns away to the river. He pushes his hands into the pockets of his jeans, pulls them out again. He bends and finds another pebble, then he drops it. "You know," he says.

His voice is small. Delia and I wait. We don't look at each other. We know this is it, everything. Pictures of Griner spin across my mind, his car hidden in the trees at the park, him driving past the house late at night looking up at Delia's window. Maybe he followed her and Bick that night. Maybe he was watching when the wild boy climbed the bluff and ran at Bick with his hands out like hooves.

Griner's arms rise straight out from his sides. When he drops them, the leather makes a flapping sound. He says, "Because you know me." His voice is almost too soft to hear. "You know I didn't do it, because you know me."

He turns and looks at Delia, and I see his love in his eyes. It's like coming into a clearing in the woods and finding an animal dying on the ground. You watch to the end, and you know that nobody will ever know, but you know it's wrong that you watched.

Delia lifts her face to the sky and closes her eyes. "You're right. I know you didn't do anything to Bick."

Griner's face is ugly now with the old scar and the new mark, but he looks so young when he says, "Will you tell your daddy?"

Delia looks down at the wet sand, then out across the living surface of the river. "I'll think of something," is all she says.

Griner doesn't thank her, but he looks like he wants to. He reaches up and touches his new mark. He looks confused touching it. Delia walks a few yards down the bank. She stands with her white tenny pumps inches from the water.

We could leave now, but I know she doesn't want to. I think about asking if we can go. I could say I'm not feeling good, the heat is getting to me. Something.

Before I can speak, she turns back to Griner and says, "You said you saw Bick. When did you see him?" She tries to make her voice just curious, but there's another sound in it.

Griner watches her, taking in what she's trying to hide—that she has to know, that she's trading what she'll say to Grandpa Hollister for this. He swallows and looks out over the water.

"Kenny?"

Griner shrugs, and the leather wings flap. He scratches the back of his neck, rubs his cheek with a rasp of whiskers. He shoves his hand back into his jeans. "Bick wudn't so bad when you got him away from Ronny. It's the difference between the town and the country, I guess. It wudn't so long ago that people of mine sharecropped for Ronny's grand-daddy. A boy like Ronny can't forget that."

Griner seems to lose his way. He smiles and says, "I guess ole Travis here'll be going back to school pretty soon."

I can't help what happens in my eyes. I've tried not to think about going back. There's been too much trouble, too much happening too fast. But sometimes at night I try to figure a way to stay. I don't think my dad would mind if I stayed, but my mom needs me. And now I know more about how to help her. Griner sees what I'm thinking. He knows I want to stay.

He shrugs and turns back to the river. "S'matter of fact, I saw Bick right here."

I can feel Delia seizing up where she stands with her white shoes inches from the brown water. Griner says, "I

don't mean right here. It was back there where we left the
cars. It was a couple days after we had our little whoop-tee-
do at the gas station."

"You said he mentioned me..." Delia looks down at her
right toe making a row of little V-marks in the wet sand.
"...and Travis?"

Griner looks up at the sky. The sun is white hot, and
there's not a cloud floating in the channel at the top of the
trees. The white light strikes back from the brown water so
bright it makes your eyes sore, and the water moves on,
throwing up cool vapors that touch our faces.

Griner says, "I was gonna swim. I felt like steam on a
stove top that day, and I wanted to cool off. I figured I'd be
alone. You don't see people out here very much." Griner
looks upstream at the white shelf of Widow Rock. "Most
folks go up there when they come to the river, but I like it
here."

He makes a quick glance at Delia. She doesn't look up at
Widow Rock. She's concentrating hard on the little row of V-
marks in the sand. He says, "Anyway, that day I wanted to
swim, and I was rolling in just as Bick came walking out of
the woods. He was walking fast, and his face was red, and
he looked real shook up. He was walking with his head
down, and he got right up on me before he seen me. But he
stopped and looked at me like he wudn't surprised, like he
expected me. Then he gave this funny laugh and said, 'She's
all yours.'

"For a minute, I thought we were gonna have trouble like
we did at the gas station, but then I could see Bick didn't want
trouble. The trouble was all inside him. I ast him who he
meant, who was all mine, but I known he meant you, Delia."

When Griner says this, he looks at her, and a red blush creeps up from the collar of his white T-shirt. Delia doesn't look up from her rows of Vs.

"But I ast him anyway. '*Who* can I have, Bick?' He went on past me to his car, walking fast. 'Her,' he said, and he pointed behind him at the river. Then he stopped and looked at me. I think it was the first time he ever really looked at me, and I guess it was the last time I ever seen him. I'll never forget what he said then. 'You can have her if you can get her away from that kid.'

"He got in that red Olds of his and drove off fast, and it wudn't but a day or two after that when he...fell."

Griner looks back upstream at the white shelf of Widow Rock. His eyes narrow and strain at the place as though they might see Bick Sifford up there, might see him falling. Griner turns and looks right at me. I look right back. I've never looked at a grown man before like I look at him now. We hold. His eyes break away first, and we both look at Delia.

She hugs herself and tries not to shiver. Her voice is small when she says, "What do you think he meant by that, Kenny?"

I remember the first day Delia took me up to Widow Rock. She told me the story of the Widow and how she jumped, and then we sat on the rock, and she tucked her blouse up into her bra and rolled down her jeans to get the sun, and Griner stepped out of the woods. He was drinking whiskey, and he caught Delia fixing her clothes, and he said, "How old you say that boy is?"

Griner says, "I don't know, Delia. I thought you might know." He looks at me again. "You and Travis."

I say, "Aunt Delia, it's time to go. We promised we'd be home at three-thirty, remember?"

Delia looks at me. She nods.

Griner says to her, "Was you here that day I met Bick? I didn't see your car anywhere. I walked in to the river, and I seen footprints and things, and maybe they was a boat way downstream just cutting around the bend toward Milton, but I didn't see anybody. Was you here? Did you come to meet Bick?" He wants to know, and he doesn't want it. I can see it in his eyes, and he wants Delia to stay here with him as long as he can keep her.

Delia says, "I don't know what Bick meant, Kenny. I don't suppose we'll ever know, do you?"

I say it again. "Aunt Delia, we've got to go."

Griner says, "Don't forget to talk to your daddy about me. Don't forget your promise."

Delia takes a last look at the rows of Vs she's made in the sand. She bends at the edge of the water and dips her hand in and scoops water out, then she washes them all away. It takes a while, but she gets rid of every trace, then she says, "I won't forget, Kenny."

She holds out her hand to me. "Come on, Travis."

I take her hand, and we start up the bank toward the woods. Griner watches us. He's watching our hands. How we touch.

thirty-six

When we get home from the river, Grandpa comes out of the bedroom and watches us climb the stairs. We're halfway up when he says, "Are you all right, Delia?"

Delia turns and smiles. "I'm fine, Daddy. It's just so hot. I can't wait for the fall to come."

Grandpa Hollister looks at me and says, "Travis, your dad called while you were out. He's got you booked on a flight next Monday."

I know I'm supposed to smile and say I'm glad. Say I miss my dad and mom, and I'm happy to be going home. But all I can think is: Thursday. Today's Thursday. That means only four more days with Delia. I'm thinking too many things at once: about finding a way to stay here, about what I'll do for my mom when I get home, about what Delia might do here without me.

Grandpa Hollister says, "Travis, I'm talking to you."

I say, "Yes, sir. Thank you, sir." I don't know what else to say. I turn and look at Delia standing a few risers above me on the stairs.

She says, "Daddy, he doesn't know what to say. A summer's a long time when you're his age, and this is home to him now."

She looks at Grandpa Hollister like no one else in the world can look at him, and he looks back the same way. The first day I came here, Delia drove the white Chevy into the garage too fast. Then she jumped out and kissed Grandpa Hollister, and his eyes said she could burn down the house and he wouldn't care. He'd do anything for another kiss like that.

My Grandpa Hollister takes off his steel wire glasses and rubs them on the front of his white shirt. He puts them back on and looks at me. "His home is with his mother and father, Delia. You know that, and so does he."

That night I go to Delia's room. It's late, and everything's quiet downstairs. I stand by her bed and wait. I can tell by her breathing she's awake. I wait, but she doesn't speak. I reach out and hover my hand over her face, feeling the heat of her skin rise through the still air, feeling her breath. Finally, she lifts her arm to her eyes, and her hand falls on her neck, and I know she's turning the gold cross in her fingers. She says, "I can't tonight, Travis. I just can't."

I say, "Please."

I'm thinking: Four days. Four days with Delia.

She lets go of the cross and turns away from me to the window, and I hear her whisper, "I can't. I'm sorry."

I stand there for a while looking at the dark pool of her hair on the white pillow, the curve of her shoulder in the moonlight from the window. I can smell her perfume and her shampoo and her secret skin, and I think this is the place on Earth I want to be when the Russians drop the big bomb. I'd die happy here.

I walk out into the hallway and see dark motion to my right, something rising from the black well of the stairs. I turn toward the bathroom, walking quietly, slowly. I open the bathroom door and go in and turn on the light. I count ten, then flush the toilet, turn off the light, and walk out into the hallway. My heart booms in my ears like the bass drum in a circus band. I see it at the top of the stairs, the narrow comb of black hair, the shaved rails of white along the sides. It's my Grandpa Hollister standing there with his eyes at floor level, skimming them at my feet as I step into my room.

The next night in my sleep I hear it, a whine and a Pop-Pop-Pop. It's coming from the corner down by the Hatcher's house, and that means he'll be passing my window soon. I swim to the surface where asleep and awake meet like water and air, and I push out of bed and start for the window. When my feet hit the floor, I stop.

Delia's in my room. She's standing at my window looking out. She's in her bra and underpants, and she's looking through the open window so hard she doesn't hear me come up behind her. When I put my hand on her shoulder, she shivers, but she doesn't look at me. I look over her shoulder at midnight-blue metal and red flames and a white T-shirt and a glowing red cigarette. I see his white face looking up at our window. When he hits the corner at the far end of our street, the rod's engine backs down again, Pop-Pop-Pop.

Delia turns to me, and her eyes are tired in the moonlight. She's lost more weight. All her jeans are loose on her. I say, "He'll never leave you alone now."

She nods. "I know."

Beulah and Caroline come over to talk about Bick. Caroline says she never knew what death was until she saw Bick's coffin. She says she's sure gonna slow down and not drive so fast.

Beulah says, "You better slow down a lot of things, Girl."

Caroline says for a week after the funeral her mother snuck into her room late at night to see if she was still breathing.

Beulah says her father read in the *Atlanta Constitution* about a high school boy who went up into the north Georgia mountains and jumped from a cliff into the Chattooga River. He kept his clothes on, though.

They both watch Delia. They want her to tell them what Bick's death means, to make it as true as the radio. Delia looks at them, and her eyes go a little crazy, and she shakes her head slow. They think she's too sad about Bick to say anything. I know she's thinking how stupid they are, and how they don't learn anything from what happens to them.

Delia gets up and turns on the radio. It's playing, "Dream Baby." I remember asking Delia if Bick was a dreamboat, and her saying I'm one, too. Delia stands in the middle of her room with her eyes closed and Caroline and Beulah watching, and she starts to sway. She sways to the music for a while, and then she reaches out her arms like she's dancing with someone. The radio says, "Sweet dreams baby, got me dreaming sweet dreams, the whole night through. Sweet dreams baby, got me dreaming sweet dreams, in the daytime too. How long must I dream?" She holds her arms out like that, swaying until even her fingers move like she's holding someone. Some dance partner in a dream. I look over at Caroline and Beulah, and they've both got tears in their eyes.

Delia and I walk downtown to pick up some things for Marvadell at the mercantile. Walking back with our packages, we pass Tolbert's. We go in for a Coke. Mrs. Sifford's there. I know Delia wants to leave as soon as we see her, but it wouldn't look right to turn and go. So we go to the fountain and ask Mr. Tolbert for Cokes and sit with our legs dangling into the room.

Mrs. Sifford sits in the same booth Bick and Ronny used the first day I met them. She doesn't touch the cup of coffee in front of her. She's dressed up like she's going to Panama City, or even Tallahassee, but she isn't. The town talks about how she's been acting since Bick died. Always dressing up in her best clothes but never going anywhere. Beulah and Caroline say she thinks nice clothes will keep bad things from happening to her. She's wearing a pink suit with big covered buttons down the front, and pink shoes made of shiny cloth, and a pink hat that looks to me like a puff pastry. She's got on a lot of makeup, but her face still looks like it's coming apart.

I'm hoping we can drink our Cokes and go before she sees us. It doesn't look like she's seeing anything but the black pool in her coffee cup. Delia hasn't looked at her since we first came in. She's drawing Coke through her straw, trying to finish fast.

When Mrs. Sifford finally looks over at Delia, there's no mistaking what's in her eyes. It's recognition. She sees in Delia something she knows well. I sit there hoping it's just sadness she's seeing. Delia hasn't looked at her yet, or isn't going to show she has. I wait. Mrs. Sifford says, "Delia Hollister, I haven't seen you since the dance at our house. I know you were at Bick's funeral, but I...I wasn't seeing very well that day. I couldn't name ten people I saw there." Her voice is so cheery and crisp, it gives me the creeps.

Delia looks over at her, and the smile she drags to her face makes them look like mother and daughter. She says, "How are you, Mrs. Sifford?"

Mrs. Sifford's brittle smile gets bigger. Her eyelids flutter, and she says, "Oh, I've been...Well, you know, I..." Her hands shake as she picks up her purse and gets to her feet. She wobbles on her high heels, steadies, and starts toward us. Behind us, Mr. Tolbert backs away. The sink where he washes glasses with his back to the counter is his usual post when people need privacy. But there's a little store room behind the fountain, and now I hear his feet sliding through the door and it closing behind him.

Mrs. Sifford stands in front of Delia and me. "Delia, you knew Bick."

Delia nods looking into the Coke glass in her lap.

Mrs. Sifford says, "For a while, I thought maybe you and he were.... Well, never mind that. But you knew him, and I wonder if there's anything you can tell me. Anything you noticed about him. Anything he said that...?"

It's all coming apart. It's still holding—eyes, voice, hair, hat, and suit—but not for long. Delia's got to speak, but she can't. I look over at her, and her face is coming apart like Mrs. Sifford's. I'm going to have to do something, say something. I decide to wait a few more heartbeats before I do, but Delia pushes off the stool and runs for the door.

I get up, dig in my pocket for some money, drop it on the counter without counting, and say to Mrs. Sifford, "I'm sorry, ma'am, but I've got to go." Then, for some reason, I stop straining toward the door, the sidewalk where I see Delia's long legs in faded blue jeans walking fast, and I say, "I'm just...sorry."

I have to pull myself out of her eyes before I drown. It's so deep and far and sad in there, I hope I never have to see anything like it again. She starts to say something back, but I'm running, and I'm halfway caught up with Delia before I realize what I said to Mrs. Sifford. *I said, I'm sorry.*

That night I wake up late with the words, *two more days*, singing in my head. It's a mad, sad song, and I can't stand any more of it. I've been thinking maybe she won't let me come to her again, and that will kill me. It's like being born and then told you have to go back to what was before, back to not born, back to alive but not in life. That night we did it together was the beginning of my life. I go to Delia's room for the thing I have to have.

It's a still, clear night with a big white moon, but I wish it was raining. I wish there was a storm, another big blue howler pounding up out of the Gulf of Mexico. I walk soft-soled to the head of the stairs and look down. The house is quiet. I don't know if Grandpa is home or out patrolling. He makes it hard to know on purpose. He's been coming upstairs a lot lately. Last night I heard his soft walking out in the hall, heard him go to Delia's door and stop and listen, heard him at my door listening, then going back downstairs.

At Delia's door, I listen. The radio's playing low: "When I want you, in the night. When I want you, to hold me tight. Whenever I want you, all I have to do is dream." I go in and walk to her bed. She's lying with her back to me. But she's like a radio, and I know my song is coming through. I put my hand on her shoulder, and she turns. Moonlight falling through the oak branches shows me her face. I think I see a smile, but it's hard to tell. I know now that a smile can say anything from hate to love. I whisper, "Can we tonight?"

She looks at me for a long time. Her eyes are wide, and her cheeks are hollow, and her face in the moonlight might be made of bone. She says, "Travis, what we did wasn't good for you. Don't you know that yet?"

I know she's right and wrong. I know that growing and knowing are good and bad. I know what the preacher meant now when he said, "The end of man is knowledge." I say, "I love you, Delia, and it can't be bad."

She shakes her head on the pillow. Black hair thrashes around her face. She says, "I love you, too, and I wish more than anything in the world that we could have been your age together or my age together. You'd be my dreamboat then, but look at us now. We can't keep doing this."

I know I have to go back to Omaha. I have to go back and take care of my mother, but I'm coming back to Widow Rock. I'm coming back for Delia. I say, "We can. We have to. I'm leaving on Monday."

She reaches out and touches my forehead. Her fingers are cool and light, and they burn the name of what we've done into my skin. She says, "I want you to leave with some good memories of me, Travis. If we...stay apart tonight, that'll be a good memory, don't you think?"

I shake my head until her fingers fall from me. I take her hand and put her fingers to my mouth and kiss them. "No," is all I say. I want her so bad I'll die. I stand there holding her hand, sending her the message of my love. Finally, she sighs and moves over and says, "All right, Travis, my dreamboat. Just once more. Once more before you leave."

I wake up in Delia's bed. I don't know how long I've slept, or what time it is, but I know what I have to do. I lift a handful of her fragrant black hair to my face and then kiss her once on the temple. She doesn't wake. I slip out of bed and go to her vanity table and find her purse, then I go to my room and dress.

thirty-seven

I kill the headlights and let the Chevy roll to a stop a hundred yards from Griner's old, tin-roofed farm house. Griner's street rod is parked beside the house, but the other car is gone, the blue Plymouth that belongs to the blond boy, Randle. The house is dark, but there's a light on in the barn. I slip out of the Chevy and walk past the house with the tattered window screens hanging down its sides. I stop beside the street rod and look inside at the fuzzy white dice that hang from the mirror and the knob attached to the steering wheel so you can steer with one hand and the white skull for a gearshift handle. There are some paperback books on the passenger seat, and I think, "His friends. He rides with these books, so he's not alone."

From here on, I have to be careful. I walk along the two-rut track to the old barn and stop under the block and tackle. An engine hangs from it dead heavy in the night, even though the rising wind is moving the limbs of the big oak that supports it. I look up at the eight empty cylinders, then down at the puddle of oil on the ground. A few steps closer and I can hear the radio playing through the two big, swung-open barn doors. I can't make out the song, but it's something slow and dreamy. The kind of song Delia says you dance to late at night, just before they turn out the lights in the gym and send everyone home.

I turn to my right, away from the music and the light that falls from the doors. In the moon shadows, I step slowly into a farmer's field until my feet hit an old, rusted-down fence. There I turn again toward the barn. I crouch and crab-walk to a side

Downstairs, I stand among the familiar shapes of the dark living room listening for any sound from Grandpa and Grandma Hollister's bedroom. When I hear Grandma Hollister say, "What? What?" and hear her roll over heavy and unrested in their bed, I soft-sole through the dining room into the kitchen. The screen door groans like a man with a toothache, but I don't care. Outside, the wind is rising, and the oak branches are singing about big weather coming.

I push the white Chevy down the driveway and jump in. I back all the way down the hill to the Hatcher's house before I start the engine.

window. I squat and then slowly rise to the windowsill. Through the dusty pane, I see a lightbulb hanging from a wire above the raised hood of an old black Ford. I think it's a '52, but I'm not sure. There are benches along three walls covered with tools, parts, batteries, rags, stacks of oil cans, and old tires. Another wire runs from a socket above the bench to a light that hangs by a hook from the open hood, shining down on the car engine.

The radio is loud enough to hear through the window: "When the night has come, and the land is dark, and the moon is the only light we'll see. No I won't be afraid, no I won't shed a tear, just as long as you stand by me." I squat at the window with the light cutting across the sill into my eyes, wondering what to do now. I can't see Griner. Maybe he's not even here. Maybe he left the light on and the radio playing and went off somewhere. Maybe it's somebody else in there, the blond boy, Randle, or one of their friends.

With my back pressed to the barn wall, I side-step to the front, turn the corner, and peek through the inch of light where one of the big doors hinges. I can see the rear end of the car and something on the floor beyond it, a boot maybe, but I can't really tell. I come out around the door and side-step into the light that falls from the front of the barn. I'm sweating now. The wind from the storm that's coming cools me, but the light on my skin feels even colder.

Someone in the house could see me now. Someone driving by on the road two hundred yards away might even see me. Crouching, I move into the barn and stop. I see the radio on the bench across from the little window. Griner's cigarettes, lighter, and a half-empty bottle of Coke sit beside it. I creep soft another two feet, and I see his legs sticking out from under the car. He's lying on a piece of greasy canvas with tools and parts spread out around him, and I can see his stomach in the white T-shirt moving up and down with his effort as he fixes the Ford.

Three more steps, and I can hear him humming with the radio: "If the sky we look upon should tumble and fall, and the mountains should crumble to the sea. I won't cry, I won't cry, no I won't shed a tear, just as long as you stand by me." I move quietly to the bench where the radio rests, and I listen for its message.

I have to protect Delia. My mind spins with pictures: me and Delia in the white Chevy cruising the night roads with the wind full of a music only we understand, me and Delia in the river, our wet mouths passing hot breath across the cold water, our hands touching secrets under the water, Delia and Bick lying like one wedded thing on the white rock in the moonlight, their bodies moving like the storm trees move outside my window, Bick dancing silent on the edge of the rock and falling the same way, the blood prints my feet made on the limestone as I ran at him, me and Delia in her bed, falling together into the wild dream of boy and girl.

Griner's Zippo lighter is in my hand before the idea is clear in my head.

I pick up a red, two-gallon gas can. It's heavy, and as I twist the cap, metal scrapes on metal. I stop when the radio stops, and the disk jockey talks. I twist the cap again when another song starts: "Hello, Mary Lou, good-bye heart. Sweet Mary Lou I swore we'd never part." I pour the gas along the dirt floor under the bench. The smell rises strong to my nostrils, and I look over quick at Griner's legs, but they don't move. He's still humming. He grunts, and his stomach muscles swell when he pushes hard on a wrench under there.

I pour the first two gallons along the wall under the

bench. I pick up the second can, wait for the music, and open it. I pour it along the front of the barn and up the far side until it runs out. The third can is only half full, so I just tip it over under the window where I first looked in.

The smell is so powerful now mixed with the fear and the music, the skin on my forehead starts to throb, and my feet don't touch ground as I move quietly back to the door. I look at Griner's legs, his greasy engineer boots, the cuffs of his jeans full of holes from putting out cigarettes. I wait. I don't know what I'm waiting for. I only came here to talk to him, at least that's what I told myself driving out here through the night fields, passing the white, astonished faces of the cattle, watching the white moon rise out of the dark land.

I open the Zippo lighter, and another song begins. "Every night, I hope and pray, a dream lover will come my way. A girl to hold in my arms, to know the magic of her charms. 'Cause I want a girl to call my own. I want a dream lover, so I don't have to dream alone. Dream lover where are you, with a love oh so true, and a hand that I can hold, through the years as I grow old."

I'd talk to him, I told myself, and I'd know what to say when the time came. But the time came, and I had no idea what to say. The time came, and the music told me love never ends, and we dream awake and asleep, and nothing can stop his wanting her. Nothing can keep him away from her.

Griner's Zippo shines in the light, and I step outside the wet, three-sided figure made of gasoline. I strike the lighter at the wrong moment. There's no music, no disk jockey talking. It's all quiet, dead air. Griner stops humming. I hear him say, "Hey? That you, Randle? Don't you be bumming my cigarettes, now."

I kneel and hold the small blue flame above the wet place in the earth. My hand is shaking. It shakes the flame up and down, and the gas awakes with a ripping sound, and it rushes right and left in front of me like something terrified, something escaping into the night. When it hits the place where the third can lies overturned, there's a boom and a rush of air, and I'm lying on my back in the dust with the shock of a fist in my chest watching the red gas can fall from the rafters onto the roof of the Ford.

I get to my feet in the dust and run to the first door and swing it shut. I run to the second and swing it shut, and my last glimpse of Griner is of a white face wide open with a scream I can't hear and blue flame feathering along his arms as he tries to fan them, tries to fly. I shut the second door and lean all my weight to it just as Griner slams his body against the other side. I can hear him screaming now. Wordless words, things without names, places in hell.

I push back at him as hard as I can, but he's winning.

There's a hand on my shoulder.

The hand throws me back, and I roll in the dust looking up at long legs in black trousers, a white shirt. Grandpa Hollister has an ax in his hands. He raises it over his head, and I know he's going to chop the door open, but then he tilts it parallel to the earth and shoves it between the two handles of the barn door.

Griner screams and pushes, and the door buckles and rumbles, but he can't fight the ax holding the two door handles together. Grandpa Hollister walks to his right, toward the little window, and I get up and follow him. I stand there beside him watching the storm of flame.

Things too heavy to float in water—cans and bottles and

tools—rise on the power of the fire. I want to run away, but I can't. I know we have to get out of here. This light can be seen for miles. I know I'll be lucky if I get the white Chevy two miles away from here before somebody comes. But I can't leave. I can't believe how fast it all goes up. The old pitch-pine boards of the barn, the greasy rags, the cans of oil erupting and exploding, the hot air driving straight up with the pounding sound of a locomotive engine.

The hand's on my shoulder again. I know it's God reaching down to take me to the place where I'm told what happens to people like me. But when I look up, it's only Grandpa Hollister. And he's not looking at me. He's looking into the fire. We stand there together, and his grip is hard on my shoulder like the first day I met him, and he stood me in front of him and told me to call him sir and said he'd treat me like my father did: like a boy who took responsibility for his actions.

It's getting hot where we are. The fire is eating up the sides of the barn in front of us now. I put out my hand, and the boards are too hot to touch. Black snakes of smoke hiss and crawl out between the slats. I look up at Grandpa Hollister, and I see him reach into the pocket of his black coat. He takes out a piece of paper. He unfolds it and holds it out in front of me. I try to take it, but he won't let go.

"Read it," he says.

I read it.

Delia,

Meet me tonight behind the gas station, 9:00. I'll be waiting in my car. Don't bring the little boy you like so much. Come or the whole town will know how you like to swim.

When I finish, Grandpa Hollister says, "Do you understand, Travis?"

I look up at him. I nod.

She took it with her when she went to meet Bick behind the ESSO station. She left it in the red Oldsmobile. And that's where my Grandpa Hollister found it when he went out to Widow Rock and brought the car back.

My Grandpa Hollister holds the paper in his right hand, he reaches into his pants pocket with his left and takes out the thing Griner called his knuckle-duster. It's the leather-covered club with the long, braided lanyard. He punches the club at the window in front of us, and the hot pane snaps like a pistol shot, and the broken glass is sucked inside, and we stand there in the wild breath of the fire. The fire tries to suck the whole windy night into the garage where Griner is trying to fly.

My Grandpa Hollister holds the paper out to the broken pane and lets it flutter there in the firebreath, then he lets it go, and we both watch it explode and rise as nothing but fine black dust in all that flame.

Grandpa Hollister puts away his knuckle-duster, and the hand comes back to my shoulder. He pulls me back from the fiery window. We walk out into the old field. When we get to the rusted-down fence, he squats in front of me and looks into my eyes. "We have to get out of here right now. Can you drive back to town?"

Of course I can drive. I got here, didn't I?

I just say, "Yes, sir."

"All right, follow me."

He gets up and starts loping his long stiff frame toward the Buick parked next to Delia's white Chevy. I run a few steps and stop. I run back to the barn doors and pull the ax from the two handles. I throw the ax out into the yard and take off running after my Grandpa Hollister's long, black legs.

We don't go home the way I came. He takes me out to the county hardroad, and we turn away from town. I follow his red taillights through a tangle of country roads only he knows, and the storm is boiling black on the horizon to the south, and the trees along the narrow roads bend and groan, and the air at my window is cold from miles high in the sky. We circle out and come back to town just as morning comes on the same road we took my first day here. The one that crosses the bridge over the Hiawassee River where the sign says, WELCOME TO WIDOW ROCK.

We get home before anybody's up, and we sneak into the house together. The last I see of him that early morning, he's standing at his bedroom door looking back at me. His eyes tell me we have a secret, and it will lie in our hearts untold on the days we die.

I'm in the kitchen washing the soot from my arms and face when Marvadell comes in the back door singing one of her over Jordan songs. She stops short, scared when she sees me. "Chile, what you doin' in my kitchen this time of the moanin?"

I say, "I got up early and I went outside and got dirty, and I'm washing up down here so Grandpa won't know." It's the voice of a boy who isn't anymore, and it sounds strange to me. But not to her.

She looks at me from way up high in the air over Jordan, and then she remembers our conspiracy against Grandpa Hollister, and she smiles and says, "All right, Travis, Honey. You get along now. I'll clean up down here."

Upstairs, I go to Delia's door. I listen. I raise my hand to knock, but I don't. My hand still smells of smoke. I think: Let her dream.

When I crawl into bed, I know I'll be getting up in an hour, and I know I won't be able to sleep. My eyes are too full of fire for that. But I close them and try anyway, and the storm breaks over our house, and over all of Widow Rock. I lie there with my eyes closed, seeing the rain roll on over the town, roll on over the farms and fields until it puts out Griner's fire. I see it wash away the footprints and the tire tracks, too, until all that's left is an accident. Something that happened to a poor boy nobody cared much about.

SEPTEMBER

Come softly darling, come to me, stay,
You're my obsession, forever and a day.

Come Softly To Me
—Music and Lyrics by Gary Troxel, Gretchen Christopher,
  and Barbara Ellis
—Recorded by The Fleetwoods

thirty-eight

I put down my John R. Tunis novel and go to the library window. Some guys are playing kickball down on the playground. It's hot even though it's the middle of September, and they don't look like they're having much fun. I like it up here in the library. I come as much as I can, nights and weekends. It's a big room with tall windows and good-smelling oak floors and narrow aisles of bookshelves. Three big paddle fans keep the air moving. If you sit still and let your mind go into a book, you can stay pretty cool.

I go back to the library table and pick up my book and try to read, but it's not working like it should. I've read all nine books about the baseball team. I'm reading the one about the catcher again now, but it's a kid's book, and I'm not a kid anymore. I know things now you won't find in this library. The books Mrs. Cohen gave Delia had those things in them. Maybe the books Griner read did, too. I don't know.

Mr. Hale, the librarian, looks over at me kind of stern. Most of the guys think he's an okay guy, but the library has a rule: if you're not reading or studying or doing something they call constructive, you have to leave. You can't just sit up here and think or feel the cool air from the paddle fans on your skin. That's not constructive. Mr. Hale calls it wool-gathering, which is all right with me. I guess I've gathered a lot of wool since I came to this place.

Dr. Janeway, the psychologist, calls it morbid self-absorption. Most of the guys here think he's a shithead. But not all of them know him like I do. I have an appointment with him pretty soon. He comes in on Saturday afternoons.

He has an office somewhere else, but he talks to the guys here that interest him. The first day they pulled me out of the furniture shop to see him, he told me he was interested in my case. I told him I didn't know I had one. He said, "You don't have one, Travis, you *are* one. You did something boys your age usually don't do." I told him not to call me a boy, so he calls me a guy when he remembers, which isn't all the time.

We have our meetings in Mr. Bronovitch's office. Mr. Bronovitch is the superintendent. The guys call him the Super, or just Soup. He was a cop before he got educated, and a prize-fighter before that. All his fingers have been broken, and his nose is as flat as Mrs. Cleary's chest. She's the night nurse. Some of the older guys here say that Soup will talk to you about boxing if he's not busy and you ask him right. They say he fought Tony Zale once, and he could have made it big but he cut too easy. I guess I know what that means.

There are some tough guys here, but they don't mess with me. They think I'm a bug, that means crazy, and I don't try to convince them I'm not. If they leave bugs alone, then I'll be a bug. Bugs get along okay. I read in a library book that bugs have been around since before the dinosaurs.

I go over to Mr. Hale's desk and hand him the John R. Tunis novel about the catcher. Mr. Hale smiles at me. His teeth are crooked and brown from all the coffee he drinks. "You finish it, Travis?"

"I read it once already. I don't think I can get through it again. The funny thing is, they're all the same. It's a different guy in each one, and he plays a different position, but they're all the same. I don't know why it took me so long to figure that out."

Mr. Hale nods when I talk. He nods too much. Some of the guys make fun of him, but I don't. So what if he's not the sharpest knife in the drawer and he doesn't make much money. Nobody that works here does. Mr. Hale's been okay to me, and I like him for that.

He says, "Maybe I'll bring in something a little more adult for you to read. Would you like that?"

"Sure," I say. "Yeah, I would."

I don't know what he means by adult, but anything from outside would be okay. Mr. Hale smiles and says, "I'll have to clear it with Mr. Bronovitch, but I think he might look with favor upon my request."

That's another thing about Mr. Hale. He talks funny, like an actor or like somebody from back in history who was dropped here by space monsters or something. I give him my most serious look and say, "I hope he does. I hope he looks with favor upon your request because I'd enjoy something more adult to read."

You have to do that in here. I learned that the first week. You have to take what they say seriously, even when it's stupid. You can't make fun of anything they do. That's the worst thing you can do in here. It's worse than fighting or getting caught in a closet with some other guy doing the reach around.

The older guys tell a story about a kid who came here, and his face was stuck in a grin. He couldn't help it. He was just born that way. He wasn't a funny guy. Even when he wanted to smile, you couldn't tell it because he was always grinning. It was written in his file, the older guys say, that the permanent grin was a birth defect, but he still couldn't make it here. The staff couldn't stand to look at him.

They didn't see the kid, only his grin. And they thought the kid was laughing at them, at the program, at all their education and good will and good works. They started finding bruises on the guy, and the injuries got worse, and pretty soon he was like the chicken the other chickens peck to death in the barnyard. Everybody was on him.

The older guys say he lasted six weeks. They say he left one night on a stretcher with the blanket pulled up to his chin and his eyes rolled to the back of his head. I don't know if that part is true. You hear a lot of bullshit in here. If it isn't true, it ought to be true.

So I tell Mr. Hale thanks again, and tell him it's time for me to go to Mr. Bronovitch's office to meet Dr. Janeway. Mr. Hale smiles and scratches his arm, and I know he'll watch me leave. I know he wonders what Dr. Janeway and I talk about, and it's fun to make him wonder. If you have to be a bug, you might as well be a mysterious one.

Dr. Janeway's waiting for me in Mr. Bronovitch's office. He always arrives first and arranges his notebook and his fountain pen on the desk and plugs in the big suitcase tape recorder and lights his pipe and leans back in Mr. Bronovitch's brown leather chair. When I come in, he's already got the room full of good-smelling pipe smoke, and he's in control. That's what he likes.

What he doesn't like is Mr. Bronovitch's office. Mr. Bronovitch is not a pipe type of guy. If he smoked, it would be big fat cigars. Mr. Bronovitch's office is decorated with framed black and white pictures of his boxing matches. There's a lot of smoke in those pictures, and a lot of it's in the eyes of the guys Mr. Bronovitch is knocking the crap out of. There's a baseball signed by the entire pennant-winning

New York Yankees team of 1956. There are plaques and trophies, too, from the organizations Mr. Bronovitch belongs to. I like the office. It's official, but it's like an old coat. You could wear it pretty well on a winter day. Dr. Janeway thinks it's low-class crappy. He only tolerates it because he's getting at some interesting cases. I'm one of them. I don't know how I fit with the other guys he talks to, and I don't care. It's okay to be interesting if it gets me out of the furniture shop.

I knock on Mr. Bronovitch's door, and Dr. Janeway calls out, "Come in, Trav." I walk into the cloud of pipe smoke that smells like flowers burning in a pile of maple leaves. I sit down in the chair across from the desk. I pull the trousers of my uniform up and straighten the creases in the brown cotton. Dr. Janeway thinks that's interesting. He calls it my need for order in a disordered world. What the hell.

He's always writing when I come in. He doesn't look up until he finishes what he's writing with his tortoiseshell fountain pen. He's got neat handwriting, I can see that. I guess the sentence he's finishing is so good he'd really lose something if he looked up when I came in.

I watch him write. He's a tall, thin guy with sandy brown hair going gray at the temples. He looks like the Hathaway Man in the ads for shirts. He wears wool sport coats and yellow or blue button-down shirts and knitted ties with square ends. He wears vest sweaters, too. I've counted six so far in all different colors. He wears saddle shoes sometimes and sometimes penny loafers, and when I'm talking he likes to lean back and pull his ankle up onto his knee and pick at the weave in his argyle socks, especially when I say something particularly interesting.

He fiddles a lot with his pipe. He empties it and refills it. He frowns when it's not packed right and doesn't burn evenly. He straightens paper clips and pokes them into it. He wears a gold key on a chain. I asked what it was, and he said, Phi Beta Kappa. He acted like I'd know what that meant.

He looks up from his notebook and screws the cap onto his pen and turns on the tape recorder. "So, how's it going, Trav?"

I don't know why he calls me Trav. Nobody else does. I don't call him Jane.

"Fine," I say, and smile, and we start through the usual list of questions and answers. I'm doing well in school. I find my assignments interesting. I'm getting along with my teachers. I like my work in the furniture shop, except sometimes I get a little light-headed from the varnish. I haven't had any problems with the other guys. I haven't had a D.R. since my first week here. I'm getting letters from my mom and dad, and I'm writing back to them. I miss home, but I know why I have to be here, and I understand that it could be a long time before I get to leave. I know it depends on the progress I make here.

Once when Dr. Janeway said that about progress, I said I wished I just had a sentence. Just time to be here and a time to leave. He frowned like I'd missed something important. "Don't you see, Trav," he said, "the indeterminacy of your time here works in your favor. You can't just manipulate the system until it's time to go back into society. Under the indeterminacy policy, the staff here can really evaluate your progress. They can put you under some pressure and see who you really are."

I nodded. I made my face look like it does when I read

something in a book I like, something that means a lot to me. But I was thinking what a rotten rat-bastard system it is. You're like an animal in a zoo, and there's a wild forest only miles away. You smell that forest on the wind at night, and you know you're wild, and sometimes you even dream your way out through the bars. But you always wake up with the bars and the fences around you, and you know you won't get out until someone who can't smell the forest decides to unlock your cage. Or you die.

While we're doing the usual questions, Dr. Janeway leans back and smokes and picks at the little squares in his socks. They're brown today, the squares. When we finish, he leans forward and rests the leather patches in his sportcoat sleeves on Mr. Bronovitch's desk.

"Trav," he says, "you look uncomfortable today. Is anything bothering you? Be honest with me."

I lean forward and smile and try to look more comfortable. I drag some honesty into my eyes. "No, really, I'm fine, Dr. Janeway. There's nothing bothering me."

Dr. Janeway frowns. When he picks up his notebook, he sneaks a look at his watch. We have to put in an hour here.

He puts down the notebook, picks up the fountain pen, and drums it on the notebook cover. "Travis, I want to go back to the day you got into trouble. I want you to tell me again why you did it."

It's not the first time he's made me do this. It's like the cops when they took me to the station and put me in a cell and talked to me before my dad got somebody from his law firm downtown to get me out. They kept making me go over it and over it. They kept asking me the same questions. Where did I get the bayonet? Where was the bayonet when

Jimmy Pultney shot the arrow at me? How many times had he shot at me before? They acted like I was lying and they were going to prove it until I pulled apart the hair on the top of my head and showed them the scar. After that, one of them started talking about self-defense.

I look at Dr. Janeway with my best Trav Trying Hard eyes and say, "I don't know what I can tell you that we haven't already talked about. I got back from my summer in Florida, and I was feeling bad about my mom and dad and things not going so well with them, and I went into the bedroom and took the bayonet from under my dad's pillow. Jimmy already tried to kill me twice, and I knew he'd do it again. I knew his parents couldn't stop him, and I didn't want to bother my dad about it."

I look out of my Trav Trying Hard eyes at Dr. Janeway. Maybe I should ask Dr. Janeway if he'd rather be sitting here with Jimmy Pultney talking about why he shot a steel-tipped arrow into my head. Ask him if that would be more interesting. Dr. Janeway is listening carefully. I know he wants something new. He wants something I haven't said before. And suddenly I'm tired of this, so tired of all this, and the Trav Trying Hard eyes blink and the light goes out in them, and I can't get Dr. Janeway back into focus, and I say, "You see, I learned some things in Florida, and so I knew what I had to do about Jimmy."

And there it is. The new thing. And the lights go on again, and Dr. Janeway's very interested face comes back into focus, and I know I'm in trouble. I don't know what made me say it. I didn't want to. I didn't even know it was there. I've memorized the things I always say.

Dr. Janeway is on my words like a cat on a baby bird

blown from a nest in a storm. He leans forward and points the fountain pen at me and says, "You learned something in Florida? What did you learn, Travis?"

I don't know what to say. Travis, the real one, not Trav Trying Hard, but Travis Marking Time, has fucked up. He should have kept to the story he always tells. I have to come up with something. I say, "To defend myself. I learned to defend myself."

"What happened in Florida that taught you that, Trav?"

I don't know what to say. I close my eyes and look back, all the way back a year and a month to Widow Rock. Ronny Bishop's mean, red-headed face appears out of the dark, and there's a revolver in his hand, and then I see Bick dancing on the edge in the moonlight, and then Griner howling in the flames. I say, "I met some guys down there who taught me how to stand up for myself, that's all. I think every guy should know how to stand up for himself, don't you?"

One of the framed pictures of Mr. Bronovitch in the ring catches my eye. I look at it now, and so does Dr. Janeway. Mr. Bronovitch is standing up for himself so well, the other guy's gonna sleep for a week. Dr. Janeway sucks so hard on the pipe I can see his back teeth through his cheeks, and he blows a lot of blue smoke into the room. Finally, he says, "Trav, Buddy, have you ever heard of a thing called premeditation?"

Of course I have, but I tell him no.

He says, "When you went into your dad's bedroom and you stole the bayonet from under his pillow, that meant you *planned* to stab Jimmy. That's what our friends down at the courthouse call premeditation. In fact, Trav, that's what got you into this place. Do you see what I mean?"

I know I shouldn't say it. I know he's not going to think

it's progress, but I say, "If I didn't get the bayonet ahead of time, I wouldn't have been ready to stab him when he tried to kill me again with his bow and arrow. I don't call that premeditation, I call it preparation." I want to tell him how dangerous the world is out there, and how you have to plan for every possibility, but I don't. Maybe guys like him don't need to know that. Maybe the world isn't dangerous for them.

I can see he doesn't like my answer. I can see we've hit a rough place on the long road to progress.

We talk for another thirty minutes, going over some of the same things we've talked about before, getting back to the people we always are with each other, getting past the moment when Trav Trying Hard turned into Travis Marking Time.

When my hour's up, Dr. Janeway looks at his watch and stands up and stretches. I know I'm supposed to stay in my chair until he comes around the desk and puts his hand on my shoulder and says, "All right, Trav, Buddy. I think we did pretty well today. I want you to think about what we said, and if you have any questions about the session or any insights you want to share with me next time, write them down and bring them in and read them to me. Okay, Buddy?"

I say, "Okay, Dr. Janeway."

He says, "You are still keeping your journal, aren't you?"

I tell him yes, I'm still keeping my journal.

I've got the Trav Trying Hard look back in my eyes, and I stand up under the soft pressure of his hand, and we walk to the door together, and I say, "Thanks, Dr. Janeway. I'll sure think about what you said today. See you next week."

"See you, Trav. And Trav. Think about what *you* said today."

As I walk through the outer office, I don't look at the next poor guy waiting to see Dr. Janeway.

We get an hour of free time before they ring the bell and we line up for the mess hall. Sometimes I go out on the playground and walk the fence line or toss a baseball around with some of the guys, but I don't feel like it today. I go back to the dormitory and lie in my bunk with my face to the window and think about how close I just came to telling Dr. Janeway about Florida, the town of Widow Rock, about Delia. It scares me so much that I almost told him, my face gets hot and I start to shake. I reach down and pull my journal out from between the mattress and the springs and hold it against my chest to make the shaking stop.

Grandma Hollister cried when I left Widow Rock. She hugged me and said she loved me, and she was glad she'd gotten to know such a fine young man, and it hurt her that such sorrowful things had to happen while I was here. She said she was sorry, too, that we never went to Panama City Beach. Any boy who came all the way from Omaha to Florida should have a day at the beach with a picnic lunch and swimming and fishing, but that would have to wait for my next visit, and she hoped it would be soon.

Grandpa Hollister didn't look at me that whole Monday morning. All through breakfast when Delia didn't come downstairs, and all through my last minutes packing and saying good-bye to Marvadell, he never let his eyes and mine combine. The phone rang early that morning with the news about the fire at Kenny Griner's house, and Grandma Hollister went upstairs to tell Delia, and we all said that was Delia's reason for not saying good-bye to me.

When Grandpa Hollister said it was time to leave for the airport, Grandma Hollister went to the foot of the stairs and called up, "Delia, can't you come down and say good-bye to Travis? I know you're upset, but you never know when you'll see him again."

Delia didn't say anything. We stood there at the bottom of the stairs. We could hear the radio playing up there soft, and Grandma looked at me and said, "Travis, Honey, she's just very upset. It's terrible, two of her friends dying like this in one month. We've had such bad luck in our little town."

She looked over at Grandpa Hollister. "John, do you want to go up and ask her to come down and give Travis a hug?"

Grandpa Hollister didn't look at her, or at me. He watched the top of the stairs, then he said, "Come on, Mother. If we don't leave now, the boy will miss his plane."

That's how I ended up leaving Widow Rock the way I came to it, sitting in the front seat of the Buick Roadmaster between Grandma and Grandpa Hollister. My plane was delayed, so we went to the little restaurant in the terminal. They had coffee, and I had a glass of orange juice, and finally Grandpa Hollister looked at his watch and said, "Mother, I think Travis can get on the plane all right by himself. We need to get on back and see to things."

Grandma Hollister cried when she looked at me then, and I remembered how she'd cried when I arrived, saying she was worried about me getting snatched by white slavers. Grandpa Hollister carried my suitcase back down the terminal to the airline desk. Grandma Hollister leaned down and gave me one of her big smothering hugs. Then she hurried off toward the Buick with her hanky pressed to her eyes.

Grandpa Hollister put the suitcase handle in my hand and tucked my ticket into my shirt pocket. Then he looked straight at me for the first time that morning. He gave me the full gale of his eyes, all the storm wind and dark night and hard rain that was in them, and he whispered one word to me, "Remember."

I wake up at night sometimes hearing him whisper that word. *Remember.* How could I forget? That Delia wouldn't see me the morning I left. That she locked her door the night before.

A week after I got back to Omaha, my mom came home from the hospital. She told me she was better. She said, "Travis, my sweet boy, I want to go and stay with my family in San Francisco for a while." She and my dad argued about that. Late at night I heard her crying and him saying she'd never come back to us. They talked and argued, and she cried all the next day, and when she started singing in Japanese again, I had to go out into the backyard.

It was like some crazy thing in a movie, the same thing happening to me again just like it happened before, just like I'd never left Omaha and there never was a summer in Widow Rock.

Jimmy Pultney shot the arrow at me, and for a second I thought I wouldn't duck. My mom was going to visit her family, and I knew what that meant, and Delia was two thousand miles away, and I didn't know what that meant yet, and so for a crazy second I thought I wouldn't move. I thought I'd let the arrow hit me. It wasn't aimed at my head like before. It was coming for the center of my chest. But not even a kid like me is that crazy.

I jumped to the side like you do in dodge ball, and the arrow buried deep across the yard. Those red and yellow feathers stuck up like flowers from the grass.

And Jimmy said, "Kid, go get that arrow. Don't make me climb over there and stomp your ass."

So I looked at Jimmy, and I think I smiled. The bayonet was there, hidden down the back of my jeans under my shirt.

Mean, stupid Jimmy was standing at the fence. He had another arrow on his bowstring to scare me with. I knew exactly what he was going to say: "Kid, I'm not going to tell you again." I went and picked up the arrow.

I brought it over and I stood close to the fence. I held the arrow on my side, then over the top, not through the wire. Jimmy was too far away. I said, "Here it is."

Jimmy still had the second arrow pointed at me. He said, "Toss it over."

I said, "No, you have to come and get it."

Jimmy's mean, stupid eyes were full of Pultney suspicion. That's what keeps them alive and multiplying though they're useless at everything else. Finally, he came over. When he reached for the arrow, I watched his eyes. When they moved, mean and cold, from my face to our hands, my left hand held onto the arrow, pulling him close, and my right hand shoved the bayonet through the fence. I could feel the meat and then the bone on the point of my knife. I drove it in as deep as I could. I tried for his heart, but I missed. If mine was going to be dead, why should this little shit have one?

All hell broke loose after that with me disappearing into the wheatfield to bury the bayonet, and Jimmy's father pounding on our back door with a shotgun butt, and the ambulance coming to take Jimmy away, and Jimmy's fat, stupid mother running around like one of those chickens Jimmy gives the ax, and my father the only one with the sense to press his hand so tight to Jimmy's shoulder that the bleeding stopped. When it was all over, and the cops had Jimmy's father in a police car and his shotgun in the trunk, and a detective arrived and told my dad he'd have to take me away, my dad stood there with Jimmy's blood drying all over him, and he looked at me like Grandpa Hollister did the last time I saw him, and it wasn't a secret his eyes were telling me to keep. It was me he wasn't keeping, not any-more. And so my Mom was leaving, and I was, too.

Jimmy didn't die. My dad wrote me that he'll never have the use of his left arm. As far as I'm concerned, Jimmy drag-ging around a dead arm is fair enough. And just a little less trouble for everybody else in this world.

I got sent here, and my dad passed the bar examination, and now he's a real lawyer. He wrote me that he thinks he'll go back to Widow Rock where people know him. He said they need him, and it's better to be a small-town lawyer than one of a thousand in a big city like Omaha.

At night, I dream of Delia.

I dream of the house on Bedford Street and our two rooms with the hallway between them and my night walks to Delia's door. I dream of her hair fanned out black on her white pillow, my night angel. I dream of the gold cross and her fingers twisting it as she lies with her arm over her eyes, and I dream of her laughter like water moving over stones. I dream the spicy smell of the river, and the thousand years it takes water to saw through rock and how the river swept away earth to bring the bones of the driftwood beast to light. I dream of Delia swimming like some river animal, her arms and legs white in the coffee-brown water. I hear her sweet voice singing with the radio, and I feel her holding me in the river, turning me around and around and singing Rockabye Travis and telling me the bough doesn't always break. I always dream of Delia.

We can't have radios here, but a guy who bunks near me knows how to make one by winding copper wire around a toilet-paper roll. Sometimes after lights out, I go to his bunk, and we listen together. The radio's no good, and the music comes from far away, but the words are still out there. I listen for the message. I listen for the songs about secrets and promises. There are people out there just like me.

I'm thirteen years and three months old now, and Delia's seventeen. When I'm twenty, she'll be twenty-four. I look at grown-up people. When I can, I ask how old they are. I watch the men and the women, and I know it will be all right for Delia and me someday.

The bell to line up for the mess hall rings.

I open my journal and find where I've written the name. Delia.

I kiss the name and hold the journal to my chest to stop the shaking. I don't write in it things to tell Dr. Janeway. I write about Delia, about the things we did. I write about the terrible thing inside me and how it grew and how I learned it was my love for her, about what we'll do someday when we're together. I've written her letters, but she hasn't written back to me. I don't know why. Maybe it's Grandpa Hollister. His way of reminding me. *Remember.*

I don't mind not getting letters. I have my dreams. Someday, I'll show her this journal. She'll read the story of her and me, the things I never told her. She'll understand what love is, and we'll always be together.

ABOUT THE AUTHOR

Sterling Watson is the author of four novels, *Weep No More My Brother*, *The Calling*, *Blind Tongues*, and *Deadly Sweet*. Watson is the recipient of three Florida Fine Arts Council awards for fiction writing and is a former fellow of The Virginia Center for the Creative Arts. His short fiction and non-fiction have appeared in *Prairie Schooner*, the *Georgia Review*, the *Los Angeles Times Book Review*, the *Fiction Quarterly*, the *Michigan Quarterly Review*, and the *Southern Review*. He has co-authored several screenplays, two of them based on his novels, with novelist, Dennis Lehane. He is Director of the Creative Writing Program at Eckerd College and has taught at the University of Florida and the Florida State Prison, at Raiford. He received his B.A. degree from Eckerd College and his M.A. degree from the University of Florida.